THE ONYX BOOK OF OCCULT FICTION

I0602458

SNUGGLY BOOKS

THE ONYX BOOK OF OCCULT FICTION

EDITED BY

DAMIAN MURPHY

THIS IS A SNUGGLY BOOK

All stories Copyright © by the various authors or their estates.
Anthology Copyright © 2024
by Damian Murphy.
All rights reserved.

ISBN: 978-1-64525-165-1

CONTENTS

INTRODUCTION

THE prospect of writing occult fiction opens up an incredible range of unique possibilities. The vast majority of occult fiction written throughout the 20th century is both somewhat narrow in its approach and hopelessly out of date. There are, of course, exceptions. Arthur Machen's "The White People", for example, would lose none of its ability to fascinate if it were published today. The same could be said of much of the fiction of Gustav Meyrink. Lovecraft's innovations were bold for their time, but his major work is nearly a century old. The field, as it stands, is ripe for new methods. Fortunately, in more recent years, a number of authors have introduced some truly noteworthy innovations to the genre. This anthology is intended to provide a sample of this work.

Upon considering techniques that might be employed toward the emergence of a new era of occult fiction, it's easy to come up with an abundance of examples. The genre, for the most part, has failed to keep up with the last century's developments in literature (the work of the illustrious Mary Butts notwithstanding; one might also include that of John Cowper Powys). A certain amount of work could be devoted to merely catching up. I could imagine an entire esoteric literary movement adapted from the circle of experimental authors in 1960s Britain—B.S. Johnson, Ann Quin, Alan Burns, and Eva Figes, among others. The circular narratives of Julio Cortázar could easily be applied to a variety of esoteric motifs—the byzantine angelology of Ismaili gnosis comes to mind, or the poetic expositions of the Kabbalistic Book of Splendor. The elegant tropisms of Nathalie Sarraute seem almost conspicuously suited to such traditional occult conventions as drawing room séances and astral projection. This is hardly the tip of the iceberg as far as possibilities go, to say nothing of the truly new.

Similarly, genre tropes not usually associated with the occult could be used to give new narratives a unique flavor and atmosphere. I anticipate a wider range of occult fiction than we've seen so far, one that employs a more extensive approach, rather than adhering to familiar horror or fantasy motifs. There are so many possibilities in this area that it would take an army of authors to exhaust them—homages to the cinema of the French New Wave or to erotic Italian crime comics such as Kriminal and Sadistik; esoteric pastiches of Roberto Bolaño, Robert Musil, or Muriel Spark; sadomasochistic locked room mysteries; poetic epics intermingled with romantic sex comedies; or the long, intoxicating monologues of Clarice Lispector. One might imagine the basic narrative of André Gide's The Counterfeiters reworked as a study of the occult application of Goethe's theory of colors. The possibilities are endless.

Might we be seeing the nascent buds of a vast new wave of occult fiction? The potential is there, at the very least. The past twenty-five years have seen an unexpected flowering of the form through the agency of a handful of small, independent publishers. The output of these presses is a little bit obscure—necessarily so as their books are typically printed in strictly limited editions—yet their dedicated following is hardly surprising, given the high quality of their material. Among these publishers are Tartarus Press, Ash-Tree Press, Swan River Press, Sarob Press, Ex Occidente Press (more recently known as Mount Abraxas), Side Real Press, Chômu Press, Egaeus Press, Zagava Books, and of course Snuggly Books, who, in addition to their focus on historical decadent and symbolist literature, have published a number of contemporary books of occult fiction. Broodcomb Press, whose standards are excellent, is a more recent addition. Many of these presses print fine, hardback editions, while others produce primarily paperbacks.

It should be noted that not all of the authors that have published with these presses have occult inclinations. Some of the most notable among them have gone in very different directions. John Howard, for instance, whose writing is replete with architectural and city-planning themes, has found inspiration in the architecture of Le Corbusier and the shifting balance of European powers that resulted from the first world war. George Berguño is another excellent example. While Berguño's short stories and novellas often dip into the supernatural, for the most part they recall the parable-like narratives of the Yugoslav author Danilo Kiš more than anything recognizable as occult fiction. There are other authors whose occult pieces have proven too lengthy to include in this anthology. Among these is Quentin S. Crisp's *Ynys-y-Plag*, which is a modern classic of the genre.

With these and other considerations in mind, I've chosen 15 pieces to represent this movement, each of which, in my opinion, is thoroughly unique. This is barely the tip of the iceberg in terms of the output of the above-mentioned presses. Several additional authors could easily have been included if the size of the anthology allowed for it. The oldest of the included stories, Reggie Oliver's "The Children of Monte Rosa," was first published in 2007 by Ash Tree Press. The most recent was published in 2022. From all indications, this resurrection of the form is still moving forward with inexhaustible momentum.

Very few common themes can be found throughout these stories. For the most part, the genre as a whole is completely cut off from occult and publishing trends that have emerged in recent decades. A number of authors have incorporated the styles and motifs of previous authors in the field—Arthur Machen, M.R. James, H.P. Lovecraft, and Robert Aickman, among others—yet there's been no shortage of original voices whose output stands alone. The pieces included in this volume were chosen for their singularity, each of them offering a unique approach to the immeasurable variety that constitutes the hidden mysteries. The stories that follow can be taken as strategies for the probing of the ineffable. Some of them look back to tradition while others eschew it as a matter of principle, yet all of them manage to cover new ground, bringing a light, however oblique, into a region of the darkness that resists rational analysis. This, in my opinion, is the single crucial factor that defines the entire genre.

THE ONYX BOOK
OF OCCULT FICTION

THE UNDERGROUND ROOM

by Justin Isis

ALL over Tokyo people were dreaming of the underground room—or so it seemed from the conversations you heard at a certain kind of club, a certain kind of event. These conversations, however obscure, emphasized the dreams' ubiquity, the strange feeling of an unsuspected shared experience, like people who played at the same park in childhood encountering each other as adults. The intensely personal quality of the dreams led to an initial reluctance to share them, which meant that they had been going on for some time before their communal nature became apparent.

It was a measure of the dreams' strangeness that it took so long, given our general openness; for years all of us had shared our lives and creations in a free and unreflective manner. The designers among us made clothes, which were circulated without any commercial incentive. The writers wrote stories and novels, the artists and coders made games, the filmmakers films, the musicians music. None of us felt the need to market these creations; in fact we were determined to keep them to ourselves. The more industrious among us, those with careers, maintained apartments—sometimes in respectable areas— but there were just as many who drifted between residences, crashing on couches or net café floors, sleeping during the day and roaming the city at night. We did not search for others like ourselves; somehow they always found their own way to us. All of us had spent years wandering through clubs and shows and parties, devoting our purest energies to fashion, music and drugs. Already decades had passed, and it was difficult to remember when we had first stayed out all night, desperate for any place but home. We had lived for years in the hope of becoming those we admired, and now that we had succeeded there was no longer anyone worth imitating.

Into this period of somewhat sterile contentment came the dreams. These first distinguished themselves from the conventional kind mainly through the sensation they evoked, lacking as they did any precise image. Principally this was a vast sense of compression and darkness. Those who reported these early dreams—I was not among them; my own visions came later—spoke of a warm feeling of weight. The only other impression was of constant movement, although no precise direction, or definite presence other than the dreamer, could be discerned. This absence of form itself became significant: all was glossy blackness. Over a period of weeks the dreams took on more details, and their serial nature—signalled by the unusual vividness of the darkness—became clear, but this sense of being present in some great unlit space remained.

As the dreams developed, certain shared and recurring elements appeared. The dreamer seemed to be moving through a labyrinth of tunnels marked by their low ceilings, dark stone walls and pervading dampness. Only a dim light existed to illuminate these tunnels, although perhaps the light itself was only the dreamer's awareness. The only other sensation was of a great rising warmth, as if the tunnels led towards some subterranean furnace.

Finally scenes of the underground room appeared. This juxtaposition—the maze of tunnels and the underground room—seemed to imply that the former contained the latter, although no one reported any definite scenes of entry, nor mentioned seeing doors or portals of any kind. The size of the room itself varied according to the dreamer, although it was usually described as being as large as two or three conventional living rooms, or in other words the average size of a public event space. The furnishings, too, varied according to the account, but almost always contained a mixture of archaic and modern elements, as well as those with no analogue in any era of the waking world.

I can recall several distinct impressions from my own initial dreams. The distribution of light in the room was inconsistent; regions of intense fluorescent brightness—existing independently of any visible source—contrasted with those of relative darkness. The walls, floor and ceiling were all of silver, and spotlessly clean. The unusual timelessness of the room concentrated itself in these surfaces: a great sense of age adhered to them, but in looking at their smooth curves I felt that I was observing a space that did not yet exist, had not yet been built, one that seemed capable of remaining frozen in place for eternity or else dissolving at the slightest touch. The walls were lined with tinted windows of crimson glass overhung with heavy dark cloth and silk drapes. A grandfather clock stood against one wall, next to a carved rosewood table supporting a ceramic vase filled with brittle copper roses. On various circular tables around the room were devices whose functions remained unclear: conical sculptures, glass cubes filled with fluid, small metal boxes with unreadable electronic displays. In the center of the room, spanning its width, was a long high table or counter, in front of which stood a row of black metal stools.

The most significant element of the room—so much so that it seemed as much a physical presence as anything else I have described—was the music, which did not resemble anything I had ever heard. Ocean music is the only term that seems appropriate to describe its weight and depth, the sense of a formless churning obeying its own inscrutable rhythms. There were no visible instruments or speakers, which added to the sense of immanence, an inherent property or process rather than anything consciously produced. This music was so much like a fluid in its consistency that all movements seemed somehow delayed, as if they were occurring underwater. I felt that the underground room existed not only beneath the city or beneath the world, but in some sense beneath the universe itself. The great warmth of the tunnels remained, so it seemed that the warmth and the music were the same thing, the internal rhythms of a natural structure, like the sound of blood pumping through veins or the echo of lapping waves in an underground cave. The organic presence of the music offset the room's formal elements, all of which seemed to have been arranged according to a precise aesthetic system. The proliferation of apparently functionless objects did not in any sense decorate the room; if anything the walls and the floor seemed mere adjuncts to the objects themselves, so that it was impossible to determine which had given rise to the other. All of this is to suggest that the underground room collapsed not only temporal distinctions but those of origination; it seemed to have both been built according to a strict blueprint and cohered organically in some unguessed-at corner of existence. In the obscurity of its origins, perhaps, the underground room resembled the universe as a whole; in all other respects it seemed entirely remote.

At this stage, discussion of the underground room centered on the possible nature and meaning of the objects it contained and what function the room itself served—that no consensus was reached only added to the fevered nature of the discussions. Employing a variety of media—clay, paint, plaster, film and software—several of us set about creating representations of objects glimpsed in the underground room.

Perhaps the most notable was a recreation of the "static pyramid," a transparent glass solid containing a cloud of swarming black and white motes. The artist who re-imagined this object in the daylight hours (his model employed a multi-panelled video monitor broadcasting white noise, encased in a glass cone) produced something vaguely reminiscent of the original, but on the whole this effort, like the rest, was unsuccessful at evoking the underground room in anything other than a purely symbolic sense. The inherent nature or atmosphere of its objects, it seemed, could not be reproduced, although we eventually decided that the failure lay less with the artists' talents than with the impossibility of isolating any element from the underground room, which, we had come to believe, was a total system and not a collection of random elements: the architectural equivalent of a biological cell. The only sense in which our artworks succeeded, then, was as an attempt to clarify that we were all experiencing the same singular phenomenon.

As the dreams continued, our interest shifted to the figures glimpsed in them, since the underground room was not empty. The accounts of its inhabitants varied more than those of its furnishings, and were generally more fantastical, sometimes to the point of incoherence. The inhabitants of the underground room—creatures, they were usually referred to, although every report stressed that they were human; some referred to them as objects, although with the understanding that they were alive in every sense that mattered—were not bound by the limitations of a single form. These creatures, or objects, were one with the underground room, so that they could never visit the surface, or "descend" (this latter term requires some explanation: although the underground room was thought to be located beneath the city, in a series of tunnels, entrance to it was always spoken of in terms of ascent). Their flesh glowed with a dim phosphorescence and their movements were slow and deliberate. Some had the marbled figures of classical statues, while others were pale sylphs, sinuous creatures with glittering eyes and translucent flesh. They seemed to be in constant communication with each other, although no form of speech was heard. The impression was of a gathering where everyone has known everyone for so long that sustained conversation has become unnecessary, a system of glances and gestures and averted eyes serving to convey all manner of subtleties: a gathering on which a certain warm lassitude rests like a fine covering of ash from some distant conflagration. Some sat at the high table, while others wandered the room in a languorous trance. They were perhaps the human descendents of the objects resting on the tables, the objects that our artists had failed to recreate with any measure of skill. As they moved about this isolated universe of warm metal and high-contrast shadows they seemed only to be expressing certain inclinations latent in the positions of the objects and their relations to the angles of the walls, tables and floor.

I dreamed of the underground room, and the impression was of a desert in which whirling dervishes spun under the stars, the sense of circular motion giving way to the room itself, which seemed also to be in motion. I walked barefoot over the floor, feeling something wet beneath my soles. The ocean music submerged me, its peculiar gravity delaying my movements, so that I seemed to linger in the air at the crest of each step. The room was crowded with countless figures moving about as if in a masquerade. I brushed past a child with skin like an open flower before encountering a man with metal intestines. This inhabitant's cast-iron guts, which were visible through the transparent glass casing of his stomach, could "pass through any number of fires" (in the dream this seemed significant) without melting. I moved forward and was embraced by a woman of glass and metal with thin lips and unbearable green eyes. Her nails were chips of jade inset in slender silver fingers. Other inhabitants resembled living collages of light and color, vaporous as ghosts. Rows of them crowded close to the high table, where a golden chalice was being passed around for them to drink "the black and pink milk." As I passed through the throng I felt an excitement mounting within me which expressed itself as an intense concentration on the movements of these figures which, I realized, were not as random as they seemed: a precise coordination existed between them all, a slow and elaborate dance uniting those crossing the floor with those seated. Nothing in the underground room, I realized, was ever entirely at rest.

I passed beyond the high table and moved to the back of the room, an area which had received little attention in previous accounts. In my own earlier dreams I had perceived it only as a black blur, a block of coalescent darkness. Now, even as it retained its pitch texture, I could see shapes moving within it, outlined forms. Against the wall stood a row of low couches on which dim figures sat. These figures, which I cannot describe in any meaningful sense, were pressed so close together that their limbs rested against each other's, hands lying on hands and heads resting on shoulders. The whirling sensation remained, but a great inertial slowness concentrated itself in these figures. I thought of the compressed matter at the hearts of stars. An atmosphere of similar compression filled the back row, black-burning and denser than diamond, weighing on each brief movement. The warmth and closeness of this back row and its seated, secluded figures assumed more importance than anything I had ever known; the only point of my existence was to move towards it, to be at one with the figures and their slow, languorous movements. It was important that I could touch them; in this their essential humanity made itself known. Anything I could learn from them would be imparted not through words, but through a more occult transmission of proximity and touch, a constellation of subtle gestures and barely perceptible movements amounting to a unified heart.

I remember waking to the darkness of my own room, a darkness which now seemed empty and unreal compared to what I had felt in the underground room. As I remembered the back row my body itself felt lighter than before, my movements hurried and brittle; I seemed to be suffocating in an atmosphere too thin to sustain me. If I approached the underground room I would feel that closeness and slowness again, and then I could enter the back row and be one with its seated figures, those embodiments of the monstrously compressed intimacy underlying all visible matter.

The others had had their own dreams, and when I met them that day a new reticence shadowed all that we said, a sense that we had experienced something impossible: as such we spoke little, moving about the city as if it were a stage set, unreal and easily dismantled. Reality had concentrated itself elsewhere. The buildings seemed unnaturally flat, without any visible perspective; the sunlight itself had taken on a parodic dullness. This sense of unreality suffused our interactions, lending them a distracted quality. While we had once shared every detail of the dreams, eager to establish correspondences that would complete our picture of the underground room, we now kept our thoughts to ourselves—even as those thoughts took on a new certainty. In place of our earlier speculations was an unspoken consensus that the underground room existed in the waking world, or was at least accessible in a more immediate sense than we had first supposed. We knew that we must find and enter it, even as we lacked any definite path.

We began by wandering the city at random. Thousands of unconscious routines moved us from street to shop to train, the routines we had accumulated since childhood. Since no map existed that could lead us to the underground room, we entrusted ourselves instead to the structural elements of the city, its arrangements and limitations of space, which had until now produced only conventional departures and arrivals. One of us suggested that the city was a language whose words we understood too well, and that this understanding would never allow us to find the underground room; only by exhausting familiarity could we hope to enter it. Like a child who repeats words until they lose their meanings, we resolved to repeat our routines until they lost their functions. Then we would receive new directions from the city and form new interactions, new routines leading at last to the underground room.

Several days passed in which we slept little, if at all, though we seemed always to be sleepwalking. We moved slowly from ward to ward, and everywhere our memories adhered to the surface of the landscape, so that we seemed to be moving less through a physical environment than through the vagaries of our own minds, passing from place to place in an unfocused drift. One of us stopped in a park, before a row of zelkova trees facing the river, and regarded the progression of white boats gliding over the surface of the water; we knew that he was seeing neither boats nor water but a scene from his past. Finally he sat on the grass and stared through the trees for another half hour before wandering back to join us. He remained silent, and nothing about his expression had changed, but this mattered less than the movement of his feet across the grass, the angle of his head as he focused his attention on the flow of traffic ahead of him. Similar interludes took place outside the east exit of a station, where a familiar vagrant, wrapped in filthy blankets, made his home; in the storage room of a convenience store, where certain obscure encounters had once taken place; and on the second level of a small and now unpopular club, on a section of the dance floor close to the bar, where one of us had stood some five years before and felt an inexplicable happiness. When the unreality we had sensed in the city overwhelmed us, we knew that we had succeeded in exhausting the routines and separating our movements from their usual functions, resolving the structures around us into mere physical arrangements freed from the associations our memories had once imposed. The names of the stations flashing past on the train monitors became unreadable glyphs. At last we were lost.

We looked around. It seemed to be the middle of the night, although no one bothered to check the exact time; in fact we had ceased to pay any attention to time at all. The structure we stood before was located so centrally, was an object we had seen so many times without scrutinizing, that in looking at it now we felt as disturbed as if we had looked at our own faces and noticed some previously unsuspected feature. We could not have missed this building with its prime location in the city we knew so well, but the fact of its centrality had rendered it invisible, so that in every real sense we now saw it for the first time. Outwardly it differed little from the buildings surrounding it, the broad base and streamlined windows resembling those of a bank tower, surmounted by a distant glass crown. The main entrance was closed, but we knew that the doors were unlocked. We stood facing them for some time. Now that we had reached our destination, the strain of wandering for days overcame us, manifesting as a sudden vertigo. Although we had ascended a hill to reach the tower, we felt ourselves to be at the bottom of a sunken valley, staring at the doors as if at the mouth of a well. This derangement of perspective we attributed to our general exhaustion.

At last we pushed open the doors and crossed the threshold. The dereliction that greeted us contrasted so strongly with the tower's shining exterior that the two seemed to belong to different buildings. The ground floor was vastly larger than we had expected, although given the total darkness it was difficult to estimate its area. We had brought electric lights, but even their strafing beams did not reach the furthest wall. The room seemed to extend forever. As we took our first steps into this absolute unlit emptiness, the only object our lights revealed was a staircase some ten yards to our left, barely more than a fire escape. Although we wandered the floor for some time, we could find no doors or elevators, or any furnishings other than this rickety skeleton of black metal coiling into the darkness above. Combining our lights into a single swathe of brightness, we stepped onto the stairs and climbed towards the second floor.

Our first impression of this floor was that it exactly resembled the one below. There was the same darkness, the same indeterminate sprawl exceeding what could reasonably have been contained by the building's facade. But while the ground floor had been empty, inspection of this floor revealed a group of objects scattered at random: wide metal tables with thin legs, all seemingly identical. Some stood upright, while others were overturned. We wandered the floor, uprighting the fallen tables and searching for any variations. While most of them seemed almost to be the same object, we found some with legs of uneven length. Others had frames that seemed longer or shorter than the rest. Some of us became so absorbed in this search for exceptions that it was impossible to pull them away from it, and they insisted we continue the climb, promising to follow on later.

We continued to ascend, inspecting each floor in turn, finding again and again the same enormous empty room scattered with detritus. Only the nature of the objects varied. Most of them belonged to various sets of themed iterations: figurines; metal cups; glass shapes, cubes and pyramids; metal chairs; artificial flowers. The variations were usually imperceptible, although some deviated notably from their parent series. On a floor of iron drinking cups, amidst hundreds of conventional models, we discovered one with its mouth twisted closed, like a woman chewing her lips in frustration. Another floor displayed a series of chairs whose seats underwent a progressive concave warping, so that the later models were impossible to sit in without sinking through the frame. It was unclear whether the various series began with these deviant models and progressed towards regularity, or whether the aberrations themselves were the ultimate end. On each floor several of us remained to complete a more precise inspection, thinning our ranks so that eventually only a small group remained. As we ascended, the angle of the stairs inclined less sharply, so that after a while we felt ourselves moving on a level plane, as if through a series of tunnels rather than stairs, compelled by a vague centripetal motion. The continuing darkness and vertigo forced us to climb slowly; even with our electric lights we could make out little more than the next turn of the stairs, and at times a sense of whirling motion overcame us. The heat increased, and with it we felt a new dampness in the air. We heard one of us call out: tired from the climb, he was now resting on a step behind us. Unwilling to leave him, the rest of us dropped down and rested for some time, feeling the warm darkness pressing against our skin. Someone said he heard music, a faint pulse at the edge of his awareness.

After an unknown length of time we continued our climb and came at last to a floor of masks. Most were simple featureless faces, empty coverings slotted for sight and breathing. Only their mouths displayed any variation, the formations of the lips registering subtle differences in expression. We began a kind of game, trying on mask after mask while spinning around the room, letting our lights roam at random, so that countless pale faces flickered in and out of existence, some seeming to smile or cry, others vague and unreadable. In this way we lost all track of our positions, and it was only by calling out to each other that we were able to re-establish contact—though after a while our voices became distant, inaudible. As I whirled through space I heard music coming from somewhere, or more accurately, everywhere; the darkness itself seemed alive with a formless fluid churning. As the music passed through me I imagined the infinite compression of the back row, so different from the endless expanse surrounding me. I tore my mask away and cast it into the darkness. Somehow I found my way back to the stairs and began to climb.

As I mounted the stairs I heard footsteps behind me; only three of us now remained, the other two following slowly. I continued to climb and thought again of the back row; of the carelessly strewn limbs of the seated figures, hands resting on hands and heads resting on shoulders, the warmth and compression and the unconscious rhythm of their slow, languorous movements. Finally I turned the stair as if to enter another one of the identical floors, but now a narrow path stretched before me. I dropped to the floor and crawled forward, casting aside my light. Eventually my hands struck something hard, and I stood, tracing the shape that confronted me: a solid brick wall crossing the width of the corridor. I began beating my fists against it until my knuckles bled and the flesh of my hands became ragged. I recalled the faces of the seated figures. In the darkness, the pain in my hands seemed to roar. I laughed, knowing I would soon enter the underground room.

ALYSSA

by Thomas Phillips

I

YOU don't make excessive noise in such an environment. You don't do it. Especially at night, or in the early morning hours. When sleep accrued to build and store energy is necessary to get through the heat of the day with its many demands. Your repertoire of noise, ever expanding, always something new, the scrapes on hardwood, the heavy footsteps, the muted banging, your dropping of objects in the night, or just prior to the sun rising to inaugurate another day, such behavior has consequences. You don't know this now, but you will.

The first floor apartment was the most spacious, the most beautiful. It gave the resident access to a sizable porch with wicker chairs, pillows in the chairs, no steps to climb when returning from the market with groceries or other items. How very nice to sit there when the weather is benign, take in the air. Nights are particularly pleasant under the moon, surrounded by other such homes, like this one, late Victorian. Taste the quietude of the night, the relative silence in the otherwise bustling city, the center of which is a mere few blocks away. It had been easy to get the piano and other items through the front door, through the plush common area by the stairwell and into her new home. There were many reasons for her to be happy here.

When you make your sounds in the dark, you demonstrate your unconsciousness. Your dumb immaturity, the solipsism of adolescence. You are only thinking of yourself, and really, at the core of your psychology, you're not thinking at all. You don't take the time to consider your neighbor. The one living and sleeping below you has a system that cannot be interrupted. She sleeps at night, operates in the world of people and other creatures by day. By all means, stay awake into the early hours, feel the immensity of stillness that night bequeaths us, utilize its power to provoke contemplation, or revelry, but do so without noise. You have been told once, you did not hear, you didn't perceive the gravity of the situation, and now the consequences.

She trudged to a specialty shop in one of the city's many neighborhoods, far from the trodden paths of tourists. Her eyes were heavy. Despite the tremendous fount of energy at her disposal, accumulated over years of service, ambition, she was no longer young. The body is of the ground, dirt; inhabit it wisely, but come to terms with its ephemeral nature; pleasure it, secure it, but honor its free fall. She felt slothful in her movement, a product of her age in combat with sleeplessness. She handed over a list and indicated to the person behind the counter her unwillingness to speak with a simple nod. The other prepared her items, small bottles of powder, stole glances at the quality of her presence, here she is, before me, her green amulet, rings, the barely hidden magnificence of her aging. She left swiftly, as if reinvigorated by the promise of powders and evocations and what she could call in all honesty a new tomorrow.

You act as though you are alone in the universe. As if your heavy footsteps and obnoxious tooling about with dropped and dragging objects in the night are warranted by the very singularity of your being, your privileged ontological status in the hierarchy of the cosmos, in the apartment above. You should have responded to the request to please stop, be still in the night, with attention and conscientiousness. You merely feigned an apology. Your weak constitution that seeks above all to smooth over such an exchange with put on civility. And then you continue to wallow in your oafish body, your stupid physicality. You should have listened and acquiesced. It would have been better for us both. Now, in the final hours, and in those unredeemed seconds before the final jerk of life that remains to you, you will understand your error.

She set to work immediately upon returning home. The process would take time. No sitting on the porch until evening, once her part was done. The necessity of being in the open air after such an expenditure of energy and materials. Under the moon, stars, bright or clouded over, breeze-swept matter of the cosmos. The night would prove perfectly clear. She arranged ingredients and pulled out an old book that one doesn't find in a library. She changed clothes. A robe for such occasions that was not uncomfortable in the cool air that blew through an open window in her living room. Every room in that space was for living. Worshipping. Devouring.

That her intention was impure from the perspective of most anyone on the margins of her Work had no bearing on her conscience or the ritual that was to precipitate a pitiless demise. Maternal, benevolent to loved ones and children, animals, a vegetarian, she considered the largest scope of life possible, its many forces, and its insects, human peons who flap in currents of this precious gift, life, with little to no understanding, or the unwillingness to understand. And from this vantage point, she acted accordingly.

The afternoon wore on and it didn't matter whether her upstairs neighbor was at home or elsewhere earning money, moving heavily through his own asinine preoccupations. What mattered was that she got everything right, the right amounts, the correct pronunciations of words in the book. She lit candles. She took her time, but acted efficiently, with incomparable skill. As it happened, he wasn't at home. There was no noise apart from the city in the distance to interrupt the proceedings. Her measurements were accurate, the words issued from her mouth with an elegant, a knowing intonation, all syllables accurate to the best of her knowledge. A longstanding tradition of incantation, fire, base elements of maneuvering men and other natural forces. She didn't stop to eat. Her phone was off. By nightfall, it was accomplished. She let out a silent, exasperated moan. Followed by time on the porch, decompression, communing with the elements of the night. Waiting for events to unfold.

In the night, sounds issued from above until the early morning hours. More sounds than usual, in fact, and she knew this was part of the process. The pacing from room to room, the habitual lack of conscientiousness coupled with a frantic, a needling constitution that dug into the base of his skull and filtered out into his coarse body, inching its way into juvenile psychology, compelling him to wonder why, urging concern, worry, mounting stress. He paced, stopped, paced some more. When the moon was bright and the stars aligned time on the porch with the magic of cinema, approximately 3am, the pacing stopped again and became a rolling, a body rolling and perhaps writhing sound kneading the floor above. The vibrations of his loathsome heft would have enraged her had this been an ordinary night in the Victorian home, had she been in her apartment attempting to sleep rather than on the porch, taking in the night, breathing the dark air. Back inside, it was nearly time. When the wood of the floor ceased to convey his awkward gyrations, and when his usual stomping was replaced by careful steps, a mechanical sorting through implements, the rope, the stool, the rope around his neck, and then the final sound of wood turning over on the hardwood floor, his final, strident, awkward moment, she knew it was over. His feet dangling a foot above the floor where he once walked, stomped, intruded upon her well-being in the night. The Philistine had hanged himself. Where he had once disturbed her being. Never to do this again. The space between floor and his ugly, still, downward-pointing toes a gift of air.

Soon it would be time to make further preparations. In anticipation of the right sort of neighbor. An unassuming, quiet sort above. She drifted in her thoughts to weigh what she had done, in His name, to the glory of the Master, and for her own health at home. She sat languidly in one of the comfortable wicker chairs on the porch. A clear, enchanting sky. Tapped her foot on the ground in a steady rhythm as the neighbor had been wont to do at inconvenient times prior to his neck in a rope.

When the body was discovered some days later, the occupants of the Victorian home that was divided into apartments expressed their perplexity. He was not one to give into the turmoil of life, they said, and she agreed. He was too *breezy*, too *devil-may-care* for that, she said. So a mystery. What complicated his inscrutable demise, however, was a pencil marking he had managed to scrawl, nearly illegible, on the wall. I DON'T MEAN THIS. DOWNSTAIRS. This was all it said. I DON'T MEAN THIS. Some of the words were difficult to make out. Not the final word. DOWNSTAIRS. As though something had driven him to do what he did not wish to do. As though he did not mean to secure the rope, place the stool, climb the stool, step off. The message increased the level of perplexity among the apartment dwellers and authorities alike. The media was soon to follow. She—she—was especially confused as to what went wrong. The writing on the wall wasn't supposed to happen. Not at all. Just stagger to the rope and the damn chair, step off the chair. But the process of conjuration is hard, confusing at times. There was another, a priest of former renown, now a relic and still in pursuit of the Enemy, who watched television and was also confused, compelled to investigate in due time, with his limited resources. She would become aware of his presence before he arrived. Though she would fail to stop him. Another knot in the many tangles of her long and compelling life.

Happiness, what is that for her? In her largely solitary life. In spite of the many people who encounter that solitude at the market, shops, the weekly meeting, concerts attended. Her mostly solitary existence among others. What is happiness for one whose maternal instincts have been nurtured in the service of an unpopular deity? Her solitary apartment a living altar to His glory.

II

She was abducted in a parking garage through which she often passed on her way to a meeting in the city center. Surrounded by concrete, cut off from nature. Approached by three masked men. Intuiting danger though she did, there wasn't enough time to evade the gun that suddenly poked in her back, not enough power to stop a bullet shooting from the gun had the priest felt the need to pull the trigger. The gun in her back, no one else around, the distinct smell of the man's hand over her mouth, the dragging to a van, departure to some unknown destination. How ordinary, how unimaginative of the priest, what a cliché of abduction, though it worked nonetheless. He had captured the witch.

For he, too, was in touch with his own intuitive processes, discombobulated and maligned as they were. Something about the suicide, the message penciled on the wall, and her reputation that preceded her in the small coterie of men who followed such things, such people and the predatory mischief of their ways. Outlaw Christians. Psychopaths. He saw it on television, read an article in the paper, felt intuitively that the Victorian apartment was home to menace. They met promptly, organized themselves and followed her. They learned her routine. She moved with more energy these days, she was resting well, the old energy was back. Though it wasn't enough to stop the abduction. She was getting older, it had to be conceded, accepted. The van smelled of cheap leather upholstery and the man's hand, still gripping her face. They drove into the night, far outside the city. To where, she had no idea.

The priest had his own problems. He rolled with the bumps in the back of the van with the rest of them, silent, contemplating the years that had taken him to this point. Watching her. A gentle but no less enforced excommunication from the church is less than ideal. It had taken its toll. He thought of his family, how they viewed him, and those parishioners he had helped or hindered in the past and the fact that he was no longer a priest in any official capacity. He now operated in an unofficial capacity. Off the grid of sanctioned holy people. Against the law. Some of his crew were lunatics, but still functional, still committed to a cause. How he became more interested in evil than in the omnipotent good of his god was a question he had pondered for many years. And there was never a satisfying answer. Psychoanalysis is futile, he thought. The other priests had been increasingly unsupportive, suspicious. His family stopped being supportive when he was first called in for questioning by the police concerning the disappearance of a young man, a cult leader. A nasty cult. From that point on, the police initiated a rap sheet, cultivated their own intuition around the former priest.

Out of the van, blindfolded, and into the building. Hold onto an arm and walk carefully downstairs, perhaps to a basement, dank new smells. Sit in a chair. The amulet, rings removed. The men talk with quiet voices, they're aware of the gravity of the situation in spite of their victory. Do not remove the blindfold. The smell and the feel of rope, rope applied to the wrists, the ankles, and around the legs of the chair. She was too proud and too angry to cry. She sat in imposed stillness. The men talked, and then, finally, retired upstairs. Alone, she writhed in the rope and, realizing the futility of movement, forced herself into a meditative, a kind of trance state. There she would contact her power, His bounty, liberation. Retribution would come later.

Time becomes something different from the day to day in trance mode, in captivity. When after an inconceivable amount of time had passed and she heard the voices again, felt their presence next to her again, she made the transition back to the physical reality of her situation, the rope and the chair, obscured vision. The priest meant to interrogate her about the suicide, her current *spiritual* affiliations, he used the word mockingly. He would inquire into the prospects of her redemption. Coming out of trance, she already knew what he was going to ask. The answers had been provided to her. Yes, I am responsible, she would say to the first question. You know where my loyalty lies, to the second, otherwise I wouldn't be here. As for the third, you know as well as I that there's a Goat's Head waiting to enter your sphincter, and there, to speak the words of the Almighty Apostate as a resonating clamor throughout your stinking corpulence for eternity.

The priest wondered about the potential for sexual violation on the part of one of the men in particular. Rape. For despite the abduction, he still held to the remnants of a moral structure. Sexual misconduct was repugnant to him. He forgave in his heart, and made every effort to aim for her redemption. In discussing the long-term plan for this ambition, he realized that the men were too afraid of such close contact with her to commit any unpardonable acts. And he knew, of course, that they were right to be so fearful. Raping her would have exposed them to torments beyond anything they could have foreseen. The abduction alone had already put them in the line of her fire, an infernal, otherworldly conflagration as he imagined it, and thus necessitated scrupulous precautions.

Then weeks. Time passing. It's hard to measure time in these circumstances. The chain that had been exchanged for rope, the limited movement in a mostly empty, dank space, the periodic visitations. The questioning, listening to insufferable scripture recitations. Not only did she once again sleep poorly, she was sleeping often, in fits and starts. Losing track of day and night, soon these meant nothing. She contemplated the tragedy of losing touch with a day's seasons, the gradual shifts, cycles, and the effect this has on the body, the ecology of her craft. Listening for their small noises above her, weighing the implications of each sound as she had done with the boy upstairs. A bucket for a toilet. She was beginning to forfeit her exceptional sanity.

He thought of the fact that in addition to her bewitchment, the indirect murder, to everything, really, she was also a woman, a human being. He lamented the fact that their daily scripture readings, one prior to each meal, the flesh and the blood of Christ, were really getting them nowhere. She had no affinity for biblical scripture. On one particularly woeful day, she spit her food at him and urinated on the floor instead of in the bucket. Allowed the liquid to stream down her leg as she locked into his vision, shared this moment with him. An essentially elegant woman reduced to such behavior. There were moments of uncertainty to be sure. What was the plan in the event that she never came round to his perspective? Release her into the wild? The authorities couldn't touch her.

But as surely as the sun gives way to the moon, she could touch them, given the opportunity of liberation and sanity, proper sleep regained.

In the moments of lucidity that also visited her with less and less frequency, she was coming to know the nature and quality of metal. The chains that bound her were, in the grand scheme, mere manifestations of the elements, designed as loops, one in the other, a kind of ongoing infinity, wrapped around her neck. A symbol of her captivity, her unendingly poor sleep, yes. But earth material to be manipulated. She was beginning to understand its properties, what made it what it was to her, there, in the troubled, empty room. It was only a matter of time. Time captured in moments of respite. The offering of His grace and vengeance.

III

Running, with some difficulty given her stagnation over an unknown period of days, weeks, running through a dense wilderness. Though the colossal trees and roots and outgrowths of vegetation that determined her course were obstacles to avoid, phenomena that impeded her escape from the building and the men, the priest currently chasing, a safe distance behind, she could only feel good in their midst, this cathedral of flora and arborescence. Animals were doubtless there as well, underfoot, in the trees. It all seemed to buoy her despite the obstacles to freedom. She ran with determined steps, careful not to land wrong, a twisted ankle would be affliction. It had taken time for her eyes to adjust to the natural light of the cathedral. She had to be careful. Fleeing the confined space, the lunatic men, the biblical indoctrination.

Her foot finally gave to the solidity of a rock obscured by leaves. The ankle bent, far beyond what is typical of its capacity, in a quick snap. She let out the cry but instinctively corrected its position. Of course by then it was too late. The parts of the ankle that normally support and encourage activity, flexibility, were furious. They seized up, commanded her to stop, inspect the damage. Of course it was bad and running was no longer an option. Time to find a discrete, comfortable spot, rest it, be still and know that He is watching. Feel His presence. Forgive Him for being conceived as male. She thought she could hear the priest fumbling in the distance. Be still. Breathe intently, subtly. Find the sanity and grip it tightly, don't let go. The faltering priest will grow tired and relent. How perfect that darkness is now imminent and that the clothes she wore on the day of her abduction are also dark. Plush, dark green, in fact.

The injury was bad. She massaged it, tore off part of her skirt and wrapped it so as to stabilize the swelling, bruised ankle. Her eyes were heavy in the night. In the dark, she began to drift. No more noise could be heard in the distance save what was clearly the work of animals, branches, wind speaking to her in drifts upon her skin, through the trees. The elements seemed to gather around her, protect her through the trial of what was ultimately an extension of her captivity, there in the dense forest. This is how she sensed the totality of her experience there, in compromised flight.

In the forest one is eventually safe from the indignities of mad priests and rapists. Nature is the great provider, it protects her, feeds her berries, foliage, branches conceal her tired and shivering body from the rain when it rains. How good it tastes, food that is of the earth rather than the body of Christ. But it also presents obstacles to health, endurance. Its safety, consolation, are not that of modern culture in the city. One recalls being in the forest as a child and eventually yearning to leave. Not all the animals there sought her wellbeing. She was eager to put the greenery and the immense trees behind her, wherever she was. But this would have to wait.

She was accustomed to moving in and out of sleep, an uncomfortable mattress in the dank, unnaturally lit room. Here the dark was natural. The moon towered above, illuminating the fact of its cold solitude. Illuminating her night in the forest, the first of many, to be followed by days of genuine light that would not disappoint in the way that summer light can overwhelm, subtract from the preciousness of the dark. She leaned against a tree, closed her eyes for minutes at a time, only to open them in fearful shock, bolt upright, a woman alone in the elements.

By the light of the sun, she moved on, afraid of the men resuming their hunt. The forest guided her, this is how she experienced particular beams of light through the trees and landing on a spot of earth, a mark in a tree signifying direction. Signposts that oriented her toward the end, which was freedom. From rape, scripture. Her killing ankle. The capacity to animate her limbs at will, a signpost. Find home. Rectify a wrong. It was not until another night, another swell into the darkness of newfound freedom, that she realized the imminence of an additional capacity. Wisdom. The men were long gone, she knew. Their howling inside with the knowledge of what she would do to them should she survive, and the lack of details informing them, their ultimate lack of knowledge and imagination. This frightened them the most, she well knew. But her freedom would require expansion beyond the forest and her revived energy. She would need to find the next level of her craft.

In the night she fell in and out of sleep, having walked long and far that next day on a still livid ankle, no civilization in sight, no roads, she cursed the men and their rural retreat.

Upon waking and foraging for plant food, the impulse to dig was confusing and strong. It spoke to her, though, with violence, dig, pick up that branch, dig yourself a hole. She dug until her hands and back ached, sweat made her frightening to behold, she knew. Her ankle was in turmoil, her other leg weary from the added weight. Dig until the blood is enough to drink. She dug at the spot where she had been instructed by the violence to stick-dig, unearth her grave, and then licked the blood from her war-torn hands.

The afternoon wore on and the hole was deep enough to inhabit. Not home, it nevertheless served the purpose of insulating her from the elements that might do harm. The men who, in fact, continued to search, who might have caught up with her by following a stream—even she needs water, they thought. By the end of the day and its blistering sun, they might have found her, bludgeoned her with the cock of an angry god, had she not chiseled out a space in the ground, woven branches to cover herself. She laughed to herself at the thought of a man falling in and on top of her. She let herself down into the hole, putting most of the pressure on one foot. She eased into this new challenge.

A womb, she conceded in the seriousness of her venture. And there the violence continued to inform. Notice the animosity and the pain, recognize these sensations with distance, now go deeper, feel the earth around you, at once remove yourself and be immersed in the final hours of your life as you've known it. The fluids drowning you in your soil sac, the thinnest cord attaching you to your former life, learn to breathe in the unfamiliar fluid. It was all very painful indeed. She was hungry. But the coolness of the earth offered comfort, her ankle was healing, the thought of the men no longer a dagger thorn in her move to freedom but a source of diabolism and pleasure. What she would do in vengeance. In the end, of course, it would be him, just him.

Time. Time passing. Clarity around time and fate. And this cavity in time, this looming presence becoming her. This woman in the earth being remade. Infinitely more than a mere hole, a sex organ for the dumb stick of masculinity to poke. Though she fingered herself there, underground, as instructed, her own fluids, the wetness on her already bleeding, wounded fingers, combining, healing. She no longer felt pain. She feared nothing. She lost her appetite. He spoke to her and she answered, in due time, by rising slowly from the grave. Her hands reached through the entwined branches, grasped the dirt, she lifted herself into the night. The moon had spoken. The forest, in all of its grandiosity and understanding, a sanctuary for her mounting power and bile. It beheld her there, floating above the hole in the ground. She was lifted, she levitated above the earth. Behold her. The forest knew, as one knows, that something original had been born into the world, again. As did the priest, in the van, on his way back to the city, unnerved, unfathomably scared. For himself, for us all.

IV

Return to the source. Before Salem. Where history is so old it creaks with the slightest shift. Still moving, practicing, evading the Law of the Twelve Tables and its modern successors with deft strategies. Europe awaits you, you'll find help there, they know how to enact the rites without suspicion intervening. With the weight of history in tow, they remove heaven's ceiling, blaspheme it open, with subtle devastation, perpetually hack away at any and all small-minded piety, uphold His vision, His present and future. They can use you. You're a survivor.

People had to be contacted from a safe distance. Wear disguises to enter her apartment so as to protect themselves from abduction, interrogation, uncalled for recitations in chains. The apartment would be paid for, don't worry, just advance, push forward. Items were sent abroad, clothes, some trinkets, manuscripts, articles of faith. Financial arrangements were made. Details in which, admittedly, she was never very interested. Now she had to be interested, direct them, her people, with beams of light and signs. She did so with the blackened luminosity of one who has been transformed in the soil, answered the call of depths. The others responded with appropriate, and astonished, loyalty. Their zeal equaled and surpassed only by her newfound authority. The recently opened portal to her Source.

The Europe paved in cobblestone, where history emanates in corners, from behind walls and mirrors. Where diverse ages of wisdom and insight flow exoterically into the new age following modernity. Over dinner, at the café, in the meeting house. Ideas percolating, theory pulling discourse away from its own bones as meat, and people understanding this process, the necessity of dismantling the *idée fixe*, gathering to speak as exercise, maneuvering thought. A variety of cuisines. Rich food. But be careful, indulge without attachment. And uncommonly beautiful architecture that speaks to the wisdom of the ages, the commitment to thoughtful, engaging space. Walk these streets, meet the right people, insert yourself, music of the spheres, with the Greater Magic inaugurate the damage that was begun many, many years ago. Lex Satanicus, Lex Satanicus, Lex Satanicus.

Her new home, a small apartment in the capital city. Its view more than acceptable. The bustle of the city below her shook with its rampant energy though it wasn't enough to disturb her sleep. She occupied the top floor of the building. She had no time to waste on heavy stepping neighbors, loud talkers, people who don't respond to politeness when asked to please contain your noise. There was serious work to do. So much more than mere homicide. Time, time spent at the edges of an abyss where no human is allowed to remain for fear of permanent dementia. Her fear was real, a physical sensation, far from the playful torment of an obsessive priest. But she had been guided there, she would be safe, instructed in the ways of time and proximity to the edge. Given the tools to navigate a well-trod path, where one encounters Elders whose immensity of collective power can eviscerate as easily as it aids the seeker in justice, vengeance, or untold education. In the space off the living room, separated by French doors, the space whose awkward dimensions correlated perfectly to the art of her craft at this new level, this mastered aptitude for human, elemental dominion. Her time was about settling in, fleshing out the accoutrements of her new home. A new, enriching chapter. The end of life as a priest knows it.

When free of obligation, she attended concerts. There are many in the city. One of the great pleasures in her life, the abundance of culturally enriching events that took on a special flavor in this city of lights, diverse people, intoxicating scenes. Though she never allowed herself to become over-stimulated by culture, people, she never forgot her aim and how she had been driven to its demands and responsibilities by an inferior wretch of a man, for better and for worse. She missed her old life. But she was strong, persistent, and really, in her new clothes, cut of soil and autoeroticism, the blood of a hole in the forest, she was nearly inhuman. Life was a different enterprise now. It floated over and above the banalities of old and new, the undulating landscapes of daily concerns. It was only the most profound cultural events that still managed to charge her with the electricity that invigorates certain elevated humans, that allowed her to share in the humanity of others, in a room, an auditorium, if only for a brief interim between extended periods of focus, ritual, preparation.

In the main hall of the Eglise Saint Ephrem, the lights lowered and she was reminded of the descent into a dark night which all must undergo before the magic really begins to materialize. She got comfortable in her seat, looked to the person sitting next to her, smelled him, wondered if they would be transported together this evening, despite his countless limitations as an adherent to some lesser faith, as a man. The pianist took the stage, bowed, everyone clapped. She intuited that something unique was about to seize them, or her, as the pianist settled into the music, began the journey. The moment of realizing that one is in the right place at the right time, the veracity of this encounter unimpeded by the cliché of its universality.

How odd that it should have come through Chopin. Nocturne No. 1 in B-Flat Minor. Or not. Another canonical cliché, a favorite of the concert hall, but its quiet shifting between buoyancy and melancholia, the elegance with which it proceeds to its gentle conclusion. These qualities lend it a certain earthy mysticism. And so it was through the music, and specifically at the piece's triumphant mid-point, the swell that signifies joy, festivity, that another, less dramatic modification to her person occurred, there in the sixth row of the concert hall. Chopin's fleeting celebration collapsed into the momentum of her aim, a joyful assemblage, and awoke in her the knowledge of what must be done. As though the notes combined with the voice with which she now communed on a daily basis, lifting that voice to unparalleled heights of decadent comprehension. This is how he will die, it said in the language of her new home, through the buoyant Chopin in the Eglise Saint Ephrem. Despite her age, she was an excellent student of language. And this is what you must do to make it so. Perhaps the most beautiful, love-soaked language on earth. For all his ineptitude, the man next to her felt the transition, the physical impact of her epiphany. He turned to face her, without volition, but she only looked dead ahead, locked into the triumph of her promise as the pianist continued to play the Nocturne faultlessly and exquisitely.

At home again, still floating on the music, the pleasure of being in the company of music lovers. Curtains drawn, it's getting late. Candles made shadows. Behind French doors in the space off the living room. Her body erect now, and blanketed, her staring into a candle and the goat's head, the items one requires to instill the ether with the force of one's aim. The pentagram means something to her. Her, what is that. Who is she when possessed, fully committed in the moment of rapture? She intonated in a low voice the commandments of her Master. The months have come down to this night, its fulfillment, Chopin. She spoke fluently, like the pianist at the keys. She sensed the swirling of energies about her, whereupon she was directed to open the curtains, throw open the window onto the city, let it out, keep speaking in that low voice, that low growl, feel His power emanating from you, into the room and beyond its walls, it travels with incomprehensible speed to its destination, keep intonating the words of the living Elders, and finally, of the fallen Son, He alone gives you what you need, fulfills your destiny if only you will welcome Him into the dreams of your heart.

Burn the priest, Alyssa. Burn the priest.

Her lips continued to mouth the words once the energy had evaporated into the night, her body on the precipice of collapse. Her lips moved with the barest sound of a chant, the lowest frequencies of the human voice falling out of her until the night was black just before dawn. The ritual complete after these many months. When she awoke next day, on the floor, overcome by the emptiness of the space and the lethargy and hunger that kept her there longer than is deemed efficient for an adult on a sunny afternoon in the city, she wept. Much time had passed since she had last cried. Tears of joy and celebration, productive, targeted exhaustion. Triumph of her holy will. She knew it without question, the side of her face impressed upon the hardwood of the floor, the candles long since melted down. Her static, aging body still clothed in concert regalia, there on the floor amidst accoutrements of ritual. It was accomplished.

<h1 style="text-align:center">V</h1>

Time moving quickly, forthrightly. What is time when temporal-spatial barriers are collapsed? When retribution screams silently through the ether and lands on a condemned man?

It was in the company of others, for better or for worse, when he first began to experience symptoms. Nobody likes a cold. Not even a guilt-laden priest. He shrugged it off to his companions, men who, like him, had reached a point of offering only their confusion and hostility to life. Some of them were better off than others. And yet the symptoms had appeared with such rapidity and ferocity. He excused himself and made his way home. He entered the rooms that had become their own monastic refuge, segregated from the living world about him by virtue of its dead, old world relics, souvenirs of a corrupted religious practice, all currently on display in the wake of recent misfortune, his museum of a home, closed to the public. The many months meant nothing to him. He carried her presence with him always. Into the night, dreams. How could he have messed up like that. What was he thinking. The other men had nearly forgotten. Not him.

The symptoms persisted in spite of an infusion of vitamin C and other conventional staples of flu battle. In fact they worsened. With even greater rapidity. They began to overwhelm his sense of embodiment in the hours following his return home, unaccompanied, a solitary man. A sore throat, now ripping through his neck every time he swallowed, or so it felt. Fever, undoubtedly. He was tired, very tired, from the symptoms and the agitated questing for peace in the wake of dubious circumstances. His neck was bothering him, just under the ears and reaching toward the collar bone, he was swelling there, he was sure of it. Odd how one identifies so intensely with the body under such circumstances. I am swollen. I am a painful throat, I am walking death. Now he was delirious. Consequently, it was unclear to him whether the white patch that was forming by the minute on his tongue was real or imagined. What is that in the mirror. I am hair on a diseased tongue. A contaminated shrinking face in the mirror, burning from the inside. He rested, finally, managed to fall asleep before the darkness set in.

Tremendously difficult to stand upon waking, in the night, far from the morning hours that inaugurate a new day, light, he had never felt so feeble, this otherwise robust priest whose powers of commanding attention from the pulpit or abducting heathens were once so secure. He made his way to the bathroom where urinating hurt. The mirror then spoke to him. With self-loathing. How can you not hate this image, it said. He had grown spotty in the night hours, rashes appeared on his face, and likely down his neck, over the entirety of his body, though he was afraid to look. His face was gaunt. He stepped on a scale. He had lost twenty-three pounds in a day. The mass of his body was falling away, it seemed clear to him. What was wrong. He needed help. Now. He called a man at this terrible hour but the man didn't answer. He gave up on help. Put on ill-fitting clothes. Dragged himself to the van. Drove the van through the empty city in search of a hospital. Parked illegally. Collapsed somewhere between the lobby and a unit reserved for minimal care patients.

The hours that passed were as nothing. He wasn't there. The symptoms were rushing into being at such an exponential rate that he couldn't distinguish himself from other objects in the corridor, and soon the room reserved for special cases. Doctors and nurses were also fevered in their emergency care. They took precautions, kept him away from others, out of sight, dashed him into the room. There was no time to contemplate the dramas in their own lives that mimicked those

the priest sometimes followed on television hospital dramas.
Their rubber gloves would protect them from him, this was
the hope. From what they immediately diagnosed as an oblit-
erated immune system. The priest had lost all immunity to
the challenges abounding in and around his body. He was
his body. No longer walking. That his condition would most
likely, the doctors suspected, be identified as that which is
most unbecoming for a priest, excommunicated or not, they
would have to explain to him once he regained consciousness.
If he by chance regained a sense of himself apart from the
condition of dying there.

It would happen. He knew. This is the plan. He must be
cognizant of his defilement. He would awaken and feel some
relief in the comfortable bed and the IV in his shrinking arm,
the attention of kind nurses. In truth they were frightened
of him. He first noted their translucent rubber gloves upon
waking, not touching him, and then their whispering to one
another, but chose to focus on the Hippocratic formalities
governing their occupations, and perhaps their consciences.
And then after an unknown period of time had passed—time
meant nothing, he was lost in its lying web, in this sterile
room that contained no flowers, cards, loved ones, not even
a blank television screen—at a particularly alert hour, a doctor would appear in the room to explain the situation. We
aren't yet sure, it was only what's known as a rapid test, further results are forthcoming, but it appears, father, that your
immune system is deficient, inoperable. You have acquired a
fatal, metastasizing virus. Your immune system is shot. There
are drugs, of course, but your condition is expanding at such
an alarming rate that we can only ease your pain. There are
specialists flying in. Your case is unique. You will have the
best. But I am not hopeful. Do you have any questions.

The priest asked if he could be helped to the bathroom.
The mirror doesn't lie, that cliché, facing him there, as a nurse

held him steady, his face at once reduced and swollen. Her subtly flinching eyes. The nurse didn't join him in confronting the mirror image. She helped him urinate, less painful now, and helped him back to bed. She whispered to a colleague at the door. There would be a time for questions regarding his behavior prior to the emergence of symptoms. A priest, a stigmatized disease, exceptional in its advance through his body. Drug needles. Behavior with other men. Boys. Father, we need to talk. How did this happen. Is there anybody who needs to be contacted, for obvious reasons. Or another priest, entering the room in his pompous, easy manner. Do you repent, do you seek forgiveness? What do you know about this, the other priest would say. A curse, he would mumble, finally, without getting too close, into the disbelieving ear of his confessor.

He understood the laws that had been enacted on his behalf. If there were any modicum of compassion in her, he would soon die. If not, or if drugs and technology intervened, quite without his blessing, he would live to embody his torment for unfathomable years to come. Now he could only speak without speaking, in the interior space of his captivity, to the willful figure before him. The other priest whose grounded, dark suit and white collar ran counter, screaming, to the tunnel, the white light, the blissful threshold on the other side he so desired, there in the hospital.

"Destroy him."

The Master appears before him when he opens his eyes. Even a priest does not truly comprehend that vision until he does. He sees the Master in flashes, in that corner, standing above him, framed in the window, better than television. Infernal shocks to a system that is nearly drawn to its embittered and godless end.

She contemplates this scene in the quietude of the night. Stands on the veranda of her new home overlooking the city of lights, the body of water that snakes through the city center, its countless amusements, people. There is perhaps no better offering of productive art and thought than what lives below her there in the museums and the lesser-known galleries, prestigious institutions. The opportunities for concerts here are so abundant as to necessitate choosing between possibilities on any given night. She takes slow sips from a glass on the veranda, listening to the music of city; a hackneyed, filmic moment that nevertheless asserts itself as authentic, immediate happiness. As real and authentic as the slaughter of a priest in the throes of his feeble, living, waking death.

The Dance of Abraxas

by Benjamin Tweddell

"GOD dwelleth behind the sun, the devil behind the night. What god bringeth forth out of the light the devil sucketh into the night. But Abraxas is the world, its becoming and its passing. Upon every gift that cometh from the god-sun the devil layeth his curse."

A peal of thunder roused Charles from his contemplation of the text before him, and he felt an involuntary shudder as the germinal flickering of a summer storm momentarily illuminated the distant mountains with a spectral radiance. The warm summer evening was cooling rapidly. As the first spots of rain, harbingers of the impending deluge, began to streak the pools of lamp light which surrounded the veranda on which he sat, Charles snatched up his book and hurried inside. The incessant twilight chatter of the cicadas fell into silence, replaced by the drumming of the downpour.

The interior of the small house was dark, but his host had kindled a fire, and was lighting an oil lamp on the mantle, its pallid glow dancing across the simple furniture and throwing long shadows on the walls. The acrid smell of the fuel contrasted starkly with the freshness of the summer rain in Charles nostrils. He felt a momentary wave of confusion, the dissonance which often swept over him since his release from the hospital. It was still disorientating to be here. Everything about Switzerland was so utterly strange after the months as an invalid in London. The seemingly endless days since his discharge had congealed into an aggregate of grey monotony, staring from the window of his London Flat over the dreary rooftops, the noise, and the smog obscuring the horizon. The journey here had been long and exhausting—a train from Paris to Zurich followed by a series of local services through the Alps. Now, however, any apprehension he felt about his new surroundings was at least tempered by the recognition which the storm forced upon him of vitality, life and experience outside the sterile monochrome of his previous enforced torpor.

All the same, he didn't feel entirely at ease here. He knew Herr Freideberg only through their correspondence, and although he was impeccably hospitable, Charles felt a certain tension hovering between them. A stillness lingered in the house, even with the tempest raging outside. Charles guessed that his host was unused to visitors. He understood that. Many men who had endured the trenches—years spent in cramped squalor with their fellow soldiers, sought the luxury of solitude when they returned home. There was, however, a forlorn atmosphere clinging to the cottage, as if it had been frozen in the past. Dust showed heavy in the lamp light upon the books which crowded the simple wooden shelves. The titles were mostly in German, but Charles spotted some English poets, as well as the Hindu 'Bhagavad Gita' and 'Upanishads', Buddhist sutras, Plotinus and more which he did not recognise. His host poured two schnapps, and they sat before the fire, listening to the pouring rain. He was a slightly built man, but emanated a strength which his physique belied, as well as an obvious sadness. When he spoke, his voice was soft, and his English excellent.

"Your sister loved these summer storms. She used to say that it was the voice of the mountains. A visitor once asked her 'do you mean the voice of God, Frau Lydford', but I remember she just turned away to stare at the hills and said nothing. She was a true Asconan in that respect, unusual for you English. The mountains and the sun were her gods, the rolling hills and the streams her faith. I apologise if I imply her to have been . . . impious, but a certain spirit prevailed here at Monte Verità . . . stills prevails, despite our losses and tragedies. She shared that spirit . . . perhaps she shares it still."

Charles took a sip of his schnapps and stared thoughtfully into the fire "My sister would abandon herself to the ferocity of the elements. She would run in the grounds of our home as the rains lashed down. It drove our mother to despair when she was like that. She was always too wild for Berkshire. That's what brought her here I suppose, that search for true abandon."

"And you, Herr Lydford?"

"I saw too much ferocity in the trenches to ever welcome it in a storm. I don't hear the voice of god or mountains in the thunder, or glimpse the infinite in a flash of lightning, just the onslaught of artillery shells over the barbed wire in the night." He felt the sudden sting of bitterness break in his words and silently cursed his outburst. They had all suffered, English and German. What was the point of dwelling on it?

Perhaps just to break the hush that had descended on them his companion asked "What do you think of Herr Jung's little book? He gave this copy to me some years back now. Do you know his visions first began here, at Monte Verità?"

"I hardly know what to make of it, Herr Freideberg"

"Karl, please."

"It's intriguing, Karl. But rather opaque. I mean . . . Seven Sermons of the Dead? I was of the impression that Doctor Jung was a scientist, but what is one make of this?" He scrutinised the book which rested on the table beside him. "The monster of the under-world, a thousand-armed polyp, coiled knot of winged serpents, frenzy." He spoke in what he intended as jest, but the thunder rolled again, closer this time, and his attempt at levity died on his tongue, leaving him again with that fleeting sense of paramnesia, the tentacles of unreality coiling around his perception for just the briefest moment.

"Indeed Herr Lydford," replied his host, and for a moment Charles had the eerie impression that his thoughts were naked and visible in the air around them, tangible, like dancing sprites. "Abraxas. Begetter of truth and lying, good and evil. The brightest light of day and the darkest night of madness . . ."

"To fear it, is wisdom. To resist it not, is redemption," murmured Charles, finishing the passage and putting the book aside.

A shutter slammed, caught suddenly by the wind, and he started violently, almost dropping his glass onto the flagstone floor. Karl leapt to his feet and secured the window against the storm, before returning to the pool of light surrounding the fireplace. He stared into his glass, perhaps deliberating the prudence of voicing his thoughts, but then continued.

"Your sister too, was . . . pre-occupied with the notion of Abraxas, Herr Lydford. You corresponded with Frau Wigman in Berlin, and so perhaps know a little of the work they were collaborating on here . . ."

"Charles—please. And, yes, I have tried to engage with Mary Wigman, but correspond would imply a measure of reciprocity. I have found Miss Wigman to be truculent in the extreme on the subject of Anna's whereabouts . . . and indeed every subject."

Karl let a brief smile play on his lips and poured them both another schnapps. "Indeed, well Mary is . . . a difficult woman. But is that not so often the way with genius?"

Charles looked briefly incredulous, but Karl held up his hand to stop him. "Genius indeed. I, and many others here in Ascona thought of . . . think of, Mary as such. She is certainly a visionary. Her work in the field of dance is without parallel. Even Rudolf Laban is, I believe, rather in awe of her. Her dance ceremonies were fundamental to life here at Monte Verità. To bring something incomprehensible into the world, to banish the tyranny of reason and restore intoxication as a universal mode. Those were her aims; those were all our aims in the years before the war. But I suppose the trenches left us all sodden with incomprehension. Perhaps we all now crave a little of the tyranny of reason."

Charles raised his glass. "To reason then."

Karl laughed mirthlessly and followed suit. "Not a toast I ever imagined joining at Monte Verità, but, to reason, and to perhaps a saner Europe."

They were silent for a moment, both staring into the fire as the rain danced across the window pane behind them.

"You said earlier that perhaps my sister still shared the spirit of Ascona? You think she may still be alive then Karl?"

"I really don't know. I last saw Anna in 1916, when I left for the war. As I am sure Frau Wigman told you in her letter, the two of them worked together closely. Mary was already perfecting her theory that movement could be . . . how can I put it. . . . A mechanism for the evocation of spirit. She sought a physical method to unify our values, our goal of *total expressionism*. When your sister arrived, they took the work further, forging a style of dance which utterly rejected tradition. They explored the mountains together, immersed in the act of creation. 'Even the wolf dances, if you have the eyes to see', Mary told me. I remember them, here outside my cottage, working with such intent and ferocity, dancing to mirror the rapture of existence."

He laughed to himself. "But I ramble. During the war, Mary returned to Berlin, Anna remained. We called Mary 'The Priestess' when she was here, half in jest . . . but there was truth to it. Anna took up that role with even greater fervour. It was that summer that Herr Jung visited, and had the first of his, shall we call them, visions? A grave illness certainly, with fevers that eventually inspired the book you were reading earlier. He and Anna talked many times, long into the night, of Abraxas. She knew of it already when she arrived here 'the unknown god' she called it, 'the mother and father of good and evil, that which we have forgotten'. I believe it may have been Anna who inspired Herr Jung to delve deeper into the subject. Did you know of Anna's interests in these . . . matters?"

Charles again felt that brief tug at the back of his mind, the tendrils of sudden cold shoot through him despite the warming schnapps he had consumed.

"I . . . lost touch with my sister. I had not spoken to her for several years after she left England, and I do not know what her enthusiasms, or pursuits were during that time, or where her travels took her. I knew that she was here in Ascona in 1912, because she wrote to me. She sounded . . . happy, so I did not pursue her, did not beg her to come home. She had a small allowance from our father, so I knew she was secure enough. Anna always had a passion for . . . the outlandish, even in our childhood years. She would urge father to tell us the stories of the old gods and goddesses—always with a taste for the oddest tales, Celtic Ceridwen, Fenris of the Norse, Astarte of Babylon, Circe. We would often sit together on rainy afternoons in his study as he read from some leather-bound tome, me distracted, wishing I was out playing cricket, but Anna, serious, absorbed, always asking questions. It does not surprise me to hear she talked of such matters with a man as erudite as Herr Jung. She would have been, I believe, in her element." He smiled wryly, remembering how her teachers had complained of her quarrels and disputations with them during class, the constant disruptions to their lessons "But, please, go on Herr Freideberg."

"Sadly, there is little else I can tell you. Most of the men of Monte Verità, including myself, had been called away to the

German or Austrian armies by the time of her disappearance, or like Gustav Gräser refused to serve and were imprisoned. It was the same for all of us. We lost so many. And we lost Anna. All I know is that she ascended into the mountains at midsummer and was simply never seen again. Not a trace. They searched of course. I sometimes . . . feel she is . . . not dead, but I really cannot explain. I just know she is gone, and we are poorer for it." He finished his drink and laid the glass on the table between them. "But come. It is late, the storm is passing. I think it is time we retired. Tomorrow is another day."

Although the ferocity of the storm had eased, the wind rattled persistently at the windows, and Charles found the embrace of sleep elusive. His mind swam with the strangeness of his new surroundings. Each time he felt the drift to slumber, he would be suddenly snapped back to wakefulness, possessed by an intense, nervous vigilance. He thought himself back in the darkness of the hospital ward, the claustrophobia of his bandaged face momentarily choking him with nausea and panic. Finally, overtaken by utter weariness, he sank into sleep. But unquiet dreams welled up, of asphyxiation, of the stench of mustard gas creeping across darkened trenches and the distant shrieks of the dying. And then something else. A voice that was not a voice, the voice of wind and of the water that runs eternally down the darkened gullies of a mountain peak, of the sun as it ascended over a high alpine meadow where sapphire flowers blazed with an unearthly inner light.

Charles woke to a bright, fresh day, the memory of his nocturnal visions now indistinct—a dimming unease which was brushed aside as his host produced coffee on the veranda. Karl seemed content to enjoy the silence of the morning, which pleased Charles, and neither man felt the need to converse. Before them, the broad expanse of Lake Maggiore sparkled in the morning sun, its surface mirroring the cloudless alpine sky. Karl's cottage was situated a mile beyond the small town of Ascona, and below them houses crowded to the edge of the water, red tiled roofs and shuttered steeples seeming to huddle together. It gave Charles the fleeting impression that they sought refuge from the steep hills which loomed on all sides. Distant snow-capped peaks quietly dominated the scene, a reminder that despite the warmth of the day, this was a region subject to the violent caprices of the mountain climes. Beside the shore of the lake, palm trees grew alongside willow, incongruous interlopers from the Mediterranean, far to the south.

On the opposite hill, Charles could see the sweeping staircase which framed Casa Centrale, the windows of its expansive front porch glinting in the morning sun. Yesterday Karl had taken him there for a tour of the building. Charles had been struck by its beauty as they climbed toward it, the fine wrought iron railings and the Art-Nouveau-style façade exquisite. But its grandeur was illusionary, for inside the central hall there hung the same neglect and melancholy which filled Karl's home. A gloomy, opaque light filtered through the cobwebbed windows, and dust lay heavy on the intricate mosaic floors. The Yin-Yang symbol which dominated the chamber was now obscured by grime. Pigeons regarded them from the darkened circular balcony above, where scarlet drapes flapped in the breeze, tattered and mildewing. Streaks of water darkened the once splendid domed ceiling, the woodwork buckling as the elements toiled with ceaseless patience to gain ingress. Karl's voice had sounded hollow when he spoke. "Casa Centrale was built as a meeting house for the community, designed to maximise the natural light, to illuminate the spirit of our gatherings. 'The clear world of the blessed souls' Elisar von Kupffer once called it. It was our focal point, the very heart of Monte Verità. I witnessed Frau Wigman and your sister dance here often, and it gladdens me to visit it and think of those times, despite the neglect you now see. The ancient Chinese symbol of Yin-Yang is the *genius-loci* of this place." He stooped to wipe the dust away from the mosaic circle. "Within the light always resides the darkness. Light has given way to shadow here at Monte Verità, Herr Lydford, but all is transient. The shade will pass again, bringing clarity, I know it in my heart." His words had echoed in the dome of the chamber, before a forlorn silence descended once more, and they left that mournful space behind them.

Charles was snapped from his recollection by a shouted greeting, in German, and Karl too was roused from his morning languor. Striding up the lane toward them, like a biblical patriarch, was a heavily bearded, longed haired figure. Almost immediately, Charles' alarm at the sudden appearance of this outlandish apparition was allayed by the stranger's broad smile and open manner.

Karl beamed with delight and held out his hands in greeting. "Gustav, you came. Wonderful. Herr Lydford, may I introduce Gustav Gräser, one of the founders of our community."

"Gusto to my friends. And the brother of Anna Lydford is most assuredly a friend. Your sister and I were very close," he effused, in heavily accented English, offering a small, formal bow that struck Charles as strangely incongruous. He was handsome, imposing—consummately Germanic with his striking blue eyes. Despite his tunic, sandals and disorderly countenance, this was clearly a person to be reckoned with. Charles briefly considered, with a flash of anger which he immediately supressed, just how close this man and his sister had been.

They drank their coffee and sat for a while in companionable silence, each gazing toward the sunlit mountains, lost in their own thoughts. Finally, Gustav stood and stretched his arms as if to salute the sun then cheerfully addressed Charles.

"Perhaps you would care to stroll with me? The view of Lake Maggiore, if one climbs a little higher into these hills, is splendid. To see it in the morning is to bask in Amida's pure light you know," he grinned, then before Charles had time to protest his fatigue, he found himself following this curious companion, whilst Karl waved them farewell and vanished from their sight.

They walked together in silence for some time, following a well-used track that wound up the valley ahead. Gustav had the wide, loping steps of a seasoned hiker, and Charles found himself breaking into a sweat to keep up. He silently cursed himself for accepting Gustav's invitation. The doctors had assured him that his physical injuries were less grave than initially assumed, but he had still not fully regained his strength. Gustav's pace slowed when he realised his companion was falling behind. They sat for a while on the grass to regain their breath, enjoying the warmth of the morning sun and watching skylarks swoop overhead, their high, trilling song chiming on the breeze. Charles felt a sudden peace, the first he could remember for a long time.

He was unused to the expansive surroundings. How long it had been since he experienced such a peaceful landscape he could not recall. Years in the trenches changed a man. Despite the beauty around him, he saw still the pitiful remnants of once verdant woodland transformed into a wasteland of cratered mud, strewn with the men he had lost. Their bodies lay twisted in ghastly repose before his mind's eye, gas mask clad faces glaring in silent reproach across no-man's land. Trying to shake the image from his mind, he realised that the green hills rising ahead of them stirred memories of childhood holidays with Anna and his parents in the English Lake district, but with the mountains hovering in the distance, the familiarity was rendered otherworldly, uncanny. Those times in Cumbria had been some of his happiest, but now he had the eerie feeling he was peering into another man's memories, a man untouched by the spectre of grief. Still, the sun was bright, the scent of the meadow and the alpine air invigorating, and Gustav seemed happy to talk for both of them.

"When I first came here, in 1900 Ascona was just a village. The place was poor. But the climate was good, there was no competition for land. Many farmers had left for the cities, tired of eking out a living in such a remote place. But that was exactly its appeal to me. One could live free, unfettered by Protestant conceit and mechanised hubris. It felt like the threshold of the old world back then, far from the pompous Burghers and their cheerless wives. I suppose I imagined my-self one of the Taoist sages of old China in those days, like Hanshan striding on the hills, my heart full of poetry and song." He laughed at the memory. "I lived in caves up there at the top of the valley, I talked with the gypsies, and cared not what the morrow would bring. You know, this has always been a byway for nomads travelling from southern climes, and I resolved to make it the confluence for, let us say, more strangely feathered birds." He smiled to himself. "Many came here, poets, painters, mystics and anarchists. I sat under the stars with Hesse and Jung, talking of the yogis of India and the theurgists of old Alexandria. I listened as Kropotkin talked of the utopia we could build if only humanity worked together, instead of as competitors. Your own Herr Lawrence stayed here, began his book 'The Rainbow' in Ascona. But your sister was the one with the brightest plumage. She was truly like no other woman I had met. She hiked here, on foot, you know, travelling part way with the gypsies from the south. I remember her, staring in wonder across Lake Maggiore when she arrived, her hair blowing wild, clad in sandals and cotton skirt. Even Mary's companions, with their ideas of rational dress looked positively conservative in comparison! She was truly a free spirit, a seeker of revelation, a hunter after truth

. . . I will never meet another like her. When she first came, I was translating the Tao of Lao-Tzu. She loved to read it aloud, with the stars glittering above us. 'Unnameable is the unending one, and nameable only the passing part'. That is how I feel now about your sister. It is only the part of her we can name that has vanished from our sight. Something for which we have no words burns brightly still, in the mountains, in all of us"

Charles saw her now, as they raced together across the hills of Cumbria, tearing off her shoes and hurling them into the bracken in a wild attempt to catch up, their mother crying out in exasperation and Anna's laughter ringing on the wind. He could almost hear it now, as he walked beside Gustav, and felt the despair rise up in himself.

"I must know, Herr Gräser. I must discover what became of her. You must understand that. I failed her. I cannot forgive myself for the thought that I turned my back on her, abandoned her. I can tell that you loved her, Gusto, perhaps as much as I did . . . do. Please forgive my bluntness, but I must say what I feel."

Gustav paused for a moment, the breeze whipping his long hair around him.

"Do you know the next lines of Lao-Tzu's poem, Charles? 'Guard, O guard the secret, then the secret will guard you, but will to see it, perforce it lays waste your life'. I think some things are better not known. Perhaps we should let the mountains keep their secrets."

They walked on together in silence, both wrapped in their memories of Anna. Once, he had been unable to see what had driven her from their childhood home, from their comfortable life to be a vagabond in the hills of Switzerland. The man he had once been could never have fathomed the impulse to throw away family for a disordered life camped under the stars with bohemians and anarchists. But that man was gone. Once upon a time he would have seen Gustav as a social menace, his refusal to fight for his country an unpardonable disgrace. But the long years on the front, the long months in hospital, had excised all his old values and allegiances. He saw now the nobility, the bravery in Gustav's refusal to fight, to reject being swept into the bottomless futility of the Great War. But he still felt a terrible emptiness, cast adrift from the values which had seemed so important in his youth. God, King, Country. Absurd. All the old sureties were gone. Even his grief seemed remote sometimes. Lost in his own abstractions, Charles realised he had barely perceived the majestic sweep of the hills through which they strode.

They were climbing a steep sided gulley, down which a lively mountain brook cascaded in a series of waterfalls. The mid-morning sun refracted through a fine mist, casting a shimmering rainbow which enlivened their ascent, and the path criss-crossed the rushing stream, requiring leaps between stepping stones. Gustav looked delighted, obviously in his element here in the back-country. Stopping to take a drink, the water icy and refreshing, they startled a wary stag. It regarded them momentarily, before taking flight, bolting upstream toward the pine forest which crowded to the edge of the precipitous cliffs. Gustav joyfully saluted the retreating creature, and stooped to fill his canteen, before sitting upon the glistening rocks to rest. "Anna loved to climb in this valley, Charles. She would swim in the pools of the canyon ahead. She often went there to study, to create the patterns of her dance, to divine movements in the water which she considered . . . . significant." He laughed. "Her beliefs were often peculiar. Many things I considered absurd, the divinations and auguries of the ancients, she studied, trusted, and integrated into her art. I would tease her when she read the old books which she brought from Spain, full of talisman, charms and incantations, 'The Ghāyat al-Hakīm—*the Aim of the Sage'.* I thought it foolish, but Anna . . . she believed in these things. Yes . . . she could be strange indeed, your sister." Gustav chuckled and shook his head. "But come, we are almost there." The canyon narrowed as they climbed higher, its sheer walls towering above them, a shadowed cavern into which the sunlight barely reached. Deep pools formed here within echoing grottos, the walls undulating with the reflected play of the meagre sunlight. It created the uncanny impression that the rock was breathing, that they traversed the interior of a colossal sleeping beast. Despite Gustav's apparent ease in these surroundings, the shadow haunted canyon made Charles uneasy. The hollow sound of their footsteps merged with the distant reverberating boom of a waterfall, creating subtle auditory hallucinations. For a moment he was sure he heard laughter, and had the distinct impression that they were not alone, that somebody was following, yet there was nobody to be seen. Stopping to peer into one of the eddying pools, Charles saw the bones of some animal glitter like pale alabaster in the depths, the hollow eyes of its skull meeting his gaze with mute distain. For a moment, he saw submerged faces, wreathed in gas masks, and snapped his eyes shut to dispel the vision. When he opened them, he noticed chalk marks on the stone floor, geometric shapes which had been carefully inscribed and then partially rubbed away. He frowned, studied the peculiar sigils for a few moments, and then hurried to catch up with Gustav. There was something eerie about these grottos and their darkened pools, a stillness that was preternatural. They seemed to demand a mute veneration, and Charles had the absurd, but powerful sensation that his every breath was an outrage against some nameless axiom. As they progressed, the tumult of the waterfall ahead became gradually louder, and finally, to Charles' relief, they emerged from this silent realm and began to ascend a series of mossy steps. The river cascaded into the canyon here, the roar of its descent exhilarating after the sepulchral hush of the chambers below. A flimsy handrail was all that separated them from the precipice and the twisting stairway was slick with spray from the waterfall, yet despite the precariousness of the climb, Charles felt liberated from some hidden malevolence. Gustav pointed to an eagle soaring high above, circling the black crags, but he barely saw it—his eyes were drawn back to the darkness. A watchfulness seemed to emanate from it . . . *A voice that was not a voice.* He shook the thought away quickly, and then they were out of that dusky abyss, bathed once more in brilliant sunlight. The heat of noon was almost upon them and Charles' legs were aching, his lungs burning, when they finally reached a promontory which offered breath-taking views of the valley below. "There!" exclaimed Gustav, delight-ed, "is that not a vista to stir the heart, my friend? I am no Christian, but I always think of the *Hortus conclusus* when I am here. 'A garden enclosed is my sister, my spouse'. There is still much beauty, despite all we have lost."

It was indeed a magnificent panorama. A sheer drop yawned before them, a vast gulf of sky and wheeling birds with the ma-jestic sweep of Lake Maggiore far distant. Peering over the cliff edge, Charles could trace the course of the stream which they had followed, and see the mouth of the canyon where it van-ished into the forested slopes. Despite the sublime scene before him, the creeping sense of disquiet he had experienced during their ascent continued to grow. The turquoise circle of the lake seemed to ensnare the snowbound peaks, inverting them in a mirrored stockade, rendering whatever secrets they contained doubly phantasmagorical. They sat for some time, sharing a simple meal of bread and cheese which Gustav had produced from his pack, recovering from the arduous climb. A gentle breeze caressed their faces, carrying with it the scent of pine.

"This was Anna's favourite spot. We Asconans called this rock 'Harrassprung', after the old story of the Knight who, pursued on horseback by his enemies, leapt into such an abyss to escape. The horse was dashed upon the rocks, but the knight miraculously cheated death."

He drank deeply from a canteen of water and passed it to Charles.

"We would come here often, me writing, translating, or both just sitting, meditating, worshipping the sun you know!" He laughed, but Charles was silent.

As he gazed into the valley, instead of transcendence, he felt increasingly insubstantial and breathless, unanchored at the sight of it. He fancied that the lake was a great eye, blue, piercing, staring straight at *him,* into him. For a few moments, he was back in the trenches, on that June night in 1917, just before the attack which had left him hospitalised, transfixed by the full moon and experiencing the same feeling of uncanny, celestial scrutiny which assailed him now. Closing his eyes, he tried to shake himself free of the vision, to return his focus to Gustav's voice, but ethereal laughter danced out of the void, as if from an immense distance, and his panic grew. There was something subtly anomalous in the motion of the clouds which swept above them, something troubling too about their appearance. Gustav was clearly oblivious to it all. The pine trees appeared inexplicably ominous, in fact the whole landscape . . . A wave of fear swept through him, he was vaguely aware of Gustav saying something, and then . . . darkness.

When he came to, Gustav was kneeling beside him, a look of deep concern on his face. "Come, there is a place I know not far from here, the home of a friend. We must get you there immediately. I think you have had a little too much of Amida's pure light, Herr Lydford." He laughed, but his concern was obvious.

"It's nothing, really. I get these spells since I left the hospital. I will be quite alright I assure you Gusto." But the confidence in his words was diminished. Hardly knowing where he was, Charles allowed himself to be led up the slope, stumbling, a distant, hollow voice still reverberating through his mind. Or was it a voice? Where had he heard it before? Words from Jung's strange book flashed to him again . . . or did he hear them ringing out, like a returning echo from the void?

"You find yourselves in endless space, in the innermost infinity . . . at immeasurable distance stands one single star in the zenith."

He must have spoken the words aloud, for Gustav stopped and looked at him sharply, a flash of fear in his eyes, then quickly regaining his composure, murmured, "Come, we must get you to a place where you can rest."

Despite the apparently brief duration of his unconsciousness, Charles felt as if he had been disembodied for a colossal period, adrift on the furthest oceans of dream. His legs were weak, his vision uncertain, and he felt, with a pang of horror the same wretched helplessness that he experienced after leaving the hospital. Still, he tried to keep his composure for Gustav's sake, but wished they were not hiking, so many miles from habitation.

As they trekked up the steeply sloping meadows, they passed an arched stone structure, apparently of some antiquity. Despite its desolate location, it seemed cared for, and fresh flowers lay about the entrance. "A shrine to the Madonna," Gustav indicated with a wave of his hand. "There are many such in the countryside here. Mary and your sister believed them to be significant to the reverence of the feminine, the Great Mother, which still clings to life amongst the peasants here. I do not believe that. These people are simple, pious, but hardly pagan. Like all Christians they have swapped the elation and defiance of Jesus' teaching for insipid resignation and guilt. Please forgive me if I cause you offence, Charles. I often read the gospels, and think them quite beautiful, but what mankind has done with Christ's teachings is an abomination." Perhaps wishing to change the subject, he strode on. "Come, my friend Ernst lives not more than a mile further, there we can rest."

Charles glanced into the shrine as they passed. The Madonna, obscured within the shadowy interior, seemed momentarily baleful, a Lamia or Succubus awaiting its prey. Then the sun touched her face, and the vision passed. It was a Madonna, like any other, beatific and serene.

Numerous empty houses and farmsteads dotted the valley, in various states of disrepair. Crows flapped away from sagging roofs as they approached, and at one, a buzzard sat imperious on the chimney top, marking their passing with watchful quiet. Instead of the sublimity that Gustav clearly perceived in this landscape, Charles felt instead a melancholy, loss and sadness. Each farm they passed had fallen into ruin, with bindweed claiming back gates and fences and the grass growing long. Darkened windows gazed vacantly, as sightless as the eyes of their vanished occupants, and the wind seemed to whisper the names of those who had once worked this land, gone to the war, never returned, and now were forgotten. Passing a cottage, Charles stopped and, almost without thinking, pushed open the door. Peering into the chamber beyond, he glimpsed furniture, books and household utensils. Despite the darkness, the house emanated an eerie expectancy, as if it silently awaited the return of its former occupants, patiently enduring the passing seasons. Charles stepped inside, the accumulated dust rising in billowing spirals, and a shaft of light which fell through the grubby window seemed suddenly alive with the flicker of its eddying motes. For just a moment he thought he beheld a vortex of miniscule dancers, which almost caused him to cry out in astonishment, then Gustav stepped into the room beside him, and once more he saw only a beam of sallow, dusty sunlight. The illusion was dispelled, and he heard the furtive scuttling of rodents vanishing into the darkness, and smelt the miasma of damp and decay. A desk faced the window, scattered with mildewing sheets of paper. Once, Charles reflected, somebody had sat here, gazing into the valley, writing, but now the product of their contemplation lay discarded, mouldering, turning slowly to powder in the indifferent embrace of the passing years. As if reading his thoughts, Gustav began to speak softly. "Lotte Hattemer and Elly Lenz shared this house for a while, composing their philosophy of *Vegetarismus*. I remember, when Emil Ludwig, the novelist visited—he was entranced by these two, living the free life up here." A smile flickered across his face, then passed away. "I thought we could build a new world here, Charles, a better world, a utopia. The boldest and brightest came. In this very house I talked with Paul Klee and Ludwig Klages, of the rapture to come, of the new age. We had such dreams. Sometimes I wonder if it really happened. A shadow fell on us, not just that of war, but . . ." He lapsed into silence, unable to say more, and they turned their backs on the forlorn room, making their way outside into the afternoon sun. Gustav closed the door with an air of finality and bowed his head as if in silent prayer, before turning to face Charles, a hesitance in his voice.

"Your words earlier, when you awoke . . . were familiar to me. I remember camping out here once with Anna. The stars, you know, on clear summer nights in these mountains are truly something to behold, Charles. That night, staring up at the sky, I recall saying that it was a vision of the ineffable mystery of god, of infinity. 'Not so', your sister murmured. 'The great sage Basilides tells that there was a time when *nothing* was, not angel, not god. He did not mean that there was nothing, but that nothing *itself existed*. The stars', she said 'which we look upon are born from this nothing, Gusto. They are mere illusion. How does one live in an illusion? There are things which are beyond ineffable, beyond any name, any word. We have one name, Abraxas, one single star in the zenith, and beyond that, only silence'. I remember those words well, and I had no reply for her. Anna was secretive about many things, especially about her past. Of her childhood she mentioned only her great love for you, her brother. Of her travels, she told, even me, very little. I know she had been in the libraries of Toledo and had read much, and that she had studied with an aged priest in Alexandria. A priest of what faith, however, she never told me. She had danced with the Sufis, and I believe that she sought more in her work with Mary than mere intoxication. She spoke sometimes of seeking the dance, the harmony which revealed body and soul were of one nature, and of how that one nature transformed itself . . . into silence. And she spoke of Abraxas. Sometimes I wonder . . ." He trailed off, and they walked on in silence.

The hills here swept up to pine forest, and beyond that, vertical cliffs fractured by steep chasms which marked the beginning of the mountains. They crossed a wide mountain pasture, with goats grazing in the distance. A small house marked the only sign of human habitation, and near it a figure, a lone resident in these eerie hills, raised a hand in welcome. "My friend, Ernst," Gustav smiled, waving back. Arriving at the dilapidated dwelling, the two friends embraced warmly and Ernst pulled up three battered wooden chairs, motioning them to sit and rest whilst he fetched tea. He had the dishevelled aspect of a man who didn't often receive visitors—his goatee beard grown long and straggling, and his dark, untidy hair falling into his eyes. Greetings dispensed with, they sat on the porch of the house. Charles felt quietly irritated to be treated like an invalid, but he gladly accepted the offer of tea, and silently appreciated the rest after the long climb. The home in which Gustav's companion lived was little more than a shack. Goats roamed the fields outside. The wooden porch was rotten, the boards warped. Strange metal sculptures hung from the beams, grotesque masks created in imitation of medieval gargoyles. Once their bronze faces would have glittered in the sun, but whatever expression they had worn was long vanished beneath encrusted verdigris. They danced lightly in the breeze, the beam creaking above them, their sightless eyes seeming to follow Charles as he nervously sipped his tea and glanced at his surroundings. At the other end of the porch was a grubby copper alembic pot still, obviously to produce homemade liquor, and the numerous empty bottles on the ground attested to its frequent use. Cigarette stubs littered the floor. Ernst clearly lived a disordered life. Inside, just beyond the pool of opaque light which fell through the dirty window panes, books could be glimpsed, some of which appeared rare and valuable, piled in untidy stacks. Detritus of all types was scattered on the porch, from the prosaic to the more arcane—discarded tarot cards and pages covered with abstruse hand-written symbols, which were possibly astrological, but not immediately identifiable. Despite Gustav's obvious happiness to be there, the house, and the friendly, though guarded welcome of its occupant did nothing to dissipate the sense of unease which had been growing in Charles throughout the day. The mountains loomed close, their precipitous blackened ramparts towering above. He found his gaze inexorably drawn to them, their soaring bulk somehow oppressive, like squatting Titans glowering down upon them. He realised Ernst had been talking, but he had not listened to a word.

"I am sorry Herr Mohr, you were saying?" He fixed his eyes on the face before him. Ernst Mohr had a distinct elfin quality about him, something oddly sylvan. He was still a youngish man, perhaps in his mid-thirties, but his eyes had a haunted look, making him appear much older.

"I was just saying that I worked with your sister often." His tone was restrained, polite, but nervous. Perhaps it was simply the isolation of living so far up in these untenanted hills that caused the uneasiness which he emanated. "We first met when I was studying dance under Frau Wigman's tutorship." Charles must have looked startled, for he quickly interjected "I no longer dance, Herr Lydford. Not anymore." His response was sharp, and there was a bitterness in his tone. It was clear he did not want to discuss the matter further. An awkward hush fell upon them, broken finally by Gustav.

"Ernst was a priest when he first came here in 1910," he chuckled, pouring more tea from the cracked china pot on the precarious, rusting wrought iron table.

"A trainee priest—something which Gusto finds most amusing. But of course, I left Christ for Dionysus the moment I saw Mary perform her . . . rites. We call this place Monte Verità, the Mountain of Truth, and I find it has the tendency to dispel illusion, whether we desire it or not. Rudolf Laban, Mary's teacher you know, told me that to dance is to inhabit the true state of being, that of flux, change. The world we believe solid, real, is illusion, he said, merely transition—no beginning or end; always the midpoint between eternity."

The voice he had heard earlier, the vision, returned to Charles again . . . that solitary star in the zenith flashed into his mind, and felt sweat break on his brow, but forced himself back to Ernst's words.

"I saw at once that Rudolf was correct. Religion is but a mirage. All deities are born within the moment of ecstasy. How can one train to be a priest if god is an illusion?"

He poured more tea. Already the day was slipping away from them, and the sun was beginning to dip toward the mountain peaks. Charles felt increasingly forlorn in this desolate spot, depressed by the bleak visage of the pine trees stretching away to into wind swept crags. He could keep his silence no longer.

"Please . . . what do you know about my sister's disappearance, Herr Mohr? I knew nothing of her fate during the war. I knew she was still in Ascona when hostilities were declared, and I wrote her letters from the front, receiving only one reply, brief, very unlike her. We were close as children, we . . ."

He broke off. Those days were so remote now, so distantly halcyon that suddenly he could not bear to think of them, let alone talk of them. For a moment he was aware that tears were welling in his eyes, and he passed a hand across his face, unwilling to let these strangers bear witness to his sorrow and distress. He felt Gustav's hand on his shoulder.

"There is no shame in your tears Charles. Please, continue."

He noticed that Ernst had produced a bottle of clear spirit, homemade schnapps, and filled three grubby tumblers. He swallowed the fiery liquid, and fought back a fit of coughing, such was its potency, but he felt calmer and able to continue.

"Thank you, Herr Mohr. It is hard for me to talk about. In 1917, my line was struck by an artillery barrage. The set of events are not at all clear to me now. I was the only survivor; my entire unit was decimated. I . . . I remember stumbling through ruins and carnage. It comes back to me now only very faintly—seeing myself covered in blood, but registering it only in a dispassionately curious way, like I was witnessing something of little importance. How on earth I made it out, I simply cannot say. The will for survival defies explanation I suppose. I ended up in hospital, back in London. Later, after I was discharged, every doctor to whom I spoke was incredulous, saying my survival defied logic, that it was a miracle. That period remains mostly a horror of blackness, faint recollections—a nurse, a female volunteer perhaps, sitting with me as I lay between life and death . . . that is all. During my later recovery, a chance meeting with an injured German in the hospital led me to Karl Freideberg's name, and through him, Miss Wigman. Karl was . . . is, a model of courtesy, and has been extraordinarily generous in inviting me here, offering me hospitality, but he cannot help me with my quest. Mary hinted a little. She told me that Anna became her student here in Ascona, and then her collaborator, that they did great work together. Her letter suggested a rift though, that perhaps they had not parted well. I felt there was a lot more she was not saying, certainly."

"Of course," replied Ernst nodding thoughtfully and pouring them all another drink, "many find Mary abrasive. She makes no secret of her volatility, that is what drives her, fuels her, and she has no time for the supercilious smiles of charlatans. You say she suggested a rift had formed with your sister? That, I know is true. There was always something of a rivalry between them. Perhaps that is not surprising where two such talented, and fiery individuals are concerned. Mary, I think, always believed Anna to be something of . . . a threat to her position here, an ally to be utilised, indeed honoured, but never entirely trusted. Sometimes I would see the way she watched your sister, an expression on her face which spoke of . . . . unease. I remember one day, as we walked to the shrines of the Madonna in the hills, they argued bitterly. I do not know the cause, I was some way behind, and could not hear what transpired between the two of them, but I recall Mary's expression vividly as she swept past me. At the time I presumed her face was taut with anger. But now I believe that it was fear which I saw in her eyes. She packed and left for Berlin that very day without an explanation."

Ernst furrowed his brow, clearly unnerved by some aspect of the incident as he recalled it again. After a few moments, Charles continued, faintly uneasy.

"When I lost my parents to the influenza epidemic I knew that there was nothing left for me in England. The place I knew had vanished, I was a stranger there, uprooted from the country to which I had given so much. I think perhaps this is how my sister had always felt, that she was a stranger amongst her own people. Do you know she ran away from every boarding school my parents sent her to? The police would always bring her back of course, days later, dirty, dishevelled, but defiant, and always like she was aflame with a joy that none of us could understand. I believe I understand now—it was the joy of escape from a culture she felt imprisoned by. She was, I think, always running from something. Perhaps right until . . . the end. So, I left England. This trip was born of sheer desperation, last resort. I swore, after losing so much, so many comrades, that I would not lose my sister . . ."

It was too much, and he wept now, his grief overwhelming him.

His two companions did not move, perhaps sensing that their intervention would be intrusive, that the Englishman needed to shed the tears. Eventually, Ernst said, quietly "Once, a visitor to Ascona, marvelling at the wildness of Anna's dance, a panegyric to the mountain wolves and the stags of the forest, compared your sister, in her mastery of the forms of the beasts, to the goddess Artemis. That struck me at the time, and stayed with me, for, of course, Artemis is the hunter, not the stag, and I glimpsed, at that moment, something profound about Anna which I had failed to previously perceive. I do not believe that your sister *was* seeking escape from her past, or that she was running from anything. I believe she was hunting *for* something—intently pursuing some definite objective, some precise *aim*. Given what happened at the end, it should have been obvious to us all from the moment of her arrival." He paused to refill their glasses.

Gustav looked at Ernst quizzically, and Charles, too, tried to absorb the meaning of his enigmatic statement. All at once, something his sister had said, many years ago, flashed into his mind. It had been one of the many occasions when the police had brought her back home, following a flight from yet another school. What exactly had it been . . . ? He could no longer remember, but surely it had been some cryptic allusion to running with the hunt, not with the hunted? The policemen had stared sharply at her, and Charles remembered too the strange look he had glimpsed in her eyes as she had said it. He shook the memory away as quickly as it had come, unwilling to acknowledge the unpleasant feeling which crept up his spine. He wished that they were not sat in such a wild, lonely spot as they discussed these matters. Ernst fixed Charles in his gaze.

"I was with Anna on that final night here, in June 1917. I cannot give you all the answers you seek, for there is still much that I only guess, but I will tell you what know, Herr Lydford. Gustav was already incarcerated, taken by the authorities because he would not serve. We both thought, still think, that the war was nothing but a devil's feast. We could not sup at that table, no matter what they did to us. When I heard you were coming here, some weeks back, I decided it was best not to tell you of that final night. Gustav also thought . . . it would be better to leave the mountains with their secrets. Many already searched, they found nothing. I do not like to talk of that night, but there are things regarding your sister which I believe you, and Gusto too, need to know. As I said—the Mountain of Truth banishes illusion—whether we desire it or not."

It seemed that fear flashed in Gustav's eyes, but he rose and retrieved a leather bound volume from just inside the gloom of the house, returned to his seat and contemplated a passage of the Latin text within. "Heinrich Khunrath, the renowned alchemist, whom, Ernst, I know you respect," he inclined his head toward the book resting on his lap, "wrote 'he who knows the stone, is silent about it.' This reminds me also of Lao-Tzu's words 'Whoever speaks does not know, whoever knows does not speak.' Please, my friend—be careful before

you say any more. I felt . . . we should not speak of this matter
. . . should not add to Charles' burden by leading him deeper
into a labyrinth of riddles. However, you are right, it is not for
us to decide. I do not really 'know'. I do not know the stone,
the truth, I too am lost in the maze. But, I somehow sense,
Charles, that your sister reached the centre of the labyrinth,
and that for her the Mountain of Truth dispelled, finally, all
illusion."

The sun was growing low now, a reddening orb that cast
lengthening shadows, as if the mountains reached out to grasp
the three men who sat there in the gathering gloom. Swallows
wheeled and dived above them, intent on their lightning pursuit of twilight prey, and the verdant green of the distant pine
forest darkened as the wind began to rise.

Pouring more schnapps, Ernst began his tale. "You could
not have met, Herr Lydford, probably have not even heard of
Otto Gross. He died last summer in Berlin, ragged, ravaged
by the cocaine, opium and hashish which had once fuelled his
ecstasy. Yet Ascona would have been nothing without him."

Gustav nodded thoughtfully, head bowed, and Ernst continued.

"Otto was a psychoanalyst at the turn of the century, part
of Freud's circle, but he quickly realised that consciousness is
not a sphere easily explainable using rational methods, and
that the path he had chosen would do nothing to help people in way he desired. Back at the turn of the new century,
Otto saw a dark path for humanity if we did not learn to
free ourselves from the suffocating straight jacket of morality,
of Christianity, of fear, of hatred—that if mankind did learn
how to burn with joy, with Dyoniasiac rapture, then surely our fate was annihilation in the inferno that a world war
would bring. It seems obvious looking back that Otto's path
to universal intoxication, his addiction to narcotics, would
lead him to despair, madness, and death, but before the war,

in more innocent days, none of us knew that the gods of rapture demanded such savage restitution from their adherents."

He laughed solemnly, and paused to light a cigarette. For a few moments he was silent, smoking and gazing into the twilight, oblivious to his companions and lost in abstraction.

"No. Back then, we thought mere delirium would be enough save the world. I thought I had found that path when I gave up the priesthood to train with Mary. Many people saw her dances as demoniac of course, but god and the devil—that was exactly what we were trying to do away with here. It was as Laban said, an odyssey through all illusion, to that midpoint between eternity, that is what obsessed us, the elemental fury, the fire within. I studied the alchemists, their arcane books and their doctrine that one cannot achieve the universal tincture, the real gold of the philosophers, without igniting the fire in the soul, and we forged our dance rites from that molten energy—*Seelentänz*. It is hard . . . to describe. Words are part of the illusion, of Maya, that we sought to break through."

He drew on his cigarette, staring thoughtfully into his glass for some moments. "When your sister arrived, she understood perfectly what we were trying to achieve. In retrospect, I see that she understood too well, that she had her own unspoken reasons for joining our endeavours, some secret design known only to herself, even in those early years. I know with certainty, as does Gusto, that she wore always a stone around her neck, engraved with Greek letters, a strange image, lion headed, serpent tailed. She claimed to have been gifted it on her journey, by travellers from the south, and she would not be parted from it. Herr Jung took great interest in it, had seen others of its kind. Abraxas, he said, the power above all, and First Principle, sacred to the Gnostics."

"I knew my Irenaeus of course," continued Ernst, "I knew Abraxas only in the role the church had cast him, as demon, dark to Christ's light. But he was neither, and from that moment on, he was our guiding light, our first principle. Those were the great years, when we believed we had found our way, when our rites of dance were truly ecstatic, joyful. A time none of us will forget. Then the war came. Otto had foreseen that dark path already."

He stopped there. So many memories were conjured for the three of them that he did not have to continue. Twilight was growing around them now. The heat of the afternoon was rapidly dissipating, the noise of the cicadas grew increasingly intense, hypnotic—an invocation to the gathering gloom. It was now far too late to walk back down the valley. Charles' thoughts swam with the alcohol he had consumed, and he tried to stifle a pang of anxiety as he realised he would have to spend the night in this strange, lonely house. A rumble of thunder sounded, distant, reverberating through the stillness.

"By 1916, many of us had gone, to the war, or to prison. The community was scattered. I remained here though, determined not to fight, evading the authorities. This was still a mountain of truth, we still pursued the vision despite the horrors on the front. And then, came Gerhard Voigt. You perhaps know him by reputation, but I saw no 'mystical truth' in his so called Verità Mystica. I recall the night of his arrival. It was late September, I lived, then, in the village. There had been a celebration at The Casa Centrale, a wonderful evening of dance, music, festivity. Anna was intoxicating, her skill, and her movement utterly elemental. I, too, was entangled in the enchantment she weaved, and I danced as if possessed, endowed with a passion, a stamina which I had never thought possible. The crowd was ecstatic. It was a moment of total gestalt and we were drunk on the perfection of our union. Afterward, I returned home, exhausted but too exhilarated for sleep. As I sat by my fire, the sensations I had experienced during the dance, began to trouble me. The feeling of . . .

possession, as if my will had been usurped by another. As the euphoria of the evening deserted me, fear grew in my heart. I was convinced that I had indeed been . . . enthralled. It had been more than mere gestalt. A knock at the door snapped me from my reverie, and I leapt to my feet, now suddenly afraid, but of what exactly, I did not know. Throwing open the door, I saw Otto, looking drawn, pale, unwell, and beside him a stranger. I bade them enter, and I remember the unease I felt when this man, Voigt, stepped into my home. He was polite, charming, well dressed—clearly somebody of means, but despite the warmth of the room, I shuddered as we shook hands. Our conversation remains undimmed in my mind, despite all that came later, for it marked the turning point. We sat by my fire and talked long into the night. At first, he spoke of general things—his work with the Order of the Golden Dawn in England, his introduction of new Masonic rites to Germany. Then, as the schnapps flowed more freely, his words began to chill me to the core and I knew everything at Monte Verità would change. 'The great Gnostic, Ptolemy,' he told me, 'wrote that as gold retains its beauty in the depths of the blackest mud, and is not sullied, so the initiated cannot be sullied by their actions in this world. The perfect', he continued, 'can commit the most forbidden acts without shame. Those who have attained perfection can wallow in every vice, every pleasure, for they are beyond the touch of corruption'. Otto was entranced, convinced that together we could scale new heights, new ecstasies. The morphine had ravaged his mind by then. I was familiar with much of which Voigt spoke, his methods and his sources, and I saw at once he was a char-latan, twisting the wisdom of the sages to satisfy his own base desires, hungry for power, a wolf amongst . . ." he trailed off.

Ernst paused to light another cigarette, obviously deeply uncomfortable with his narrative. The thunder rolled again, Charles realised sweat was dripping from his brow. He fought to regain his composure, but from deep inside could feel panic rising. The dangling bronze masks began a livelier dance as the wind freshened, twisting and cavorting as if animated by some inner intelligence. Whispers seemed to pass between them, like fellow conspirators in some macabre covenant. Out in the field, the goats bleated, low, nervous as they sensed the coming storm.

"We had always worshipped nature, sought the intoxication of purity. Not so for Voigt. He may have preached Otto's message of liberation, but he practised nothing but the most depraved seductions—the desecration of all which I held sacred in our community. Many, initially at Otto's behest, attended his . . . rites in the Casa Centrale. I did so just once. I arrived toward sunset, the appointed hour, and all appeared dark from within. The sun was dropping toward the mountains, bathing the hillside crimson, and I heard the low hum of voices . . . I mounted the stairs with deep trepidation. My mind went back, as I entered, to the celebrations on the night of Voigt's arrival, the overpowering beauty of that experience, but also its haunting aftermath. That feeling gripped me again as I walked into the chamber. A bewitchment, as if my limbs were not my own. Many were there, many I considered friends, but I felt remote from them, unanchored. Scarlet drapes obscured the windows, filtering the evening light to a bloody hue on the faces around me. Braziers flickered red, the intoxicating fumes of incense filling the air and Voigt stood before us. A hush fell as he began his ritual, the domed chamber ringing with his shrill voice. Anna sat at the side of the stage, impassive, watchful as a hawk, her eyes fixed on Voigt throughout, whether with distain or admiration I could not tell. From my study of the ancient Gnostics, I recognised the source of his words. He borrowed liberally from the teachings of the Ophites, their doctrine that the serpent of Eden was the initiator—bringer of pleasure and knowledge, not sin.

This was the room in which I had marvelled at Mary's most breath-taking performances, where I wept as Ida Hofmann played Wagner's music, such was its beauty. It had been the heart of Monte Verità, and now I witnessed there . . . abominations. Elly Lenz joined him on the stage, like a sleep-walker, casting off her garments to enact the seduction of Eve—not as corruption but as liberation."

He laughed mirthlessly. "Liberation . . . I saw no liberation that day. I will say no more of what followed, except that I felt the same bewitchment, the same compulsion to stay until the bitter end of that depraved farce. I found myself filing out with the others, past midnight, dazed, my mind reeling from all I had witnessed."

Gustav was silent throughout, still as a statue, and Charles waited for his host to continue. He had little choice.

"That summer of 1917, Voigt planned a great festival. I knew our vision had been usurped, yet I did nothing. Gustav was, of course imprisoned by this time and . . . does not know much of what occurred. Really, I hardly know where to start, can hardly find the will to speak, it was so inexplicable."

He closed his eyes for a moment, and then looked to his friend as if seeking consent to continue. "Anna had been spending more and more time with Voigt toward the end. He may have been a charlatan, a wolf, but he had also delved long into arcane things, taught Crowley in Paris, travelled to strange shores. He had a power certainly, and Anna was drawn to it. I believe your sister felt that she had travelled as far down the path as she could with Mary, that there were deeper secrets in the labyrinth through which she walked, and that perhaps Voigt held the key she sought. Otto grasped too late the malefic force which he had unleashed by allowing this devil into our community. He sought nothing now but the obliterating embrace of Morphia, and could be of no further help to me, so I visited Voigt alone on that final evening of the festival, in his rooms, determined to confront the man. The air was perfumed with the scent of hashish as I entered, and perhaps herbs more obscure. It was well known that Voigt made use of many drugs to navigate the dark waters in which he sailed– *Psilocybe*, opium and stranger things he brought back from foreign shores—*the flesh of the gods*. All was shrouded in darkness, a few candelabra providing the only illumination. Black velvet drapes shimmered in the dimness and the most baleful atmosphere permeated the air. I felt dread creep through me as I entered, and I was again the timid, superstitious priest of my younger years, hardly the joyful Asconan I had thought myself. Voigt lounged before me, cigarette holder gripped between his fingers, a narcotic cloud gathered before the thin smile of his greeting. He was courteous, but icy, and bade me sit before him, as if I were pleading a case before a king of the ancient world. Indeed, so I felt for just a moment. He held out the cigarette to me, lazily, from sheer habit perhaps, uninterested whether I accepted or declined, so I took the latter course, needing clarity of purpose as I never had before. He inclined his head, narrowed his eyes, and waited for me to speak. Anna was kneeling upon a scarlet Persian carpet, as if in a trance, but clearly conscious, staring unblinking toward me. She held me fast in the savage clarity of her gaze, and I felt the strength drain from me, coldness seizing my body and utter terror begin to creep through my soul. I tell you, it was perhaps the most frightened I have ever been, and I simply could not explain the cause. Still, somehow, I regained my courage, found again some of the spirit of Monte Verità, and I stood to confront Voigt, tensing my posture as the Yogi's of India do, for mental protection. My mind was swimming from the hashish fumes, but I fought to free myself from the . . . really, I can say only the bewitchment under which I knew I was gripped. I remember seeing Anna again, her eyes fierce, and forcing her from my mind, as if physically pushing her away. It was a feeling the like of which I have never experienced, and I shudder to recall it. I told Voigt, as plainly as I was able in the suffocating atmosphere of that room that he was poison to your sister, to all of us, that I would go to the authorities if he did not leave the country. Then Anna was beside me, her hand on my shoulder. She said nothing, but fixed me with another look from those glacial eyes of hers. It was not anger, nor beseeching, but an absolute command. I knew then that this was a path she walked of her own volition, and also, with appalling certainty, that I would obey her, no matter what she asked of me. I have never told this to another soul, but I saw at once that it was Voigt who was the servitor, not your sister. She was the hierophant, he . . . nothing—merely a self-important vizier. Your sister was the director of all that transpired—she had been since the moment of her arrival. I walked out of Voigt's rooms, my heart like stone, sickened, knowing we were, had always been, mere leaves before the power of a tempest, that her aims were obscure, frightful, and that I could do nothing to stop whatever events might transpire."

A profound, chilling silence fell upon the group until Ernst at last, reluctantly found his voice, and continued.

"Anna had spent the weeks before the festival in deep contemplation, brooding over the books in Voigt's collection. The wisdom of the old masters, their speculation on the mathematics of harmony, she studied long—Pythagoras, Iamblichus, Proclus, and the arcane whispers of Paracelsus, Trithemius, Ficino. Exactly what she sought, I can only guess at, but she prepared a new dance, more intoxicating, more exacting and more bizarre than any I had seen. Mary had rarely danced with male partners, more often a demoniac unreal consort, her Animus, her own shadow self. For the finale of the festival, Anna would do the same. She seemed . . . calm, but, distant, like a woman turned to stone. As darkness drew in and the moon began to rise, we made our way up there." He indicated the head of the valley. "It was still, hushed, like the night was holding its breath. I remained numb from the horror of what had occurred in Voigt's rooms, and I walked, like a sleep-walker, with the rest. Our procession carried flaming torches to light our way, and as we ascended, Voigt urged the musicians to play, an uproar of flutes, drums ringing into the sky, the stars wheeling above. Many had drunk from the cup of sacrament he proffered, and now the potion it contained was taking hold. Their voices grew euphoric as the serpent *psilocybin* uncoiled itself within them and they tore off their clothes, blind to their surroundings. I felt the very mountains join our rapture, and knew we were stepping into the inferno, the annihilation that we had striven so hard to evade. This was the culmination of our vision quest, and the vision would be monstrous. Anna led us onward, shouting words of invocation, inciting us as never before . . ."

He stopped now, head hanging down, his energy spent, lost in the memories of that rite, his cigarette burned down to his fingers.

"I can talk no more of the bacchanal that followed. As the dawn broke, the sun appearing in the east to cries of joy from my companions, I saw Anna coldly survey us from atop a promontory of boulders, and I knew we had all been mere pawns, serving some obscure purpose, for her and her alone. She fixed me in her gaze for just a moment and vanished from sight. That was the last I ever saw of her. I believe, as Gustav hinted earlier, that she found what she sought up there, that she penetrated finally to the heart of the labyrinth. There is not much more to tell you. Voigt left Ascona a few days later. I heard he suffered a stroke in Zurich not so long ago. I did not grieve to hear it. The week that he left us, the authorities came, arrested many, and I joined Gustav in prison. The community was fractured, was finished. Our dream was over, and we awakened to a harsher reality, the illusion broken, the magic dissipated as if it had never been. When the war finished I returned here. I had nowhere else to go. I keep goats now, Herr Lydford, a simple herdsman. I have no appetite for ecstasy any more, and I have not danced since 1917."

Silence fell upon them for some time, and then Ernst held out a glittering object. "This is yours now Herr Lydford. I discovered it in the high meadow as I grazed my goats—just days before I heard you were coming. There is a preordination in these events, I am sure of it, and they come together now, for better or for worse. There is a continuity at work here, and, I confess, I am deeply afraid of it. I have feared it ever since I first looked into your sister's eyes." He dropped a pendant into Charles trembling hand, and he caught a glimpse of the lion head, the serpent tail. Abraxas.

The storm broke now over the mountains, unleashing its burden of rain. Lightning flashed, and thunder boomed above them. Gustav looked pale and drained, hunched upon his seat, but Charles sat perfectly still, the pendant resting in his palm. It was dark now. Ernst rose slowly and began to kindle an oil lamp hanging from a beam. The feeble pool of light and the sagging porch roof seemed, suddenly, scant protection from the elements, and the night that pressed in upon them.

As Charles took the pendant, he knew, suddenly, everything that he had tried so hard to keep hidden within himself, and a veil of deceit dropped away from his eyes. The labyrinth opened before him, a hidden path which he knew he had always walked, the maze his feet had unknowingly trodden, ceaselessly since childhood—to bring him just to this moment. Now he approached his destination. The flood gates of his memory opened, and he lurched from his seat. Before Gustav or Ernst had the opportunity to stop him he was plunging headlong into the night, toward the pine forest, the storm thundering before him. Despite the darkness, and his unfamiliarity with his surroundings, Charles' feet knew the path on which he ran, as if an invisible thread pulled him on.

Ernst's desperate voice cried out. "Please Herr Lydford, come back, it is dangerous to go on any further in the darkness." Gustav joined his call—"Charles, come back, please!" But he could not stop, he could not go back. As he ran blindly through the forest, branches cutting his face, he felt the inexorable pull of a remorseless truth, its invisible fingers grasping his throat. He had felt it on every one of those days, lying in blind horror in the hospital. He had known it from the first, blocking it from his mind, not daring to stare it in the face. He knew it now, with terrible certainty. All illusion was finally banished.

He was back in the trenches again on a clear summer night in 1917. A sergeant and two privates sat nearby in the dugout, smoking, brewing tea and murmuring quietly over a game of cards, whilst a dazzling full moon gleamed above them. Charles was oblivious to his companions and stared, transfixed, through the barbed wire toward no-man's land. A recent summer storm had flooded the violent patchwork of craters, leaving them brimming with stagnant water. Now, however, they were brilliantly illuminated, burnished silver and transfigured into crystalline pools, their grisly contents rendered invisible. Charles was enchanted, lost in the hallucinatory beauty of the scene, and inhaled deeply the sweet night air, allowing himself to be intoxicated by the illusion. Gone was the taint of decay on the breeze and closing his eyes, a vision of Anna came clearly to his mind. She was reaching out, ready to take him by the hand, her smile beatific, and his heart was glad, knowing finally that she was somewhere safe, somewhere she was happy. It was then the artillery shells struck. He failed to hear their tell-tale whining approach through the still night air, so lost was he in inner vision. The impact must have been immense, for when he next looked around him, the trench was annihilated, a turmoil of shattered wood, wire, sandbags—and human-beings. Smoke curled around him, mixed with the choking stench of burning flesh, and he rose to his feet, ears ringing from the force of the detonation, his skin lacerated and burnt, but otherwise apparently unharmed. How he was still alive he did not have the ability to comprehend, but he felt himself being taken by the hand, gently, and led through the pandemonium, through the horror of his eviscerated comrades, their strewn body parts marking a scarlet avenue through which he processed. He knew his own limbs should also have formed part of that ghastly tableau, that there was no earthly way he could, or should, have survived a direct artillery hit on their position. He had known it then and refused to believe the truth. It was Anna who led him to safety, their hands entwined, her soft voice telling him to walk, to just keep walking, away from the death which should have been his that night.

Now Charles ran, toward the darkened canyon ahead, to be with her. His face was lacerated from blind collisions in the forest, and the torrential rain obscured his vision. It mattered not—he no longer needed sight—an inner voice called, a gentle hand held his own. Whatever Anna had done to these people, this community, was suddenly meaningless. She had leapt into the void and they had been dashed upon the rocks. It was unimportant now. That he loved her was all. He loved her and had let her go, and now they would be together again.

He remembered, as he ran, the long months in the hospital, swimming between life and death. It had been her who sat with him, hand resting in his, stroking his brow, willing him back. He saw now the endless space, the innermost infinity in which he had swum, and, at immeasurable distance, that one single star in the zenith. Abraxas, Anna, himself—salvation. She had brought him back, so they could be here, together, on this very night in the mountains. How right Ernst had been, he found himself laughing. The world of solidity, reality was truly mere illusion, transition—the midpoint between eternity. From ahead he heard the same joyous cry he remembered from childhood as Anna had run in the bracken, and he hurried on, heedless of the elements, tears streaking his face.

At last, the canyon walls fell away and he stumbled into a darkened natural amphitheatre, a high alpine meadow surrounded by towering rocks. High above, he sensed the snowcapped bulk of the mountains, towering to heaven. He had reached the *Hortus conclusus*, the garden enclosed—the heart of the labyrinth. Opening his hand, he saw the pendant there, the image, lion headed, serpent tailed, glinting cryptically, half perceived in the darkness. The lightening lit the scene for just a moment, and Charles wept as he saw Anna standing before him, radiant, her hair whipped high by the wind, coiling like a nest of serpents around her shoulders, her eyes blazing with unearthly inner light. She reached out to him and he took her hand, tears of gratitude flowing down his cheeks. They walked together, across the meadow, through the flowers, as they had done so many times in his dreams. Before them rang out a voice that was not a voice, the voice of the wind, and of the water that runs eternally down the darkened gullies of a mountain peak. "We run now Charles, with the hunt," whispered Anna. Then they were gone, like the smoke above the herdsman's fire, who through the night keeps silent watch over his flock.

IN SEARCH OF THE HIDDEN CITY

by Thomas Strømsholt

> *"I am half sick of shadows," said*
> *The Lady of Shalott.*
> (Tennyson)

SOMETIMES it seemed to her as if reality hesitated in a superposition of infinite possibilities.

She saw the city flicker like a crowd of grinning ghosts in the violet hour: buildings trembled, their featureless façades flaked away like old skin to reveal the brittle bones beneath; a concrete block of flats opened its flat gaze towards the pale blue sky, its tiles swelling to form a voluptuous cupola; an office building was slowly enveloped in an embrace of lush ivy and blossoming periwinkle; and whichever way she turned her eyes, walls grew extravagant ornaments and carved figures, balustrades stretched upwards, and balconies bloomed forth, gushing white oleander trees and pale green palms; lank towers and golden spires rose toward the sky, verdigris domes mushroomed; streets and alleys melted away like glaciers, and water flowed freely through the city's decalcified vessels; and from the unveiled canals, whose dark surface was sprinkled with the silvery flakes of the sharp morning sun, a faint, melodious sound of lapping water was heard.

Then she felt a violent pull, and the possibilities collapsed in a mad, spinning motion, and she was awake in the crummy apartment, cracked ceiling, empty bottles and dirty curtains, awake to another pale morning in the same old city. And yet not quite the same.

A smile played on Elene's dry lips as she looked out of the open window. A non-human change had come over Copenhagen; she felt the change pulsate through her body, she could smell it in the air and hear it in the modulation of birds' voices: the sun had passed through the vernal equinox, and winter had turned finally to spring.

It is with houses and people as with dogs and dog owners; they frequently share characteristics to an unnerving degree. The boarding house was scruffy, the walls bled with damp, and it reeked of old sweat. At a desk across the main entrance sat a man watching TV, probably the host or caretaker. He was balding at the crown, and the pomaded comb-over failed to conceal it. His shirt, wrinkled and unwashed, was unbuttoned to reveal a hairy chest, obviously his pride. At the sight of Elene, he licked his lips and smoothed the comb-over. Elene hastened past the man, acknowledging his presence with a slight nod only, and climbed the stairs to the second floor.

It worried her that it had been nearly three weeks since last she heard from Lubb. She knocked on the door. Although she had not really expected him to be in, the silence of the room was dispiriting. She tried again. Her bowels contracted into a hard knot as the silence turned to fragile glass. Now it happens, she thought. The glass will shatter, and there is nothing I can do about it. But the panic attack went away as suddenly as it had risen, leaving her with a sense of shame. The door was locked of course but she had to try before giving up.

Downstairs again, the balding man addressed her: "Been calling on Mr Lubb, have you?"

Outside the cold November rain battered down, but the lobby felt like a hothouse full of rotting organic matter. Elene wanted most of all to return home, and maybe try another day, or wait for Lubb to contact her. Yet she halted and replied with a nod.

"Mr Tomas Lubbert hasn't shown himself for more than a fortnight," the host went on. "See, honey, I keep an eye on my lodgers. Can't be trusted, especially not his kind. Not that I'm racist, but I've been around long enough to know what I'm talking about. They're here today, gone tomorrow—without paying the rent of course." He scrutinized her. "Wouldn't be surprised if your boyfriend just up an' left."

Elene just let the words slide past. She said, "I assume there's a spare key?"

"Sorry, honey, it's against house policy."

Elene produced a crumbled bank note from her hip pocket and placed it on the desk and said, "Perhaps exceptions can be made?"

"Only in the case of relatives."

"He's my brother." Another note was sacrificed.

The host licked his lips. "Must've been blind to have missed the likeness," he said.

※

The factory building lay like a rotting whale washed up on a desolate shore, a ruin surrounded by debris, waste, and vacant lots. The upper floor windows stared blankly into a night of coffee grounded darkness. The lower windows were boarded up, and the metal doors were locked. But there is always a crack, a hole, a secret passage.

The oil-stained concrete floor, long ago stripped of machinery, was covered with broken glass, screws, nails and litter.

A stench of urine and moisture pervaded the air. Crumbling pipes crept like delicate bones along walls bleeding rust. A fragile silence ruled the building. Earlier, a heavy rain had fallen, and the silence was occasionally broken by discordant droplets. It was a silence so fragile that she hardly dared breathe. And yet she whispered:

"We're faded memories on the threshold of amnesia."

"Saprophytes sucking nourishment from the dying," he said.

"Touch me here."

Lubb stiffened, his eyes twitching in the pale light of the moon. She watched his pupils dilate like gushing ink, almost drowning the brown irises, and she imagined herself submerged in that inky blackness. She took his hand, put it under her blouse, and the touch of his cold fingers made her shiver.

"Fissures run through the foundation. I'm afraid to look down for fear of what I might see."

"If nothing is real there can be no illusion."

"Show me that the floor is firm."

"As firm as rusty nails and broken glass."

"Do you love me?"

"No."

"Good. Now touch me here . . ."

And they left blood in the hard, dusty concrete.

The cramped room consisted of a small table, an unmade bed, and books piled on the floor along the walls. Below the table was an old, almost antique computer case with gutted insides. The wallpaper was faded to a nondescript colour, and the window overlooked a narrow backyard. On the windowsill was an ashtray that brimmed with cigarette butts. The air was stuffy and damp-stained, and the rain that drummed against the window made the room even more sad.

Lubb always came to her place, and it was the first time she saw his room. The lack of order was consistent with certain aspects of Lubb's personality: his erratic behaviour, experiments with drugs, his insomnia and frequent mood swings. But there was another side to Lubb, a radiant purity like a sunflower growing on a heap of junk . . .

She seated herself, lit a cigarette, and stared into the dusty face of a large CRT monitor. A yellow note was stuck on the dead black screen:

> *When the moon tide rises, the corners corner you, streets lose their way, and houses quiver and crumble away.*

The scrawled note reminded her of something he had once said, or perhaps written, but immediately she failed to place it.

Apart from the bulbous monitor, the table was a clutter of battered paperbacks, papers, and sepia-coloured prints of panoramic cityscapes. Conspicuous among the paperbacks was a large octavo in a red binding which she recognized immediately as *Copenhagen Peregrinations* by Gregor Schulz, 1877. Lubb's copy abounded with inlaid city maps, and the margins were filled with notes in his cramped longhand. This volume had been his dearest possession, or perhaps his obsession, and it was hard to believe that he would leave it behind . . . unless it was a clue meant for her to discover.

Then again, something awful might have happened to him, and as she tried not to imagine the manifold ways of violent ends, an icy draft began to rise, and she heard the familiar muted howl of the abyss.

✳

Ever since the tragedy, she had walked on brittle glass. There were days when she was afraid to lower her gaze lest she should see the cracks spreading beneath her feet. Restless and sleepless, she began to drift like an empty packet of cigarettes caught by random winds through desolate night streets, across squalid squares, past empty churches, and culs-de-sac, until exhaustion would finally replace anxiety. But for a short while only.

One night she was brought to a towering black, ramshackle building in a plain of concrete. Afterwards she would tell herself that it was curiosity that made her trespass when in fact she entered the condemned office block believing it would somehow offer release, or comfort, or sanctuary. Inside the abandoned building, among rows of emptied file cabinets, ruined furniture, and broken coffee cups, she experienced a quiet which nestled her body and filled her haunted skull out with a deep, deep calm. The next day she returned with a camera in order to document this strange, soothing calm.

From then on, she began to explore the condemned and forgotten buildings and spaces above and below the city, quickly developing dependence. Via the Net she came into contact with an obscure society of people whose one common denominator, beyond a prevalent disposition to insomnia, was an attraction to abandoned urban spaces, the silence of ruins, and the aesthetics of decay. This was how she met Lubb who despite his youth had acquired a reputation as a veteran urban explorer.

The streets were flooded with sodium and neon Christmas lights, streams of late shoppers and vendors hurried senselessly about. Elene felt her throat contract and turned her gaze upwards as if to escape, but above her, the multitudinous city lights had turned the cloudy night sky into a soiled orange shroud or a veil behind which the waxing moon was faintly seen as a blurry white blotch. Elene walked the dark side streets. A cold breeze blew trash across the cracked pavement of Aagade, a transparent plastic bag levitated past her like a butterfly. Lubb had told her: "Many of the old streams, brooks and canals still run beneath the asphalt and flagstones. If one listens carefully, they can be heard as a faint murmuring." She knelt on the cold ground and listened. But although Aagade was desolate and quiet, she was unable to detect the coursing of the underground brook; she had not really expected to.

Tired and depressed, she sauntered about the sleepy district. A slightly curved and badly lit lane brought her past a narrow passage blocked by a wooden fence. Framed by decrepit buildings on each side, the half rotten fence was painted with sigil-like graffiti tags. She framed the scene with her hands, cocked her head, thinking it would make a nice motif if only she could capture its decaying aesthetics. She was about to reach for her analogue camera when the edges of the fence began to shimmer like gold. She watched, astounded, as a strong yellow glow bled through the cracks in the wood as if the fence were lit from the other side by a light projector or a rising sun. The vision was of short duration, a mere flash wherein the passage expanded, and in the far distance she glimpsed an organic geometry—long colonnades and weird curves; arches turned into cupolas; viaducts sprouted towers that shoot spires; marble and gold washed in blazing sunlight, reflected and intensified by the waters . . . silvery, murmuring. . . . She blinked, and immediately the marvellous scene lapsed into drab commonness.

Back in her apartment, she searched through Lubb's city maps. Using thick red and black felt-tip pens, he had meticulously traced the canals, waterways and brooks that once ran through the old port city, adding the projected or imagined waterways. Aagade dated back to the end of the eighteenth century but supposedly the brook still ran its now hidden course. According to Schulz' *Peregrinations*—Elene had secured Lubb's copy—it had been proposed to transform the brook into a canal connected to the then existing main canals. Consulting the maps again, she discovered that the connection ran through the unnamed passage with the fence.

At the coming of dawn, Elene stumbled into bed, but in her dreams she proceeded to peregrinate through the occult layers of the city.

She was in Riga when Lubb mailed his last message. An acquaintance had offered her a lift to what was supposed to be a short trip. But her stay was prolonged when she was caught by the *policija* and had to explain why she was trespassing in an abandoned orphanage to photograph dusty rooms, mouldering beds, and mutilated dolls. The problem was not so much the language barrier, for few people comprehended the fascination of these pockets in time and space where nothing happened but the slow decay which would eventually reduce everything to nothing; and as a mere observer of that process, she took care not to disturb anything. In the end she was released only to find her acquaintance had moved on, and with little money left, the homeward journey was long and hard.

Lubb wrote:

Remember that passage from Schulz' work wherein he writes of the influence of the waxing moon on the 'forgotten aqueducts'? He knew the secret of Copenhagen, the city's hidden cities, and in his psychotopography he left clues, codes, hints. If I understand him correctly, the chances of finding that which is implied or veiled by the present city will be greatest around the ecliptic. I believe that my research is nearing some kind of end. Wish you were here. Forget the ruins and their silence, for theirs is the whisper of death: there is another *place.*

Since then, he had been off-line; since September he had not set foot in the boarding house; since autumnal equinox no one had either seen or heard from him.

The January sun spilled its blinding white light over the city. It had rained during the night, and the dull black asphalt of the streets was transmuted into rivers of melted gold; when she screwed up her eyes, the streets looked like the canals from her dreams, the canals coursing through a Copenhagen that was not Copenhagen. What is a city? *In present day Copenhagen, one may discern the remnants of former epochs,* wrote Schulz: *The yellow wings of Christian IV is a tale told in stone of times lost but not completely abandoned although new vistas grow everywhere. If we take a walk from Thott's Mansion to the Royal Theatre, a few minutes by foot, we cover a distance of around one hundred years. Such it is with any old city—such it is with anything perceived by the naked eye—it is all quite trivial. So much is invisible to us: The old canals, cancelled streets, buildings lost to fire and neglect; backyards and squares that were destroyed by new plans for the city; lost palaces, churches, houses. A whole city, or cities, lost in hazy memories and sediment of dirt. But a city is more than stone and ashes. Hidden and conserved in its deepest sediments we discover all the architectural reveries and plans which were never realised:* the Citta del Sole *of Christian V, the canals of Axel Urup, the spire that was supposed to adorn Vor Frue Kirke [. . .]. In order to behold a city in its entirety, one must make use of more than one's corporeal senses.*

Through the din of morning traffic, she could hear the gentle lapping from the canals on Slotsholmen. With her back to the canals, the short fishwife stood in granite melancholy, a monument of past times like the sooty murals of healthy workers on the façade of Thorvaldsen's Museum. The slate grey surface of the water was ribbed by the cold wind, and she shook herself involuntarily.

Little was known of Gregor Schulz. He was of Eastern European origin and had travelled via Germany to Copenhagen in the early eighteen-fifties where he was employed as secretary to Professor Hans Jørgen Koch, the architect. From the years between Koch's death in 1860 to the publication of *Copenhagen Peregrinations*, the information was scant; he was unmarried and lived, it seemed, in obscurity.

The banks and ministries of Slotsholmen huddled together like petrified frigates and heavy barges, their verdigrised copper roofs scraped against the clear sky. Above the old Rococo stock exchange the stone dragons twined their tails while eyeing the pedestrians streaming by. Neptune, standing in front of the Rococo building, cast a questioning glance at the patron of merchants and thieves who answered with a deceptive smile. Elene, peregrinating Copenhagen in search of Lubb and the cities within the city, went on.

Lubb had been on the track of something: *there is* another *place*. His annotated city maps provided a guide; unfortunately, his lines and circles made little sense, and Elene wandered in darkness. Doubt would sometimes come over her. Gregor Schulz was fifty-seven years old when he presumably committed suicide in 1878—it was said that he suffered from "nervous fever"—but a body was never found. Tomas Lubbert was thirty-three years old when he, seduced by Schulz' hints of another city, disappeared. If not for Elene's persistent and very vivid dreams, it would be easy for her to dismiss it all as utter nonsense.

What was she supposed to do? *In order to behold a city in its entirety, one must make use of more than one's corporeal senses.* On her walks through the city, she observed the few remaining canals and listened to the course of the water. But compared to the canals of her dreams it was as if the real canals lacked texture and colour: in fact they lacked the most essential qualities of things real.

She admitted to herself that she had been unaware of how much Lubb meant until the vacuum of his absence had enveloped her. It was absurdly banal, yet without him there was but the abyss, the icy draft and the muted howls like perverted sirens singing. The one thing that kept her back from the edge, and spurred her on, was the recurring dreams of a strange cityscape.

At a glance, *Copenhagen Peregrinations* seemed like a topographical and historical work done in a dry and rather pompous style, except for a few jarring Romantic or mystical passages. Lubb did not care for the so-called 'nerve fever'. He insisted:

"It's a mystical Baedeker."

"Or the delusions of a sick man."

"Very elaborate delusions. Look at Plate III . . ."

They were seated at a thronged and noisy café. Every other moment people jostled by, and the close proximity of strangers made Elene edgy. Lubb seemed to block it off, his whole attention absorbed by the red octavo on the table. Elene tried to concentrate on Plate III, a poorly reproduced engraving of the city anno 1745 viewed from a northern hill.

"What's wrong with this picture?"

"The perspective? Scale?" tried Elene.

"Strictly speaking, it is geometrically incorrect. The engraver, unknown by the way, wasn't interested in realism. In fact, the engraving is a work of imaginative art. Now, try to look again, this time with a magnifying glass." Thus saying, he reached into a bag at the floor and produced the optical instrument.

"What is it exactly I'm supposed to look for?"

"The extraordinary."

Puzzled, she moved the magnifying glass across the engraving. Her gaze halted at a building placed in the old city centre: it was a Gothic cathedral with five conical towers and abundant flying buttresses. Engraved in a slightly lesser scale, the cathedral was almost hidden to the naked eye by the surrounding buildings. Looking closer it seemed to her that the buttresses raised the whole building above ground.

"Now look at Plate V."

Presumably the said Plate offered a view of the city anno 1779, but here the artist had added a viaduct which curved and bent its way through the city's topography like a long caterpillar. Leafing to the next Plate, a panorama from 1830, she discovered a row of tall, narrow houses which twisted impossibly around their own axes.

"Please notice the many canals," remarked Lubb. "Every plate is like this," he proceeded enthusiastically, "abundant with surreal elements in the real; a psychotopography!"

"What does it mean?"

"Think about it, Elene. As secretary to Koch, Schulz had free access to the archives of the Academy of Arts. All the town planning that for some reason or other was shelved. All the architects' dreams and fantasies . . ." His dark eyes glowed.

"So, *Copenhagen Peregrinations* is a fantasy?"

"In a sense, yes. Like the surreal prisons of Piranesi or the gothic churches of Schinkel. Except here, the phantasies are placed on the map. We may say that a map isn't the territory, but we still navigate by it. Notice how the title suggests a pilgrimage. Rather unusual for a work of topography don't you think? This book is a map."

"A fictive map of a fictive city dreamed up in a feverous brain."

"There isn't one real city of Copenhagen, there's numerous, but separated in layers. Schulz' map indicates the points where the layers intersect. At first, I thought the abundance of waterways were a kind of metaphor but now I'm not so sure. Many of the old streams, brooks and canals still have their course beneath the asphalt and flagstones. If you listen carefully, they can be heard as a faint murmuring. It is, I believe, the sound of the hidden city or cites."

"You're mad."

"This is what we're longing for."

"No, Lubb, this is what *you* are longing for."

The last days of February saw Elene walking in one of the old quarters. The worn paving stones were a hard shell, covering layers of waste and refuse three meters deep. It was in this part of the city, not far from Aagade and the mystical passage, that an unnamed engraver had erected a surreal Gothic cathedral around 1745; and also, it was here, according to one of Lubb's maps, that two imaginary canals interlocked.

Most of the streets were narrow and curved, characteristic of a Medieval town. The earliest houses, single-storeyed with black tarred bases and yellow plaster walls, dated back to the early seventeenth century; around them lay the imposing Baroque and Classical apartment buildings interspersed with a few dull looking blocks of flats from the twentieth century. It was a quiet and relatively small quarter, almost like a small town hiding within a metropolis. And yet, after three days of meandering about the curved streets, Elene had a nagging feeling that the quarter was larger than it should be: firstly, the number of streets was inconsistent with the latest printed city map, but then every time she counted, she arrived at a new number; secondly, she often experienced disorientation.

As she became more familiar with the quarter, she discovered that this disorientation increased at certain street corners, it was as if the angles flickered in and out of focus. There were days when she felt like a half-blind idiot with no sense of direction at all, and on other days she would think of herself as a fool chasing a morphic delusion with the conviction of a madman. But such days of dark despair were invariably followed by dreams of almost hallucinatory lucidity which renewed her hopes.

By degrees, she realized that these ups and down followed a pattern, for the hyperaesthetic peaks of her dreaming seemed to correspond with full moon and new moon. She recalled Lubb's enigmatic note: *When the moon tide rises, the corners corner you, streets lose their way, and houses quiver and crumble away.* Convinced that this sentence described the old quarter with its weird streets and corners, she continued her peripatetic explorations.

Blades of sunlight cut through the lead grey thunderclouds, and the din and rumble of the city sounded like a distant surf. Elene haunted the old quarter, restless and with a feverish look in her eyes. Some of the local shopkeepers still eyed the lonely stranger with suspicion, and some parents would hurriedly take their children across the streets whenever they saw her, but mostly she was ignored.

She rested on a bench and began to study a creased map. On this morning a non-human change had come over Copenhagen: the vernal equinox, the arrival of spring. She unfolded the map and walked on.

Shortly afterwards she rounded a street corner and walked down a street where she knew that the degree of disorientation was unusually intense. This time it came upon her suddenly like a strong gust of wind. She halted, confused and dizzy. In front of her was a narrow passage that she had never before noticed; and from that passage issued the faint melody of lapping water.

Excited to a delirious degree, she followed the seductive sound into the passage. Dark and winding, the passage proved to be a cul-de-sac, and she was just about to turn when she noticed the door. It was a black painted door of a size so small that it appeared constructed for children. The door communicated with a large backyard, but there was nothing of that shut-inness, sadness and greyness one usually connects with these city enclosures; rather, the shape and appearance of the backyard brought to mind a Roman atrium or an artificial oasis of a Near Eastern palace. It was shaped like an octagon with very tall, white-plastered walls without windows. Almost all the surface of the walls was covered by a sea-green carpet of ivy which flowed out of the ground and mixed with wild growing plants, scented flowers and small bushes carrying violet berries. The luxuriant flora met in the centre of the yard where the sea-green cover nestled around and up the sides of a broad well, creeping round its neck and down into the black depths. And from the depths of the well rose that faint sound of water that haunted her dreams.

A cast iron bench was placed next to the well, and here, overwhelmed with the mystery about her, she sat down. Hesitating, she reached for one of the violet berries. She feared it would dissipate like a fata morgana, but when the berry lay in the palm of her hand, she feared it would transform, like the gold of fairy, into a lump of coal; but the berry tasted juicy and sweet. The weather was mild, and she removed her jacket.

She picked up a rock which she let fall into the black throat of the well, counting the seconds, straining her ears for the sound of—nothing. Nothing but the rise and fall of small waves from the subterranean canals.

For a long time, she just sat with her eyes closed, listening to the subterranean streams. She thought of Lubb: *Forget the ruins and their silence, for theirs is the whisper of death: there is another place.* Suddenly the sound of distant thunder woke her from her pleasant reveries. She was averse to leaving the enchanted backyard, but night was falling.

She was unable to recall exactly where she had entered the backyard. The low door was not immediately visible through the thick ivy carpet, and after having traced the octagonal walls three times, she was still unable to locate it. She tried to call out as loudly as she was able but received only the echo of her own voice.

Again she traced the walls, searching behind the ivy cover and finding but knotty tendrils and mouldering bricks. With rising uneasiness, she wondered how many others knew of this spot. Were the dwellers behind those tall walls even aware of their wondrous backyard, or did it exist only in the weird engravings of the *Peregrinations*? If the latter was true—however absurd and fantastical that truth appeared—it was probable that Schulz had known of this place. Likewise, Lubb might have entered this backyard on a day where the celestial bodies worked their influences in strange ways—as they did on this very day. Suddenly the backyard felt like an enchanted prison, a place where people disappeared without a trace.

Not knowing what to do, she once more returned to the bench. Luckily it seemed that the bad weather had passed by. But night had fallen, abrupt like the change of scene in a theatre. The night sky was black as onyx sprinkled with the white of whirling star clusters. The ripe large moon had an intense glow, and the yard was veiled in a bluish, shimmering light. The temperature was almost balmy. But for the tranquil sound of lapping water all was quiet.

The moonlight made the backyard appear larger. The walls had changed into dark-blue shadows fusing with the night sky above, and the ivy quivered like a veil suggesting unknown worlds. Something behind that veil arrested Elene's attention. Peering into the shadows, she saw, by slow gradations, the black outline of the small door emerge. She wondered how she could have missed it. Bending low, she reached for the handle, but the touch sent shivers through her body. What lay on the other side?

For a moment, reality seemed to hesitate in a superposition of infinite possibilities; then she pressed the handle.

THE CHILDREN OF MONTE ROSA

by Reggie Oliver

I

IT was my mother who first noticed Mr and Mrs de Walter as they strolled along the promenade. She had a talent for picking out unusual and interesting looking people in the passing crowd and often exercised this gift for my amusement, though mainly for my father. He was a journalist who was always going to write a novel when he could find the time.

My parents and I had been sitting in a little café on the front at Estoril where we were on holiday that year. In 1964 it was still unusual to see English people in Portugal, particularly the North, and the couple my mother pointed out to us were so obviously English. "They're probably expatriates," she said. As I was only eleven at the time I had to have the term explained to me.

They must have been in their late sixties, though to me at the time they simply looked ancient. They were of a height but, while she was skeletally thin, he was flabby and shapeless in an immaculate but crumpled white linen suit. He wore a "Guards" tie—this observation supplied by my father—and a white straw Panama with a hat band in the bacon and egg colours of the M.C.C, which I, a cricket enthusiast, identified myself. A monocle on a ribbon of black watered silk hung from his neck. He had a clipped white moustache and white tufted eyebrows which stood out from the pink of his face. His cheeks were suffused with broken veins that, like fibre optic cables, were capable of changing the colour of his complexion with alarming rapidity.

His wife was also decked out in the regalia of antique gentility. Her garments were cream-coloured, softly graduating to yellow age at their edges. Their general formlessness seemed to date them to the flapper era of the 1920s, an impression accentuated by her shingled Eton Crop which was dyed a disconcerting shade of blue. Her most eccentric item of dress was a curious pair of long-sleeved crocheted mittens from which her withered and ringed fingers seemed to claw their way to freedom. The crochet work, executed in a pearl-coloured silky material, was elaborate but irregular, evidently the work of an amateur, making them resemble a pair of badly mended fishermen's nets.

My mother who was immediately fascinated was seized by an embarrassing determination that we should somehow get to know them. I have a feeling she thought they would make "good copy" for my father's long projected novel, or a short story at least. My father and I went along with her plans, not because we approved them but because we knew that resistance was useless.

We were staying at the Grande, one of the big old Edwardian hotels on the sea front, but my mother noticed that "the expats", as she was now calling them, often took a pre-dinner aperitif on the terrace of the Excelsior, a similar establishment adjacent to ours. Accordingly, one evening we went for a drink at the Excelsior, positioning ourselves at a table near to where my mother had seen the expatriates drinking.

For once, everything went according to my mother's plan. The couple arrived shortly after we had, sat down and ordered their drinks, gin and Italian Vermouth, a fashionable pre-war cocktail. ("Gin and It!" my mother whispered to us, "it's too perfect!") My mother who had been an actress in her youth was the possessor of a very audible voice, so our conversation was soon overheard. Presently we saw that the lady was coming over to us. She seemed to hesitate momentarily, looming over us, before saying: "I couldn't help noticing that you were speaking English." Her mouth was gashed with a thin streak of dark red lipstick, of a primeval 1920s shade.

So we joined them at their table and they introduced themselves as Hugh and Penelope de Walter. I was a well-behaved boy at that time and, being an only child, had no siblings with whom to fight or conspire, so I think I made a favourable impression. Besides, because I had either inherited or acquired by influence my mother's appetite for human oddities, I was quite happy to sit there with my "sumo d'ananas" and listen to the grown-ups.

The de Walters were, as my mother had correctly surmised, expatriates, and they had a villa at Monte Rosa, a village in the foothills above Estoril. De Walter had been in the wine trade, hence his acquaintance with Portugal, and, on retiring in the 1950s had decided that England was "going to Hell in a handcart" what with its filthy music, its even filthier plays and the way the working classes generally "have the run of the place these days". De Walter conceded that Salazar, the then dictator of Portugal, "might have his faults, but at least he runs a tight ship". I had no idea what this meant but it sounded impressive, if a little forbidding.

Their life at the Villa Monte Rosa, so named because it was the grandest if not the oldest dwelling in their village, was, they told us, more serene and civilised than any they could have hoped to afford in Worthing or Eastbourne. I wondered, though, if it were not a little lonely for them among all those foreigners, but said nothing.

I think it was after a slight lull in the conversation that the de Walters turned their attention on me. In answer to enquiries, I told them where I was presently at school and for which public school I was destined. De Walter nodded his approval.

"I'm a Haileybury man myself," he said. "Are you planning to go to the 'varsity after that?"

I looked blank. My father came to my aid by informing me that "the 'varsity" meant Oxford or Cambridge. I said I hoped so without really knowing what was meant.

"Never got to the 'varsity myself," said de Walter. "I was due to go up in '15, but a certain Kaiser Bill put the kibosh on that."

The First World War was ancient history to me, a series of faded sepia snapshots of mud-filled trenches and Dreadnoughts cutting through the foggy wastes of the North Sea, a tinkle of "Tipperary" on a rickety church piano. Trying to imagine a young de Walter going to war all those years ago silenced me.

"Do you have children yourself, Mr and Mrs de Walter?" my mother asked.

There was an unpleasant little silence. My father, who was frequently embarrassed by my mother's forthrightness, passed a hand through his thinning hair, a familiar gesture of nervous exasperation. The broken veins in de Walter's face had turned it a very ugly shade of dark purple. Mrs de Walter seemed about to say something when her husband restrained her by tightly grasping one of her stick-like arms.

"No," said de Walter in a lower, firmer voice than we had hitherto heard, "we have not been blessed with that inestimable privilege." There was another pause before he added: "We couldn't, you see. War wound."

With old world courtesy, he cut off my mother's abject apologies for raising the issue. "Please, dear lady," he said. "Let us say no more on the subject." Soon we were discussing the present state of English cricket in which de Walter took a passionate interest, even if he could not quite grasp that Denis Compton was no longer saving England from the defeat at the hands of the Australians, or some people whom he called "the fuzzy-wuzzies". My father, an enthusiast whose information was rather more up-to-date, was able to correct some of de Walter's misapprehensions while Mrs de Walter told my mother how she had all her clothes made up and sent over to Portugal by her dressmaker in England. Everything passed off so amicably that we found ourselves being asked to take lunch with the de Walters the following day at the Villa Monte Rosa.

The next day a taxi delivered us to a pair of rusty wrought iron gates in the pleasantly unspoilt hill village of Monte Rosa. The gates were situated in a high stone wall which surrounded what looked like extensive grounds; a drive from the gates curved into the leafy obscurity of palm and pine trees, and other overgrown vegetation. We were about to push open the gate when down the drive came a wiry middle-aged woman in overalls. Her head was tied up in a bandana and she had a narrow, deeply lined face, the colour and consistency of an old pigskin wallet. Silently she shook our hands with an attempt at a smile on her face, then gestured us to follow her up the drive.

The grounds were not well kept, if they were kept at all, but we saw enough of them to guess that they had once been laid out and planted on a lavish scale. Once or twice through some dense and abandoned screen of leaf I caught a glimpse of a lichened piece of classical statuary on a plinth. Then we turned a corner and had our first sight of the Villa Monte Rosa.

It looked to me like a miniature palace made out of pink sugar. Both my parents were entranced by it, but, as they told me later, in slightly different ways. To my father the ornate neo-baroque design evoked a vanished world of elegant

Edwardian hedonism. Had it been only a little more extensive, it could have passed for a small casino. To my mother this rose-coloured folly encroached on all sides by deep, undisciplined vegetation was a fairy-tale abode of the Sleeping Beauty. It reminded her of illustrations by Edmond Dulac and Arthur Rackham in the books of her childhood.

The de Walters were there to greet us on the steps that led up to the entrance portico. Lunch, simple and elegant, was served to us on the terrace by the woman who had escorted us up the drive. She was their housekeeper and her name was Maria. The terrace was situated at the back of the villa and looked down a gentle incline towards the sea in the distance. What must once have been a magnificent view was now all but obscured by the pine trees through which flashes of azure tantalised the spectator. Mrs de Walter informed us proudly that the Villa Monte Rosa had been built in the 1890s by a Russian Prince for his ballerina mistress. It might not have been true, but it was plausible.

The conversation did not greatly interest me. It consisted largely of a monologue on wine from de Walter who obviously considered himself an aficionado. Though my father knew more than enough to keep up with him, he had the journalist's knack of displaying a little judicious ignorance. My mother and Mrs de Walter, who appeared to have less in common, sporadically discussed the weather and the flowers in the garden of the Villa Monte Rosa. After lunch Maria wheeled out a metal trolley on which a large selection of ports and unusual liqueurs were displayed. De Walter proposed a tasting to my parents and then turned to me.

"Why don't you go and explore the grounds, young feller? We won't mind. We'll hold the fort for you here, what? All boys like exploring, don't they? Eh?" This project appealed to me and was acceptable to my parents.

"Don't get lost!" said my mother.

"It's all right," said de Walter with a raucous laugh. "We'll send out search parties if you do!"

So I walked down the shallow steps of the terrace and into the gardens of the Villa Monte Rosa. After crossing a small oval lawn with a lily pond at its centre, I took a serpentine path which led down through shrubberies. Great tropical fronds stooped over me. The gravel path was riven with weeds and more than once I tripped over a thin green limb of vegetation that had clawed its way across it in search of nourishment. I imagined myself to be an archaeologist uncovering the remains of a lost civilisation.

It is often a great shock to find one's fantasy life confirmed by reality. I came down into a dell to find a structure consisting of a statue in a niche above a stone basin in the shape of a shell. It looked like the fountain at the gate of some ancient city. The statue was of a naked woman, lichened and weather worn, holding a jar, tilted downwards, from which, water had once fallen into the basin which had been dry for a long while. The figure I now think was probably modelled on Ingres' *La Source* which made it mid to late nineteenth century in origin. On its pedestal was carved the word DANAIDE. This meant something to me even then. I knew from the simple gobbets of Greek prose that I was beginning to study that the Danaids, because they murdered their husbands, had been condemned to fill leaky vessels for all eternity in Hades, the Land of the Dead.

I stared for a long time at this ancient conceit, turning its significance over in my mind, but coming to no conclusion, until eventually I decided to follow the path round it and travel further down the slope. After a few minutes I came to another clearing where I received my second and more prodigious shock.

Within a little amphitheatre of box and yew, both rampant and unpruned, was a hard floor of grassless grit in which was built out of smooth, dressed stones a low circular wall that I took to be the mouth of a well. On the wall sat a pale, fair-haired boy of about my age. He wore grey flannel shorts and a white flannel shirt, of the kind I was made to wear out of doors in the summer at my school. We stared at each other for a long while: to me he was horribly unexpected.

One reason why I spent so long looking at him was that I could not quite make out what I was seeing. He was a perfectly proportioned flesh and blood boy in all respects but one. He seemed smaller than he should be, not by much but by enough to make him seem deformed in some subtle way. As he sat on the wall his feet dangled a foot or so above the ground when they should have touched it, but he was not dwarfish: his legs were not bowed or stunted; his head was not too big for his body. Apart from the extreme pallor of his skin and hair, he was, I suppose, rather a handsome boy. I could have come closer to him to confirm my suspicions about his size, but I did not want to.

"Hello," I said, then recollecting that the boy, his appearance notwithstanding, was almost certainly Portuguese, I said: "*Bom Dir.*"

"You're not Portugoose, are you?" said the boy. "You're English."

"Yes," I said. He had a voice like mine. He belonged to the middle classes. He asked me my name. I told him and he said his name was Hal.

"Hal what?" I asked.

"Just Hal."

"What are you doing here?"

"What are *you* doing here?"

I told him and then I said it was his turn to tell.

"I come here sometimes," he said.

"Do Mr and Mrs de Walter know?"

"*Of course*, they do, you ass," said Hal. "Anyway, what's it got to do with you? Mind your own beeswax!" *Mind your own beeswax*. It was a piece slang I had heard once or twice at my school, but even there it had seemed dated, culled perhaps from a reading of *Billy Bunter* or *Stalky & Co*.

Hal asked me about my school, in particular about games. I boasted as much as I could about my distinctly average abilities, and my exploits in the third eleven at cricket. He kept his eyes fixed on me but I wondered how much he was taking in.

He said: "When I grow up I'm going to be a cricketer, like Wally Hammond."

"Who's Wally Hammond?" I asked.

"Crikey, don't you know who Wally Hammond is? You are of blockheads the most crassly ignoramus."

"Is he a cricketer?"

"Is he a cricketer? Of course he's a cricketer, you utterly frabjous oaf! Don't you know anything?" As I was one of those boys who had learned by heart the names of the entire England cricket team together with their bowling and batting averages I took great offence at this. Later in our conversation I slipped in a reference to Geoffrey Boycott. Hal said: "Boycott what?" I did not reply, but I felt vindicated.

It was not long after this that I began to feel that my company was no longer a pleasure to Hal. Something about his eyes were not quite right. They seemed to be darker than when I had first seen them, not only the irises and pupils, but the whites had turned a greyish colour. Perhaps it was a trick of the fading light which may also account for the fact that he was beginning to look even smaller.

Suddenly he said: "Who are you anyway?"

"Who are you for that matter, and what are you doing here?" I said, taking a step towards him.

"Go away!" he shouted. "Private Property!"

The sound of his cry rang in my ears. I turned from him and ran up the path to the top of the slope. When I had reached it I turned again and looked back. Hal was still sitting there on the lip of the old well, his heels banging against the stones. He was facing in my direction but I could not tell whether he was looking at me or not. The light, which was not quite right in that strange garden, had turned his eye sockets into empty black holes. I turned again and ran: this time I did not look back.

For a while I was lost. In that dense foliage I could not tell which way was the sea and which way the Villa Monte Rosa. I remember some agonising minutes during which I could not stop myself from going round in a circle. I kept coming back to the same small stone statue of a cat crouching on a plinth. It was perhaps the tomb of a pet, but there was no inscription. I began to panic. The cat looked as if it were about to spring. I decided that the only way of escape was to ignore the paths and move resolutely in one direction.

Surprisingly enough this worked and in a matter of minutes I found I was walking across the little lawn towards the terrace where my parents were. I was about to set foot on the steps to the terrace when I saw Mrs de Walter at the top of them, scrutinising me intently. She came down to meet me.

"So you've found your way back," she said. "We were beginning to wonder if you were lost.'

I shook my head. She laid her thin hand lightly on my shoulder.

"Did you meet anyone on your travels?" she asked. It was a curious way of expressing herself and I was wary. "You did, didn't you?"

I nodded. It seemed the course of least resistance.

"A little boy?"

I nodded again.

"An English little boy?"

I gave her the same response. The pressure of her hand on my shoulder became so great that I imagined I could feel the bones in her fingers through my thin shirt, or was it the cords of her strange crocheted mittens? She said: "We won't mention the little English boy to anyone else, shall we? Not even our parents. This shall be our personal secret, shan't it?"

I was quite happy to agree with this suggestion, because I had a feeling that my parents would not believe me if I did tell them about Hal.

"Come!" said Mrs de Walter. "I want to show you some things which will amuse you. This way!" Her hand now pressed firmly against my left shoulder blade, she guided me anticlockwise round the villa to a part of it which I had not seen, a long low structure with tall windows abutting onto the main building.

"We call this the orangery," she said. "But it's many years since anyone grew oranges here." She took out a key and turned it in the lock of a door made from grey and wrinkled wood to which a few flakes and blisters of green paint still adhered.

"Who is Hal?" I asked Mrs De Walter.

"Come inside," she said. "There are some things here which I'm sure will amuse you."

We entered a long, dingy space feebly lit by the tall dirty windows that faced onto the garden. At the far end of the orangery was a curtain of faded green damask drawn across a dark space, and along the wall which faced the windows was ranged a series of rectangular glass cases set on legs at a height convenient to the spectator.

"These are bound to amuse you," said Mrs de Walter. "All boys like you are amused by these." Her insistence on my reaction was beginning to make me nervous.

At first I thought that the glass cases simply contained stuffed animals of the kind I had seen in museums, but when I was placed firmly in front of one I saw that this was not quite so. There were stuffed animals certainly, but they were all mice, rats and other rodents, and they had been put into human postures and settings.

The first tableau depicted the oak panelled parlour of an old-fashioned inn. A red squirrel in an apron was half way through a door bearing a tray of bottles, glasses and foaming tankards of ale. At a table sat four or five rats and a white mouse. Playing cards were scattered over the table and on the floor. The white mouse was looking disconsolately away towards the viewer while the rats seemed to be gloating over the piles of coin which had accumulated on their side of the table. The white mouse wore an elegant embroidered sash of primrose coloured silk while perching on one of the finials of his chair back was an extravagantly plumed hat. The setting and costume accessories suggested the Carolean period. Two moles wearing spectacles and Puritan steeple hats were watching the proceedings with disapproval from a corner table. It was clear that the rats had gulled the wealthy but innocent young mouse out of his cash at cards.

The tableau looked as if it had been made in the Victorian era and had, I am sure, been designed to amuse, as Mrs de Walter kept reminding me, but there was something dusty and oppressive about the atmosphere it evoked. Perhaps it was the implied moralism of the display, a sort of *Rodent Rake's Progress*, that disheartened me.

In the second case the scene was set outside the inn. The two moles were now observing the action from an open first floor casement window to the right of the inn sign which bore the image of a skull and a trumpet. On the road in front of the inn a brawl was taking place between the white mouse and one of the rats. Both were being urged on by groups of their fellow rodents, the mice being smaller obviously, but more elegantly equipped with plumed hats and rapiers swinging from their tasselled baldrics. The rats had a proletarian look about them and had leather rather than silk accoutrements.

The third tableau was set in a forest clearing where the mouse and his comrades had just ambushed the rat with whom he had been brawling in the previous scene. The mouse was plunging a rapier into the belly of the rat which was now in its death throes. I was slightly surprised by the graphic way in which the creator of these scenes had shown the blood. It surrounded the gaping wound which the mouse had created; there was a dark viscous pool of the stuff on the yellow soil beneath its body and great splashes of it on the mouse's white fur. One could just see the faces of the two moles peeping out from a dense belt of undergrowth to one side.

The final glass case depicted a courtroom, presided over by an owl judge. Other participants were all rodents of one kind or another. The white mouse, his coat still faintly stained with blood, stood in the spike-hedged dock between two burly ferret policemen. A rat in a wig was interrogating one of the moles whose head was just visible above the wooden sides of the witness box. The entire jury was composed of rats and, as if to confirm the inevitable outcome of the trial, I noticed that a small square of black cloth already reposed upon the owl's flat head.

"I thought these would amuse you," said Mrs de Walter who was standing behind me. I started. In my absorption I had quite forgotten her presence. Amused was not the word, but I was held by a morbid fascination. These scenes with their lurid subject matter and their dusty gallows humour, were redolent of long-forgotten illustrated books and savage Victorian childhoods.

"Ah! But you haven't seen behind the curtain, have you?" said Mrs de Walter with a dreadful attempt at a roguish smile. It was then that I became very much afraid. I can only account for the suddenness of my panic by the fact that uneasiness had built it up inside me over the course of the afternoon, that it had reached a critical mass and was now in danger of erupting into sheer terror. One thought dominated: I must not see be-hind the curtain, and yet, at the same time, I knew I could not look away. Mrs de Walter appeared to take all this in, but she showed neither concern nor indifference to my state of mind, only a kind of intense curiosity. She bent down and looked directly into my eyes.

"I wonder if you should see this one. It might shock you." She approached the curtain and put one hand on it so that in an instant she could pull it aside. There was a pause before she asked me a question.

"Are you by any chance a pious sort of a boy?"

For several seconds I simply could not grasp what she meant. Of course I understood the word "pious". It was the name of a recent Pope; monks in the Middle Ages were pious; but I had never heard it applied to a living human being, let alone myself. I said I didn't know. She smiled.

"All right," she said, "the tiniest peep, then," and she flicked aside the curtain. It was only a few seconds before she released the curtain and all was hidden again, but my impressions, though fragmentary, were all the more vivid for that.

It was a glass case like the others, but the scene within it was very different. I remember the painted background of a lurid and stormy sky, torn apart by zigzags of lightening. Against them the three crosses on a grey mound stood out strongly. I cannot say too much, but it was my impression that the three toads had still been alive when they were nailed to the wood.

I can remember nothing after that until Mrs de Walter and I found ourselves on the terrace again. I saw a table strewn with little glasses and open bottles full of strange coloured liquids. Mr de Walter and my parents appeared to be having a lively discussion about race.

"I've knocked about the world a bit in my time," de Walter was saying, "and I've met all sorts, I can tell you. And of all the peoples I have met, the best, for all their faults, are the English. 'Fraid so. Modesty forbids and all that, but facts is facts. Next best are the Germans. Now, I know what you're going to say, and I'd agree, your bad German is a Hun of the first water—Dammit, I should know!—but your good German is a gentleman. Your Frenchie is an arrogant swine; your Arab is a rogue, but at least he's an honest rogue, unlike your Turk. Don't waste your time with the Swiss: they all have the mentalities of small-town stationmasters. Nobody understands the Japs, not even the Japs, but your absolute shit of hell in my experience is the Bulgarian. Scum of the earth; sodomites to a man; rape a woman soon as look at her, but not in the natural way of things if you understand me."

"Hugh!" said Mrs de Walter reproachfully indicating my presence.

"What about the Portuguese?" said my mother quickly, in an attempt to smother any further revelations about the Bulgarians. "You must like the Portuguese. We've found them to be absolutely charming."

"Your Portugoose is not a bad fellow, I grant you," said de Walter rather more thoughtfully than before, "but he's a primitive. You've seen the folk round here: dark, squat little beggars, stunted by our standards. Well, there's a reason for that in my opinion. It's because they're the direct descendants of the original Iberian natives. There's been no intermingling with Aryan races, not even the Romans when they invaded, or the Moors for that matter. They're like another species. I call them the Children of the Earth."

My parents did not know how to respond to this without either compromising themselves or causing offence, so there was a silence. It was broken by de Walter's suggestion that he take us on a tour of the house.

The rooms were luxuriously furnished in an opulent Edwardian style with heavy brocades and potted palms. On side tables of dark polished wood were ranged treasures of the kind that used to be called "curios": ostrich eggs mounted in silver, meerschaum pipes whose bowls were shaped like mermaids or wicked bearded heads, little wild animals carved in green nephrite by Fabergé. On a side table was a gold cigarette case of exquisite workmanship with the letter E emblazoned in diamonds upon it. De Walter opened the case for us. Resting in its glittering interior was a charred and withered tube of white paper that might once have been a cigarette.

"I'd blush to tell you how I got hold of this little item, or what I paid for it," he said. "This case once belonged to a very beautiful and tragic lady, the Empress Elizabeth of Austria. And that little scrap of paper was the last cigarette she ever smoked. I have the documents to prove it. She was assassinated, you know. Stabbed by an Italian anarchist in Switzerland of all places. Ghastly people, the Italians: blub over a bambino while holding a knife to your guts under the table."

The books that lined the whole of one wall of what he called his "saloon" were nearly all leather bound and had curious titles which I did not recognise. They were not like the miscellaneous collection of classics and popular novels to be found in our house.

"Here's something that might amuse you, old man," said de Walter to my father, pulling out a gilt tooled volume in red leather. "Crébillon fils. The engravings are contemporary."

I saw my father open the book at random. The right hand page was an engraved illustration of some sort, but he shut it too rapidly for me to see what it was.

My eye was attracted to a group of silver framed photographs on a bureau. Several of them featured younger versions of the de Walters which showed that they must once have been elegant if not exactly handsome. Others were of strangers, presumably relatives or friends, usually formal portraits, and of these one stood out. It was an old photograph, pre-war at a guess, of a bald man with a short nose, determined mouth and a fierce stare. He looked straight out menacingly at the camera and, it would seem, at us: it was like no photograph I had ever seen before.

"Know who that is, young feller-me-lad?" de Walter asked me.

"*I* do," said my mother with evident distaste.

"Yes," said de Walter, sensitive to her reaction but unruffled. "He had a certain reputation. The Great Beast and all that. Queer chap, but he knew a thing or two. Know what he said? Remember this, young 'un. "Resolute imagination is the key to all successful magical working." That's what he said. Well, Crowley had the imagination all right. Trouble was, he lacked the resolve. Drugs and other beastliness got in the way. I'm afraid he wasn't quite a gentleman, you see. I visited him once or twice during his last days in Hastings. He was in a bad way because the drugs had caught up with him, as they always do. Ghastly, but useful. Got some handy stuff out of him about the *homunculus*. Ever heard of that, little man?" he said with a wink. I said I hadn't.

"It means 'little man', little man. Except he doesn't come out of a mother's tummy, he comes out of an egg. But it's a special Alchemical egg." I was baffled, but I took comfort from the fact that my parents seemed to be equally puzzled. De Walter went on: "Making the egg. That's the hard part. Now, here's another. Have you heard of a *puerculus*, my boy?" And he winked again. I shook my head. "Well now, use your nous. Puer in Latin means—?"

"Boy."

"Good. Right ho, then. So if *homunculus* means little man, then *puerculus* means—"

"Hugh, dear, hadn't we better be getting on?" said Mrs de Walter.

"Ha! Yes! Call to order from the lady wife!" De Walter led us out of the room and down a whitewashed corridor towards a stout iron bound oak door with a gothic arch to it quite unlike the others in the house.

"Now then," said de Walter putting his hand on a great black key which protruded from the door's lock, "my grand finale. The wine cellars! This way, boys and girls!"

My mother, who had become increasingly nervous throughout the trip, suddenly burst into a stream of agitated speech: "No really, that's awfully kind of you, but we must be on our way. Do forgive us. It's been really delightful, but there's a bus from the village in ten minutes—I consulted the man, you see—which we will just be able to catch. Thank you so much, but—"

"Enough, dear lady, enough!" said de Walter. He seemed more amused than offended, though even then I recognised the amusement of the bully who has successfully humiliated his victim.

When we were safely on the bus, among a troupe of uniformed schoolchildren and three black clad old women who were carrying cagefulls of hens into Estoril, my mother said: "Never again!" My father whose courteous soul, I thought, might have been offended by our hastily contrived departure, said nothing. I think he even nodded slightly.

II

One Sunday morning, a year or so after our holiday in Portugal, my parents and I were sitting over breakfast in the kitchen. Sunday papers were, as usual, spread everywhere. One of my father's indulgences, excused on the grounds of professional interest, was to take a large number of the Sunday papers, including the less 'quality' ones, like *The People* and *The News of the World*. I noticed that my father always picked up the latter first and often read it with such avid attention that my mother had to address him several times before he would comply with a simple request, like passing the butter. I had no interest in newspapers at that time and frequently, with my mother's permission, took a book to the breakfast table.

On this occasion I happened to notice my father turn a page of *The News of the World* and give a sudden start. My mother asked if anything was the matter. "I'll tell you later," he said and left the kitchen, taking the paper with him. When, later that morning, I found *The News of the World* abandoned in the sitting room I noticed that the centre pages were missing, but my father had failed to observe that among the exciting list of contents to be found on the front page were the words: HORROR AT THE VILLA MONTE ROSA.

I forget how I managed to get hold of another copy of that paper, but I did, that day, and I made sure that my parents did not know about it. These little discretions and courtesies were part of the fabric of our life together.

Across the centre page spread was sprawled the familiar headline: HORROR AT THE VILLA MONTE ROSA.

Much of the space was occupied by a large but fuzzy photograph, probably taken with a long lens from a nearby vantage point, of three people being escorted down the drive of the villa by several Portuguese policemen. Two of them I could clearly make out: they were Mr and Mrs de Walter, their expressions stony and sullen. The third, a woman in an overall, had bowed her head and was covering her face with both hands. I guessed this to be their housekeeper Maria, an assumption which was confirmed by the text.

The article itself was short on detail, but long on words such as "horror", "gruesome", "grisly" and "sinister". The few clear facts that I could ascertain were as follows. Over the course of about eight or nine years, a number of boys, all Portuguese, aged between ten and twelve had disappeared from the Monte Rosa district. The last boy to vanish, from the village of Monte Rosa itself, had been seen on the day of his disappearance in the company of the de Walters' housekeeper, Maria. A police search of the Villa Monte Rosa and its grounds resulted in the discovery not only of the boy's corpse "hideously mutilated," according to the article, but to the remains of over a dozen other children. Most of these had been found "at the bottom of a disused well in the grounds." The de Walters, said the article, had "been unable to throw any light on these horrific discoveries," but were still helping the authorities with their investigations.

Some weeks later I confessed to my mother that I had read the article. Her only comment was that I had had a lucky escape, but I am not sure if she was right. The de Walters would not have touched me, and Hal, whom I had met by the well, had not been one of the boys who were killed because they were all Portuguese. Hal, you see, had been English like me and not a *Portugoose*.

III

I am writing this now because I have been told to, by my wife and the others. Not that I have any complaint against her. We have been married for over twenty years. We have no children: that inestimable privilege had been denied us, and adoption would have been impossible. I could not have taken an alien being into my house. But we have plenty of occupation, my wife and I. We are great collectors; in fact, I am a dealer in antiques and am recognised as something of an expert on Lalique glass.

One afternoon, about three months ago—I think it was three months; it may have been two, or perhaps even less— we were in Bath. Naturally we did our rounds of the antique shops. There is a little place in Circus Mews, not far from the Royal Crescent, which we often visit, rather shabbier than the rest; at least not tarted up in some awful way. I won't say we pick up bargains there because the owner knows his stuff, but he has a way of discovering rare and unusual items which I find enviable.

It was a bright summer day and shafts of sun were penetrating the windows of his normally rather gloomy establishment. That is how I believe I had a sense of what was ahead of me even before we opened the door to the shop, and as soon as I was inside I saw it.

It was one of Mrs de Walter's glass cases of stuffed animals, the second one of the series I had called in my mind "The Rodent's Rake's Progress," and it was exactly as I had remembered it. In fact, it surprised me that it did not seem smaller to me, now that I was myself older and larger.

The scene, as you remember, is set outside the Inn with the sign of the Skull and Trumpet. There were the brawling mice and rats in the foreground, and—yes!—the Puritan moles in steeple hats are peering out of a diamond leaded casement on the first floor to the right of the inn sign. There are windows to the left but these are not open. And yet—this is something I cannot remember seeing before—there is something behind those windows, and it is not another rodent. It is the pale head and shoulders of a boy in a white flannel shirt, a boy no more than six inches high. I cannot see him too clearly through the little leaded panes of glass, but I think I know him.

I swear that the head moved and turned its black eyes upon me. They tell me of course this is rubbish, and I want to believe them.

Under Different Stars

by Avalon Brantley

*T*HERE *is a necessity to feel . . . not a necessity to live.*
Words I pirated from Plutarch's Pompey, ships idle in the harbour, hulls full of Iberian grain. His sailors cowed before the tempest's sudden manifesting, out of the blue. Worried for their lives, they sought to wait it out.

What were their names?

Where are their shades?

The Great general strode aboard, demanded his men weigh anchor, and stentorian into their paling faces: "There is a necessity to sail, not a necessity to live!"

I took his words to be my own. Because *scribo, ergo sum.* It is needful to feel. But not to live.

That is why I would talk to you. The non-living.

I thought of that there. In the darkened parlour. I would let *centurias* of entities command me, fill me up. Like a ship. A fleet of ships. Their holds all full of different mouths, different minds, disembodied speakers, whispering with different voices, in visible chorus, conjured on the page.

We, that is to say I, as well as Aunt Ana, her children Mario and Maria, the bearded gent from Cascais and his pretty niece Amadora, and Auntie's friend Flor, all sat at Auntie's circular table. I'd transiently hoped that Amadora would sit next to

126

me, but I would have to hold the sinewy hand of her uncle instead.

My fingers felt cold in that room; I kept them clasped until it was time to hand them to others beside me.

There lay skeletal covering of cutwork lace on the table, under my hands. I looked at it. The thought appealed to me: an extraction of scraps and threads, one at a time, from the whole cloth with which one started. So many holes, so many retractions. Yet a most aesthetic end, don't you think so?

But . . . only stretches of broken white? To be left lying on a table?

Yes, at best, we all end up that way.

Looking down from above the table. When I try, really try, to remember, that's where I see how it was. There is Amadora, shy smile, auburn curls. There is the thin black hair of her uncle, balding in two symmetrical spaces toward the upper back of his head, and on Amadora's other side, Mario. There is Auntie, dark coffee eyes, a thick head of fine grey hair. And Maria, her eyes the same, dark as her hair, dark as Auntie's once was. And Flor between us both, to my right. Yes, I see me there. Because I am not that young man but the older, different man whom he will learn to know. And yet I can somewhat remember how he felt, how he invited this multiplicity, this life-long division of himself. And consequently, me. My, what a power over me that young man down there has!

And how detached he is from the rest of the séance . . .

This is what he witnessed happening for a while.

Flor's thin lips began first to tremble, then to mumble. She beetled her thick brown eyebrows over pinched-shut eyes, the muttering growing faster, faster, yet also ever quieter. Between indecipherable word-riddled gasps her teeth chattered, a char-nel sound. Cold marble. Bones.

Then there commenced a strange, drawn-out call and re-sponse between her and Amadora, little whispers, almost as if Amadora were drawing in the words in reverse, speaking on inspired breath. The unknown words felt almost visible, palpable; spheres and spirals.

I watch my eyes, those of the young man at the table. He doesn't open them, although I know Flor and Amadora had ceased their strange anti-conversation, indeed all their movements, the very moment that the bearded man opened his eyes to gaze rigidly down on his niece.

Amadora opened her eyes, stared up at the nothing about the table. Where I locked eyes with her for a moment.

She spoke in broken sentences, stuttering over words she never finished. She seemed not quite inside her own eyes as she intoned, "He is not *wurdum!* He is a man who made *guasnpsst!* He is *mediumpty. MORE!*"

"NO, NOT MORE!" her bearded uncle inexplicably bellowed. His jaw gaped open like the *Boca do Inferno*, but the tidewaters in the cavern settled again. He said nothing more; just glared emptily, yawn-mouthed.

The circle broke. Hands fell. On paper and pens. Like jackals. A storm of writing arose—swirling scritches, jagged jabbing written jabbers, pens scarring the wooden surface, or punching through pages on account of the holes in the table linen.

The young man I was was the only one not writing. He merely watched, detachedly, while the others all came suddenly alive with spontaneous, convulsive scribbling. Spirit-written pages—covered predominantly with numbers, though some bore pictures, symbols, or sentences of doubtful legibility—began to spill from the table, were strewn about the floor, proliferating unstoppably from the single tiny pile with which we started, like bread in Bethsaida. There were only the sounds of writing, and breathing, and the rain outside. The frenzy continued, as if our company were a desperate printing house run by hydrophobics, and when blank paper was suddenly not to be found, they turned to the walls, to the ceiling, to even each other.

Auntie finished scratching on a sheet, turned it so I could read. Her eyes were half open, showing only white slivers of sclera. She made an expression like a person unpractised at smiling, although my sweet, devoted, actual aunt could do nothing more naturally than smile.

The turned page read: *You are not mad, nor even mad-seeming. You're under the presence of a very evil spirit. The unknown Master has chosen to impose upon you a higher existence than that of these others. Your destiny falls under different stars, a different Law.*

She'd written it in my hand. My trembling, wavering, different hand. But my hand all the same.

Abruptly they stopped writing, perhaps suddenly aware they had each run entirely out of ink. All turned to face me. Their eyes were hollow; the women's hair, young and old, was half-undone and dishevelled. In the gloom shining through the thin white drapes across the picture window, I could see the bearded man's mouth hanging open like a cave. And his eyes: even emptier than that. Flor gave a lifeless grin around an illegible tangle of ink scrawled deep across her face and up one cheek; in doing so she presumably dissected the uncertain word into its root morpheme and a bleeding desinence.

They swayed closer, surrounded, chins down toward their chests, as if their heads were far too heavy.

And I suddenly felt featherweight as paper.

Each raised his or her stylus high overhead.

The pain burst like light, all over my body, but I felt as if I were bleeding the wrong way, as if my inner space were a vacuum. All the unseen airborne *somethings* surrounding us, attracted by the séance, sought the holes the pens had made in me; they wormed into me, most of them disappearing from my awareness like ephemeral faces in a crowd observed from a quiet café balcony, a cigarette between one hand's cold fingers, a cup of cooling coffee beside the other, warmer one, the one writing. Writing this, and much of the rest that I, we, wrote. There are *so* many voices, clamouring, commenting, criticizing, even at times doing battle. At other times, one will come with quiet thoughts all his own, or even a silent soliloquy. But that rain-muffled afternoon in Auntie's peaceful little home, as my companions all repeatedly stabbed me, cold crowds swarmed inside, and settled, and slept. Their voices come to life, each in its season or time, some more outspoken than others. They were me, yet not me, not identity nor progeny. And yet reminiscent of each.

Reminiscent of *me*.

Whoever *that* is! Or would have been.

Who might I have been?

It seems strange, to sometimes think of someone, long for someone, who has never been *anyone*. To have such *saudade*— for oneself, who never was.

And meanwhile, who are these many, who think with my brain and write with my hand, who make me *me*, this uncertain demiurge I Am? Whose are these voices, really, which rise from me as if from vast, unending fields composed of open wells, over which a lonely wind has risen to wander and blow?

I remain very changed from that day, and yet I realize that no one really moved, that I still held hands in mine. Everyone was still seated, eyes closed, a small furrowed "V" between the brows of the bearded man, and frowns on the faces both of Flor and Amadora.

Auntie sighed, letting go of the hands that she held. She spoke to the others, although she looked longest at me.

"It's not working. Nothing's coming."

"You feel nothing?" Amadora asked, glancing around.

"Nothing," Flor sighed. "And we've had such successful sessions before."

"There is a delaying element present," the bearded man posited.

"But Miguel, how could that be? My children and I have been with both you and Amadora at your sister's home, and there was generous spirit activity in your presence. So we know it cannot be you! And Flor, why, Flor and I have met with successes at this very table. . . ."

She trailed off, again meeting the eyes behind my glasses.

"I'm sorry, *carinho*, but it could only be you."

"Me?"

They nodded sombrely.

"I'm the delaying element? I'm the reason the spirits are silent?"

"I think so."

"Yes."

Nods around me.

But how? What am I?!

Glancing around, I forced myself to shut my open mouth.

They hadn't seen. I had lost myself there for a minute, and in the interim something powerful had happened to me, and yet for them, none of it had happened; instead I became an impediment to their efforts.

My own séances had been conducted all along, in secret, even from me. Inside me somehow.

Composing myself, I stood. Dignity. Poise. Quiet.

"I'm terribly sorry. I shall retire to my room to do some writing, but I should be glad to hear of whatever activity you may . . ."

"It's better you should leave the house when there is a séance," pretty Amadora advised.

"Amadora," the bearded man chided, though not very forcefully. "It's raining today."

"As a matter of fact, a walk through the city might be just the thing!" said I. "I have a very nice, wide umbrella. Perfect for days like today. The world under rain is different. Special. It appeals very strongly to someone in me."

I depart, clicking the door softly shut behind me, the sound like entering a new frame of mind. The rain is falling hard, it is difficult to know if I really hear its click, but of course, regardless, I do. It is a peaceful, symmetrical noise, rectangular and final, like the only photograph taken in the very second it is taken, before that second flies minutes, decades, millennia, backwards, taking the world as it was and all that was in it with it. And did I live in that moment? Or rather, as I begin to suspect, do I live it more truly now, here, on this page?

I make my way from the house, selecting directions at random, yet finding myself returning to familiar territory again and again. The pavements slope downward, towards the sea. Beneath sheets of rainfall, yellow trams loiter in a quiet queue; they seem like spectres of unspent sunlight, stored north of the wharves so to wait out the storm.

My feet meander me southward, down the *Rua dos Douradores*, past the familiar firm whose doors will open tomorrow to swallow me and my time. Its sarcophagal windows hover silent in the Sunday rainfall. Shaded. And seeming even sleepier than usual.

Onward along the *Rua da Alfândega*, to the close, rueful little streets around it, where the ceramic rooftops stop, lending glimpses of an oblivious sky above the waterfront.

I stand alone at the docks. Through curtains of misty precipitation, a ship is rolling in. A small black steamer? My glasses are misted, I cannot tell. Perhaps instead she is a carrack, returning some ancient conquistador home with his treasures? Perhaps even Great Pompey himself, or some other venerable argonaut whose name we have forgotten? Give to him new names, unique and innumerable, as many as the stars by which he still sails. They aren't quite like ours, those other stars.

There is no storm at the moment; only rain in millions of light-like filaments, like the threads left from openwork. I lower my umbrella, remove my hat and glasses, tilt my face upward, and stand there to feel it washing over me. Without breathing.

THE WITCH IS THE BODY

by Farah Rose Smith

SOMETIMES I wonder why the witches I left behind as friends did this to me . . . why their curses and spells riddled my body with pain and deformity. Then I remember that there is no greater witch than this body *I* am in. Guinevere warped my jaw, crushed my hands. Anais made my hair fall out, like snow sliding off of a gable roof. Valerie made my voice sound like broad hooves on shattered glass. Then the others, quieter, made little kinks and cuts, bruises and blood, arthritis and bursitis and the subtle stirring of dementia. I am only twenty-three years old.

My husband was allowed to visit me today. He says that I am more powerful than the memories of their wickedness, but he doesn't see as I see, feel as I feel. Witchcraft brews at the cellular level, streams through the blood. Jackson sees me as I was. When I look in the mirror, I see who I have become.

Guin was the first to admit she had done something wicked. On the phone, she told me she burned a friend's book and turned it to black salt. I stopped talking, discomfort growing in me. I wanted her to be better than that. She felt the fear, the rejection in that silence, and assured me that it wasn't a big deal. Soon after she would tell me of strange prayers she said on my behalf—that the flame of her candle reached out and burned her in that very prayer. She said there was a "bad spirit" around me. She hadn't realized there were many, and she was one.

We had first met in the city at a poetry reading. Guin looked like a Manson girl mixed with a runway model. Sickly-sweet, with a glaze in her eyes that stared right into my lonely heart. We wrote a few emails back and forth for months, which led to phone calls. She was always digging into someone, calling them ugly. I was quiet in those moments, since so much of the time she spent calling me beautiful, honest, true. I'd been love-bombed before, but never by a woman in such a platonic way, never by someone so beautiful, like a flickering candelabrum.

Our last fight was in a hotel in Boston. She'd frightened me so terribly that I ran back to my room on the 24th floor, locking the doors and the windows, and called Anais to tell her what she'd done. The window flew open with a sucking motion, pulling me towards it, a devilsome attempt to plummet me and my disapproval to the depths of the city sidewalk, blood spattered like Pollock on cement. Guinevere didn't know that I could fly.

Anais was different. Her hair was the color of a rotten eggplant, which contrasted sharply with her sickly skin and frail frame. There was a time before Jackson, my husband, when other men had shown vague interest in me. Anais thought her partner was one of them. That's why she befriended me, I think. That was her tactic, to keep women close whom he may have used to betray her. She was a lot older than I was, despite her love for gossip and snake-like hatred of younger women. She turned like a barracuda in night water when she heard that I'd cursed her weasel of a man.

I had met Valerie long before either of them, when we were both sixteen. We were like long lost sisters, but a strain of a desire for intimacy lingered in me like an infection. She never knew that, and I cut her off when she married the man who had had his way with me. She wore tattoos like talismans and had my name torn out of her skin. Valerie became famous, polished face and features gracing every magazine in every store, a glamour and confusion the likes of which I could never reconcile.

Friendship with women was its own cataclysm since childhood, free of witchcraft. Bethany stole my earrings, Serena hurt my dog. Katryn was an idiot, and Asa was on Klonopin at age 6. Angelina brought witchcraft to my doorstep in the seventh grade, luring me in gently with a series of books about high school witches. I bonded more with the books than I did with her, with any of them.

Every day is a new discovery, a betrayal of senses. The scent of the magnolia tree in front of our Church turned to hot sewage. I can no longer see red or its adjacent hues, so that when I bleed, I don't know. Migraine auras flourish into paradoxical hallucinations. Walls stand where there are none, windows stare out into primitive, pagan landscapes. Voices a simpler torment. Guin, Anais, and Valerie, reminding me of my ill gains and missteps. That I was not redeemable in the eyes of God. All this because I chose to leave them.

We were women, through and through, caught in the complexity of conflict as densely as being submerged in dark honey. Guin liked to humiliate me in public. Anais liked to control what I said. Valerie worshipped men. Each, in turn, had corroded my former beauty into a despairing heap. My greatest passion, sex, had been stolen from me. It didn't matter that my partner told me I was beautiful, that I would always be beautiful to him. Every glance in a mirror was a reminder of my own personal Waco—a disaster. I didn't know who I really was, not physically. Not after that. The doctor said it was psychosomatic, or some form of body dysmorphia. I was young and spritely and wide-eyed, lost in my own over-contemplation of contemporary life. One can't diagnose a bewitching.

We suffered from my lack of passion. Penetration felt like a machete infiltrating the womb. There were no orgasms. Not for me, and soon enough not for him. You can't fuck someone in mourning, in permanent estrangement from themselves, can you? Not when you really love them. I remembered telling Guin about our passion, that he said I was the best, the sexiest he ever had. It was one of few things I could hold to my heart with pride. Of course she took it away from me. Is there any greater betrayal from one woman to another? She painted a cage between my legs, a barrier to life, to children—an abyss through which nothing can sweetly enter or exit. I hated her. But still, no more than I hated myself.

I consulted with a plastic surgeon about my jaw, but he said the symmetry was near-perfect, that he saw no injury. I bought bottles of Rogaine to no avail, as Jackson said my hair flowed like a stallion's mane. Always scarring, always pain. No matter the effort, I couldn't see it. I only saw the erosion of my former self, a calcification of grief, a mourning of flesh.

I often looked back at life before the city, before the witches. In mother's house, I didn't have to be beautiful, or even functional. I just had to be. I stopped pricking my skin with needles, stopped all communication beyond the confines of the house. There was a silence there like whipping cream . . . all-consuming peace. I didn't miss needing to be good enough, to feel good enough to be loved. In confinement, there is an ambivalence to all called ugly. Mother remembers the names they called me, the curses sewn into my bones. I am among only myself in a body, therein flesh remembers wickedness. What had happened to other, elder witches? Had the world turned against them, before they turned towards the natural world?

I didn't tell Jackson that I'd booked a one way ticket to the Azure Coast, to contemplate this body, this mind in a sea of blue. He didn't know the depths of my despair, the reasons for this desire to leave, other than a barren womb and the deep cosmic despair of material erosion. He only knew the letter I left, telling him I would be back when I was right again, whatever that meant.

✳

Much of their hate became nothing in the natural world. Gnarled hands crushed the wood of the rower, splintering life lines, heart lines of my palms, extending them to the outer wrist, like a hearkening for everlasting life. Crickets, frogs, night birds, and gunk stirred up from the foot of the riverbed, stirring out the sounds in my own head. One can't be ugly here, only different. The August heat goads my tongue when my jaw drops to pant. There are the makings of sanctuary here, at the end of the river. The old boat is sticky, the wood growing thick in the humidity. Calls from the canopy hearken the eyes. There are no stars, only great silhouetted leaves swaying, despite stillness beneath. There are thirteen names I could carve into the skin of the trees, and I will. The names will live beneath my feet, the groundwork of my body. Someday they will come, and like Ginny Greenteeth emerging from the muck, I will reach beyond the will of their contempt and show them the unerring mettle of the witch.

I am not caught in a witch's spell. I am, rather, caught in the absolute evolutionary betrayal of our kind, *to know thyself.* A dog doesn't know they're ugly, do they? They can sense something wrong when they're ill, but there is no great contemplation of their condition. Not like man. Not like me.

In the wilderness, I become part of a hybrid ecosystem. One that connects me to the animals, the trees, the mud.

There are no mirrors in this place. The water is too murky, too covered in lily pads. The croaking is too loud, so beautifully loud, that the voices in my ears dim, like faint dust on a crumbling mantle.

✳

On the third week of my rewilding, a young man knocked on my door, seeking direction to more civilized grounds, away from the sticky heat and oppression of August. He spoke to me with a mesmeric look. I laughed at myself and thought he perhaps saw the glimmer of a late grandmother, or a character in a storybook. The man was enchanted. I basked in a momentary forgetfulness of my condition. How? One can't forget a condition in the arms of those they love, but the matter is different in the arms of one you will see once, and never again.

Passionately and readily, blood boiling with magic. I swallowed semen like lemonade. He thanked me and departed with his directions to the civilized world, and I had a momentary reprieve from two existences; the one in which I rotted like meat on a counter for my previous indiscretions, and the one in which I desired to be alone for my remaining days. This fantasy would expire, when the swamp water became red like blood, and the croaking of frogs became screams, like women drowning in a river.

✳

I don't know how long I have lived here. My body is the same. Warped jaw, knotted hands, bald head, scar-swept, with a voice like the destruction of the moon. I could be one hundred and three years old. How old am I? I still bleed in concordance with *a linda lua*, and have breasts that sit high, despite their rot. It doesn't matter on nights like this, when

I write nonsense on shredding parchment of the nature of a certain and lurking betrayal. Guinevere said she loved me. Anais said she loved me. Valerie said she loved me. I never loved myself. Their voices grow loud again, as the natural world fades. I know they have found me. But how?

The rustling of leaves grows loud outside of the cabin, and I imagine Guinevere's long chestnut hair slithering through the branches like Medusa's crown serpents. I peak through a crevice in the shoddily built wall to see long, inhuman legs. Four maned wolves are circling the cabin, sniffing the air, then the ground. No witches to be seen. None except for me, slowly returning to myself with dark enchantment. I have stolen everything from them, as they had from me. The canine hooves become white steam. The maned wolves evaporate on the forest floor like radiation victims, only bones clattering against protruding tree roots. They pull together as though magnetized and reform into the body of the visiting man, the man I fucked with so much passion and forgetfulness of fate. I watch. I watch closely.

Are they coming, I ask myself. *Or are they already here?*

Of course they're here, I think. They've always been here, lurking about. They are attached to me like a spiritual umbilical cord, my cosmic responsibility. I bear the hideous marks of that which rots in a dissolution of hexes.

Red light rises from beneath the floorboards, igniting my feet into flame. The wall planks peel like sardine cans to reveal them. Guinevere, Anais, Valerie, not in flesh, but the fluid of spectral resurrection, their spirits free from the bombardment of hexes and spells that had kept them from my door for all of these years. They approach with pleasure, intention glowing from eye to lip. I do not care what they do to this body. It's not something I can see. Not something I fear any longer. My soul is not the witch. The witch is the body, sewn cell by cell with cosmic magic, made to repair, made to emerge. Heaven help the harridans who let this spirit loose upon the world.

FLOWER OF THE SUN

by Colin Insole

> You do wrong to take me out of the grave,
> Thou art a soul in bliss but I am bound
> Upon a wheel of fire, that mine own tears
> Do scald like molten lead.
> (*King Lear*, Act IV, Scene VII)

I will defy my late husband's wishes. I refuse to destroy his journal. Someone should know what was done to him and to our daughter, dead these sixty-four years. But of the other object, the instrument of his ruin, I will reflect and decide later.

I never met his masters, as he called them, nor did he discuss the nature of his war work. He was based at Mortlake on some strange secret assignment. They recruited him in 1939 after he gained academic renown and transitory fame as an undergraduate when he located three missing pages of "The Dream of Rhonabwy" from the "Mabinogion" in a remote parish church in Merionethshire.

We were married in 1943 and blissfully happy. And then, in 1945, the year of hope, all changed. John spent the last sixty-four years of his life in a hospital for the incurably insane.

I visited him only once. It was during the bitter winter of 1947. The hospital was remote in the Surrey countryside, unmarked on any map. We travelled by horse and cart down a maze of farm tracks with the snow piled waist-high in the hedgerows to an anonymous converted Victorian farmhouse.

The inmates had the air of broken monks worn down by study and loss of faith rather than mental incapacity. As we approached they scuttled back to their rooms like cockroaches when the light is turned on in a darkened kitchen.

The orderlies heated housebricks in the hospital ovens and wrapped them in rags to heat the beds but there were icicles on the inside of my husband's room. He looked like a man asleep for a thousand years waking to a private hell. We barely spoke. Oppressed by the silence, I went outside to where a frozen stream passed his window. I picked up a black pebble and idly threw it onto the ice. John pulled me back inside.

"Do you not know why we are kept isolated?" he said. "That same water will flow from here through towns and cities where they gather in cafés and listen at bridges. Wolves can sense a stricken human ten miles away. They tracked the stragglers of Napoleon's army and picked them off from Wiazma to Vilnius. I would welcome the quiet kindness of beasts. But at night, when the hospital is silent, I hear the murmur of voices, savage and angry, far beyond the hills and trees of our seclusion. The tumult and clamour will come, roaring over the fields. Burning, burning they will come."

He did not permit me to visit him again. I thought of the man in Rimbaud's "Song of the Highest Tower", plagued by the wild buzzing of a hundred filthy flies. He had endured so long that he had forgotten everything. John was denied even that one consolation. He remembered everything.

I paid little heed at the time to his words. In post-war London, violence bubbled and simmered under the surface, occasionally erupting in brutal affrays and riots. But when I moved to the country, seeking solitude and consolation, I understood.

My cottage was accessible only by a long winding lane with impenetrable thorn hedges on both sides. I spent hours there, exercising my dogs and enjoying its silence. Once, after many years of tranquility, I heard a noise far in the distance, but closing fast and I was afraid. It sounded like a great crowd of people, angry and dangerous. There was no escape for the hedges were thick. It was not my imagination for my dog sensed it too and drew closer to me. The sound of birds ceased and the landscape seemed to pause and wait. At any moment I expected them to come roaring into view around a bend in the lane and engulf me. But there was nothing. The sensation subsided.

Over the years I experienced that feeling many times, often during periods of civil unrest or rumours of wars. Sometimes, as if in mockery, a cyclist or rider would appear, seemingly innocent and benign. But always there was a knowing prescient edge to their smile or greeting. And I knew that one day, something terrible would come.

I was sure my husband's madness was connected with his work. The only hint I ever had was when we spent a few days in Wales in June 1942. John wanted to escape the attentions of his assistant, Derek Dawlley, foist upon him by his masters. I hated the man. He was a creature of mud and slime, leering and winking at me. Quilp, I called him.

We tramped miles over the Welsh hills. Once we stopped at a farmhouse and were given milk still warm from the cow and freshly-baked rough unleavened bread. Walking home in the dark, we carried a glow-worm wrapped in a lily leaf when the moon—a flower moon in mid-summer—was hidden behind the clouds. I've never been happier.

One rainy evening, John was digging at a deserted house in Denbighshire, near to the Shropshire border. Under the hearth he found some documents, black stones and two earthenware flagons. Surprised and delighted, he wrapped them in a cloth of red and blue and strapped them onto his rucksack. Then, almost as an afterthought, he dug deeper and pulled an object from the ground. It was a gold bracelet. There was something fluid and elusive about it for strange colours and lights shone in the bones of the metal. In the grey twilight he fastened it to my wrist. I only wore it once despite its beauty.

We quarrelled that night. I was in a foolish sulky mood and saw the worst side of John—his self-absorption and secrecy. I pictured him lost in his work with me as his mock widow. Everyone angered me. I saw the lechery in the faces of the drinkers at the inn where we were staying and the landlord's furtive cunning. Of course I never linked my irritation with the bracelet. But its associations were painful and I left it in an old jewellery box at my parents' house. I've never worn it since. When they died I deposited it at my bank.

During his incarceration at the asylum John never answered any of my letters. But every year, on the anniversary of our daughter's death, a painting, featuring one of the characters from *King Lear* or *The Tempest*, arrived by special delivery. Each figure was shown framed in a solid stone arch. Even the villains—Goneril, Regan and Edmund—were depicted as noble stylised actors.

They seemed fragile and vulnerable—protected only by the wall. For outside that arch were hideous human figures—kicking, biting and gouging each other. Every human depravity was enacted. In the early paintings of the sequence, those figures were self-absorbed in their lust, violence and destruction. But gradually, they turned their attentions to the actors behind the arch, cocooned in their world of colour and beauty. Some began hammering with chisels at the stone, sending little plumes of grey dust into the main picture.

In the penultimate scene, King Lear was crouched in a corner, terrified not by the lifeless body of Cordelia at his side, but the howling mob, about to break through. The final picture, painted in the year of his death, was entitled

"Sycorax"—"I have set you loose like vermin to contaminate the world." It showed no witch, but was a self-portrait, a defeated tormented man in his cell, food-stains on his clothes. The one character he had never painted was Caliban.

At the funeral it snowed—flakes falling on us like the dust in the pictures. Apart from the family and a handful of token nursing staff, there was only one guest—a flabby man with large milky eyes who stood alone—humming or whistling to himself. I noticed the tune. It was the song John and I danced to when we first met in 1938.

That night, empty and exhausted by the funeral and the futility of John's life, I re-examined his "Sycorax" self-portrait. Almost hidden in the depiction of his sparse hospital cell was a tiny reproduction of the very painting I held in my hands. Using a magnifying glass, I observed what seemed to be a small pamphlet or magazine, sticking out from the frame of that picture. With a palette knife I probed the ornate gilt and there it was—not a magazine but John's wartime journal with a note attached.

"My Dearest Wife, This is a faithful record of all that happened at Mortlake. You will recognize its truth. Read it and destroy it along with every token and memory I gave you from those years. I fear they are not finished with us yet. John."

Below, I reproduce the most salient entries from that journal.

September 6th, 1939

Today I was summoned to an anonymous government office in Whitehall. The letter "cordially invited" me to come but I understood at once the tone of authority. I traipsed through a warren of dusty corridors to a room which resembled a broom cupboard. Only one man was waiting for me. He introduced himself as "Mr Wells" although I felt it was not his real name. His clothes were frowsy and unkempt like a schoolmaster who is ragged by his pupils. Partly obscured by his frayed shirt cuff was a gold bracelet. His demeanour was weak and evasive but when he spoke I recognised the type of voice that is used to command.

"You are aware of Dr John Dee, the Elizabethan alchemist—Shakespeare's model for both Prospero and King Lear—and his charlatan assistant, Edward Kelley, who claimed to summon spirits and angels. It was said that Dee himself raised the storm that sank the Spanish Armada. You laugh? Do we dismiss this as primitive superstition from an age that believed witches could change the destiny of kings? Or, do we probe and investigate? As I speak, the mystics, clairvoyants and dreamers of Russia, France, Germany and Britain—yes, we here in Britain—are as busy and active as the military men. We wrestle and compete in thought across the oceans. Did you know that Himmler is morbidly terrified by rats? Our psychics gnaw into the tunnels of his dreams. And Hess? We have great hopes of Hess. You'll see.

"Your task is to dig and search the grounds of Dee's old house in Mortlake. Who knows what you will find? Entire documents of alchemy or laundry lists. Flagons of golden dust or old mutton bones. We expect nothing but hope for 'the very flower of the sun, the perfect ruby, which we call elixir.' You have the subtle instinct for the work. You are a scholar but also have that rare gift of imagination. Do not neglect the river. Our forefathers revered it and threw offerings to it. You will, of course, reveal nothing of your work to anyone, not even your delightful fox-trotting fiancée. Yes, I am aware that you dance like angels. Let us hope, that like Dr Dee, you can summon them.

"We will send you an assistant—a Mr Derek Dawlley. He is a coarse but engaging fellow who knows every blue joke by

Max Miller and will sing, if permitted, the entire repertoire of George Formby. But he has his uses. He worked in a chemist's shop and has some rudimentary skills with powders.

"Naturally we will send you all of Dee's extant papers together with his specula for summoning angels. Make of them what you can."

October 21st, 1939

I have been sent Dee's diary, his papers collected by the antiquarian, Sir Bruce Cotton, the later history of the house, together with his specula—a lump of highly-polished candle coal and a pink crystal that resembles a pomegranate in Mr Smedley's greengrocer shop before the war.

Dawlley oppresses me. He reminds me of Henry Mayhew's descriptions of the old London sewer-hunters who braved floods, poisonous gases and hordes of ferocious rats before Bazalgette designed the present sewerage system in the 1860's. 'Toshers' they were called. They travelled miles underground, recovering bone, rope, jewellery and coins washed by the rain and floods from streets and cesspits. They shared his florid good health. I've never known Dawlley ill—not a cough or sneeze. Like the toshers he rakes the mud with a long pole, delighting in the useless fragments he scrapes up. He is lecherous too—asking after Alice—playing with the sound of her name with his tongue and fleshy lips.

It was Edward Kelley, Dee's crop-eared assistant, who pretended to see angels. What shadows would Dawlley invoke? No pretty lisping Madimi, flitting between the bookcases but some filthy Thames mudlark clothed in the skins of sewer rats perhaps.

January 24th, 1940

While fishing in the river today I found a human skull. Like a metaphysical poet I will place it in my study as a reminder of my own mortality. I will look in the mirror which flatters not. Scrubbing it clean of the river tar and sludge, I found a tiny bottle tied to the jawbone. Inside, was this inscription. "I am the head of Thomas Clinkshaw—waterman and famed balladeer of Mortlake. Died 1842. We are the dream singers of the Thames. Our voices will echo down the ages, through the mists and fogs of the estuaries and marshes to the open sea. The nymphs are now our companions."

It is said that many of the watermen balladeers could sing for hours without ever repeating the same song. Their music haunted and enchanted the river for centuries. The tongue of Thomas Clinkshaw is mute. The boatmen and river workers are silent now except for guttural croaks and curses. The song of the river is dead. I feel that nothing of John Dee remains. There are no golden or silver mysteries left. It has been picked clean. Only the bones remain. Eliot was right. The nymphs are departed.

May 20th, 1940

There are two pubs close to our lodgings—"The Alchemist's Beard" and "The Green Cat". Sometimes Dawlley and I sit lugubriously in the latter, drinking weak beer and playing dominos. The walls are festooned with dark prints and engravings depicting scenes dating back to Tudor times. The pub regulars have nicknamed us "The Archbishop" and "The Gargoyle". The landlord's son, a spoilt ten-year-old, baits and taunts Dawlley by pulling grotesque faces. He even abused my master, Mr Wells, during his solitary visit to the pub.

"Look," he said. "It's old po-face from the pictures on the walls."

Rimbaud drank at "The Green Inn". He wrote that the froth on his beer was turned into gold by a ray of late sunshine. I am denied even that rude alchemy.

May 25th, 1940

The landlord's son at "The Green Cat" is ill. He is delirious in bed, tormented by the flapping sign at his window, claiming that the cat is alive. The doctor attending him, an erudite scholarly man, knows the legend told by Elizabeth Cotton to Dee, of the Staffordshire schoolboy terrorised by a witch, who claimed also to see angels at his window. The doctor thinks our boy may have overheard barroom gossip.

"Poor lad," he said. "He sees no angels. Keeps saying, 'The tatterdemalions and the moon-men are coming. I can see their shapes on the river-bank. Burning, burning, the house by the river is burning.' Curious words those. He spoke to me in the polari of the Elizabethan underworld. Strange how that canting slang seeps into the folk-memory."

May 29th, 1940

I feel like a mountebank in a Victorian fairground, with the consolation that no-one, except Dawlley, who watches me toad-like with a mocking smirk, can witness my folly. While our world crumbles in France and Belgium, I am dressed in a hairy dressing-gown, holding a pink glass pomegranate and chanting cod-Latin. Whereas Dee raised a tempest in 1588, my masters request that I calm the Channel while our broken expeditionary forces crawl home from Dunkirk in destroyers, fishing boats and pleasure dinghies.

The landlord's son has been taken away still screaming of those imaginary wretches. His father, despite his grief, asks about Mr Wells, saying that his face and the golden bracelet are half-familiar to him. He keeps his own counsel though and is reluctant to confide in me further.

June 10th, 1940

My troglodyte assistant has unearthed a metal contraption from the mud. It is a wheel of some sort, about a foot in diameter, with a hollow rim, quite intricate in its own way. My guess is that it's Victorian—probably used for sewing or coarse weaving. Dawlley insists that it is older.

"I reckon that old quack Dee used this in his witchcraft, summoning up his angels. See how it spins."

And he set it whirring. It rattled away like a rusty old steam engine, showering dirt and dried leaves in our hair, for at least two minutes. It is certainly robust, surviving decades in the foul Mortlake mud.

The landlord of "The Green Cat" has disappeared. Two days ago he took an early train to Central London, carrying with him two of the pub's Elizabethan prints. He told his wife he was visiting the British Library.

February 14, 1941

Whilst studying the history of Dee's estate, I encountered a strange and sombre tale. In the early nineteenth century the house was converted to a girls' school. One dark November morning, as twelve year old Charlotte Bedmead lifted up a dormitory floorboard where she'd hidden some ham, she pulled out a tiny phial which broke in her hand and showered her in yellow dust. For a few seconds she shimmered, golden and transformed.

"Look, Lotty's an angel," someone said.

That morning, while the other girls laboured over their spelling and syntax, Charlotte Bedmead wrote first a poem and then a scene from a play. The schoolmistress, sour and crabbed, beat her once for copying and harder when she read the bitter sexual imagery of both passages. On hearing of the golden phial they dragged her screaming from the classroom, scrubbed her with carbolic soap, forcing her mouth open to purge her of such filth.

Her writings however, were kept. Decades later, a curious clergyman examined them and realised she had transcribed a recently-discovered Shakespeare sonnet from the Dark Lady series and dialogue between Edgar and King Lear which had been omitted from all folios.

And what became of Charlotte Bedmead? She never spoke another word. Cheated and reviled, she recoiled into herself. She had glimpsed something golden and magical from another world. She had held it in her hand and now it was gone she could no longer bear reality. She had communed with angels. Over the years, she was confined, beaten, strait-jacketed, visited by priests and poisoned with medicines. She died, aged forty-nine, mute and defiant, in an asylum for lunatics.

May 11th, 1941

A visit from Mr Wells. He is triumphant. Rudolph Hess has parachuted into a Scottish field.

"We have played and reeled in Hess like a trout on a line," he said. "We convinced him he had the power of words to awaken the lost Celtic warriors. He would summon them from their slumber and sweep east—driving all before him.

Poor Hess—prodded with a farmer's pitchfork and babbling of stars. The dead are more subtle. They slip like quicksilver through our hands. But he will learn that in the long years to come."

The success of Mr Wells' plans led him to confide in me. I had long wondered how many other deranged souls are employed in similar work to mine.

"Many," he said. "There are 'The Seven Sleepers'—men and women who, in the past, have foreseen and avoided ruin and disaster. Every night they record their dreams in pale blue notebooks which are posted to a nondescript sleepy pub in Dorchester where the landlord's wife analyses them for patterns and similarities.

"Then there is 'The Goosewoman'—you remember how the geese warned the sleeping Romans of impending attack. She has the body and movement of a huge pink slug but a mind as sharp as a chisel. She senses rumour, anomalies, quirky little things out of kilter and alerts us."

November 28th, 1941

When the Armada was sighted, beacons were lit across Southern England—points of light that illuminated the defenders within a circle of defiance. Last night I dreamed of a blazing rim of fire, like a gigantic Catherine wheel, here upon the mud of Mortlake, which sent up sparks like stars. And one by one, the beacons were lit again, as the stars fell upon the hills and valleys. But then spatters of mud and yellow London smog seeped into the heart of the fiery wheel and, as it spluttered and fizzed, the darkness spread to all corners of the world. I woke trembling and distressed. Outside in the darkness, shadows race across the chimneys and rooftops. All is cold. All is gloom.

When Dee returned penniless from Europe in 1589, his library burnt and ransacked, and memories of the "Golden Street" in Prague a bitter joke, he was taunted and harried by the mob of Mortlake. He was however, befriended by Mrs Thomasin, the Queen's dwarf, who used to ride out carrying a bottle of sac and fruitcakes she'd baked herself in the ovens at Richmond.

Sat one afternoon by the river, discursing on the meaning of dreams, they were approached by a group of travelling beggars or moon-men. They were the same wanderers that plagued the imagination of the landlord's son. One waved in triumph a looted manuscript. It was 'The Thief of Kent's Boast'—a lost and suppressed Canterbury Tale.

On the night before their arrival in Canterbury, at an inn near Chartham, the pilgrims, content and at ease with each other, met a "soft and sallow churl", dressed in black, who boasted he would steal from each, the thing, bar life itself, they valued most. Each one hugged close his most treasured possession—the Pardoner, his relics; the Nun's Priest, his sacred scrolls and the Merchant, his bag of gold.

But while they talked and sang, the thief secretly contaminated their food and drink with a subtle black philtre. By midnight he had stolen their wits. The next day, the entire company capered naked, blasphemous and profane to the shrine at Canterbury where the contagion spread throughout the streets until the whole populace became a Holy city of fools and madmen. Dee described the tale as being full of bleakness and despair with language "corrupt and fantastical". Shakespeare knew of it and the heath scenes in *King Lear* echo its strange imagery.

Having tantalised Dee with the manuscript, one beggar tore it into fragments before his face, cramming a small handful into his mouth and throwing the rest into the Thames. Mrs Thomasin dealt the oaf a heavy blow with her walking stick and the group dispersed.

May 28th, 1942

It was generally believed that Dee unearthed his powders digging at Glastonbury Abbey but an obscure reference in one document hints at Wales for the source. One of the apparitions, Lundranguffa, had a Welsh name and Dee himself was from that country—possibly Denbighshire. I will investigate this alone, leaving Dawlley to his mud-trawling. I am due a holiday. Alice and I will visit Wales.

June 15th, 1942

A remarkable day walking In Denbighshire with Alice. I had given up all hope of finding any relics of Dee when, asking directions from a farm-hand, I was told of the 'Black House'. Hoping for a ghost story or dark tale of murder or witchcraft, I was told instead that it was simply the name of the old family that vacated it centuries ago. In Welsh, "Dee" comes from "Du" and it means "black".

The house was hidden at the end of a long bridleway. We surprised a vixen snoozing in the brickwork of the old kitchen. Hunch, luck or instinct but under the hearth I found two flagons of powder, two black opals—presumably specula—and documents. A final desultory search produced a strange and beautiful object—a gold bracelet which I gave to Alice. She is unaware of its antiquity. A torque would be rare enough but this was fashioned for a Celtic princess. It has panels which interweave like the scales on a slumbering golden dragon. God, how it glows. I should, of course, humbly present it to the nation, but I am a diffident sleazy romantic. Alice shall wear it when we fox-trot and cha-cha-cha in the sweaty dance palaces of Richmond while the ghost of Queen Elizabeth sulks jealously in the wings.

June 20th, 1942

The documents I found in Wales are disappointing. Dee offers no instructions on how the powders are to be used. Instead, he is deeply troubled by the black opals. He urges the Queen to ban their possession and offers to hide them from dangerous mountebanks and meddlers. He fears even casting them into the Thames, lest they be retrieved by witchcraft. He associates them with evil, saying that the opal is the most fragile of all stones and easily rendered into dust. A worrying thought occurs to me. Could it be that Dee hid those objects I have discovered to keep them away from some malign power?

November 20th, 1942

I have the impression that up until now I have been humoured. The apparently successful charade with the Dunkirk weather was luck of course. I played no part. And my masters knew it. Still, they indulged and encouraged me. I hear them laughing at my robe of tuft mockado. The specula are baubles to tempt a curious child—frills like the fake ectoplasm the bogus mediums employ to impress the credulous. Today though, everything changed.

From the dirty twitching chrysalis you expect a dull blundering insect to emerge—clumsy like a daddy-long-legs. But when our butterfly had stretched the blood into its wings, it was crimson and gold, and stars flew when it took the air.

I knew my assistant had been polishing and mending his contraption—"Dawlley's Rattling Jenny"—I nicknamed it. But when he placed it on the table next to the flagons of powder, I realised I'd misjudged him. It no longer seemed like a Victorian sewing machine used by the slatternly wife of a Thames bargeman but an exotic artefact wrought by Byzantine craftsmen.

I had been asked by my masters to exert some influence on the progress of the war in the east. Nudged by Dawlley and using a silver spoon carved in the form of a dragon, I poured a small amount from each flagon into the rim of the wheel and set it spinning. I needed no specula or robe. I stood in my corduroys and boots, stinking of sweat and the river. Words came unprompted. I am a good linguist but I have no notion what language I spoke.

As the wheel spun, the powders caught fire. Sparks flew from the rim, passed through the walls and out of sight. I gazed hard into the fire and through a host of colours, saw the great city of the east stretched out on the plains beneath. I was part of the tempest as it met a great wind blowing from the opposite direction. We felt the force of that wind but drove it back, scattering it like drops of rain, until it was no more.

November 23rd, 1942

Dee's diaries interweave the wondrous with the mundane. After accounts of Kelley discoursing with angels, he praises his dry nurse Marjory Stubble for her industry in preparing twelve pots of medlar jelly. A day after my successful intervention at Stalingrad, Alice and I enjoy a tinned salmon high tea at the ABC restaurant in Piccadilly.

We returned to Richmond to find that her lodgings have been ransacked. Her landlady is in tears, hinting darkly at fifth columnists and saboteurs. Mercifully, there is little damage and only loose change has been stolen.

May 25th, 1944

A visit from Mr Wells. The invasion of France is imminent. We will be busy in the weeks to come. The wheel burns. We have become thrifty in the use of the powders. A few grains are sufficient to work our magic. The war swings in our favour. Mr Wells tells me of some breaches in security.

"'The Goosewoman' is troubled," he said. "Lately, she has noticed our codewords appearing in the crossword clues of the august Daily Telegraph. And there is a medium who has been most indiscreet in her revelations. Steps will be taken. 'The Assyrian will come down like a wolf on the fold.'"

Our daughter was born yesterday. Dee named his child "Madimia" after the ghost girl summoned by Kelley. That was a surrender. I will not have my life infected with this witchcraft. Our daughter's name is Susan.

November 12, 1944

Daylight is furtive, apologetic, eager to make its excuses and go. I read Thomas Dekker's 1609 work *The Bellman of London*, which tells of the city watchman walking the streets, with his lantern, illuminating the growing mobs of cheats, thieves and plunderers. It is a tour of hell. These are the wretches the landlord's son imagined on the shore of the river—the moon-men, tatterdemalions and roaring boys. They are the ones who burned Dee's library and taunted him on his return from Europe. Their poison swells. They are urged to "creep into bosoms that are buttoned up in satin and there spread the wings of thine infection, make every head thy pillow to lean on, or use it like a mill, only to grind mischief."

February 11th, 1945

The poet and essayist, Sir Thomas Browne, wrote that his friend, Dee's son Arthur, swore that he had witnessed his father use the grey powder to turn pewter plates into silver which were sold to the smiths of Prague. Why then did Dee not make his fortune? I believe he quickly grew tired of such cheap conjuring tricks as I am growing sick of this war and my own rough magic. If the powder works upon base metals and can influence events far away in every theatre of conflict, why should it not work upon the human soul, turning coarse and vulgar actions into something fine and strange? Perhaps Dee himself laboured with this intention and caused his own ruin.

The dark opals, whatever their function have disappeared. I suspect Dawlley has pawned them to buy black market whisky.

June 2nd, 1945

I write this last entry locked and constrained within the bedroom of the lodging house I share with Dawlley, waiting for the car which will take me to a remote and forsaken location. There I will be confined till the end of my days.

This morning I resolved to use a substantial portion of the remaining powder. The war is won. The wheel and its burning dust have thrown back armies and destroyed cities. But my masters spoke on the first day of creating "the flower of the sun, the perfect ruby, which we call elixir." That was my intention today. To send out in waves of fire the beauty and truth that Dee attempted and failed.

I waited until the time when Dawlley spent two or three hours queueing with our ration books in Mortlake High Street. The room was still and quiet but outside a rare song thrush sang sweet and plaintive. I loaded the powders, set the wheel spinning and breathed my spell into its hub. Again, the gold and crimson stars flew.

But before they had even reached the grey rooftops of the nearby houses, Dawlley and Mr Wells burst into the room. Wells cast a handful of black dust into the heart of the wheel. The stars I'd set loose broke like a million fragments of a shattered mirror, distorting and corrupting the images they reflected. Then waves of shadow seeped from the machine— darker and more insidious than all the melancholy smogs of London.

Dawlley restrained me and fixed me to a chair. He seemed hurt—disappointed and shocked at my treachery. Mr Wells spoke.

"Like you, Dee was an interfering fool. He desired knowledge only for its own sake. I offered him power but he laughed out loud. Quoted Bacon at me. Told me I was copulating with clouds and raising centaurs and chimeras. I gave him chimeras alright. I flung the black dust of the opals into his blazing wheel of knowledge and I created the spirit of Caliban and set him loose. I led the mob that burned and pillaged Dee's library. Tatterdemalions, roaring boys and moon-men they were called. The malign spirit and the brute body of Caliban that Shakespeare so eloquently plagiarised. One oaf defecated, laughed and wiped his steaming rump on a sheaf of poems by Li Ho—each one the bitter sweet moods evoked by the thirty-four colours reflected in the scales of the golden dragon of Liang.

"Who are we? We are the bones and sinews of your world and we break and make mad those who defy us, those who seek the 'flower of the sun'. Rimbaud was another who sought hermetic knowledge. We harried him and broke his spirit. Where do you think the cancer that claimed his life at thirty-five came from? And that rat of a girl, Lotty Bedmead, lusting after ham in floorboards and finding angels. I was the doctor who committed her and delighted in my regular visits to her hell.

"Your own success with the 'Mabinogion' was remark-able—intuitive and inspired. We felt sure you would locate the remaining powders and the opals that Dee hid from us. We should have destroyed him utterly before he had the op-portunity to bury them but he had something else we wanted.

"You have observed my gold bracelet. Do not deny it. I have watched you. Embedded within it are minerals which show us the virtues and benign qualities of anyone we meet. Its powers led us to you. But there is a companion piece which reveals weaknesses and frailties. Dee acquired it and concealed it from us. A man who wears it will see his wife's infidelities and deceptions before she has even contemplated her own adultery. We wish to find it and believe you know of its whereabouts.

"You have served us well and would have been allowed an untroubled life—what you call happy. But this folly today and its knowledge will earn only madness and seclusion. With the powdered opal you unearthed, we will stir humanity like a wasps' nest, continually agitated with a stick. We have enjoyed this war immensely and look forward to the darker times still to come. In your isolation, year on year, you will sense the growing chaos and clamour. You will hear them coming."

I was returned to my lodgings and await the car that takes

me away from the world. Propped against the bed were the two missing prints from "The Green Cat". Both depicted Francis Walsingham, Queen Elizabeth's controller of spies and puppet master. But in these engravings, he was a craven and subservient errand-boy. Surrounding him, were the real masters. Mr Wells was in the foreground, unmistakable with his soft eyes and gold bracelet.

June 4th, 1945

They have destroyed any consolation or solace I might find from my family. Mr Wells encouraged me to phone Alice. Our child, our Susan, is dead. Through her tears, Alice told me that the infant spent yesterday cowering and whimpering in a corner, holding up her hands as if to ward off an unseen blow. That blow has come. Alice, first blaming herself and now me for my silence and inactivity, is a dried straw, blown by any stray wind.

I brought Caliban back into this world. Through my vanity and conceit an age of barbarism is upon us, beginning in whispers but growing in fury until it engulfs us all.

December 28th, 2009

I take no small risk for your safety in writing this final entry. Throughout my incarceration, my journal has been left untouched in the hope that I will reveal the whereabouts of the bracelet. I know only that you wore it once. I remember our quarrel and understand now that it was the cause. I can only guess at the place you discarded it, finding its memories painful.

When I am dead, their interest in you will be redoubled for it is their only hope of recovering the bracelet. From their

remarks and innuendoes I know they have watched and harried you.

However, they have grown accustomed to my paintings
and take pleasure in their increasing despair. Their vigilance
slips as they savour the imagery of each picture and I will
take the chance of hiding this journal in a cavity in the frame
of the next canvas I send. It will be the last for I am dying. I
know that you will act swiftly and for the best.

Footnote March 21st, 2010 by Philip Karby

The above manuscript was found in the luggage of my great-
aunt, Alice Karby. Aged ninety-one, she collapsed and died
on board "The Star of the Sea", whilst crossing the Atlantic
on a cruise. Prior to her death, she was seen to throw a golden
object into the ocean. A fellow passenger, Mr Ed Kelley, a
pharmaceutical salesman, was initially arrested after observers
described an altercation with my aunt, immediately before
she died. He was released without charge.

MOONPATHS OF THE DEPARTED

by Adam S. Cantwell

THE eyes of the Baroness strained heavenward through closed lids as she turned the bone flute in long, pale fingers. Only her dignified and solemn aspect—straight black hair plunging down either side of a patrician face, like curtains flanking a mysterious stage; the veil of violet gauze deepening the shadows under the broad arches of her brows and in the hollows of her throat—only this kept me seated. Out of respect for her I held the hands of strangers on either side and did not break the spell of the séance. I glanced around the table. I saw no scorn or skepticism to answer mine, only anxious avidity or near-sensual anticipation. Worldly and cynical as the other guests were, they were as transported as the Baroness herself by imminent contact with the spirit world.

The Baroness set down the fragmentary artifact and took the hands of those on her left and right, completing the circle. Was it Slovenian she spoke now? I couldn't tell, but the rhythm of her incantation worked on me. In the purple gloom, aided by the close air, I lapsed into a drowsy reverie.

If the Baroness had not insisted on my presence, I never would have taken part. She'd averred, at the outset of the séance, that this length of perforated thighbone was a spiritual link to the Stone Age people who had dwelled in the caves beneath the Castle. To my mind, if some primordial man had lent his breath to this object, as accompaniment to whatever rude triumph or dim pain or inconceivable ecstasy, that act did not constitute music, at least not as I understand it. And of course this supernatural exercise was ludicrous. But to express my true feelings would have been rude and may have endangered my commission.

When her chant was joined by the faint, ragged sound of an unseen flute, the others gasped, but I could only grimace. I had seen the facsimile flutes that were displayed alongside the true artifact in the Castle's exhibit room. Obviously a player was concealed behind the heavy velvet drapery and we were being subjected to a variation on the Spiritualist trick of the "spirit-trumpet."

But I was committed, with no means of escape; so I indulged the chain of thoughts and associations that spun out from the lorn tones. The player had, at least, imagination. If troglodytic man had in fact ever played upon this bone flute, the result would surely have been as grotesque. If beauty in Art results, as I believe it does, from man's highest effort—the struggle to understand the universal principles revealed in the heart of nature—then this idiot flute-song was an expression of man at his basest and most benighted, a reminder of his most helpless inability—or staunchest refusal—to perceive the universal harmony.

Though we felt no draught, the candles flickered, evoking the fire around which the flute's makers had crouched. The Baroness began to speak, her voice low and flat.

"Members of the circle . . . those who have gone long before . . . are here again. They speak without tongues in the language of the soul. O forbears, I hear your weary, wordless song . . . you travelers seeking refuge under stern northern skies . . . here everything was strange, the animals and plants, the stars themselves . . . you found cold shelter within the

earth itself, so deep within . . . you found solitude . . . safety .
. . and after hard seasons and much sorrow, you found pride .
. . a sharp land had sharpened you . . . you new people of the
land of sun's setting . . ."

"O voyagers, favor your children once more with your
song, so that we might carry on your rites, that we might
never forget the striving that brought us forth from the cradle
to this land of trials and triumphs . . ." On cue, the flute let
fly with a hectic call that raised my hackles. Then it broke
into a sort of mad dance as all the candles but one flickered
and died. The Baroness began to sway to the uncouth cadence
and was joined by the others, their shadows lurching on black
velvet. I was looking for an opportunity to discreetly extricate
myself when I saw the pained grimace on the Baroness' face.
I could just catch her words: ". . . but why the cruel rites . . .
they never brought anything our good and cruel Mother did
not bring in season . . ."

Then the Polish artillery captain at the Baroness' left was
up out of his seat and barking obscenities. The look of his
protuberant red-rimmed eyes warned me that he was on the
verge of lashing out physically at the Swede seated across from
him. In an instant, it seemed, some past slight between the
two men had flared into aggression. The tension in the room
spread swiftly, borne upon the maddening flute-song.

The Swede stood and invited the Pole to back his churlish
words with action, but still he held the hands to his left and
right. Indeed, though its members were close to trading blows,
the circle of the séance remained unbroken. Like bobbing
candle-shadows on the draped walls, anger leapt and danced
on contorted faces. The Pole showered insults on the Swede,
spittle flying from his lips; a rich Venetian widow in antique
lace cackled derisively at the two of them, egging them on,
while the Contessa to my right wept bitterly, histrionically
imploring the men to cease. An inebriated Greek viscount

brayed mad laughter; tears ran from the eyes of a Danish shipping magnate.

Then the last candle went out. I jumped from my seat and moved to protect the Contessa, should it prove necessary. I heard a babel of shouts, the table legs scraping across the floor, and the sound of a fist striking flesh—but the flute had at last stopped.

The curtains parted and a servant rushed in with lamp upraised. The Swede gripped the knife handle that protruded from his shoulder; the Polish captain slumped in his seat with a vacant expression. The Contessa screamed. The rest looked at each other with dull, bewildered faces, like drunkards coming to after a bout; then they fled, leaving the pale and silent servants to tend to the stricken man. The Baroness herself stood aghast. She gathered the flute, now spotted with blood, into her wide sleeve.

The staff stanched the Swede's wound and removed him. I remained to offer help and to watch the perpetrator until the men-at-arms arrived. But the Pole was no further threat and sat mute, not seeming to understand where he was.

When at last the situation was in hand, I murmured a vague apology to the Baroness and moved to leave. She reached out, grabbed my arm, and said with an unaccounted urgency, "You are still coming with me to the caves tomorrow, Doktor?"

I have more than once regretted my decision to come to Castle Strmsko, but in the end I could not turn down a commission.

My first misgivings came during the long and arduous journey through the mountains. I had not taken in much of the famed Carniolan scenery on the journey from Ljubljana, the emerald lakes and verdant marshes that Kokoschka had described . . . The fact is that my anxiousness had grown quite acute since I left Vienna, Wilhelmine, and my girls. I feared a return of my nervous illness and had terrible visions of myself relinquishing the commission and begging for passage home. Then Strmsko came into view.

The magnificent Renaissance-era Castle is uniquely situated: under the eaves of, and partially *inside,* an immense cave mouth that is the point of entry to one of the most profound systems of caves in Europe. Its history, as related to me by the driver, involves robber barons, the wrath of Holy Roman Emperors, and many a siege weathered in its mighty redoubt, surrounded as it is on three sides by solid rock and connected by secret shafts to a practically endless subterranean refuge. The edifice made a sublime and terrible impression, tucked in its lofty niche between soaring limestone cliffs and partially screened by a waterfall whose waters are tinged green by certain unique mineral properties of the region.

Despite its somewhat severe and martial façade, it seemed to me a kind of dire fairy castle; for who but capricious spirits would build their fortress within such an infernal yawning gateway to the interior of the earth?

Dinner did not improve my mood. Here was a large and distinguished cohort, many of them noblemen and –women from every corner of Europe, as well as scholars and men of commerce, artists and musicians; all seated in a richly paneled sixteenth-century hall of rustic opulence, with massive carved oak beams suspending dazzling chandeliers. We were surrounded by priceless artworks ranging from Greek amphorae to Renaissance tapestries and even to canvases by Klimt, but the conversation seemed to me shallow and vapid, or else self-satisfied and smirking.

Only my inquiries about the Baron were met with uniform sincerity and politeness—all spoke respectfully of the man, who was not present.

Having escaped to the music library, I was unexpectedly greeted with a charming little performance of Wolf *lieder*, very ably sung by a young Swiss soprano and played by the Baroness herself. I could feel the tension of the day easing, leaving me gratefully transported by the music.

On display was a truly magnificent illuminated edition of Isaac's *Choralis Constantinus.* I would have suspected my hosts of flattery—also displayed was a copy of my own dissertation on Isaac, as well as the numbers of *Der Ruf* and *Der Blau Reiter* in which my songs appeared—but the Castle's collection also includes everything that Schönberg and Zemlinsky have published, and a surprising quantity of other new music. Kokoschka had assured me that Strmsko's commissions were legitimate (he himself had visited last fall) and that the acumen of the trustees was sharp and far-reaching, but I had not expected quite such an exhaustive collection.

As the small group gathered there dispersed, the Baroness bade me sit with her. After a time of listening to her melodic voice and gazing upon the noble planes of her face, I was able to wrest my attention from the musical treasures lining the walls and displayed beneath crystal panes.

A more gracious and sensitive hostess I could not have hoped for. Her lineage is Greek, but her family has held positions of power and influence here in the south of the Empire for centuries. Her education is extensive, her specialties history and archaeology (that she plays so beautifully yet regards music as a pastime is evidence of her substance). She was on Crete and aided in the excavations at Knossos, during which she showed prodigious insight that rivaled or surpassed that of Evans himself.

I learned from her that, geologically speaking, this is a region of "karst" geology, which refers to the bedrock's tendency to form sinkholes and caves.

"The caverns here rival any in Europe in size and extent. Really only the remoteness of our location keeps them from being the kind of destination for curiosity seekers that Postojna has become," she said.

"That sounds fascinating," I said, "for geologists—but for you as well? Forgive my ignorance, but there are no great temples, no Greek history down among the stalactites, are there?"

"No, there are not, but there are subtler monuments. I've become interested in the art of prehistoric man, and there are some unique examples in the caves below. I believe they are some of the earliest in Europe."

The Baroness was referring to the sort of thing that has been found in Spain and France, primitive images of animals and the like, thought to have been executed by Stone Age man. Her belief was that Strmsko's petroglyphs were different, however, that they revealed the nature of these unthinkably distant Europeans in a way that the others did not.

I asked how these paintings were different.

"I would be very grateful, Doktor, if you came with me to see for yourself—the fact is that your expertise could be very illuminating to certain aspects of my research." Further inquiries were politely deferred. If anyone else had asked me to cut into my precious work-time, I would have refused, but the Baroness was persuasive.

A short time later, as I made to excuse myself, the Baroness invited me to the séance, saying that it was a different way, unscientific perhaps, of illuminating the mysteries of the caves. I was surprised that a person of her intellectual caliber went in for Spiritualism, but again I accepted. I reminded myself of what Wilhelmine always told me, to reserve judgment, to "try to get along once in a while."

Of the séance I have already told. I have inquired about the Swedish man, but none of the staff have helped with any information.

I have begun sketching the work, a group of pieces for cello and piano. I have been asked to finish the piece and prepare it for a performance to take place before the end of my stay. I am unaccustomed to such pressure, and have no intention of rushing the music, but I will make the effort in good faith. My rooms are comfortable, the piano is excellent, and I am assured that all my needs will be met for the duration of my stay.

Now to work!

✳

Just a brief note before my trip to the caves with the Baroness.

My nerves have eased and I made excellent progress with my sketches.

If one ventures into the halls of Strmsko one is bound to encounter some eccentric person or another, but within my chambers there is solitude and blessed silence. My windows look out from beneath the eaves of the great cavern over the high mountain valley. Even if I had felt I could take time away from composing, incessant rain has kept me from exploring the surrounding peaks.

Everywhere in the Castle fires are kept roaring, so that the damp from the waterfall in front and the caverns behind is kept considerably under control. All the same, one can sense the cold depths below. The plaster sweats and the heavy oak doors swell and stick in their frames. Twilight comes early; the sun hides among the surrounding peaks and its diminished rays strike fleeting rainbows from the waterfall's mists.

I have found that the mournful aspects of the setting are in tune with some material already in my notebooks. I am developing it along lines that perhaps would not have presented themselves to me in the tumult of Vienna or in the pure air of the Preglhof.

In fact, composition has been going so well that I rather regret my promise to accompany the Baroness into the caves. But I shall try to make the best of it, knowing that I can look forward to returning to my work soon enough.

I don't know what day it is or how I came to be here in the Castle's empty infirmary. Scattered about me are sheets of paper with unfinished letters to Wilhelmine, to Schönberg and Berg and to my sisters, incoherent ravings and apologies and warnings . . . there is spilled ink on the nightstand and crumpled music paper beside the bed . . . I cannot get up to investigate, my legs are stiffened and the left one is splinted. My entire body is wracked with dreadful aches, worse than those I have felt in the depths of my nervous illness. No one has come to tell me what happened, the only answer to my calls comes from the nurse's assistant, who speaks no German. There are no windows.

I am afraid. Why did I come so far from home, so soon after I got well? Where is the Baroness, the only face I feel I know here . . . why do I trust her? Didn't she leave me somewhere?

God, what madness took me, and will it come again? I have found a letter to my dear departed mother!

It has come back to me: the memory of what went terribly wrong in the caverns, all that I saw and felt and the madness that took me and seems to hover over me still, despite the sedatives. I cling to the lessons of Dr. Adler's treatment and the well-being it brought me after the last terrible year: the death of my nephew, the breakdown . . . But that hard-won wisdom is shaken profoundly by the ugly intimations I was given under the earth. The horror I felt there threatens to sweep away all my gains, and drives my thoughts before it like a black wind . . .

In the early morning hours the Baroness met me in the gloomy courtyard behind the Castle. She was attired in heavy canvas jacket and trousers and equipped with electrified headlamps and other spelunking gear. I was amused to see yet another aspect of this fascinating woman, and to place myself in the hands of her expertise.

Though I am no mean mountaineer, the appeal of delving into a hole in the ground was never apparent to me. I have accompanied my father into mines in the course of his explorations and work, but those trips were brief and relieved by walks in the surrounding mountains.

The Baroness provided me with a helmet mounted with a headlamp, delivered a short lecture on safety measures, and then we set off.

Near the surface the going was easy. A walkway had been built for visitors, with electric lights strung above. Here the cavern was voluminous, like the interior of a great church or palace, with high ceilings from which the smallest sound echoed interminably. I remained silent, inhibited somehow from adding to the wash of sound that was an unseen presence walking with us.

After a few turnings the light seeping in from the day disappeared altogether. The electric bulbs could not completely dispel the darkness which hid everywhere among the fantastic folds and ripples of rock. Gradually the passage shrunk, pressed down from all sides by bulging limestone, until we had to duck to cross a kind of threshold. After a short time underground I had come to find that my ears were telling me more about the volumes and surfaces around me than they did in the world above. I knew before we crossed the threshold that a great chamber opened beyond.

Here the electric lighting was more plentiful but less equal to the task of illuminating the vast space. Grotesque columns of stalagmites in irregular groups surrounded a wide central area. Like fountains of rock they surged up and sometimes met the stalactites that crashed motionlessly down from a dimly glimpsed ceiling. Myriad faces of rock reflected every sound—our hesitant steps, dripping water, seemingly the stirring air itself—in a shifting sea of echoes. A passage directly across from us led out of the chamber. Off to one side, a deeper blackness glimpsed through the stands of stone was an abyss as much felt as seen.

We paused at the center of this limestone cathedral. The Baroness said that plays and concerts were sometimes staged here, and that it was a popular destination for the occasional tour groups that the Baron allowed into the caves. Once one left this chamber, there were no more lights, the going was rougher, and casual explorers rarely ventured much farther. I asked how far we were going.

"We'll be leaving the main path shortly and heading down." We moved toward the exit. Our monstrous shadows wrapped over boiling rock-forms as they moved with us. "It seems that a new fissure opened some years ago, or, I should say, re-opened. These caves have been well-known for centuries, but until recently the galleries which hold the paintings were unknown."

I expressed surprise that these seemingly frozen landscapes were subject to change. "Oh yes," she said, "cave-ins, earth tremors or quakes . . . these are rare but they do happen. The earth down here is alive."

We exited the chamber and switched on our headlamps. I felt a tightening in my chest and wished fervently that I was exploring the mountains rather than creeping through these airless passages.

As we made our way forward we had frequently to duck, or turn sideways to fit through narrow passages, or climb up over large stones. The way was twisted, there were branchings, and I was utterly disoriented within minutes. My awareness shrunk down to the area revealed by my headlamp as it scanned the ground for safe footing or followed the Baroness' progress. Rock, smooth or rough, jagged or with forms like water, swelled out at us from every angle.

Soon the Baroness paused and took her bearings, then seemed to press her body into a pool of blackness in the wall. Before she disappeared completely to leave me in the trackless darkness, she turned to me and beckoned. "The way down. A tight fit, I'm afraid." I too pressed myself through the narrow fissure. I hadn't imagined this sort of squirming about in the soil would be required, and was surprised that the Baroness was doing it without a thought.

The way forward was less a tunnel and more a series of gaps between masses of stone and sandy soil, often requiring progress on hands and knees. I can only suppose the Baroness had not warned me of the wretched conditions because she did not want to dissuade me from coming. But there would have been no way to fully convey the horror of dragging one-self on one's belly through the cold blackness, as we had to do for a stretch that seemed endless but was probably only a few meters. Though I felt my heart beating in its cage, thudding against the cold rock to which my chest was pressed, I said nothing. And, as I struggled to bring rationality to bear, I saw that there literally was no turning around in this strait passage and the only way was forward.

What gave me the strength, or at least distraction enough, to continue was the attempt to evaluate the experience and the emotions it engendered for philosophic or musical cor-relatives. I have turned worse horrors than this into Art, or at least I have attempted to. I began to separate my conscious-ness from the figure that scrabbled through darkness.

I have had experiences in the Alps in which strenuous effort purges mental chatter and frees the mind for higher things; and there in the heights one can gaze upon wildflowers and other Alpine flora whose harmonious forms seem to unfold before one's eyes the secrets of Creation. But here the air was vile and there was nothing but blackness and dirt and stones that had been pushed down toward the fundament by everything that rises. The only things that lived and burrowed here were simple, ugly, crawling chthonic things, centipedes and worms, whose forms spoke of lowly beginnings, not divine strivings. My consciousness floated out to some indeterminate point in space to view the Baroness and myself: two tiny creeping figures burrowing endlessly through inexhaustible grim solidity, ants following the strokes of a twisted calligraphy that only God could read.

When the way widened and we could once again walk erect, it was like waking from a dream, and I responded to the Baroness' promptings with the slowness of a roused sleeper. I had to ask her to repeat herself.

"I said, we have arrived, Doktor. This is the first chamber of the gallery." She took a battery-powered electric lamp from her rucksack, switched it on, and set it where it shone upon the wall.

The light revealed crude depictions of animals, stags and wild cattle, rendered in ochres and dull yellows. As my eyes adjusted to the meager illumination I could also discern other forms: hand-prints in outline; a human figure holding a spear; and other less-defined shapes.

A slow, silent examination of the paintings allowed me time to recover myself. "Really remarkable," I said. "Was there some ritual purpose served by locating the paintings in such a remote place?"

"It's likely that it was not so remote at the time these were made. There was probably an entrance in the hillside that was covered over at some point. It is, however, set apart from the dwelling-caves, and I have reason to believe that the pools gave this particular complex special significance. Please, come, I will show you the pools and then the other paintings."

A short time later we crouched on a sandy hump of earth in a large, low-ceilinged chamber and peered across the mirror-like surface of the water. Our lamps glared off its surface out to a meager distance, beyond which unrelieved blackness stretched on. The cave was filled by a silent expectancy far more profound and lugubrious than that of a calm bay or pond. A cold weight seemed to press the water's surface to an infinite flatness and stillness.

I turned to the Baroness, who herself was peering at the pool expectantly, to make some comment, anything to break the spell of the water. Then came a tiny splash, a flash of white out in the black pool at the edge of my vision.

My headlamp revealed nothing where the ropy twist of white had shown for a fraction of a second, only faint ripples radiating outward and disappearing. The Baroness laid her hand on my arm. I suppose I had jumped. "Oh Doktor, that is only an olm. I'm afraid I didn't think to warn you, there are so few animals down here—usually only a few beetles and the like—and they are all quite harmless. The olm is a sightless amphibian. Strange in appearance but also harmless."

My nerves were getting the better of me and it was showing. "Might we not see these other paintings of yours, Baroness?"

"Certainly, it's this way. Please watch your step."

We skirted the pool and proceeded through a narrow passage for perhaps another forty meters, first sloping upward and then down again. The cavern widened and we were in another gallery filled with paintings.

Some handprints were there, and animals, but in configurations very different from those in the other gallery, and they were joined by abstract markings that were nothing like what I had seen in photographs of the caves of Spain or France. Some branched and ramified like the antler-racks of stags, some writhed like the tracks of termites in wood; some spread like the outlines of lichens upon bark or stone, but always with some detail or unnatural turn that indicated that there was a human intelligence behind their design. When animals were depicted, they were not the creatures of woodland and valley, but those of the cave-dark: beetles and worms, fish, centipedes with teeming legs, and, in a central position, a kind of serpentine, puny-legged lizard with a ragged crown at the back of its elongated head, looking like nothing so much as a heraldic dragon. This last creature was rendered in a unique color: not a flat chalk-white, as it first appeared, but in fact a very subtle and modulated hue, like that of a pale yet slightly flushed human skin tone.

Beside me, the Baroness broke the silence softly. "Slovenes call the olm *cloveska ribica*, 'human fish.' When seen in the light, their flesh is remarkably human-like in appearance."

"I see. Clearly, as you say, the works in this section are very different than the others. So will you tell me now what the significance is?" My examination of the bizarre depictions had done nothing to improve my disposition.

"Of course, Doktor. You have seen the flute, at the séance. Again I must apologize for the other guests, there is no excuse for the way they comported themselves—"

Here I tried to interrupt her, to say that all had been forgiven, but she went on: "I say that there is no excuse, but the fact is that I have to believe there is power in that flute, and it was my fault to invoke it as I did. But in any case—the flute was found here, the oldest anyone has seen, as well as fragments of wood whose shape suggests a log drum of the sort that are used by still-extant Stone Age peoples like those in Australia and South Asia. Herr Doktor, I think the non-figurative elements of these paintings may be a kind of depiction of *music*, if not a system of notation. What if I could show that, thousands of years before man wrote, he composed music? You may be right to scoff, but this is why I brought you here, and I would consider it a personal favor if you would examine the evidence closely and give me your professional judgment."

Nothing I had seen or heard during the séance or after had inclined me to believe that ancient man had the capability to truly create music. And now that I had spent time in their sunless abodes, I was less inclined than ever to believe that their noisemaking was to modern music as the infant's babble is to adult speech. Rather, I took as a guide the evidence of my senses, which told me I was in a loathsome place, whether it had been shelter or no, and that those who inhabited these caves necessarily partook of the dank and dark and evil; and, as such, whatever sounds they produced upon their crude instruments were merely the cries of animals, and likely functioned as incitements to violence or celebrations of sacrifice.

But I agreed. What else could I do?

After cautioning me to watch my step, the Baroness drew my attention to some grid-like markings near the edge of the main body of the paintings. I removed the heavy headlamp, set up one of the electric lamps and began dutifully to make notes.

The Baroness had ensured that I was as comfortable as I could be, seated on an empty wooden crate left behind from a previous visit; then she excused herself, explaining that she wanted to look in on some of the outer galleries and that she'd be in earshot should I need her. In solitude I was able to become absorbed in my notes.

To my eye, the scratchings could have been accidental, or they could have referred to some organization of sound or of anything else. At first I didn't much care. If I used my imagination I could perhaps see some vague parallels between this "ur-notation" and some of the earliest and rudest medieval systems, or those of the early Greeks. I would stop short of positively identifying the markings as music, but perhaps the speculation would be enough to satisfy the Baroness.

As I sketched the grids, my eye was continually drawn away by the swooping lines and crackling clouds that surrounded them. It was a kind of blessing that I could see only that which the narrow compass of my light-beam showed me; this was an aid to concentration and kept my mind off the profound, unrelieved lightlessness around me. But my eye was continually drawn by snaking lines and twisted wedges of color toward the edge of the lamp's light, beyond which the central white image of the cave-salamander glowed faintly.

I pondered the sketches I had made and hummed under my breath a fanciful interpretation of its "music." It was a bit like sitting down at the piano and sight-reading the cracks in the plaster. The sound of my voice in the dark was unpleasant, like a lunatic maundering to himself in a cell. My eye followed the patterns mindlessly and it occurred to me what a preposterous and dangerous situation I was in. Here, how many hundreds of meters into the earth, beneath tons of rock, in the company of an eccentric noblewoman who I had known for a few days—where was she, anyway?—and engaged in a most asinine, pseudo-scientific pursuit. The quality of the air, as I took notice of it, seemed to thin appreciably with every breath. The cold crept up my cuffs and over my collar. I found myself wiping my hands on my trousers, unable to get rid of a gritty sensation that coated them. I resented the inescapable aromas of clay and of obscure molds that filled my nostrils. It was in this state of increased agitation that I realized there was something familiar about the tune I was humming. It was nearly the lurid tune of the spurious ghost-flute at the séance.

I leaned toward the wall to see whether the intervals of the ugly tune could actually have been written there. The crate on which I was seated crumpled with a dry *crack* and sent me sprawling.

The fall precipitated me down the treacherous slope into a pool of water that had lain hidden at the foot of the wall. In my attempt to check my fall I severely bumped my head and painfully hyperextended my shoulder. My lamps clattered to

the rocky floor. I lay half in and half out of the icy pool, dazed
and unable to move, and watched the light of the damaged
portable lamps slowly fade. The light failed completely but I
did not understand for a moment that its afterimage was still
in my eyes, seeming to relieve the darkness slightly. Then that
phantom light too was gone and I was adrift in an unprece-
dented, living blackness that seemed to mold to my eyes and
even to my hands and to smother them with insensibility.

I would not shout for help, not yet. I placed my hand in
the freezing water in order to right myself. A slimy form that
seemed colder than the water itself moved in coils over my
hand. I jerked the hand away, lost my balance and toppled
face-first into the pool. The ridged and infinitely repulsive
form of an olm brushed against my eyelid. In that submerged
instant, in that blind gulf at the bottom of a blind gulf, my
mind's eye saw a squad of the undulant monsters approaching through the pitch-black water, their vestigial limbs and
fringed gills waving malevolently, flying like pennants with
the purposeful motion of the serpentine bodies.

It was then that I lost my senses. Somehow my body,
injured though it was, propelled itself out of the muck and
through the caves. I have a fragmentary impression of tumult
in the blackness as I caromed off walls and hauled myself
from the floor again and again; flight from the creatures in
the slime was all that mattered. All at once my footing failed
me and I slid down an incline, fully expecting to drop out of
existence into a nameless crevasse; instead I came to rest in a
tight pocket of stone that embraced me like a grave.

The sound of my ragged breathing filled my ears in the enclosed space along with something else. I couldn't tell if it was
my whimpering or the sound of the Baroness calling for me.
I tried to control my panting because I had, in that moment,
an inexplicable terror of being detected. I had become sure in
my mania that the Baroness had plotted the evil that befell

me, had lured me here and that she commanded the olms by arcane means.

I huddled in that cold wet enclosure and hid myself from the only soul who could have helped me. I clamped my eyes closed on the void, so at least phantom afterimages would play before my vision, and I drew myself inward. I vented my frustrated rage and fear in silent curses on this subterranean realm and the twisted things that survived here. I tried to console myself with thoughts of the pure air and angelic plant-forms of the Alps. I retreated from externality with all my might, as though I could fall through myself into a high meadow on the Hochschwab, there to exist bodiless forever, gazing on the wonder of God's unity as expressed in a wildflower or an edelweiss . . .

I heard the faint echoes of the Baroness's voice and I blocked my ears. In the dead air of the caverns, sound itself was an affront, even her sonorous voice became a grotesque clanking thing.

Borne by mounting waves of panic with no outlet, I fixed upon morbid and nihilistic ideas, one after the other. I thought that, after this dead air and these cold echoes, I would never again be able to hear any sound with pleasure; so, without mental reference to pitch or timbre, I began compulsively to invent a dumb music without tones, thought-structures made up of abstract durations, articulations, and rhythms counted in purest silence . . .

The dank immovability of the tons of soil and rock under which I was buried had infected me with hopeless inertia. Here beneath the earth there was no differentiation, there were no lines or shapes, nothing but compression of that which once lived, the accumulated putrefaction of plant and animal, the grains of mighty rock weathered away, succumbed to the action of encroaching entropy . . .

I suppressed a sob. I was wrapped in cold and despair in the bowels of the earth, I had given up when Wilhelmine and the girls waited for me, so many miles away . . .

I crossed into a zone of terrible hallucination or vivid dream. In the blackness behind my eyes I saw the dwellers in the cavern cowering around smoky fires and grubbing for vermin. They fearfully served a pale matriarch who hollowed bones as she lolled in the pool of the white lizards and emerged only into the moonlight to keen her hideous song and plot treacheries against their neighbors, their enemies . . .

The Baron has just left my bedside. He showed me a manuscript in my own hand which I do not recall writing—three small pieces for cello and piano. I fear that I will not be allowed to leave the Castle until I perform the piece for his guests.

I took the man treating me to be the Castle's doctor. He examined me carefully but answered my questions diffidently. It was only after my condition improved that he revealed his true identity.

"Herr Doktor, please accept my sincerest apologies, and those of the Baroness. I was very unhappy to hear that you had been injured in the caves. It's rare that anything like this happens. The Baroness has been down to her sites hundreds of times without incident. I will spare no effort or expense to see that you are fully recovered in the shortest time possible."

I politely thanked him for his concern and indicated that I wanted only to regain enough strength to return to Vienna so that I would no longer be a burden on his household. I apologized for my stupidity in becoming lost in the caverns.

"But it was more than that, I understand? As your physician and host I of course interviewed the Baroness thoroughly, and had a look at the writings you produced in your delirium.

If I may be indelicate—you had a breakdown in the caves, did you not?"

I informed my host that I had indeed recently been cured of a nervous disorder but that my health would no longer be his concern once I was strong enough to depart. I sat up in bed but could not conceal the grimace of pain that my injuries caused me.

"Herr Doktor," the Baron said, "your upset would be understandable, if I didn't know that you are a true artist, and therefore strong. You live for your Art. What happened to you was trying, but you survived, then penned this brilliant work. Indeed, you should be proud." He reclined in his chair. "Doesn't all art come out of trouble? I regret the circumstances but I confess I'm glad to have the chance to talk with you. The movements in Vienna, the music of your teacher—these have fascinated me for some time. The Empire is fading away and no one knows what is next. Artists like you try to alert the world to the multiplying dimensions within, the mysteries, the glory, the horror . . . my guests need to hear these new truths, Herr Doktor."

In that clean, mellowly lit room, with a worldly and well-born man praising my overlooked work, I should have been comforted, but I was confused and frightened. I had trouble focusing on his words. Why was he cajoling me so? I had no memory of my rescue from beneath the earth, no memory of composing the piece. I feared for my sanity. I felt in danger of falling off the edge of the world again, where I could do nothing for my family or for Schönberg, nothing to carry out my soul's sworn duty to worship and propagate beauty.

My feelings must have shown on my face. The Baron's eyes flashed beneath lowered brows and he went on.

"Herr Doktor, I know this all must seem strange to you, and I will tell you why I am so adamant. Men like myself are still necessary in Europe. Governments change, commerce takes its due, but without those of us whose understanding of this continent is both overarching and particular, without the time-honored understandings between us, Europe would be no better than a scattering of tribes in the jungle. We allow the bringing together of the things that truly matter. Ideas are symbols and they are power. I do not wish to aggrandize myself when I tell you that my business, my very nature, is to understand and wield power. It is not necessary that I agree with every idea but all must fall beneath my gaze or I abdicate my responsibility and deny my nature. And you know that your ideas are genuinely new. I understand artists, and I see the doubt in you, the self-doubt. I can do nothing to change that for you. But I must ask—what can I offer to persuade you to fulfill your commission completely, to perform the piece and share your strange new tidings with my guests?"

How could I, in clear conscience, present as my own a piece of music that for all practical purposes was the work of a madman? I told the Baron that I was not sure I could stay to perform the piece, out of concern for my health and the well-being of my family. Trying to change the subject, I inquired whether word of my accident had been sent to my wife.

"No, it has not. It could . . . but I should think that such a communication is for you to initiate. It could cause severe distress indeed should one of my envoys appear unannounced at your home to convey news of your imposture." The Baron's manner had changed suddenly. He stiffened where he sat.

"No," I replied, "I trust that you and your agents could handle the news appropriately—if you should have the opportunity to get a message out . . ."

"And would it meet with your approval if my messengers also paid a visit to Schönberg? I am sure your master would be interested to know that his most avid pupil had so narrowly avoided disaster?"

184

For a moment I imagined there was an unpleasant meaning behind his words, but I could scarcely credit the idea. I needed time to think. The Baron's eyes glared out at me from beneath lowering, craggy brows, seeming to suppress my will and powers of reason.

I asked the Baron if I might give him my answer in the morning. His gaze bored into me for several uncomfortable moments more.

"Certainly you may. Let me know as soon as you decide. The Baroness would be disappointed indeed if she heard that you could not carry through."

I had made the decision to leave the Castle as soon as possible. The music written in my hand was strange and sinister, and the threat behind the Baron's words had grown in my mind.

On my way out of the infirmary I paused in the darkened reception area. I heard voices outside conversing in low tones.

"I do hope we can find something to do with him," said the Baroness.

"There will be something," said the Baron. "We've seen it before, the kind of avant-gardism that looks within. If he has followers they'll be too busy unlocking his codes, they won't be the sort to take to the streets or sing his songs as anthems. And if they are, well, that is also useful. But he's so fragile, all those failed conducting engagements . . . "

"Yes, he's a nervous case, but also tenacious. And there is real beauty in his work. And the new piece—even without the dose, I think he might have given us something of use."

"If he can be worked with, with or without the dose, we will work with him."

"Darling, do not use him too harshly. All that grief and regret in his music—it's beautiful in its way and I think it will please them. His dirges are like theirs, in their way."

"As you say, Europa. We'll see tomorrow. Notes on the page can't tell us if his work is capable of affecting people."

"You think he will say yes?"

"He can be induced."

As I backed into my room, fearful of detection but doubly convinced that I had to escape as soon as possible, I blundered into a table lamp. It smashed on the floor and the sound of voices outside ceased. I retreated here to bed to await another chance to escape.

The sound of footsteps from within the walls—

I will record what happened that last night at the Castle, though I will subsequently destroy this document, or cause it to become lost—no one will believe its contents and I would not persuade them to.

I came to my senses slumped in an armchair in a sort of small tent or pavilion. The Baroness was standing over me, as were the nurse and two men-at-arms. She was holding music: copies of the strange pieces I had written in my insensible state.

"Herr Doktor. How are you feeling? You should be much better shortly, I think in time to perform. I am so sorry it came to this, but it is nearly at an end and then you will be free to leave. Here is the music, I have checked the copying myself, everything is in order."

I felt the fading effects of whatever drug they had used, and they were not altogether unpleasant. To think that I would be called upon to perform a sham piece with no rehears- al—this sort of thing was the stuff of my nightmares. But in my half-drugged state, as the red velvet draperies stirred, a crowd murmured, and the Baroness' beauty was quickened by expectation, I felt inclined to play, if that was all it took to secure my freedom. How could this audience be worse than the clods in Danzig and Stettin?

I stood, as steadily as possible, took the music from the Baroness and offered her my arm. Her smile was like moonlight on the waves. "Do you think I shall be capable of playing my parts, Baroness?" I asked as we parted the curtains and walked together into the cavern's echoing cathedral chamber. "I daresay you know the music better than I at this point."

"I think you shall. I think the state in which you created the pieces is not so far below the surface as you believe. You think you don't remember, but memory is like any other sense, it has its deceptions."

Another performance was still in progress. The young Swiss soprano, singing something I didn't recognize. I looked over the music but it was difficult to keep my eyes off the crowd gathered there among the columns of living stone.

Even in Vienna a more cosmopolitan crowd would have been hard to find. Some faces I recognized from the Castle's dining rooms and salons, but there were a great many that I did not. Some were in uniform, most in evening wear; there were priests and dandies and a few bohemian types in slovenly dress, openly passing a wine bottle. A handful were costumed, in gay or macabre garb, for what costume ball I did not know. There seemed to be a contingent of the local villagers as well, conversing in Slovenian. I recognized a group of German businessmen, very rich men, enjoying their cigars in seats near the front. Slavic and Mediterranean and Nordic features were present along with others that defied easy classification. Countrymen were sometimes seated together in groups, sometimes apart. Couples shared looks and caresses. Men, women, young and old were represented, though older men were predominant. All were taking in with avid eyes the performers and each other.

"What kind of place is the Castle, Baroness? Who are these people?" I whispered.

"These people are our guests, Herr Doktor, and the Castle is our home. I don't know what you heard last night, but my husband and I believe in the idea of a nation beyond nations. We surround ourselves with all of Europe's people when we can. Some love music or art, some come to talk business, others love only luxury. We believe their presence makes us stronger."

But there was no time to penetrate beyond the surface of her reply. The music finished and was met with an enthusiastic ovation. The Baroness and I stepped upon the low riser and were greeted with polite applause in our turn. The cello was a fine instrument, and I found that my hands were acquainted with it though I had no memory of having played it. The Baron appeared and addressed the audience.

"Beloved guests and friends, I now present to you a new piece composed for the occasion by our very esteemed guest, the Viennese composer and Professor of Music, Doktor Anton Von Webern." Here another polite round of applause. I cleaned my glasses and again beheld the crowd. Distractions had been put aside and all eyes were upon the Baron. Some expressions were rapt and affectionate; some were strained and nervous.

"The form this music takes may come as a surprise to some of you. I would remind you that we come together to enrich ourselves and each other with the new experiences we share. As citizens of the Continent, we occupy a unique position at the head of a dark world, leading the way forward with the torch of enlightenment. Inspiration sometimes comes in flashes, like the lightning, and we must have the strength to change on those occasions when genius shows us a new way forward. Our forefathers, without a doubt, had that strength. But let me put no further burden on the performers. I now present to you Doktor Von Webern's *Three Pieces for Cello and Piano*."

All that remained was to make this strange music beautiful if I could. The expressive demands of the piano parts were formidable but the sensitivity of the Baroness' playing was a marvel. Though unaccustomed to performing my own music on cello, I found that my modest technique was equal to the demands placed upon it. The music unfolded its colors and gestures deliberately. The mood was wary; there was that element in it of mourning and remembrance, imbuing the colors with a shading of gray and making the airy rhythms brittle and evanescent.

The piece ended after about a minute and three quarters and I turned the page. I heard murmurs of surprise from the crowd and then, scattered through the chamber, grumbles of disapproval and stifled laughter. I betrayed little emotion, I think; I have heard much worse in Vienna.

We began the second piece. A clotted texture was woven by dissonances between the piano's left hand and the cello's muted glissandi. The palette was darker, unrelievedly so. Then an uncouth rumble arose from the profoundest notes of the piano and built threateningly. They stacked atop one another in a tightly complaining mass. I bowed ghastly harmonics in a rapid tremolo. Soon there was no shape to the music; the piano's blocks of sound became the airless fabric of the piece. All ten of the Baroness' fingers plied unheard-of chords of claustrophobic hemitones; the cello picked a twisting and frustrated path. Portrayals of horror in music were nothing new but this was something else, a refutation of movement and freedom, the abolition of line and the abandonment of development.

The piece came to a stop with a demented *trugfortschreit- ung*, but not before I realized that some in the audience were already loudly expressing their disdain. Some had risen from their seats to shout at the stage; others rose in defense of what they had heard. I do not know whether the wine that had been consumed was a factor, or whether the parties' feelings for music truly ran so deep, but not a few of them seemed ready to go to blows. The Baron appeared on the riser.

"Dear guests! You will please give the performers the respect they deserve. You may not agree with their ideas but there is no call to dishonor the ideals of civilized intercourse over a matter of taste. It would be disagreeable if we did not allow the Doktor's piece to play out."

The Baron's presence—his glare as much as his words—persuaded the combatants to take their seats again.

As strange as I had found the music to be, I had not been prepared for the reaction and could not help but feel affronted. While the murmurs died down I looked over at the Baroness. Her eyes were on the keyboard but an unmistakable smile of satisfaction played about her lips.

A moment of echoing silence, a breath, and then we began the final piece.

No tonal center anchored the tapestry that the piano and cello weaved; something in the lingering tones seemed to superimpose a forest dawn upon empty night streets in Vienna and cramped, Spartan quarters in Prague. But then the score demanded of the cello a tune alien and uncongenial, lopsided and vulgar, like something a child might thoughtlessly hum while absorbed in pointless play. It was the flute's tune from the séance. The piano briefly probed for meaning, then offered a sardonic commentary before giving in and setting up a percussive rudimentary dance.

I looked out from the stage. The crowd in the great echoing cave had been exasperated by the music of the opening section. When the vacant tune began, scorn, confusion, fear or anger ran through the crowd in waves. The reaction of one listener provoked the next to the opposite reaction. Those who had been on the verge of fighting were now over the brink. Punches were thrown as echoes blurred in the cold air.

The reverberations of the appalling tune seemed to take on a new timbre—then I realized that the bone flute had joined. The Baron stepped upon the riser and sounded the flute with all he had. A fat, well-dressed man who had been trying to shout us down noticed the Baron; his flushed and angry face suddenly broke open in a howl of laughter. The participation of the man of power had changed the musical travesty into a hilarious jest. The man and his row-mates set up a stomping, clapping accompaniment to the cracked and fearful racket. Some were too far gone in their rage to be assuaged by the appearance of the master, however, and they pummeled each other with renewed gusto; others danced lasciviously. Seats were overturned and pie-eyed drunken revelers blundered into angry knots of combatants. For a moment I feared the retribution of my hosts should I desert the stage; but they were utterly absorbed in the music and the tumult and trouble it had awakened in the assembled throng. I turned another page of music and saw that the repeats had been replaced by weird diagrams and scribbled, undulating lines like those on the cave wall. Seeing that the master and mistress of the Castle were insensible of my presence, I looked for my moment to move off the back of the stage, in hope that I could circle around unnoticed by the wild crowd and make my escape.

As I made my move the electric lights were extinguished. Darkness swallowed the revel in an instant. But the duo on-stage hardly faltered. The bawling of the crowd transformed in unison like the utterance of a single beast, first to an aston-ished gasp, then a wail of fear, then an unholy mix of raging bellow and hysteric cackle. I dropped to my knees, suddenly acutely conscious of my proximity to the yawning gulf to the rear of the stage. But to move away from it was to move closer to the raging crowd.

Before the lights went out I had been facing the little pa-vilion erected for the performers; so I continued on what I hoped was the same course. Running footsteps slammed past my head and fled on. I blundered on hands and knees into the heavy velvet of the pavilion. I ducked within, felt my way to the smoking stand, and took a handful of matches. Soft sounds of movement and the wordless voices of a man and a woman came from the nearby couch.

I set off in a direction I thought would allow me to make a circuit around the chamber. The terrible cacophony filled my ears. Lusty voices had joined in to chant wordlessly with the song of the flute. I tried to circle the stalagmite blocking my path and I was soon completely disoriented. Soon I felt a draught of dank cold that warned me I was edging closer to the abyss.

I tried to strike a match on the ground. I scrabbled abjectly, unable to find a surface that served.

A drunkenly shouting, chanting group drew near. I crept sidewise, avoiding their advance, ever vigilant should I come too near the chasm. They moved off, one of them singing the Marseillaise to the flute's depraved tune.

I attempted another match. Finally it caught.

The flare of ignition nearly blinded me, so that I almost doubted I had seen the fish-pale limbs that flashed away from the flame and ran toward the cold draught of the abyss. I dropped the match. I am certain that the corona I thought I saw trailing from its head was only an afterimage.

The dropped match landed on red velvet pooled on the floor and caught. I must have circled back to the little pavilion unknowingly when I avoided the drunken group. I lit another match from the growing flame and moved off as quickly as I dared.

I set off away from the chasm and skirted the edge of the main floor. The chaos there was unabated. A few chairs had been set aflame, and the little pavilion was now burning steadily and brightly. The Baron's guests wept or roared, pleaded for help or mocked the abject pleas, all in a babel of languages. Some had made for the exit as I was doing. Others headed in the opposite direction, toward the deeper caves. Some gathered around the low stage and still others could be seen by the light of the burning pavilion, gathering at the edge of the rift.

I had almost made my escape; I stood at the low arch beyond which the dim lights of the Castle showed the way out. But the fires within drew the eye inexorably.

The flame of the burning pavilion mounted to the ceiling, licking the molten forms of stalactites. A capering figure with flute upraised could be glimpsed at the center of a writhing throng of celebrants. The sound of a piano pummeled indiscriminately by many hands echoed and echoed again, until the reverberations seemed to precede the struck notes. And through the throng passed impossibly white man-shapes with quicksilver movements and animal postures.

I hastened out of the cave mouth and past the antique artillery pieces that I thought could have so easily been wheeled around and brought to bear on the cavern mouth; but the muzzles had had been spiked a hundred years ago, the shot was rusted, and I would not have known how to load, prime, and fire them in any case.

The environs were sparsely peopled. No one paid me any attention. In moments I was out of the gate and walking the moonlit road toward town; the next morning I was on my way to Ljubljana for the train to Vienna.

I have been vigilant the whole way, unable to gather my wits enough to read or write music or do anything but make these notes which no one will ever read. I will try to forget this nightmare; I must not assign any meaning to my experience beyond the madness of my hosts and my own folly. I worked so hard with Dr. Adler to conquer my illness, to accept responsibility and stop blaming a malign destiny for my failures. The implications of this strange interlude might paralyze me, if I permit it, but I will not. I will do all in my power to put it behind me and cling to my wellness, to protect my family and pursue my art.

The year is half gone now, but I swear that, whatever happens, I shall make the most of what remains. I can sense that 1914 will be a momentous year for me.

THE CHYMICAL WEDDING OF
DES ESSEINTES

by Brendan Connell

HOLIDAY was not all it was made out to be and he was no longer a young man and it was difficult for him to find pleasure in tramping about the streets of some foreign city with his nerves grated on at every turn.

Des Esseintes sat wearily in the café, gazing out at the pedestrians as they passed, marvelling at how ugly they were: women like giant lizards strutting about in silk, men with stovepipes balanced on their meagre craniums, children who looked like over-sized rodents and went by nibbling on apples, their eyes darting around suspiciously.

But then, he reasoned, he was no beauty himself, his once handsome face lined with wrinkles, his head bald, his body thin and covered with loose flesh.

He sipped at his glass of slivovitz, knowing very well he was beyond the time when such things could possibly stimulate his mind.

He wished he had been back in Paris, not because he liked the place, but at least there he could exist without effort. Here on the other hand it was all wrong. His digestion had been violently upset for the past three days due to the concoctions of cabbage and old meat he was served up nightly, which he was forced to wash down with some acid beverage the hotel keeper tried to pass off as wine. He had looked over the architecture and tried to keep from yawning, but in the end, the inertia of the man who has seen too much overcame him.

"French?"

Des Esseintes looked over at his questioner, who sat at a table next to him: a small individual with a neat brown beard and large eyes that stared at him from behind spectacles.

"Yes, I suppose so," he said in a tone that did not invite further conversation.

"And do you like our city?" the other persisted.

The Frenchman smiled bitterly. "Like would be a strong word."

"But you have come here."

"Arbitrarily."

"Nothing is arbitrary. The world is guided by karmic principles. Human beings ebb and flow according to the laws of gravitation."

Des Esseintes was silent. He couldn't very well disagree with that. He had exhausted all of life's pleasures many years earlier, but due to some force he himself could not explain still found himself lingering about, waiting without interest for something, though he knew not what.

The man introduced himself. "My name is Harro. Harro Pernath."

Des Esseintes murmured his own name and watched as a waitress deposited a glass of slivovitz in front of the other man, who winked, pulled out a little flask and poured a few thimblefuls of its contents into his drink.

"Ether, sweet vitriol, or, as some call it, the astral light, which mixed with spirit becomes earth. Capricorn and Taurus meet Mercury. The quintessence of matter."

The man began to interest Des Esseintes, who took a swallow of his own drink and observed the other's eyes, which

196

flashed with an odd intelligence. The fellow reminded him vaguely of a Japanese curio he had once had at his house in Fontenay.

"So, you have seen the sights of our city?"

"I suppose so. I have seen what is around me. But . . ."

"But?"

"Nothing. I have not been caught much by the motif."

Pernath looked at him with what seemed to be genuine pity.

"If you wish to be entertained . . ." he suggested.

"I don't."

"When you need food, you make a calf."

"And you know how to make a calf?"

"Well. . . . But, have you ever been to a Prague wedding?"

"No."

"A dear friend of mine . . ."

"They would not mind having a stranger among them?"

"If you are with me, you are no stranger. You will be welcomed, and no doubt impressed, because not everyone can see . . ."

Des Esseintes, though not terribly tempted by the offer, acquiesced, as much out of a sense of boredom as anything else. Anything would be better than going back to his hotel and placing himself in the hands of its cook.

He paid for the drinks; they rose and left the café.

Night had fallen, and a reddish moon had risen up in the sky.

"There are four ways to get there," Pernath said. "The first is short, but unpleasant. The second is quite nice, but takes a long time. The third is really beautiful to go by, but I am not sure you would appreciate it."

There was silence.

"And the fourth?" Des Esseintes asked, without a great deal of curiosity.

"No, better leave the fourth alone," Pernath said hastily.

"Well, you decide."

"I'll take you by the first. It is a bit rough, but we'll get there more quickly."

He pulled the flask of ether out of his pocket and took a swig.

"Go on," he said, handing it to Des Esseintes.

"And why not," the latter murmured, taking the flask and lifting it cautiously to his lips. He felt the beverage slip down his throat, move about in his stomach like a live frog.

They made their way into the Josefov. Des Esseintes had been under the impression that a great portion of the ghetto had been destroyed, but the area they went through seemed vast and there was no evidence whatsoever of rehabilitation.

He was being guided through narrow lanes. Disagreeable looking prostitutes hung their heads out of the windows of sooty dwellings and offered their services in strange tongues but unmistakable terms. Children with intelligent faces walked by and winked and showed mouths of moon-coloured teeth. A man with a beard dripping down to the ground sat at his doorstep constructing human figurines out of clay by the light of six candles. On the doorway behind him, beneath a mezuzah, was a small sign which read:

HERE LIVES ZAMBRIO, MAGICIAN

Des Esseintes looked at his guide questioningly.

"No," Pernath said. "You don't want to be caught up with him."

A dog with a long, thin muzzle walked by and Pernath weaved his arm through that of Des Esseintes and led him on.

They turned down a remarkably narrow alley, which led up a series of steps, which were moist and very slippery. The alley dead-ended abruptly in a high wall in which rested a small door.

Harro Pernath opened the door and the two men stepped into a tavern in which the shapes of men could be discerned amidst great clouds of tobacco smoke.

"This is a shortcut."

They moved through the low tables, around which men were hunched, drinking glasses of brandy, slivovitz and beer; smoking pipes and long cigars. Then along the counter, behind which were ranged beer engines, huge bottles of liquor with Hebrew written on the labels and a table on which sat baskets of bread and three or five cooked cow tongues.

A huge man with broad shoulders and a bristling black moustache came and clapped Pernath on the back, crying out in a language Des Esseintes assumed to be Yiddish.

"This is my cousin Lipotin," Pernath said shyly. "He insists on treating us to a drink."

Before Des Esseintes had time to say anything, a huge tankard of beer was thrust into his hands.

"Drink!" the man said in a guttural tone.

The Frenchman lifted the pecan-brown liquid to his lips and swallowed down a draught, which tasted vaguely of mushrooms, of old earth—of something dug up from the ground. He looked around him, fascinated to some degree by the people he saw. Men who existed behind moustaches the size of brooms and in whose eyes he could see reflections of far off lands. A white-haired gentleman who propped up an enormous black hat with his head. A very intelligent looking woman who sat in a corner, flanked by two stout fellows fondling long knives.

Des Esseintes swallowed down his beer and gave his guide an enquiring look.

"I have to buy a round now," Harro said. "Otherwise it would be impolite."

Three more tankards of beer made their way into their hands. Lipotin was growing merry, reciting some story in

Yiddish, chuckling, showing formidable rows of bay-coloured teeth and continuously taking Des Esseintes by the shoulder and shaking him affectionately.

"He says you remind him of an old girlfriend of his," Pernath said.

"Flattered. But shouldn't we . . ."

"Yes, yes, we can't be late for the wedding. You treat us to a last round and then we'll be on our way."

Des Esseintes was beginning to feel dizzy. But, smiling grimly, he held up three fingers to the barman.

When finally they stepped out the back door, he trod on the tail of some unknown animal which screeched and then bolted off into the darkness.

The two men wandered down narrow lanes, with unsteady steps, until they found themselves in a claustrophobic square with a well in the middle.

Above them were windows, the yellow-painted shutters of which were all closed.

Pernath called up, and the shutters to one of the windows was flung open and a knotted rope let down.

"Up we go," he said, grabbing hold of the rope and, with great ability, climbing to the top and through the window.

"Come, come."

Des Esseintes frowned. He did not feel comfortable engaging in such acrobatics, but in the end did struggle up the rope and through the window.

The room he found himself in was quite large, the walls hung with elaborate tapestries depicting green lions, crescent moons, heavenly birds and golden crowns. A number of large canvasses hung on the walls: one of Yehudah ben Bezalel Levai, another of Ramban.

A very small, very old man who wore an odd-shaped hat the colour of spring onion greeted him.

"We have been expecting you, my child," he said, taking Des Esseintes by the hand and giving him a look of great kindness.

"I have come for the wedding," the other said with some embarrassment.

"Why, of course you have!"

"Let him see the bride," Pernath commented.

"Yes, yes! Let's take him to Vyoma."

The old man gently pulled Des Esseintes by the arm into an adjoining room where a young woman sat on a satin divan staring into space.

She was small and pale. Des Esseintes had a hard time determining whether her face was beautiful or the very opposite. She had a blood-red ribbon wrapped around her throat with the words TEM. NA. F. written on it in purple.

"Maiden's milk," Harro Pernath said slyly and then chuckled, poking his guest in the ribs with his elbow.

The Frenchman was just beginning to mumble some awkward words of admiration when a very fat woman with large ears carrying a pink feather duster came bustling into the chamber shouting.

"Out! Out! You men are always too eager. Better to first purify your hearts!"

She thrust the feather duster at them and they retreated from the room.

"In time, in time," the old man murmured as he led the others into a small closet and then up a long ladder into a room which was crowded with clocks, a piano, a brass elephant and bric-a-brac. In the middle of the room was a table, covered with food. In one corner, in a large cage which sat atop a marble pedestal, was a curious bird, with yellow feathers and a long neck. A terrarium filled with African mice sat on a shelf.

Crowding the middle of the room was a large oak table on which were piled formidable cheeses and enormous pies; plates of smoked beef and pickled fish; bottles of Szamorodni wine and brightly-tinted liqueurs.

Des Esseintes lit a cigarette and sat down.

A group of musicians burst into the room and, after helping themselves freely to wine, began playing at their instruments violently. Harro jumped over to the piano and started to pound at its keys. A thinnish man with a moustache scraped away vigorously at a violin while another fellow, whose sleepy eyes relaxed behind a pair of spectacles, hammered on a cimbalom. A brooding looking man in his thirties blew on a clarinet.

Des Esseintes tried to follow the rhythm, which reminded him vaguely of certain passages of Christoph Demantius, but in the end gave up and turned his attention to the table.

A sudden hunger had come over him. He cut himself a huge slice of cheese. There was a bowl of hard-boiled eggs and, peeling the shell off one, he dashed a bit of salt on it and shoved it in his mouth. Then he cut himself a piece of rhubarb pie.

The violinist looked at him and shouted, "Feed the bird."

Everyone took up the theme and all began shouting uproariously for him to feed the bird.

Des Esseintes, tearing a piece off a loaf of bread, took it to the cage and let the bird peck it out of his hand, at which everyone clapped and screamed in delight while the bird began to coo and run around its cage in excitement.

The violinist introduced himself.

"My name is Gustav."

"Yes?"

There was a strange light in the eyes of the musician.

"Do not be so sure."

Des Esseintes was baffled.

"He is talking about the transformation," the clarinet player said in a bored tone. "Complete non-discrimination. It's like last night. I dreamed of a man with huge antlers playing the guitar."

"And how did he play?" asked Gustav.

"Better than you, only I couldn't hear."

"Then how do you know?"

"The same way I know that the bird is happy."

"Don't talk nonsense Alfred," the cimbalom player said. "The bird might be the body, but it's not the blood. The height of feeling leads to the path of God. No question that there is beauty in ugly pictures, but that doesn't mean our French guest here should have to endure the worst. Let him have a glass of wine and be on his way."

"He's here for the wedding," Pernath said.

"We all are!" cried Gustav. "Max is just trying to annoy us. He doesn't like to celebrate. He's waiting to return to the promised land."

"Ah, you occultists . . ."

"Hush, hush!" the old man interposed and then, approaching Des Esseintes, kissed him on both cheeks.

"She's ready now."

"Ready?" the Frenchman asked in astonishment.

"Don't be shy my child. She likes you very much."

"Make sure to kiss her on the lips," Pernath whispered in his ear.

Before he knew it, he was mounting an elegant spiral staircase of brass work.

The room he made his way into was totally round with an imposing bed stationed in its centre. She was lying there, with a blank expression on her face. He moved closer, and opened his eyes wide with surprise.

"Great God, she's——!" he said to himself.

Yes, she was there, a man past his prime, with a balding head, face lined with wrinkles, body thin and covered with loose flesh.

He stood for a moment in indecision as the fellow looked up at him. Reasoning that at least he could not accuse himself of mediocrity, he leaned over and placed his lips to his, fed on his own substance. The figure on the bed, some strange, perverted mirror-image of himself, shrugged its shoulders.

A shiver coursed over Des Esseintes' body and he was considering what course to take when the door to the apartment was flung open and everyone entered in a storm. The musicians were banging on pots and swinging their arms in the air. Harro Pernath carried the caged bird on his head and the old man was dexterously juggling the hard-boiled eggs. The African mice were mounted on Gustav's shoulders.

Everyone sang in unison:

> Now likewise
> He brings joy
> To the nuptial ceremony
> Of D.E.
>
> All is gladness
> That he is equal
> So the betrothed
> Will multiply.

Des Esseintes' body broke out in a wintry sweat. He began to bite his nails, while the figure on the bed gnawed at his.

"Let me take your jacket," the woman with the large ears said.

"No, no," Des Esseintes murmured as he backed towards the door.

He turned and ran out of the room, down stairways and ladders and then stumbled down some dark steps and through a groaning door.

He found himself outside. The night was chilly, and he pulled his coat around himself.

Looking down, he noticed a dirty-looking girl tugging at his sleeve, putting an empty hand forward. He threw some money at her and moved off, towards his hotel, to pack his trunks and portmanteaux as quickly as possible.

The pleasures of foreign cities certainly were exaggerated, he noted as he hurried on with the elastic steps of a much younger man.

A WALLED GARDEN ON THE BOSPHORUS

by Mark Valentine

THE walled garden on the Bosphorus had a narrow blue door opening out onto the waterway, a few stone steps descending from this and, affixed to their side, an iron staple where a boat might be moored. Here was kept one of the one-man sailing boats used on the water, with their single sharp triangle of white cloth. At times, I later found, the boat would be taken out to lonely islands and harbours, for its pilot to talk to the fishermen, goatherds, inn-keepers and priests, and to explore the scattered stones of ruined temples and shrines that he heard about from them.

The garden itself was perhaps twenty paces long and rather less than that wide: a walnut tree dwelt in one corner and in another, a medlar with, in spring, its bright silver-green leaves and white flowers, and, in autumn its tight, tawny little fruits. Much of the garden was cobbled, and old moss grew between the cobbles. But there was also a minor rank meadow of wild grass and in this stood an ornate bench painted blue, and a round table on a single elegant stalk: its top was just big enough to accept a coffee tray. Around the bench there were overflowing pots of mint, tarragon and rosemary. A rectangular lead cistern held brackish black water: it was decorated with the dark head of an heraldic panther whose mouth held an arid iron spout

Glazed doors led from the garden into the modest single storey studio-house attached to it: the glass in the doors had a green tinge. The room beyond the doors was restful, with worn couches, octagonal inlaid side-tables, an ugly old black-and-gold ormolu clock, a brass coffee pot, an umbrella stand, possibly used more now for parasols or walking sticks, and made from a deep brown oak like the bindings on old leather books, a glass rose-water flask with a deep spout, and a few shallow blue ceramic dishes which were sometimes graced with rather dusty comfits.

Above the arched fireplace, on the stone of the chimney, there was an unusual picture. In a simple frame of thin black wood, preserved behind heavy glass, there was a sepia photograph. It showed a stretch of sea and then billowing illumined clouds rising above a city whose outline was now jagged and haphazard. In the lower left corner there was a caption in white text: it read, "The Doom of Smyrna". Turkish acquaintances who visited the owner of the picture noted this evidence of their re-taking of the city: but when Greek acquaintances called they took it as a commemoration of their loss. The truth was that the owner simply admired the composition and drama of the piece, and the contrast between the eruption shown and the subdued, elegiac light. He liked too the epic resonance of the title it had been given, and it gave him cause, when he mulled over it in his studio, to reflect upon the "doom" that had come, or was yet to come, to other cities, or to men. Although its gunpowder mills had been bombed during the Great War, in its more recent history Constantinople had suffered none of the fire and destruction whose bloom the photograph had caught: it had become, indeed, a place of refuge. Its doom, perhaps, was a slower fate: the encroachment of twilight.

It was because of the refugees that I had come to the city. I had been sent to do work for the League of Nations. The former Ottoman capital had, since the Russian Civil War and the many minor wars that followed it, taken on the reluctant role of a kind of entrepot for fleeing humanity. Thousands were encamped in makeshift shelters on its margins or tried to burrow into its dense interior. The work of seeing to even the simplest of their needs was tiring and incessant. Yet even an international official is permitted some time to himself and it was while I was buying myself a tin of Marcovitch cigarettes one day that I chanced to meet the Frenchman who lived in the studio with the walled garden on the Bosphorus. He was waiting for a special order to be made up, and was willing to linger in talk. He gave himself the name of Felix Vrai—and I never knew any other—and we seemed to hit it off straightaway, as strangers sometimes will. It was rather as if we were resuming a friendship and a conversation that had happened before. I said as much during a brief lull in our talk, and Vrai seized upon the notion, saying certainly there would be those who believed in encounters in a previous, or different, existence. The remark interested me: and he could see that it interested me.

He invited me to accompany him to his quarters, which were not distant, and as we traversed the streets we passed the forlorn shells of the old pashas' palaces, which were grand but not vast, with deeply arched windows, unfurling rooflines and rusting gates, now drunken on their hinges. Cypress, Aleppo pine and juniper lingered in the wild gardens, in their mournful groves. The impression perhaps prompted Vrai to explain his presence in the city. He was studying, he said, the obscure faiths of the old Ottoman Empire. No belief, I gathered, no sect, was too curious to excite his interest, provided it was, or had been, or was reputed to have been, practised within the shimmering boundaries of the former trans-national state, the empire without a true Emperor, which had sprawled across the Levant, the Caucasus, the Balkans, and beyond, for so many centuries. The Druze did not escape him, nor the Alawwites, Maronites, Jacobites, Ismaili (those reputed descendants of the Assassins), nor the Bogomils (peasant dualists), the half-pagan Huculs (mountain folk of the Carpathians, with their carved axes), nor the Sabbatians (who revered in secret a 17th century Jewish messiah), nor the Hasidim and their wise Zadiks, nor the last lingering lines of the Sephardi, who had come from Castile and Andalucia centuries ago under persecution, and ended in Salonika, nor even the Lipovanians (Ukrainians who were perhaps also pagans, or Old Believers, or both).

About all these, singly or in such groupings as suggested themselves, Vrai (as I afterwards saw) would compose essays reflecting upon their beliefs, not burdened by learned footnotes, not vitiated by scepticism, but written rather elliptically, in what I think of as the typically Gallic way. It was as if he were turning over in his fingers a carved gem, remarking upon how the light and the dark played upon each facet. He did not, of course, I soon learnt, attach himself to any of these beliefs: nor indeed, could it be said, to any belief.

Ensuring that I was comfortable in his shaded study, with a mint tea to one side and a little dish of walnuts-in-rosemary to the other, Felix Vrai spoke rather of what he saw, or glimpsed, than of what he thought. For all his studying of those rare and strange beliefs, it seemed to me that he found his own solace for the soul, such as it was, in the incidental encounters of the city. He said that when the moon shone upon the dark waters lapping below his gate, it would produce an uncanny sheen which sometimes made him shiver for a reason other than the chill of the night air, though he could not say what. He knew too that the streets of the abandoned capital (for the Kemelites had acclaimed Ankara, that dull provincial town, instead) held soft shadows that caused a certain pleasurable trepidation in him. His gaze was certainly drawn, he conceded, to the celebrated domes and minarets of the city, of course: yet he said that even a single bead of rain-water, iridescent upon a tram-wire, could cause him to stare in a kind of abstract wonder. All these things, he implied, gave him reason to consider afresh the stubborn mysteries of the world: but not to form any definite conclusions, still less to assert those to strangers, as the founders and followers of the faiths he studied had been moved to do. As he spoke of these things, though, his grey eyes glimmered and his lean form in its suit of twilight blue became tense and brittle.

When I called upon Vrai more often, eager to hear again his peculiar speculative conversation, I found out more too about his diurnal routine. Once a day, usually when the golden dusk was settling on the city like a fine pollen, he left his studio and went out to frequent the few shops he favoured. On a few rare occasions, I even accompanied him: and it was a joy to witness his little pleasures. There was a stationer where he never failed to find delight in the yellowing reams of octavo and folio paper; in the fat glass bottles of inks, shaded from perle noir through gris nuage to bleu nuit and then suddenly vivified by vials of scarlet, viridian and even Imperial purple; in the little printed wads of blotting paper bearing the stationer's name and crest; and especially in the jars of fine silver sand, for those ancients who still preferred to dry their writing in this way.

Second only to the stationer was the shop of sweetmeats, with its array of pastries flavoured with almonds, preserved lemon peel, Lebanese honey, Anatolian raisins, cardamom or even Zanzibar cloves. It was rare that Vrai did not permit himself to select a few of these.

Thirdmost, before the shops of more mundane wares must occupy his attention, there was the fragrant humidor of the old tobacconist Ghazan, where we had first met. Here he selected the precise and precious mingling for his personal blend, which would later be fed to his little amber-stemmed pipe and offered as an incense to the evening air, as he sat on the scrolled blue bench in his walled garden on the Bosphorus, and listened to the liquid ripples playing beyond his gate.

I say all this so that it will be discerned that Vrai, for all his recondite studies and speculations, was no ascetic, but loved the little pleasures of life, which made all the more mysterious for me, later, his sudden absence from them. Nor was he one of those scholars who are oblivious of their surroundings. Vrai did not fail to discern the signs of neglect and decay that lay about him as he made his way through the shadow-scented streets. On certain days, indeed, he once confided in me, they almost appealed to him more than the offerings of the shops he visited. It was as if, he said, another form of merchandise had been devised for him, one made of melancholy and dust, of hollowness and fallen hauteur: all these lost ruins of a vanished empire were for him to taste on the tongue of his imagination. If there were also mortal relics in the niches of the streets, he gave them coins and no further thought. But the tawny powder of crumbling stone, the stark green stalks of the ascendant weeds, the ochreous moss that clung to the unsteady roof-tiles, these preoccupied him sometimes, on his walks at dusk.

After we had met many times in the studio or in the walled garden, Felix Vrai explained to me, at first with hesitation, that there were three faiths, the rarest of all he had found in the former Ottoman domains, that troubled him the most, and which he had not yet been able to write about. With my permission, he said, pouring me out a rose-water cordial from his graceful glass vessel, he would like to tell me what he knew. These, he said, he had not been able to discover from his usual sources or from reference works, but had relied upon chance words and rumours, and the piecing-together of fragments of papyri. Soon, he would have to seek out more about them, if his study was to be complete: but he did not know how, or where. That the answer would come to him, though, he felt sure, for (if he did not put his trust in any particular beliefs), he had a certain sense of how fate fell. He allowed me then to take notes about what he said, indeed I think he hoped I might do this. I have not added anything to them, and I do not advise anyone else to try.

Of all the sects he had heard about, he said, few whispers fascinated him as much as the suggestion that there existed still a clandestine following of the 10th century neo-Zoroastrian movement, the Qarmatians. Acting upon the conviction of the sovereign importance of the 1,500th anniversary of the death of the prophet Zarathustra, which was also coincident with a portentous conjunction of Saturn and Jupiter in the heavens, the Qarmatians had in those days sacked Mecca and captured the Black Stone, the Q'aaba. Under a young renegade Persian prince, they had revived the worship of fire, and used it to destroy many cities: and in his ninety-day rule, some said seventy, preparations were made for the return of the great Zoroastrian emanations. Whether they had indeed returned was now disputed. But the strongest assertion made by Qarmatian legend, in recounting these epochal events, was that, during its captivity the Black Stone had been pulverised, ground down, and its dark grains dispersed across the world so that Ahriman, the evil entity, would be confused by the holy veil now covering all things (the Stone miraculously recreated itself).

The safety of our world, the Qarmatians averred, depended upon this vast zaimph, like the veil upon the glory of the goddess Tanit, which safeguarded the city of Carthage. What we see now, therefore, is visible only through this sombre skein, this protective cloak: the true world in all its infinite splendour is richer far in its vivid colours and radiant light. Once it was understood, this myth explained much that was otherwise obscure, for example why the ancient poets, before the dark and sacred masking, were able to convey the world with more simple vigour; why Sappho saw brightness where Dante saw gloom.

And when he walked the streets of Constantinople, Felix Vrai said, he saw the justice of the Qarmatian belief: for everywhere wore a discernible skimming of black, a habit of decay. Even when the high sun searched out the city's innermost alcoves and arcades, the brass beams did not seem to disperse a certain kept veneer of shade. He supposed it might be the same in any city. It was possible, however, the most secret of the sect's writings suggested, to see beyond the dark chalking that lay upon the world, and behold it in its true brilliance; but such a step was fraught with danger, for it attracted the attention of Ahriman. So that when, as happened in rare revelations, he found himself contemplating a tree or stone or fountain made suddenly illuminate, there was always also a keen edge of trepidation, in case the brightness should bring a greater darkness in.

A second sect, still just possibly existing, that possessed his imagination at times, was that of the Archonites, founded by a heretic hermit in the deserts of Egypt. They held that God was indifferent to the fate of the world, which was the preserve of seven ranks of Archons, or demi-urges. These powers had but one sustenance: the souls of men; and it was their will to draw these to them by all the lures and vices of the world, each having charge of several of these. Only the untempted, such as an ascetic hermit, could avoid their greed and find a way through their avaricious ranks to the eternal. Vrai said that in picquant moments he would muse upon which particular of the Archons, who had all once been named, with their kingdoms, by this sect, had charge of (say) opium, or bhang, or the complex postures of the seraglio. Certainly, he thought that the city offered a fecund hunting-ground for the voracious Archons, and he could not claim to be free of the things that might excite their appetite.

There was a third arcane school of belief, Sethian perhaps in origin, but inflected by late Alexandrian Neo-Platonism, which held that, putting the point simply, "everything is also something else" : that there is no being nor object upon the planet that does not have a different nature to the one obviously before us. What we see on the surface, therefore, these Zenosophists held, has significances which we can hardly discern, in another, co-existent order. Vrai knew this to be true of a kind, he told me thoughtfully, on the days when the light changed the slim limbs of his medlar tree into forms of soft silver, or when the dark waters in the carved cistern in his garden seemed to reflect back upon him depths far greater than the tank could in fact contain.

Yet Felix Vrai wondered if those Zenosophists knew more, unsaid. For surely if all things we know about in our world have an "other", or are also an "other", then it follows that the reverse must also be so: that this "other", who is also us, must be searching for us, seeking the glimpses that we also long for. We might be interlocking circles where only in an eye-shaped almondine zone where the two overlapped could any connection be made with what we truly are.

And this might explain for him the feeling that he sometimes had, and not he alone, he supposed, of being watched or followed or anyway not quite alone, even as he rested in his garden regarding the night. There was a Breton doctor, he said, Victor Segalen, a scholar of the Orient, who put it succinctly: "things half-seen can never be seen."

I can still recall the stillness of his studio room as silence fell after he had outlined to me the essence of the beliefs of these three sects that still eluded him. A lucent haze seemed to fall upon the air as the sun in the last of the dusk gave out its dying embers. The picture upon the chimney piece brooded in its brown light. I saw a glint upon the agate orb of an ornate cane in the oaken umbrella stand, like the spark of a struck flint. White rays emanated from the rose-water vessel. And in the grey eyes of Felix Vrai too there was a light I had not seen before.

I did not see my friend again. I noticed at first that we did not meet in chance encounters in the quarter where he lived, as had happened often enough before: nor, I found, had the humidor heard of him for a while. He had given me a key to his studio so that I might let myself in if ever he was late for our conversations. And so, with some deference (for I did not know if he was deep now in his studies and did not want to be disturbed), I entered the place to seek for him. He was not to be found, and nor (when I permitted myself to search his desk) was there any note indicating where he had gone. I looked desolately around the room for any clue about him. It was no longer as it had been when last we had met: it might have been empty for days; a frail fur of dust had settled upon it and the picture, the cane, the glass vessel, had all lost their remembered lustre.

I look for him still, or for his other, in the dim shadows of the streets of Istanbul, as it must now be called: and sometimes he seems to appear to me in the simulacra of faces and limbs seen in stones or trees. Perhaps somewhere, behind the veil, his bright form has found its home, eluding whatever lies in wait. But I think too how I stood that day at the top of the stone steps leading from the walled garden on the Bosphorus, above an empty mooring: and I looked out across the water to where the pale pennants of the sailing boats plied in the wan rays of the sun. One of those might, I hope now, have been his, at the start of a stranger voyage still, even than those he had found in the fallen capital and its empire of visions.

THE FOUR STRENGTHS OF SHADOW

by Ron Weighell

THE STORM, which had been prowling the lagoon all morning, fell with a roar upon Venice just as Summers alighted at the *fondamenta* of Ca' Mortensa. As he raced the rain to the marble encrusted water gate, he saw Signor Bramanti waiting for him, his bulk dwarfed by winged lions of corroded bronze that flanked the entrance. A cordial shaking of hands, a gesture of mock despair to the heavens, and Bramanti led the way into the Andron.

Skirting an ancient wellhead, they climbed a winding marble stair into the *Portego*, an echoing space that ran the depth of the building. It was floored with *terrazzo*, its walls decorated with once exquisite architectural features in stucco, now crumbling into picturesque ruin. The space struck cold, but not, Summers noted with relief, particularly damp.

Having been told that Ca' Mortensa was unoccupied, he was surprised when a door opened and a woman every bit as round as Bramanti, but resplendent in a flowing gown, and what looked like a fright wig of bright red hair, began to shout in a dialect too thick for Summers to follow. Two pairs of short, fat arms waved madly on the air as Bramanti shouted back. At length the woman withdrew with a parting curse. Bramanti shook his head.

"I must apologise, Signor Sommer, this woman, she was the—*compagna*—of the Contessa who was the last occupant. This woman, she should go, she has no right to be here, but here the Law!—Festina Lente—make haste slowly, as they say. She is convinced we have come to steal the Contessa's things." He grimaced, and gave a shivering shrug, as if the woman's belief was a contamination of which he must rid himself.

Summers nodded. He was all too familiar with the myth of that last descendant of a noble line, withdrawn into a single room of the Palazzetto, holding court among the remnants of her art collection in a huge gondola bed, her growing bulk swathed in Fortuny fabrics, tangled mane covering her pillows. Her companion had evidently adopted the same uniform, down to the untended hair.

"Well you can inform her that I am here only to research the life of Sigismondo Mortensa. The Contessa, or any other past occupant of the house, is of no interest to me. By the way, no one recognised the name of this place when I gave it to the taxi men. I got here by describing the location, but they kept calling it something else."

"*Ca' Maledetto*—accursed, damned." Bramanti flushed and examined the floor.

"It is a local name—no doubt because the fortunes of the Mortensa family have fallen so low." He led the way into a shuttered space haunted by melancholy, contemplative ghosts of marble and bronze. The walls were decorated with panels cut from ancient Roman sarcophagi, reinforcing the sepulchral atmosphere. Bramanti seemed to read Summer's thoughts. "I will of course have the rooms aired and a heater brought for you. No fires, I am afraid. We must be strict about such things. And I must ask you please to be most careful about turning it off before you leave each day." A distressing thought seemed to strike him. "You were of course informed that it is not possible to sleep here?"

"Oh please don't worry about that. I have lodgings arranged, I am well aware how privileged I am to get access at all!"

This seemed to please Bramanti. He nodded and allowed himself a tight smile.

"Now, I think you will want to see the library!"

The room was very dark. Bramanti began to throw open shutters, revealing a glorious, if rain-lashed, view of the Church of San Bartolomeo. Summers realised that his hero, Sigismondo Mortensa, must have stood where he was now standing, looking proudly every day upon the Baroque structure that was the architect's greatest work.

The library was even more beautiful than he had imagined. The ceiling and walls were covered with frescoes faded to the colour of autumn fruits, except where immense bookcases in Palladian architectural form climbed, by Corinthian columns and wrought-iron walkways, to the painted heavens, their shelves a treasure trove of velum and calf.

The most remarkable object in the room was a clock over ten feet high, a kind of miniature Torre dell'Orologio, with a clock face depicting Saturn devouring his children and a group of automata on top.

"Do you think it would be possible to get this going?" Summers asked.

"I could try to locate the key." Bramanti replied doubtfully. "If I can, I will have it left here for you."

When Bramanti was gone, Summers pulled off a few covers, releasing clouds of dust into the slanting shafts of light that fell through the tall Serlian window. A gigantic desk, big enough for six people, was revealed, along with some very beautiful and surprisingly comfortable chairs and couches. With some form of heating he would be quite at home.

This was one of his favourite moments, before the hard work began, when he could give himself up to the pleasures of his surroundings. This was doubly true in Venice. He was as susceptible as anyone to what Henry James had called "the sweet bribery of association and recollection". Crossing to the window, he took in the mellow golden splendour of the church façade, a late Baroque extravaganza of columns, scrolls and statues, with rain pouring in cascades from every slanting surface. Behind the glassy sheets of water, the shadows gathered under the entablatures and arches which seemed cavernous, looming spaces in which the carved figures of stone seemed to move uneasily.

"*Terribilità.*" Summers intoned to himself Mortensa's own favourite word for the architectural effect he sought to create. "*Terribilità* in spades!"

Turning to the nearest bookshelf, he took down a volume at random. The complete works of Angelo Ambrogini Poliziano, tutor to the son of Lorenzo de Medici, the first edition in its original binding! Again a book at random; a treasure from the Press of Aldus Manutius, a Greek bible of 1518. More, a copy of the Aldine Editio Princeps of Aristotle's works; and a 1495—6 Idylls of Theocritus. Many bore the mark of the Florence Academy.

A beam of sunlight broke through the storm clouds and penetrated the chamber, turning the dancing motes of dust to gold. Summers smiled contentedly to himself.

"*Ca' Maledetto!*" Accursed, damned! If so, then let me be accursed and damned forever!"

In the days that followed, Summers settled into a pleasing routine. A bracing walk from his lodgings to Via Serpente, where he entered the Palazzetto by the much less salubrious landward entrance. Bramanti had been as good as his word, for he found an adequate if unsafe looking heater in the library. Two large keys, joined with string, lay on the desk, one quite plain, the other beautifully ornate, with a gorgon head embossed upon it. Summers assumed that the more ornate one would wind the clock, but it was the plain one that worked. The hours struck with a mellow sound, like distantly-heard church bells, and the automata moved. On examination, Summers concluded that the scene was the flaying of Marsyas. On the left hand side stood Apollo playing his lyre; on the right the *Arrotino,* or knife sharpener, crouched to wet his blade. Between them Marsyas hung by his wrists in preparation for his bloody punishment. At every hour Apollo plucked his lyre, the crouching figure sharpened his little knife, and Marsyas opened his mouth in a silent scream, turning his head stiffly from side to side. The clock was charming, and the sound pleasant, but Summers was aware at every chiming that a gathered silence of many years was being disturbed.

Every morning he researched among the Mortensa books and papers, had lunch at a local trattoria recommended by Bramanti, wandered back through the convolutions of Via Serpente, spent the early afternoon browsing over some interesting volume, then worked again until early evening. On Sunday he went to Mass in a local church, but not Mortensa's, a visit to which he was saving as a special treat.

Rain swept in waves over the roofs and cupolas of Venice, but lost in his work, Summers hardly noticed. On days of particularly foul weather he took to bringing his lunch with him and not leaving the Palazzetto at all.

The library was a delight. Once he approached a door alongside the great clock and only realised, as he reached out to open it, that it was a staggering piece of trompe l'oeil. The bibliophilic joys, too, were unending. One afternoon he wasted hours, lost in a 1499 *Hypnerotomachia Poliphili,* the velum binding and heavy, hand-made paper of which were just as ravishingly sensuous as the adventures conveyed by the text and illustrations. With a pang of envy, he came upon a long shelf of books on

Anatomy by the likes of Guido Guidi, Realdo Columbo and Gabrielle Fallopio, though surprisingly [and for Summers disappointingly] not a sign of an Andreas Vesalius *De Humani Corporis Fabrica*, the one book on the subject he would have bet on finding.

Perhaps the explanation for this last mystery lay in an annotation in one of the other works.

"Arteries are long and hollow with a double skin to convey the vital spirits; to discern which the better, they say that Vesalius the anatomist was wont to cut men up alive."

Had that rumour offended the devout Mortensa's Christian spirit so much that he would not allow a copy in his library?

Every day something memorable occurred. Once he took down a set of matching "volumes" with no labels and found they were false books full of mounted cameos and intaglios, each set enriched at the centre with a gold Tiberius. Most exciting of all, when he examined the section of the shelves devoted to Architecture, he found that the copies of Vitruvius, Alberti, Palladio and the anonymous Sepulchres of Etruria, were all annotated by Mortensa himself!

At least they were in part so annotated. Summers found two similar but distinguishable hands, and realised with a flutter of excitement, that here before him was the first record of a relationship mentioned by Vasari.

For surely the second hand must belong to Antonio Borsini, Mortensa's protégé, who had been groomed to take over the master's mantle, and had so spectacularly betrayed him by disappearing with their work on San Bartolomeo scarcely begun, escaping just before anonymous denunciation for heretical and blasphemous activities.

On first reading Vasari's account, Summers had been humbled by Mortensa's Christian forbearance. Such a blow might have justified a bitter denunciation from the great Architect, but this was a man who habitually dressed in skull cap and cassock, and donated many holy relics to the churches he built. All that he had allowed himself was a gentle statement of disappointment and a heartfelt offer of forgiveness and support, if only the young man would return.

The two hands were similar, but Summers thought he could discern which was which by the tone of the annotations. This surely was Mortensa, writing of "The Knowledge of perfect proportions, the harmony which produces beauty", and beside an exquisite little sketch of the human form within a church ground plan, the words "The interior of the body is a divine secret." The character of Borsini, on the other hand, was readily identified in such passages as "Some divide demons into nine degrees, standing contrary to the nine orders of angels. The first of these are called false gods, who would be worshipped as gods and would demand sacrifices and Adorations." Another example, on sculptural decoration, recorded, 'The rams heads refer to the power of destruction as the ram is the acknowledged symbol of Pluto, Lord of the Dead.' And perhaps worst of all, "Even as our brother in the divine Counsels of Night, Morto da Feltre, descended into the subterranean fastnesses of Rome's ruins, there to draw the grotesques, and from such inspiration invented *sgraffito*, whereby a design in white is only delineated by the presence of its black ground, so do we seek the ancient wisdom that we may build in marble that which depends, for its true meaning, upon the Four Strengths of Shadow."

Perhaps Mortensa had been too kindly and naïve to recognise the dangerous drift of such comments.

Summers came upon another troubling example of Borsini's influence on the Mortensa Library during these first days, a huge canvas-bound folio among the architectural volumes. As he turned the pages he found a fabulous scrapbook of carefully tipped-in drawings, on *carta bombasina*, of mythological scenes. The style and the medium—bistre, Chinese ink and chalks—were so reminiscent of Tiepolo that a less academic mind might have become excited. Summers had seen enough of such works in researching his books to know that drawings in the style of great Venetian artists had been a speciality of many highly talented contemporary fakers. Nevertheless, even if these works were to be categorised as "After Tiepolo", they were still very fine.

What did shock Summers slightly was the subject matter. There must have been twenty or more studies of the Centaur Nessus raping the nymph Dejanira, and a very large number depicting what he could only describe as families of satyrs eating, dancing, making sacrifice to their gods and even making love.

Now this would not be surprising in the library of almost any other architect of that era—all of whom were in some way products of the classical tradition—but Mortensa had been such a devout man, all but saintly in his embodiment of the Christian virtues.

The clue lay in the annotations that accompanied certain drawings, quotations from Pomponius Mela on the subject of satyrs, and extensive references to the *Diversorum veterum poetarum* in Priapum Iusus, an Aldine edition published in Venice in 1517. All were in the same hand as the previous annotations on demons. Summers recognised here, quite literally, the hand of Borsini.

A single bell began to toll mournfully from the tower of San Bartolomeo. The clouds had parted and the sun was beating on the rooftops of Venice. He would get some fresh air, and perhaps visit Mortensa's church at last, before a bite of lunch.

Crossing the canal by the nearest bridge, Summers navigated a tangle of *Calli* and *Cortes* to the church. Before entering, he could not resist a look back at the windows of Ca' Mortensa, thinking how strange it was that he had been inside that beautiful building only minutes before. A shadow passed across the library windows. It was so fleeting that he could not tell its shape. The source must be some passing bird, but it troubled him enough to pause and satisfy himself that there was no recurrence before entering the church.

If Mortensa had been aiming for *Terribilità* with his exterior, the intention inside must have been very different. Summers had never seen a more pious, contemplative church interior in his life. Austere enough indeed to justify the claim once made that Mortensa was the Savonarola of architecture! The green, yellow and black marble created a soothing, submerged atmosphere that suited the rippling greenish light from outside. Summers wandered around in quiet delight, wondering why this architect had never been numbered among the great. Perhaps it was the obvious piety and Christian virtue of the man that was out of step with the tenor of these cynical times. There were no concessions to irreligious sensibilities.

There was a particularly gruesome martyrdom of Saint Bartholomew after Tiepolo (a good deal further "after" than the drawings in the library), and Summers' eye was also caught by an oblong of murky light that turned out to be a case full of sacred relics. These included some implements of torture, a few leathery rags of skin stretched over ornate frames, and some shrivelled, unidentifiable body parts including a delicately beautiful human head, all mummified by time.

Kneeling there, he tried to see them devoutly as holy objects, but found that he could not banish from his mind the guilty idea of condemned meat in some nightmarish butcher's window.

There was a danger that this would spoil his lunch. In any case, a cleric in a cassock was approaching, no doubt with some prepared lecture he did not want; he left swiftly.

On his way to the trattoria, Summers thought the cleric had followed him as far as the bridge, but the dazzle of the low sun was playing tricks, for the shivery reflection in the waters below showed a bridge but no figure.

A good meal and a half carafe of red wine later, Summers made his way happily back to the Palazzetto. The late Contessa's devotee was leaving as he let himself in by the landward door, and she tried to engage him in conversation. He could understand little of her quickly-spoken Venetian dialect, and merely nodded politely as he pushed by. Clearly, Bramanti had failed to pass on the message that he was not out to pillage the relics of her devotion. In her distressed state, the oddly pronounced slang was all but impenetrable, but he caught enough words to feel offended. She seemed to be calling him an uninvited intruder, and used words such as monstrous and horrible. The pleasant mood created by his lunch was quite ruined.

In the murky light within, the Venetian mirrors distorted shapes, so that a bronze Antinous or Furietti centaur of red marble glimpsed in their mottled depths seemed to shift and gesture as he passed. In the library he was troubled to find that his books and papers on the desk had been disturbed. At once the idea came to him that the mad acolyte had been snooping, and had acted out her show of welcome merely to throw him off the scent. If so, he was at a loss to know what the faintly reddish mess was that dabbled the papers and books. Could it be henna, rouge or lipstick? A volume of classical verse lay open, and a smudgy stain lay like a clumsy underlining on the page.

> *"The dappled worm is the murderer*
> *within the eye of blooming vines—"*

A veiled threat? Or was she mad enough to see anyone who threatened her shrine as a murderer? He would make sure he locked the door from now on.

And so he did. The papers and books were undisturbed next day. Pleased with himself for having thwarted her, he worked well all morning, lunched contentedly and returned to the library rubbing his hands in anticipation. While all of Venice lay under a spell of sleep, he would select some choice volume and browse away an hour or two. Almost, he was tempted to take down the folio of mythological drawings, but after a few drinks the subject matter might turn his thoughts in unwonted directions, so instead he chose a treasure of Venetian printing that was hardly conducive to lascivious thoughts: *The Feast of the Sensa*, being an account of the ceremony of the Doge's ritual espousal of the Sea on Corpus Christi day.

Summers had heard of this charming ritual enacted yearly, when a wedding ring was cast by the Doge into the waters to ensure the favours of the ocean, so necessary for a seafaring empire. That indeed was how the account began, but when the Doge set off in the ceremonial splendour of his Bucintoro for the open sea, a second Doge similarly clad was described leaving in a covered gondola through the canals to a certain house, named *phytonteo*, where he descended by secret ways to a chamber deep below the level of the waters, a dark and noisome place, hung with weapons of torture. There, at an altar raised to other, older gods, he performed a very different rite.

Summers considered his Italian better than adequate, but the strange archaic mixture of Italian, Venetian dialect and Latin in which the book was written confused him. Which of the two Doges was the real one? What did *phytonteo* mean? Did the rite culminate in the Doge sacrificing a victim to the waters, or was it the Doge himself who died in monstrous butchery? The tone and subject matter of the book brought to his mind some words of Lawrence on Venice with which Summers had felt no empathy until now:

"Abhorrent green slippery city, whose Doges were old, and had ancient eyes."

The day was beginning to fade down the long reaches of the library. He should really turn on a lamp, but his surroundings were more than usually beautiful at this time, disclosed and concealed in perfect measure, and even one lamp might spoil a light so richly insufficient. Letting the book slip into his lap, he dozed.

The chiming of the great clock awoke him. He was looking downwards at a shiny expanse of frozen swirls and eruptions of faded colour, fired to life by a strange, tawny light. Faint, reflected images hung inverted just below the smooth surface, but he knew he was not looking at liquid. He was slumped forward in his chair, looking down at the terrazzo floor of the library, now ablaze with the last, low shafts of the setting sun.

There was a sound of movement across the floor in his direction. He remained still, in the posture he had assumed in sleep. If it was the Contessa's acolyte, she was in for a big surprise.

He could recognise the sound now, bare feet slapping wetly on the cold, marble floor in an uneven, shambling step that seemed too light for one of such rotund form. He became aware of a smell, like stagnant well water, a reflection swam over the undulating surface, into the range of his downcast eyes, and he knew with a horrible certainty that it was not her. The outline he saw was much taller, and much, much thinner, with a head hairless enough to form a bony outline, and gnarly limbs trailing ragged shreds that the figure was attempting to gather around itself with weak, ineffectual movements. It shook and shivered as it moved, and Summers heard a low moan of pain or despair. He was unable to move, or raise his eyes to look fully on what approached him in a wave of ever-colder, ever-more foul air. As it drew closer, he closed his eyes and clenched himself, still unable to move or breath.

Nothing happened. He risked opening his eyes.

The shape was passing to one side of his seat, towards the nearest bookshelves. By peering out of the corner of his eye, he saw the dimly reflected figure reach towards the books, touch one, and resolve itself into the veins and swirls of colour in the stone. Forcing himself to look up, he confirmed that the figure was gone.

It was just possible that he had confused sleeping and waking, and what he had just seen had not really happened. The test of that theory could hardly be avoided. Crossing to the spot where the reflection had last been, he examined the books before him and found—let him admit it at least to himself, with no real surprise—a familiar dabble of reddish dampness on one of the vellum spines.

Summers drew it out and looked at the title page. It was a volume of Herodotus published by Gregorio de' Gregoriis. Returning a little shakily to his seat, he examined it.

There were no annotations or apparent insertions, but the book would not close properly, springing open at a page with no obvious significance. The cause was a piece of paper slipped into a split in the vellum at the head of the spine. It was written in a hand that Summers now recognised, but was a rough draft for a letter, and therefore difficult to decipher. The writer could no longer tolerate the blasphemous and cruel actions in which he had been forced to participate, and unless they ceased, he would have no choice but to denounce the perpetrator, destroying his high renown.

The choice of words was a little convoluted, and the writing scarcely decipherable, so perhaps his translation was faulty. What he had found must be a last attempt by Mortensa to warn Borsini of the consequences of his actions. Yes, that was surely what it must be. In any case, it was high time he got away from this place for a while. With some relief he returned to his lodgings.

✳

That night sleep did not come easily to him. The events of the day replayed themselves in his head. Frightened as he had been by the moment of its appearance, Summers felt that the apparition had done nothing to suggest it meant him any harm. On the contrary, the whole effort of the poor creature had been to draw his attention to the letter. Was it then Mortensa who had returned? But if so, why had he ever hidden the rough draft, and why was it so important that Summers be shown its hiding place?

The water taxi was late, and he had an urgent letter to post. To make things worse, the water level was rising, lapping the steps of the *fondamenta* and soaking his feet. It was his sense of urgency rather than whim that led him to hail a gondola, a ridiculous extravagance he would not otherwise have countenanced. Still, he had to admit, as he settled back into the dark leather seat, that his decision had been the right one. For all its image as a tourist cliché, the gondola was undeniably the essential Venetian experience. For a while he lay back and watched the slow, hypnotic parade of elegant bridges, scarred brickwork, crumbling plaster and peeling shutters, his senses lulled by the slap of water on weed-smothered stone and the rhythmic swish of the oar.

The people leaning over the pergoli were all in Renaissance costume, because of course it was Carnival, and everyone had joined in the spirit of Masquerade. Even he had not forgotten, for on looking down he saw buskins, hose and the rim of his cloak. Some people were taking the festivities a little too far, for they had lit fires on the rooftops, and as Bramanti had made so clear, the regulations concerning fire in Venice were strict.

Was it, he wondered, really necessary to travel by such a convoluted route just to post a letter? It had not occurred to him before, but the canals of Venice were nothing more or less than a gigantic aquatic labyrinth with Mystery at its heart.

Was it the sunset which turned the sky blazing red, or those fires, which he now saw lined the canal, licking over ruinous buildings, silhouetting figures who teemed around vast engines that turned and swung in the glare? They were clearly devices of torture, hoisting bodies by the neck or stretching them cruelly between chains. And what he had taken for ruined houses were gigantic sarcophagi towering to the sky, mausolea raised by giants, burial chambers of the gods, all lit by the glare of funeral pyres.

Bodies were being broken upon wheels, torn apart, flayed alive. Fortunately, the gondola had become a funeral barge that carried him swiftly, nearer and nearer to the massive bridge, hung with gargantuan chains, that was his destination. Yes, there it was, the keystone carved into the form of a great face swathed in shroud like folds of cloth gathered on top of the head, its mouth the slit into which he must post his message.

Just as he was wondering how to reach the slot, the whole face began to grow, to fill the space under the bridge. Now he wondered how they could navigate the slit of a mouth. When he turned to ask, he saw that the gondolier had been replaced by something whose outline, so black against the glare, he did not wish to see. In any case, the problem was no more, for the stone head on the bridge, which now resembled Sigismondo Mortensa, had grown snaky hair, and the mouth was gaping wide. Blood rained down from the machinery of death on either side as they swept on, into the gaping maw of darkness.

Summers awoke gasping and running with sweat. Even at that moment he confronted the truth he had not wished to admit to himself, and knew what he must do about it. Why would a successful architect write a letter to his apprentice threatening his high reputation? The answer was that he had not. The apprentice had threatened the Master. And if that was so, then the hand, and the dark utterances, he had taken for Borsini were those of Sigismondo Mortensa.

The implications were inescapable. Vasari had been wrong, or intentionally misleading. The darker annotations had come from the hand of the supposedly saintly paragon. Borsini's threat of denunciation—the first draft of which he had concealed—had been forestalled by counter denunciation and "disappearance". Mortensa, it seemed, had not even risked leaving Borsini to the judgement of the Council of Ten, for fear of what might emerge. And now the mills of a very different kind of Venetian justice were grinding on, while lawyers droned like blowflies in courts and offices, and the hand of decay spread a grey benediction of dust over the furniture and statuary of the Palazzetto. If an unquiet spirit haunted Ca' Mortensa—or *Ca' Maledetto* as he now agreed it must be— there could be little surprise. Unquiet it would remain until someone at long last exposed the truth.

The next day he returned to Ca' Mortensa and worked all morning as usual. At noon he ate and drank nothing. Then he waited. He would make himself available for any further communication the apparition wished to reveal about its fate. And he would change the book on which he had been working from the naïve hagiography he had intended to an exposé of the true nature of Mortensa and his heritage.

To pass the time, he read more of what he now knew to be Mortensa's annotations in the works of architecture.

"For by our use of full columns, detached columns, half columns and pilasters, so are the formulating shadows summoned or banished, starved or fed, and these are the four strengths of shadow. There can be no beauty of detail without shadow, and out of shadow comes all things. There is no Wisdom without the science of shadow and light. The architect can form no shape of meaning or purpose were his Orders not defined by darkness, nor offer to heaven what rises in light above, if not for what lies in darkness below.

"Thus no Temple was raised by the Ancients without its sacrifice immured beneath, this and other *more exquisite* methods devised in the knowledge that success in such a work of creation requires the help of those who draw life from that particular vitality liberated by the fear and agony of a living human being. Were not the dismembered limbs of Dionysus boiled beneath the Pythia's tripod?"

It had not escaped Summers that the previous event had occurred at the striking of the Great Clock. As the same hour approached, he tried to keep calm, repeating inwardly to himself, "I am ready, if there is anything more you wish to show me."

The silence of the library was eventually broken by the striking of the clock, and Summers was afraid. If he was approached again, would he be able to raise his eyes? What would he see? He waited breathlessly, but there were no slapping steps, no stagnant smell, and above all, no swimming, rippling form pouring horribly across the marble floor. He felt a mixture of disappointment and relief. Perhaps the message had been delivered, and the need for visitation ended?

He rose from the chair, turned, and there it was, there at the other end of the library, as though looking at him. It turned stiffly and moved through the shadows with slow, agonised steps. Passing the shelves with no effort to touch them, it walked deliberately up to the trompe l'oeil door and disappeared through it. This was so surprising that Summers stood for some seconds before collecting himself and followed its path through a channel of foul, bitterly cold air, to the painted door.

He examined the door more closely this time. The rippling canal light played over medallions and swags of muted purple and brown, over the old reddened gold of the door, scalloped and guarded by garland bearing cherubs, for all the world like marble. The panels were studded with metal bosses so real that he had to touch one to be sure they were illusions of paint.

He noticed something else, too. The painted keyhole was formed by the mouth of a little gorgon head, and the effect of shadow in the hole was remarkably real, even by the door's stupendous standards. He put his finger to the place and found a real keyhole.

At once he remembered the two keys on the string Bramanti had left, one of them with a gorgon head decoration. It was still connected to the one in the clock. He retrieved it, and unlocked the panel painted with a fake door that pretended to be real in order to conceal the fact that that was just what it was. The fleeting question of whether a Venetian painter could be correctly described as Machiavellian rose in his mind and was brushed aside.

The pressure it took to open the panel suggested a spring or counterbalance closing mechanism. No light switches met his fumbling hand so he concluded that the room had been unknown when electricity was being installed in the twentieth century. His heart pounded with the thought that no one had entered the door for so many years, and of what might be there. Lighting a lamp, he stepped into the space. The door swung closed behind him on a counter balance. Stopping it before it closed fully, he satisfied himself that there was a handle on the inside and that it would open the latch. Only then did he let the door close, tried it once more for peace of mind, and gave his attention to the room.

The first sweep of lamp light revealed a kaleidoscopic rush of strange objects to his sight. He knew at once it was a *wunderkammer* or cabinet of curiosities; a cramped, oppressive space whose walls were lined with pitted Venetian reflecting glass, at least in those places where it was possible to see the walls at all. Here Mortensa had gathered the dark mysteries of the world into one place. He saw the branches of corals and the tusks of narwhals, festoons of bones, stuffed reptiles. Everywhere stood jars of preserved specimens, some stewed by time into unspeakable broth, others still clear enough to reveal heads with too many mouths or eyes, claws, or humped backs. Magnificent écorché, surely the work of Ludovico Cardi, capturing every sinew and tendon of their skinless torsos in marble. Chalices of bone and many books, some with great metal clasps, and all bound in the same pale hide.

There were foetuses, human and animal, mandrakes and baby dragons, dry withered mermaids and other unrecognisable monsters. Summers was horrified to see sections of human bodies and internal organs, but realised that they were far too highly coloured and solid, too sharply, glitteringly fresh to be anything but perfect wax models. It was a treasure trove, even for a building such as this. "Keep calm," he told himself; "remember this moment". For if his lungs and nostrils were sending accurate messages, no one had entered this space for a very long time.

He glanced over the titles of the books. Liceti: *De Monstruorum Causis Natura et Differentiis*. Aldrovandi: *Monstruorum Historia*. Giovanni Rinaldi: *Il Mostruosissimo Mostro*. Despite the tension and fear, Summers had to smile at the last of these titles, at the linguistically monstrous idea of the expression "monsterest of monsters."

The next book was a once-sumptuous elephant folio of Andreas Vesalius, *De Humani Corporis Fabrica Libri Septem*. Clearly that dark rumour about Vesalius's methods had not put Mortensa off after all; quite the reverse it seemed. On examination it proved to be no ordinary edition of the work. Bound in that troubling, pale soft hide, not quite like pigskin, the pages finest velum that had resisted the atmosphere of some damp place sufficiently to retain a kind of warped, chlorotic integrity. The printing was blurred in places but was quite decipherable.

The contents were quite unlike any copy of Vesalius that Summers had ever seen. The known work is unforgettable enough, a haunting combination of beauty and horror produced by those images of flayed, dissected bodies strung up on cruel systems of pulleys, twisted into elegant contortions on ropes, or just gracefully walking, muscle and sinew hanging in shreds from delicately poised limbs, a dead parody of graceful sentience. But those plates seemed to have been intended to serve a noble purpose, to unlock the mysteries of human life. This black, occult Vesalius, stamped on its title page with a head of Tiberius, depicted its frayed, skeletal bodies in parodies of The Stations of the Cross, and delineated tortures devised for one purpose only: the infliction of insufferable pain. The text was equally grotesque. One chapter entitled, De Monstris was devoted to the creation of monsters, and told how demons assumed the form of their tortured offerings. An architectural sketch in the margin showed a body laying below the foundations of a church accompanied by the words *Aufer caput, corpus ne tangito*. (Carry away the head, but don't touch the body).

The illustrations gradually descended into madness, depicting anatomical specimens slaughtering and butchering each other, skeletal figures locked in cannibalistic embraces, a world in which the tortured and the torturer had become indistinguishable.

Summers put down the book and wiped his hands along his sides. His first instinct was to leave that oppressive, foul-smelling place, but something had caught his eye. A small doorway stood in the wall opposite the entrance. So there was more. The door concealed a cramped stair that coiled down into darkness. Cautiously descending the slimy steps, he came into a chamber constructed of huge stone blocks.

The walls were disfigured with a lacteal canker of mineral damp. Slippery mosses flourished on the floor, forming a spongy, saturated carpet under foot. What he could see of the roof was covered with dripping stalactites and tumorous green humps. At intervals around the walls were gruesome variations of the Karyatid, marble figures of Marsyas suspended by his wrists and flayed, the torn raw condition of the body depicted with repulsive skill by the choice of red and white porphyry.

Between the figures, the walls were hung with mirrors but not the Venetian glasses of the cabinet. These were huge, irregular, dully tarnished as sheets of old corroded steel, but still throwing back contorted reflections of strange tools or weapons that hung from the walls or lay in heaps. In the middle of the chamber stood a Roman altar, once finely carved with tritons and nereids, now worn until its figures looked deformed or maimed, its darkly-stained top rounded off and scarred by countless cuts that made it resemble the butcher's block it undoubtedly had been. Setting down the lamp, he peered around him.

Now he could make out some of the protuberances jutting from the ceiling, corroded metal rings that still held fragments of chains and pulleys.

From the moment he had entered the chamber it had been strangely familiar to him. He knew it from something he had read recently. Then it came back to him. The book of the secret ritual of the Doge.

As he stood wondering over the purpose to which those rusty tools had once been put, a wave of chill, stagnant air swept over him, and a cold hand clamped around his wrist. He cried out and struggled to pull away, but the grip was at once sinewy and slick, five bands of clammy steel around his arm, radiating a chill that flooded through him like an evil injection. A redly-glittering, veinous head came thrusting towards him, its thin lips working as they whispered something unintelligible. Reaching the other sinewy claw to the surface of the altar, as though drawing strength from contact with the place of its last pain and ruination, that which had once been Borsini seemed to burgeon for a second into human likeness, so that Summers found himself looking into the face of a young man still full of hope and belief. Something very like a human mouth opened, and a single word issued like sirocco through parched grass.

"Guistizia."

The hand fell from the altar, and humanity dropped away from the figure as quickly as it had come. Summers last vestige of nerve broke then and, pulling free, he fled. By the light of the lamp—which he was leaving behind at every step—he just about made the foot of the stairs, and buffeted his way up through a narrow, slippery spiral of darkness.

The cabinet was, of course, pitch black, and he scrambled blindly through that cluttered space, his hands falling upon objects whose yielding or bony contours felt more horrible for being indefinable. A glass jar toppled with a deafening crash, spilling its contents in a wave of unutterably nauseating odour. Slithering through the spilled mess, he overturned a stack of books and fell against a panel with a handle on it, which he turned.

The panel would not open. He threw himself against it, but it would not give. As he struggled a voice close to his ear whispered, "Guistizia!"

In desperation he tried pulling instead of pushing and was released into light and space. The panel slammed behind him as he fled from the Palazzetto. He was dimly aware of running beside water, then nothing until, some while later, he stopped and looked around.

It was as if the fate the world had long dreaded had come to pass, and Venice was already fathoms deep in stagnant water. The city was engulfed in a fog that swirled around a crumbling well head and a saturated line of clothes strung across a *corte*. He had absolutely no idea where he was. His mind was a flood of confused images and realisations. This was the full truth of the saintly Mortensa and the villainous Borsini. He knew now the fate of the young man who had disappeared so abruptly. That dreadful, tragic wreck of a thing had lead him, weakly at first, then with growing strength of purpose, to let the world know what had occurred, the real nature of the relics they worshipped, and what lay buried beneath Mortensa's church. Summers shivered, clutched his thin jacket about him and began to look for a sign that would tell him where the hell he was.

After some minutes of searching he came upon a wall of yellow plaster crumbling away to reveal ancient brickwork, in the centre of which was a great face of stone grimacing out of the fog at him. Carved folds of fabric swathed the head and were gathered at the top like a shroud. Below, familiar words were carved.

> *"Denontie Secrete*
> *Contro chi occulterà*
> *Gratie et officii*
> *O collunderà per*
> *Nascon der la vera*
> *rendita di essi"*

He was standing before the Bocche di Leone, its mouth a slot into which accusations had been placed. That he should stumble upon this of all places at that moment could hardly be chance. This was the very mouth into which Mortensa had posted his denunciation, and by so doing saved his own skin by blackening the name of his innocent victim.

With an overwhelming sadness he thought of that wretched spectre walking the dusty shelves of the library through how many years, clutching his own ragged shreds of skin around him like the mantle of some acolyte in agonised devotion to the cruel god who had torn him from himself.

Summers found some comfort in the thought that he at least had the power to set the record straight.

Perhaps, he reflected, the Contessa's companion might not be as mad as she seemed. Had there not been a desperate tone of warning in those weirdly expressed effusions? She had been speaking of something horrible, monstrous, an intruder, but she had not meant him. Something other than eccentricity had driven the women to the cramped confines of one barricaded room. They had seen what he had seen.

Finding the way around Venice was hard enough on a clear day. In the fog it was impossible. He stumbled upon a café and sat for a while, warming his chilled hands around a cup of coffee. The fog began to clear. Armed with detailed directions back to the Via Serpente, he became lost again almost immediately, and may have wandered off his course but for a cleric in a skull cap and cassock glimpsed through the thick veils of mist. When he called out the name of his destination the figure pointed the way. Passing through the narrow *calle* indicated, Summers came to a halt, facing the mist—wreathed waters of a canal lapping at the green step before his feet. The smell of rotten vegetables was on the air. Evidently, the cleric had directed him into an alley used for loading and unloading barges. Now he would have to retrace his steps.

A bell began to toll very close by, and he recognised it: San Bartolomeo must be directly in front of him. At that moment the mist parted to reveal the pale façade of Mortensa's creation. So he could be no more than a turning or two from the Palazzetto, perhaps almost alongside it, though the view was a little different.

The tolling of the bell was subtly hypnotic, bringing to mind the movement of weed in ocean swell. The mist was dispersing swiftly and the great façade was becoming clearer. In the growing light the shadows on its surface shifted like expressions on a vast, pallid face. What had Mortensa written about the power of shadows? They certainly made the church façade look deep and hollow as a cave, an infinite distance out of which a familiar cassock-clad figure emerged, gesturing rhythmically to the tolling of the bells.

And Summers saw then who—or what—was approaching him with those hypnotic passes of the hands, and realised too late how naïve he had been to think that so formidable a being, capable of raising a temple to the ancient gods under the very noses of the Council of Ten, would allow him to destroy a reputation so cunningly created, and so ruthlessly preserved.

Summers felt compelled to look down and saw on the slimy stone between his feet a symbol or hieroglyph deeply carved. He peered at it, the bell booming through his head, as the symbol filled his vision. It was as if the very stones of Venice were speaking through the cold metal tongue of the bell, telling him to come down and learn what only the stones could know, what they kept hidden from the eyes of man.

He was dully aware that he was toppling into water, was sinking. Despite the bell and the hieroglyph that filled his mind, his desire for life was strong. Gulping in foul water through nose and mouth, he kicked desperately, felt himself sucked down, kicked again and felt his face, a mask of green slime, rise into the air. He took a mouthful, half water, and went down again, his limbs working madly. But something in him could not deny the cruel knowledge of the bell and the symbol. Even as his body struggled, he continued to sink, deeper, it seemed, than a canal could possibly be, down past hieroglyphic-carven walls and shattered columns and vast, impassive faces of stone. The cold arms of the sea embraced him, and still he seemed to sink, married forever, like the Doges of old, to the dark green Waters.

THE BEARING

by R. Ostermeier

TINTON was founded centuries ago to provide cottages for mine workers and their families on the high moor. Parish records have the area as part of Cubton district before being gradually inhabited as new tin mines were opened, becoming a parish in its own right one hundred and forty-seven years ago. The village's birth is all there in the records: mine owners provided the money, cottages were built, workers moved in and Tinton came into existence.

Folklore, however, tells a different story. Folklore says the first cottages were built after seven coffins were dragged over the moor by seven mysterious black goats. Bushes were flattened for a dozen miles round, farther than a goat might travel in one night. The coffin wood held a *queer glow*, the ropes and halters attaching the cargo to the goats being *of woven red human hair*, and the heads of the bolts holding the coffins together impressed with *a fell mark* that looked like the imprint of hooves. Local myth said the seven black goats lay down at dawn between the two great sunken tors and six died with their heads resting on the coffins. A lone miner slit the throat of the seventh for meat, and that same morning hit a seam of tin that lasted a decade. And so Tinton was founded—

Cynics say the story is confection, a supernatural money-maker, viewing the details—the devilish hooves straining through the moorland furze, the door-eyed goats' dead stares, the dread image of black coffins dragged through thorn and gorse—as local colour, the touristic equivalent of the greyhound's hare.

Yet seven coffins containing human bones still reside at Tinton, and the villagers believe they are the original seven corpses dragged there by the black goats. The larger tor, Dovecot, has a number of caves near the summit—thought to be the source of its unusual name—and to this day seven of the larger caves each have a coffin pushed deep within to shelter it from the weather. These coffins are made of machine-cut pine, which is nip to the cynics, but no one in Tinton denies that the coffins are new, for the boxes are replaced yearly at a midsummer rite called the Bearing.

I was gripped when first I heard of the Bearing. A man I knew from the settlement of Mind, Naheev, had told me about the rite. He'd been trying to take part for years but was always refused, ostensibly because it was a village affair only, yet I suspected because his motives for asking—to debunk—were not well hidden. In June, however, a friend from Tinton telephoned Naheev saying they needed bearers that year. I asked him to take me along.

"You'll be working a good few hours," the contact, de Frees, said. "Heavy weights, and we start at dusk."

"There's a medical as well," Naheev put in.

I laughed. I believed he was joking.

Come the evening, I was nervous. From the moor road nothing of Tinton can be seen. The dale is small, and the two great tors rise into visibility, and only at the edge of the dale where Leaping Tor falls into the depression does the visitor see the roofs of the village. The dwellings look drowned in gorse. Two streams carry rainwater from the moorland, the largest leading through the valley before diving under the ground towards Annesdock. In the village, the streets wind around the two monoliths and the baby, New Tor, is circled entirely by cottages like a carousel. As de Frees showed us the village, I was struck by how enclosed everything appeared, the ring of hills above and the presence of the two huge tors dwarfing all. I felt I was walking between two Neolithic cathedrals.

As de Frees showed us around the village, he pointed out the original cottages, renovated now with thatch and tiny, each whitewashed. Through one cottage a boulder had once fallen from New Tor, killing all inside one dark night. Although re-built, the house retained the slight twist the knock had given it.

About a third of the houses were on the level ground around the tors, the green in the centre holding the village focus. Where the dale rose in the east, three crescent terraces formed the remainder of the dwellings. The houses were functional, as expected from old workers' cottages, and not neatened with the touristic lipstick of trimmed lawns, hanging baskets, drawn curtains. The tiny supermarket had no trinkets or souvenirs or information leaflets. Tinton was nowhere and wanted nothing from outsiders.

There was a post office, a small supermarket, two pubs and Kenneth's Shop. Kenneth's Shop was a place of no use and all: the long-dead Kenneth had opened his rooms to whoever had a trade. The seller-of-woven-things had once worked out of the shop. Kenneth's grandson was now a shoe mender, key cutter and a fixer of odd things. De Frees told me the grandson charged one pound for a customer to tell him what problem needed fixing, and for this pound he'd give an honest appraisal of whether he could help. He could rarely help, de Frees said, and he kept the pound. The man was generous with space, however, as other rooms currently housed a hairdresser, a charity shop and (sharing) a reflexologist and a person-centred counsellor.

The villagers I saw were contained, not unfriendly as such but a stranger was noticed. A noticing eye has a fraction more weight than another eye—certainly a city eye—and the wary attention soon built up to something I could feel on my skin.

I assumed Naheev had taken me along for company. He didn't appear to like me very much. We met at the good pub, The Shadow (short for In the Shadow of the Dovecot). Naheev's pose of world-weary doubt began to wear on me at once. Little is more tedious than a full-time cynic. In the Mind community where we'd met, he was ignorable as he was part of a crowd. Here he was ever-present and unendurably brash. Conversation with him never seemed to sit right in the air, and it took time to realise he was angling for a place to compete. He looked for subjects we had in common, not so we could discuss but so he could probe for gaps in my knowledge or understanding that he could then gnaw at. Unsatisfying for him was my refusal to engage, and lack of competition baffled him, leaving him angry and peculiarly hurt.

"Why did they allow us to take part?" I asked.

"Hubris," Naheev replied. "It gets them every time."

This was not true as we soon found out when the promised medical came. In the middle of a pub we were told to roll up our arms, scales were brought out, a stethoscope. In a pub, the sight was ridiculous.

"This is necessary, is it?" I asked.

De Frees smiled. "A number of the villagers failed the fitness test this year." There was iron in his eye and voice. "If they hadn't, you and your friend wouldn't be here. We would have no need of you."

He took my height and weight and asked the strength of my glasses. He took my blood pressure, then had me run from the pub to the massive tor three times before he measured how long it took my breathing to return to normal. Strangest, he used a T-square to assess the slope of my shoulders. Throughout, he was polite but rigid.

"That was undignified," I muttered to Naheev.

"I'm fitter than you," he replied.

At dusk de Frees collected us. We walked out into the gloom of the high summer evening to find the green between Dovecot Tor and Leaping Tor filled with villagers. I knew no one else, and the exposure to so many silent and ill-seen strangers was disquieting. I counted the figures on the grass, which was difficult at dusk where clothes and bodies vanished into the shadowed earth and faces were indistinct.

"What is that? Fifty?" I whispered to Naheev.

"Forty-two," he replied, "including us."

Our contact beckoned us onto the green. We were all adults from late teens to sixties, more men than women. From Dovecot Tor, now a black mass in front of the evening sky, came scraping sounds like wood long sawn.

"It is the night of the Bearing," intoned a woman at the edge of the green. Her voice was low and carried. "We've new bearers tonight, and our thoughts go to the villagers who can no longer participate. Treat our new friends well, and remember they are not familiar with the village so do not hurry them. Especially as night falls."

Laughter, a sound that fell dead in the air.

"What is the request we make on the Bearing?"

No one replied. An old man made an exasperated noise and called, "Who is home, goat foot, who is home? Awaken if you're alive alone. Who is home, goat foot, who is home?"

Naheev, under his breath, said, "Bloody hellfire."

"Thank you, Eric," called the woman.

Eric kept the chant going, speaking with mustering arms trying to get all together in chorus. The chant was repeated once, twice, the crowd getting louder and louder until the woman called halt, laughing. Applause broke out like a scattering of hail on glass.

From Dovecot Tor, the scraping and muted swearing

continued, with odd moments of distant bellowed ruin as something fell and cracked on the dark heights.

De Frees and a fellow walked through the crowd. Certain of us were indicated with a touch on the shoulder, six per group. At first it was the tallest, then a six of the second-most tall. The sixes were sized to be as similar in height as possible. On the third pick, I was touched and pulled away from Naheev. He shrugged as I questioned him with my eyes. He was among the last picked.

By now, I understood what was happening. The noises at the tor were the seven coffins being brought down from the high caves, and we seven sixes were pallbearers. Night was falling, and the high striated light of midsummer was beginning to fade. I could see little, and when my pall group introduced themselves—four men, one woman—I doubted I'd recognise any of them by day. I said my hellos. I must have looked nervous as a man called Zoellick said, "It's fine. Everything is fine."

Nothing felt fine. I was both excited and in a high state of alert. I knew no one save Naheev, now separated from me. I'm naturally sociable, but somehow the sociability did not click in given that the faces of the others in my group were so indistinct. Reduced of senses, the human mind fills in fears and kicks out composure like a dog burying its bone in the brain. I felt nude, exposed, and I wished there was more light so I could see the faces of my fellow pallbearers well.

"I'm from Sevenston," I said to Helen.

"I'm from here," she replied.

One by one the coffins that had been tugged from the high dark caves of Dovecot Tor were carried on to the green. I had never been close to a coffin, not even open caskets when young. The rough wooden lozenge was a hazy blonde presence between the six of us. It struck me that where a spider's legs meet a flat surface outlines a coffin. I bent to touch an area of dark in the lid near the foot. The mark was a brand identifying the wood as originating from *Bippin's DIY*.

Zoellick was the head of our pall. "You know this, I'm sure, but just to repeat," he said, nodding at me, "outside hand grips the handle. Inside shoulder and hand takes the weight." He mimed the lift. "Feel for the cutaway on the underside with your fingers. The head and the foot of the coffin will be most stretched. We'll rotate to the middle if need be. Just call to say *middle* or *change* if you're feeling the weight. But beware of the changeover." He looked at me. "One hand must be on the coffin at all times. Each house must be visited once. There are sixty-three in the village. When each has been asked, we return to the rock." He pointed to Dovecot Tor, the huge mass stark against what was left of the summer light, his arm all but invisible against it. "I propose we start at Trelith Street."

The pall laughed. The man behind me saw my lack of understanding. "It's the top of the village," he explained. "All downhill from there. Half the houses are in three terraces." He saw that nothing of this was reaching my understanding. "We always start at Trelith Street," he said. "That's the joke."

"Did he say *sixty-three* houses?"

"Yes."

De Frees had said *heavy weights* but what was being suggested—to carry a coffin to all those houses—seemed without hope of success. To call a halt was impossible, however, both for social prohibition and because I was an invited stranger, but also because the other coffins were already going up on shoulders. Each one had six candles waxed onto the spine of the lid, each candle a different shape and at a different rate of burn. Zoellick handed me one to prepare the end for gluing to the box and, like the others, I screwed and held my candle until the wax stuck it to the roof of the coffin.

Other palls were moving now, the lights robbing what light there was left in the day, their bodies in shadow until they reached the light cast by the burning candles. Their movement was awkward as they found their feet and began to walk up the hill to what I assumed was Trelith Street. Each procession was a giant insect stalking off into the night, fire along its spine. I should have been rapt, but in truth my mind was baulking at the effort it was going to take to complete the night. *Sixty-three houses*, I thought. It would be hours.

Zoellick spoke. "On three," he said. He mimed the lift again. "One, two, three—"

I imitated the movement: a lift then fingers feeling for the wooden nook underneath as the weight hit my collar bone. We were moving before I fully had either grip or weight.

I'd never before had to carry a coffin. Tradition has the only word on who shoulders the weight at such times and I was never so called. For the slow climb up to the corner of Trelith Street, my mind paid no attention to the weight or the darkness or the (to be frank) pain of the rough wood and biting angles of the box. My head was overtaken with the urgent need to learn how to walk in a group. I'd been placed in the middle, kindness to the novice I assumed, but this was confusing as I neither led nor followed. I had to learn the pall's speed and stride length, yet also not take any time to think in case I dawdled into the feet of the bearer at the rear. This reality took all of my mind, and the experience was terrifying. At any moment I thought I'd stumble and bring all of us down. Occasionally I connected with the bearer behind, his toe to my heel, and a flood of panic pooled into my belly that this was it: we'd tangle and fall to the ground, our cargo shattering open on the stones.

Zoellick kept up a patter motivating and warning. "Pull right," he said. "Mind shoe cleaning irons outside houses.

"We're on the last fifty yards of the hill.

"Pothole.

"Nettles.

"*This* is the last fifty yards.

"A wanker of a cat on the right.

"Steps.

"Last fifty yards now."

"You're a swine, Zoellick."

Between one step and the next, a rhythm came upon us. It felt miraculous, imposed from without, but my rising panic and skittering steps found order and we were one. We'd become a unit by virtue or vice of necessity, and this rhythm never left us again for the whole night, even when directly threatened.

Turning onto Trelith Street was a sight I will not long forget. There are nights when the vision is integral to my dreams, and other nights when I see, despite the central focus of my dream, the procession on a high distant hill. We were sixth in a line of seven with the five ahead of us moving slow and mysterious, candles stotting and guttering in the night. Some flames had already been blown out. Below the handles of each coffin nothing was visible so each seemed a boat floating in the night with human heads bobbing alongside, three per flank, like buoys or tyres tied to protect the sides. Because it was near full dark, our time and place in history vanished as if a holding pin on the year had been pulled and the village had fallen centuries into the past.

Yet to the ear, everything was today. Voices, laughter and shouts of encouragement fed back as the coffins ahead of us began to call at the houses. Objects were being passed out, and children held up by adults relit candles whose flames had been extinguished by the wind or the journey—

"Stop," said the man next to Zoellick at the head, a man whose face I couldn't see.

We stopped. The man swore floridly. Now that my mind had shaken off the fear of falling, new realities were free to move into my awareness. The first was that I was panting with exertion: the threatened breath of lungs not deep enough to hold the air needed. I was drenched with sweat and my throat in the summer night held a wheeze from pollen and a dryness from the dust in the air.

Once stopped, my breathlessness was a fright, and still we had to hold the coffin aloft while we caught our breath, which is where I became aware of a thing true all along but not fully acknowledged. As we breathed, out of rhythm and still, the bones in the coffin moved with the rocking.

The reality of the occupant came home with a shock. In truth, the coffin was not as heavy as I'd imagined and the bulk of the weight was clearly the wood. That the box held something inside I'd successfully put out of mind, but now we were breathing hard the presence of bones became horribly real, and most real and most horrible was that the rocking movement given the skeleton inside could be read by my shoulder and hands.

Next to my ear, an object shifted how it sat inside. I read it as a three-legged stool with one short leg teetering as we panted. It must have been the head of the femur, or the leathered pelvis. Elsewhere inside the box were related shiftings, some like a mug poorly set on a table and tapping as it settles, others like chocolate snapped in the wrapper. A vivid memory came of seeing a prank in school. A football had burst and become useless, and some lads had filled it with mud then encouraged a boy they thought a fool to take a run up and kick it. The boy took his run and when he connected with the ball, his foot stopped dead, his whole body pitching forward until he took the ground with his face. Something like that mud-weighted burst football was inside the box, and I could read these movements through the wood: images of bones, rubbing spurs and hollows, leather and heavy dust that I imagined I was inhaling.

Soon we were moving again. A surprise was at house number one, the first in Trelith Street. We lined up at the door, the interior unlit. My breath had not fully returned and I did not take part in the chant—

> *Who is home, goat foot, who is home?*
> *Awaken if you're alive alone.*
> *Who is home, goat foot, who is home?*

The answer returned fast, one child's high voice gleefully and lustily calling back at us—

> *All's abed. No one's alone.*
> *No one's awoken. No one's home.*

A man came out with a boy on his shoulders. Some of our candles were out so the little lad relit them. His father held a small tray. Zoellick ensured his weight was taken on his shoulder, reached down and took a glass from the tray. It was tiny, holding perhaps a shot of black liquid, and he knocked it back fast, replacing it on the tray.

The father came to me. "What is it?" I asked.

"Black porter," said Zoellick. "Drink it."

Refusal didn't sound like an option. I knocked it back. It had the dark, urinous kick of an ale in the seven-per-cent range.

The same happened at the next house—

> *Who is home, goat foot, who is home?*
> *Awaken if you're alive alone.*
> *Who is home, goat foot, who is home?*

> *All's abed. No one's alone.*
> *No one's awoken. No one's home.*

If this was a pattern, I thought, we were looking at over six pints each by the end of the houses. I took my hand off the handle and tapped Zoellick. "I'll be hammered if I drink that much," I said.

"Change," he said.

He motioned for me to take his place at the head. As we delicately swapped, Helen opposite me moving forward as well, he told me, "You don't feel it. I know it seems a lot. It's mostly hydration and energy."

I doubted this as I was already feeling it. Porter is black and bloody, and I could feel it in my stomach, hot as if the brewer himself was in there rubbing his hands.

Ten houses, twenty houses, thirty houses came and went. I was in torment. There was no light save stars and candles, and by the third hour of the Bearing my internal tally put me at around three pints, yet it was impossible to tell if my unsteady legs were the result of the black porter or the pall. Worst of all was the pain. As time went on there was less energy to keep the edge of the coffin from rubbing into the skin. Now I was at the rear I could see the man Brian was bleeding from where the edge had bitten into his neck, and I was convinced I myself had blisters and splinters. I wanted it all to end, yet I could not be the one to call halt. I would not for pride, especially not to lose face in front of Naheev, but mostly because I was determined to succeed. The rite felt like a communal triumph and one that spoke of sacrifice and ordeal. There has always been something in me that is drawn to the ordeal. The labours of Hercules. The Christ. Marathon.

The coffin shifted and I felt something—cloth—tear at my shoulder. "Change," I called.

Zoellick read my face. "What say we hold with our feet," he said. "Take a minute. Switch sides. Do the next bit on a new shoulder."

The move was complicated. Lift, two hands, lower and shuffle our boots under the base of the coffin. My shoulder swelled into its pain.

"Remember. The coffin cannot touch the ground. We must protect the soil."

One by one, we stepped over the box while the others held the weight. Soon we'd all swapped sides and places, and I was again in the middle. To be free of the weight was bliss before the pain set in. Zoellick relit the candles and in the light I saw clearly the faces of my fellows for the first time: sweat-stained, red, dusty. Brian's shirt front held a line of red where he'd bled from his neck. He seemed pleased with the stain.

"We can go through the ford," Zoellick said, "or over the bridge and round to Leaping Tor."

"What's easier?" I replied.

Laughter. "Much of a muchness," Helen replied. "It's level from here, but the houses are further apart."

Endurance and a refusal to submit kept me going. The effort was the kind that required mind management to ignore, the setting of incremental goals on breath and feet. *The next house. The postbox sunk into the stone. That tree. The next house.*

"There's the bridge," Helen called.

Another coffin was going over now. I could hear the creak of the wooden ties. Naheev's pall. At either end of the bridge, torches burned and as the group passed into the light I saw Naheev's face. The man looked like he'd been crying. He looked ruined.

We were now at the oldest part of the village. I was drunk, no disputing it. The night began to dislocate my awareness to the point I felt outside myself. Somewhere in the darkness a part of me untethered from my human mind and looked back on my suffering. When Zoellick called fifty houses, I wanted to scream, just scream into the night because I'd gone through all possible stations of pain and was without impetus to take another step, yet somehow I found the wherewithal to go on.

> *Who is home, goat foot, who is home?*
> *Awaken if you're alive alone.*
> *Who is home, goat foot, who is home?*

> *All's abed. No one's alone.*
> *No one's awoken. No one's home.*

The taste of the black porter made me feel sick. It was hitting us all now. Dimly, I remember thinking this made sense as we were all picked the same size. At house fifty-one, hilarity kicked in. We passed another pall resting their box on their boots and abused them cruelly, jeering at their laziness. Fifty-two, fifty-three.

We fell into giggles on the chant at fifty-four—

> *Who is home, goat foot, who is home?*
> *Awaken if you're alive alone.*
> *Who is home, goat foot, who is home?*

—and were told, somewhat sternly by the woman of the house, to *do it properly.* This made a second then third attempt even more ragged.

> *All's abed. No one's alone.*
> *No one's awoken. No one's home.*

I was pissed now, numb of mind and limb and scarcely of the world. Fifty-five, fifty-six. We were at the oldest cottages that ring New Tor, thankfully close together. It was past midnight. High on Dovecot Tor, lights flickered where the first coffins were being hauled to the top. Their torment was over.

From our vantage point the transport up looked like a detail from *The Wreck of the Medusa* or André Derain's *Calvary*.

"Do we have to do that?" I managed to get out.

"Yes, though once we reach the rock, the others will help."

We stopped at the fifty-seventh house.

Who is home, goat foot, who is home?
Awaken if you're alive alone.
Who is home, goat foot, who is home?

A bang came from inside the coffin behind my head.

I was at the front. *A candle has fallen*, I thought. I laughed. The family at the door did not respond. The mother began to moan. *No. No. Not us.* They didn't repeat their side of the chant. My smile faltered—

"Shouldn't you—?"

A little girl at the door hissed, "No one *wants* you."

The door slammed. Behind it, the mother began to scream.

"Isn't it—?" I began.

"Brace yourself, Ravenel. It's us. We are the Bearing."

I turned to Zoellick. We were both at the front of the coffin, and he was hunkering down, forcing me to lower with him. The first notes of alarm took hold of me. The others were lowering behind and across from me, putting a bracing weight onto their outer foot and leaning into the coffin. I had about done the same when three hard knocks came from inside the box.

A candle, secure for hours, fell and rolled off spilling burning wax on my face.

The box was suddenly live as if the body had awoken within, but the presence within was larger, stronger, and in moments hammering mad inside. Nails scraped the inside of the coffin, roaring past my ear on the other side of the wood. The weight became impossible to balance as the force within moved from side to side and corner to corner.

256

What had been pain and endurance became a battle. Much of the last section of the ordeal is missing because the need to keep upright, but also not face whatever was inside the box, gathered my memory into a knot of panic. The *thing* within shrieked and hammered, unsettling our balance and centre of gravity.

We fought to the next house. Zoellick was the only one with wherewithal to call—

> *Who is home, goat foot, who is home?*
> *Awaken if you're alive alone.*
> *Who is home, goat foot, who is home?*

—and again there was no answer. The door was open, but the man standing there did not greet us. He let his tray of black porter fall, the glass shattering at our feet. The family looked at us with contempt and when we turned to leave, slammed the door.

We were passed by the last coffin, the seventh, as reposeful as all the others. Passing was not easy as we were buffeted side-to-side, all fight and adrenaline. The seventh pall looked terrified and despite their obvious weariness began to jog to outpace us.

> *Who is home, goat foot, who is home?*
> *Awaken if you're alive alone.*
> *Who is home, goat foot, who is home?*

The *thing* within the coffin began to scream.

The presence seemed to be moving inside so the voice—if it can be called such—felt as though it was calling in turn at all six corners of the coffin. There were no words. Certain syllables were repeated, but my memory tells me the screams were more animal than human, yet structured as the calls of a bird might be. A goat syllabary or hyena-like hunt-songs.

"Shuffle," called Zoellick. "On three—"

I cannot now stop thinking of the coffin as a boat, a boat where the physical universe was inverted and the storm was within the vessel. This was my experience, like a sailor at battle with the elements except the battle was not to ride out the storm but to contain it within the timbers.

We could not keep still at the houses, and the hits from inside and the noise bellowing through the wood made it hard to hear our chant. This did not seem to matter as the inhabitants, with stares of hatred, held the shot glasses out and poured black porter on the ground. After each silent rejection the force within got louder and stronger.

One hit, as if all of us had been rammed by a bus, felled me. "Hold," Zoellick shouted. "Hold, hold." My leg gave and I landed on my knee, the coffin weight driving down onto that pivot, the others fighting to keep the storm from touching the ground.

The pain worked through my drunkenness. I looked up at the man who was standing in the dark doorway. "My knee," I said. "Can you help me up?"

He spat on the ground in front of me, backed into the house and shut the door. The same absence: silence, ceremonial denial of the black porter, and the feeling we'd turned into the most loathed of beggars because of the load we were bearing.

The turn in the night filled me with embarrassment and fear. Nothing is more socially awkward than finding the laughter has stopped around you, and you can't help but search for something that you have done to explain why the goodwill of others has so suddenly been snatched away with no understanding of why it has been withheld. I saw the man's spit bubble on the ground, a grub of phlegm in the mess of it like birdshit. I was wounded. I didn't understand why we had to go on. I was in pain, embarrassed, terrified and angry all at the same time.

I cannot recall the last houses with any clarity. My knee barely held and the pain travelled everywhere in my body. Our buffeted progress was slow. Behind, under the muted shrieks from the wood, one of my fellows was weeping. To this day it is impossible for me to understand how we kept going. I also ask myself why I continued. I had no investment in the rite, and I could have walked away, but something held me and not just the lock ritual puts on a person's will: the immense inhibiting power of a social shackle. The reason for my persistence was that I was observed, and that if I failed in my task my failure would be witnessed.

Later Naheev described how we looked as we moved away from the last house, away from the rejecting silence, and carried the thing across the green—

"It was like a runaway horse I saw when I was travelling in South America," he said. "The farmers there had no tranquillisers so if a colt ran wild, hordes of scared men paced alongside the panicked horse until they had it pressed against a wall or a building. They were gentle but maintained the pressure on it, holding it from moving and desperate not to be kicked, until it gradually sank to the ground where they could pacify it. You looked the same, but for you there was no wall."

Now there was only the stretch over the green to Dovecot Tor. Behind us lay a silent village, all houses locked. We staggered towards the light on the rock: thirty-six people on the tor, each holding a candle, staring out at our approach.

The storm increased its raging, trying to make us fall. The end was there before us, however, and in no time we'd rushed our burden to the foot of the tor and rested it on the rock.

"We have her," said de Frees.

I looked up at his face. He seemed rested now, but with the beer-beady eyes of someone drunk.

The banging and the screams grew louder and, without us six bracing, the box shifted bodily on the granite ledge. Ropes were fixed to the side handles and the coffin dragged up and up, past the caves to the top of the tor.

We climbed too. In the darkness, it was petrifying to be drunk, limbs like old celery, climbing ladders set into the rock. At the top, above the village, forty-two people stood, packed into the space and only a lightless drop to death all around us. Stars and moon and finally the chance to breathe easily. We were filthy, and stank, and now the effort was gone cold set in. At the edge of the tor the seven coffins were lined up, one still moving as whatever was in there shrieked.

I kept close to Zoellick.

"What happened here?" I asked.

"The necessary."

"What woke in the coffin?"

"Not the dead."

"What came home?"

Zoellick touched my arm. "No one knows the answers to those questions now, Ravenel."

I looked down at the village. The house where the coffin had awoken was so dark it looked gone.

"That house is dark."

He hesitated. "Yes. Yes, I'm afraid it is."

"Someone screamed inside."

"Yes."

Six people stepped forward. They took hold of their coffin for the last time and threw it off the top of the tor. Far below the box smashed, and inside the splintering sound of the wood there was a softer clatter. The body. Again, again. When we stepped forward, I took a look over the edge. There was a promontory perhaps fifteen feet below us and twenty feet above the ground. This place was ringed with candles, a boneyard with all the broken coffins and the contents spilled within the circle of light. We took our battered and still moving coffin and threw it over the side.

An unnaturally white creature, not human, fell from our coffin as it shattered. It righted itself on its feet and fled into the night. I heard it canter down to the bottom of the tor then out into the darkness.

I wanted the thing to run out of my life, but it did not. Once far from the tor, the creature stopped and turned back to regard us, just intuitable in the dark, a stag-like quality in its stance, a swept-back sharpness to the skull, eyes with a green glint in the night. Whatever it was regarded us, sometimes pacing but always returning to stare as we climbed down to the boneyard for the bones.

My muscles were stiff now, my skin cold. I kept looking out there into the darkness, fearful that if I turned my back on whatever had fled, it would come for me, come in revenge. Seven new coffins stood upright against the cliff wall. They were lowered and the bones were passed in: seven bodies in all, shattered after so many rites but still held together by mummified leather and what cartilage still had grip. I could not touch the corpse so I helped gather the wood of the broken coffins into a bonfire. Hammers knocked nails in and some men who had remained aloft pulled the new coffins up by rope and slotted them into the caves for the next year.

I could still see the one dark house.

I was cold as meat now. Naheev avoided me, and I did not want to talk to him. I did not want him to talk to me. I did not want him to question me for I'd no answers for that last half an hour where we were transporting a *thing* at the end of its tether to the gallows. A *thing* that was not human but that understood mortality. Naheev would want me to doubt, to argue, to discuss how the trick been achieved. There was no trick. I'd passed beyond all doubt. We had carried something that feared its own death and at the end of my life, if not lucky enough to die in my sleep, I would one day face that same terror myself. We'd driven it demented and then we'd freed it.

I then saw all the villagers approach the tor and stand in the shadow. Silent, they waited. Hundreds of people in the darkness. They'd left all their lights burning and their doors open, but one house remained dark.

Zoellick put his hand on my shoulder. "It's out there," I said, "looking back towards the village. Watching."

"It'll move on soon enough."

"When?" He didn't answer. I said, "There's something about the dark house. Something you won't tell me."

"Yes."

"The dark house is its home."

"Yes."

"It was like a stag," I whispered, "but scalped. As if a knife had cut at its eyes and pulled backwards, taking off its velvet, horns, even ears."

"Yes. Or no." He shuffled his feet, looking at the rock. "You saw a stag. I saw a girl, sleek and hairy as an otter." He nodded to Helen. "Helen saw a goat. One year a bird like a bag of hooks circled the fire." He shook his head. "It's a thirst incarnate. Havoc. The soul of the moor. We don't know. We only know that the ritual is necessary."

The old coffins were in the bonfire. The flames grew high. The smell was peculiar: new wood but something else, something sweet like plum wine. The burning wood loosed curious colours in the flames. I wondered if they were contaminants, human dust, perhaps tin and rock filth. I realised the smell must be the odour of the ancient bones the coffin had inhaled for a year before the Bearing. The thought made me sick, but by this time more of the black porter had been circulated and I was drunk, drunk and seeing only the green glint of whatever had been freed staring at us as it moved towards the still dark house.

ST. SEVERINA'S FIRE

by Damian Murphy

"Saints live in flames; wise men, next to them."
(Emil Cioran, *Saints and Tears*)

6 November

IT seems that my disease has again been resurrected. Yesterday, in the quiet hours of late evening, my symptoms returned to me. I spent the night in the embrace of a dispassionate god and have emerged into a world renewed by antipathy and paperwork. This has been the first such incident in several months. The attacks go dormant on occasion, as if the font of Heaven's vitriol runs dry from time to time and must replenish itself. This marks the fourteenth instance on which I have undergone the deluge. After the waves rolled back and I had more or less recovered, I was moved to purchase a journal. I have not written about my episodes before, for fear that doing so would somehow taint them. I will write about them now.

Beneath the stairway that rises from the foyer of my employer's house lies an intimate little sitting area enclosed by panels of stained wood. Several niches open up in the latter, housing books, mounted globes, framed maps, and alabaster statuettes. A single table and two wooden chairs reside amidst the modest decoration. After my first night in his house, Kasper invited me to sit with him in this alcove and to share a bottle of wine. He is a taciturn and lonely man, not given to intimate friendships. Though he knows not a single thing about me, I can be certain that he's grateful for my company.

We sat beneath a profuse arrangement of bright yellow bulbs, their garish light reflected in the Sylvaner in our glasses. Kasper had pulled a slender volume from between two horse-head bookends in one of the niches. He placed this face-up on the table before him, pushing it across the surface for my perusal. "Not infrequently," he said with some amusement, "I find that this particular item has been put back in a different place upon the shelf than where I'd left it." The front of the book, which was perfectly square, betrayed little more than a textured red surface, in the center of which was found a square of black paper with a title in gold letters: *Indiscretions of the Sacred Heart*. "I suspect that Ignacius sometimes pulls it out and peruses its pages," said my host. "No doubt he does this while his mother is fast asleep. I can only imagine the pleasure he felt when he'd first discovered the collection. The boy's dreams must be visited by the most delightful visions."

Opening the book to a page near the center, I was greeted with a photograph of a woman attired in the official raiments of the Church. A section of her tunic was unbuttoned and held open on one side to reveal a naked breast. Her eyes were cast toward heaven as if her pose was part and parcel of the sign of the cross. On the opposing page was found the name of St. Adelina of Segovia along with her feast day and a short, salacious prayer. A decorative icon, in full color, appeared just above the text, an illustration in gold and scarlet of the licentious woman exactly as she appeared in the photograph. Turning to the following page, I found a similar arrangement, this one for St. Méline. Here, an entirely different model revealed her uncovered backside as she bowed low upon her knees to kiss the foot of a white altar.

"It was purchased in a Catholic bookshop in Bruges," said Kasper, both hands folded on the table beside his glass. "I can't imagine that the proprietor knew what lay between its covers. He took my money with good cheer as if I were buying a medal of St. Christopher."

I tried to picture my new employer paying a visit to such an establishment, with his trim beard and circular spectacles. One immediately becomes suspicious in his presence. While he's incapable of seeing beyond the surface of the world, he seems to wield that surface as a mirror. This he makes use of in insidious ways, much like a schoolboy will sometimes wield the glass in order to peer beneath a woman's dress.

I flipped through a series of lascivious images, only vaguely interested in what they had to offer, until I came to the entry for St. Severina. Beyond this point I could proceed no further. There was nothing in the photograph itself that was radically different from the others. The woman pictured was no more evocative than those on the previous pages. She was seated in an open confessional beneath a statue of the crucifixion. Her fingers stroked the intricate formations of the wooden screen beside her, her eyes peering through the tiny openings as if in observance of a cardinal sin on the other side. Not a stitch of clothing concealed her body. A little light shone from overhead, its meager glow caressing her immaculate flesh like the descending hand of grace.

I was certain that the saint, whose name was previously unknown to me, had been with me in spirit from the time I was a child. Though I'd not laid eyes on the image before, it was as familiar to me as the lines in my own face. It didn't matter that the model had no relation to the martyr that she was supposed to represent. If the latter chose to speak to me through such an unlikely medium, I was left with little choice but to receive her revelation.

"There are sins that I would happily confess to if only I could manage to commit them," sighed my employer. I gave a brief nod of concordance as my eyes remained riveted to the page. The tendrils of my disease had already begun to take hold of me. My vision grew crisp. The surrounding hues became more vibrant. My body began to recede into the distance as my thoughts grew crystal clear. These sensations were not new to me. I had an hour, at most, before my nervous system slipped entirely from my control. I was unable to take my eyes from the icon of the saint—an unclothed woman that cradled the languid petals of a white poppy in one outstretched palm while a flame rose from the hollow of her opposing fist. The symbolic depiction appeared to me to codify my condition, just as my current symptoms seemed to emanate from the body of the saint herself. I hadn't breathed a word about my illness to my new employer. I'm still not certain that I want to do so. I rose from the table without further delay, excusing myself under the pretense of fatigue exacerbated by the effects of the wine.

"Of course," said Kasper. "You've had a long day of training, after all. Tomorrow morning, we continue."

I ascended the wooden stairway beneath a row of yellow bulbs that overflowed their containing lamps. They seemed to multiply above me as if reflected in a mirror, losing nothing of their effulgence as their number grew. The light they shed lent substance to the anaesthetizing fire that spread throughout my body. By the time I reached the topmost stair I was aflame from within. I slipped around the corner as if pulled on threads of gossamer, entranced by such trivialities as the variation of the wood grain on the paneled walls.

Just before I stepped into the safety of my tiny bedroom, I saw Emma emerge from hers. For nearly a decade, I'm to understand, she's lived in the exact same quarters. Her son sleeps in the room with her. The latter more or less has the run of the house during the daytime—Kasper remains sequestered in his upstairs office as the boy's mother tends to an endless array of minor tasks and repairs. Mute since birth, Ignatius is an enigma in impeccable dress. Endowed with an acuity that far surpasses my own, he is anything but mentally impaired. Where Kasper comes off as untrustworthy, this young man seems positively dangerous. The two tend to avoid each other as if by a natural antipathy.

Having no desire to confront the stolid maid, I ducked into my sanctuary and softly closed the door behind me. My fingers fumbled for a while in the darkness before locating the lamp on the dresser opposite the bed. Already, the coloration of the lamp's marble base had begun to give rise to a rich tapestry of images. I let myself gently fall back onto the bed sheets, propping myself against one wall as my symptoms continued to run their course. They'd progressed more swiftly this time than they had before. I suspect that the icon of the saint acted as a sort of catalyst. In a matter of minutes, the sun that was dawning inside of me would completely eclipse my senses.

Closing my eyes, I was dismayed to find that I had lost my capacity for darkness. In its place extended a solid sheet of pulsating white flame. This stretched to all sides, consuming the horizons and continuing without end. Fragmented images appeared before me as if etched into its surface: cathedrals circumscribed by processions of holy men, city squares illuminated by the high flames of open lamps, an insurrection in a swiftly moving railway carriage, a catacomb besieged by a contentious swarm of doves and sparrows. Each vision emerged only briefly before giving way to the next. I knew from experience that these were little more than phantoms, similar to the imagery that passes through the mind on the threshold of unconsciousness. This notwithstanding, I was unable to stop myself from seeking meaningful connections within them. They carried the weight of aberrations in the architecture of Heaven. As I had so many times before, I began to long for the simplicity of idle thoughts.

There are certain phenomena that remain constant throughout every instance of my attacks. The first, and perhaps the most dire, is an escalating sense of loss of control. This is followed by a loss of self-perception, giving rise to the impression that the visions are witnessed not by me but by themselves. As my hallucinations grow more dense, the sequence progresses into a single, continuous transmission—unchanging, timeless, and monotonous. This all-consuming signal appears to be endowed with neither beginning nor end. The experience is of such immensity that, were I capable of thought, I would reflect that the world had exhausted its continuity.

How long this phase of my illness lasts, I cannot say. I lose all sense of time as the malady progresses. There is only an indifferent and impersonal Absolute. This comes to subsume everything, dissolving every measure of eternity into an ocean without bounds. Eventually, I find that I've returned to myself, though I have no sense of when this may have happened. Several hours have gone by in the meantime. There is a slight sense of astonishment that everything in my environment is precisely as it was before.

Within an hour after my return, I find that my faculties have restored themselves as if they'd never been disrupted. The uncreated fire seems to pass right through me, leaving nothing of itself during its passage. I seem hardly to be affected at all by these experiences, except in one particular regard: I'm left with an unshakeable conviction that the thread of history has been prematurely severed. The world that I return to has no precedence, no past, no relation to the one that I inhabited before. It would seem to have emerged, fully formed and with its own internal logic, directly from the mouth of the ineffable. This notion gradually loses its hold on me as time progresses, yet it never leaves me completely.

There are other minor deficiencies that have remained with me as a result of my fugues. I've become increasingly distracted by irrational obsessions—the existence of rare ores beneath the surface of the earth; the prospect of an uncommon and ignoble blood; the effusions of a distant star; subtle changes in magnetic charge; and the affinities of particular minerals. Certain classes of phenomena are not sufficiently refined to be apprehended by the intellect. There is an unspoken language of impulse and conviction known only to the body. Through this mechanism alone have I come to be attracted to a star in the northern heavens above the shoulder of Auriga, the charioteer. It seems to broadcast unintelligible tidings from its place above the constellation, eliciting subtle responses within the depths of my body. This morning, as I came back to my senses on the bed of my windowless room, I was given to a fixation on the bond between this distant star and the pornographic image of my saint.

The remainder of the day was passed in the rapid acquisition of legal terms and technical procedures. It came as somewhat of a relief, in the wake of my experience, to be able to apply myself to something of such minor importance. On my lunch break, I procured two notebooks on the pretext of recording the salient points of my instruction. Had I the slightest bit of interest in international customs and trade law, I might hope to replace Kasper's former assistant. As it is, a life devoted to a single profession is unthinkable to me. I am impervious to ambition, preferring to indulge in the luxury of a life without aim. I treat the world as if it were a sanatorium, and it, in turn, receives me like a convalescent.

I await, with trepidation, the onset of another attack. After the serpent has lain dormant for some months, it tends to wake from its slumber with an insatiable thirst. If past experience is any indication, I can expect the unruly beast to rear up and strike several times in quick succession. Once it's satiated, it will again pass into a narcotic trance and leave me in peace for a season or two.

My preoccupations have not diminished in tenacity or intensity. St. Severina's star becomes visible in the late evenings if the sky is clear. At the approach to midnight, she sheds her rays over the house from directly above. I can sense its radiation as I lie in my bed, though my little room is entirely cut off from the outside. This star alone, so I'm half-convinced, is immune to the fires that periodically incinerate my world.

I've taken, this past week, to pilfering eggs for Ignatius. He made his desire for them known to me late one evening after dinner. His mother, who, so far as I can tell, is entirely unaware of my existence, had already retreated upstairs. By the use of subtle gestures and insinuation, he managed to convey to me precisely what it was that he wanted.

Ignatius makes use of the silence that afflicts him like an instrument. He's able to wield it with astonishing delicacy, imparting complex shades of meaning that cannot be communicated with the spoken word. Mere speech seems intolerably crude next to his intricate command of facial expressions and hand signals. The boy is possessed of a degree of wit and acumen that makes him seem a good deal older than he is. All of this is kept well concealed from Kasper. As far as the latter is concerned, Ignatius is as senseless as he is dumb.

Following his unspoken request, I dutifully descended to the pantry and fetched a pair of eggs. He took one in each hand, his eyes conveying a frivolity of such sophistication that

I was unable to suppress a wry smile in response. He's since made it understood that I'm to deliver him a single egg each night. It pleases me to conspire with the young savant. There is a dubious prestige in acting as an accomplice to something that lies entirely beyond my comprehension. What he could possibly want with them, I haven't a clue. Something tells me that he doesn't intend to eat them.

Not infrequently, as the household sleeps, I creep down to the sitting area beneath the main stairway and revisit the pages of Kasper's book of saints. I was initially apprehensive at the prospect, lest my voyeurism trigger another attack. Thus far, I've managed to escape the onset of the familiar symptoms, though the icon of my chosen saint continues to elicit a peculiar response within me. There's something disarming about the painted woman's gaze. She seems to look right through me, training her attention instead upon the holy fire from which my world has so recently emerged. The flame that rises from her fist appears to surge and shimmer beneath the glow of the lamp above.

The images in the book are far more complex than they at first appear. While the majority of viewers will limit their attention to particular regions within the prints, the roving eye is rewarded with a surprising range of unexpected features. It's a simple matter to discern, based on the consistency of the décor, that the photographs were taken in a single church. A number of the images feature unexpected anomalies—open books left conspicuously lying on the floor, tapestries draped over the edges of benches, icons engraved directly into smooth white marble, among too many other things to mention. These items tend to lurk in the shadows and are often placed with considerable subtlety.

This is not the first time that I've noticed incongruent features concealed in erotic images. Often a model, bored to tears by several hour's worth of posing, will slip a book or a child's toy into the scene unnoticed. Sometimes the photographers themselves do the same. Publishers are not always ignorant of these measures. Much of the time they simply don't care, knowing that these things will be noticed only by the very few. The commercial world is rife with evidence of petty sabotage for those who know how to look.

The misplaced items found in this particular volume reveal a degree of strategy that rises above mere subterfuge. A tiny prayer book can be seen propped up against a pillar in one of the images. Such is the angle at which it leans against the base that the cover hangs open and a single page is visible. The shadow of the model herself lies like a shroud across the item, making it slightly difficult to discern its contents. A close inspection reveals an illustration of a wolf with a star between its jaws.

Other photographs reveal further oddities. A series of lurid paperbacks can be seen under the shelter of a wooden pew on one page. On another is found a decorated handkerchief beneath the circular base of a smoking censer. A series of lithographic images ingeniously placed behind a row of hanging stoles has left a particularly vivid impression upon me. The most pertinent among these include a lily suspended in a starless night sky above a house with no visible doors or windows, a circle of bees in flight around a flaming pillar, and a heavy key hung from a chain emerging from the mouth of a stone lion. So far as I can tell, St. Severina's page is the only one that remains unaffected by these abnormalities, though I can't escape the notion that something has been hidden inside the priest's compartment of the confessional. Perhaps the most startling of my discoveries is found in the image of St. Marquesa. What appears to be a hummingbird can just be discerned flitting behind a row of blazing candles, its tiny body slightly obscured by the blur of motion. The flames rise some distance above the body of the saintly woman as she kneels on the floor in prayer stance, a white shawl covering her pious head and shoulders while two petite white breasts remain exposed for all to see. The bird suggests a holy messenger, having taken on a sheath of feathers to deliver an epistle of the spirit to the faithful servant below.

For the most part, the other items on Kasper's shelf reveal little of note about the character of the man. The sole item of interest that I've managed to find is a short treatise on epilepsy housed in a tiny, yet luxurious edition. The banality of my employer is evident in nearly every aspect of his house. While his eye for ornament is impeccable, just as his taste in wine is above reproach, I can't help but feel that the entire world contains not a single thing that might excite his passion. His soul thirsts for a sacrament that doesn't exist, yet his longing is so constant that it passes unnoticed. The same could be said of myself, but for a single saving grace—I am pursued by the delirium of spiritual ecstasy. Were my derangement purely secular, it would be nothing more than mere pathology. The fact that I've framed it as an expression of the Absolute exalts my condition to a crowning of the spirit.

My training period is officially over now. I spend the long hours of my days engaged in gloriously tedious tasks. In the evenings, I dine out. A simple tavern is a house of God, a café a sanctuary of the inmost Mystery.

16 November

Still no trace of Heaven's fire. It appears that Severina would prefer to make me wait a little longer. I don't quite know whether I'm grateful or resentful. Whatever the case, I remain apprehensive. At any moment, the thread that binds one instant to the next may be irreparably cut, leaving me to drift like a ship without a rudder into the annihilating arms of the beloved of the saints.

Ignatius has adopted the habit of wielding an elaborate stick puppet. Where he might have obtained the thing, I can't begin to speculate. It seems to be of Southeast Asian origin. A colorful gown of silk and faux rubies conceals its body from the waist down, while the wooden head bears the unmistakable features of a monkey. Two arched eyebrows and a wide, chinless grin lend a markedly sardonic appearance to the creature. A decorative crown of gold and crimson rises from its brow. I'm given the impression of a cross between a comic villain and a duplicitous fakir.

The boy is nothing less than an adept in his control of the audacious toy. Though the face of the puppet is unchanging, Ignatius manages to make it imitate an impressive range of expressions. This, he accomplishes through an ingenious use of posture, angle, and motion. The figure is thus capable of displaying cruelty, mirth, consternation, or piety at the behest of its controller's skillful hands. Just this morning, as I sipped coffee with my employer in the nook beneath the stairs, the boy dashed recklessly past us as if in pursuit of the puppet. The thing almost seemed to move on its own, frantically rushing from one part of the house to another. An egg was cupped before him in his tiny wooden paws. He looked as if he held a time bomb that might detonate at any moment and desperately sought a safe place to dispose of it before the inevitable explosion. The frivolous image elicited a raise of my employer's eyebrows—a rare acknowledgement on his part of the boy's existence.

The puppet's actions are far more graceful when Kasper's eyes are turned away. In addition to a remarkable sophistication of wit, which inverts itself to the point of buffoonery in the presence of my host, Ignatius is given to an unexpected tenderness of hand. The subtlety of his manipulation elevates his control of the doll to the level of an art. His enthusiasm for his craft is absolute. Having not a single task or chore to divert his attention, his every moment is devoted to achieving progressively greater degrees of mastery.

The puppet carries with it the same infernal familiarity as do the icon of St. Severina and her star. I find myself imagining that its origin lies on the priest's side of the confessional in the photograph. I can almost imagine Ignatius retrieving the toy from the box, slipping in between the interstices that divide one world from the next by way of a mechanism known only to himself. His mother, far from discouraging her son's newfound obsession, seems tacitly to approve it as she dusts the crevices behind doors and polishes their elegant handles.

My interactions with the boy have been cast into a slightly different light following a recent encounter with Emma herself. Two nights before this one, as I lay atop the sheets, I was startled from my reverie by a light knock upon my bedroom door. I hardly had time to rise before the phlegmatic maid herself slipped in uninvited. She closed the door behind her and regarded me without a word, the illumination of the desk lamp falling like chalk dust upon her pale, expressionless face. She seemed so certain of herself that I wondered for a moment if we had previously agreed upon the meeting. I remained before her as if paralyzed, unable to find the words with which to ask her what she wanted. Scarcely taking her eyes off mine, she lifted her plain white maid's dress over her head with a single, inelegant movement and let it fall onto the floor beside her. She stood naked before me without the slightest hint of modesty, her body slightly inclined toward mine as the light left little to be concealed.

Emma, while not exactly unattractive, is far from glamorous. With her heavy frame and passionless face, she comprises a stark contrast to the models in the book of saints. Her measurements convey a density which is in no way conducive to the arousal of desire. She is rather like a monolith—onerous, irrefutable, and endowed with an exquisite minerality. I rose and let her embrace me, we proceeded to the bed, and within a few scant minutes our ordeal had reached its conclusion.

Not an ounce of tenderness passed between us in the aftermath of our perplexing act. She sat upon the end of the bed as she slowly clothed herself, her gaze trained on the dark wooden panels of the opposing wall. By that time, I'd retreated beneath the covers, my back supported by the single paltry pillow. I was not entirely unhappy to be in her presence. She appeared to me like an anchor, immovably bound to the heart of the world and all that it portends, whereas I tend to drift along the surface of the waters without a single decisive aim. Were the onset of my symptoms to steal over me in her presence, I feel certain that I might cling to her and thus escape their fury. At last, she turned her gaze toward mine, her face as impassive as ever. "We've always been lovers, you and I," she said, before rising once more to take her leave.

I remained just as I was for upwards of an hour, savoring the bitter aftertaste of our brief coupling. Her parting comment echoed through my thoughts as I attempted to place it into a meaningful context. At last, having come to no conclusions, I switched out the light and put myself to sleep.

23 November

In the later hours of the morning, as I sifted through a seemingly endless array of registers, charters, legal inquiries, and affidavits, a fully formed memory of my most recent attack was restored to me all at once. I don't know with any precision when the event may have taken place, though I'm certain it transpired within the last few days. It's possible that I dreamed the entirety of the episode from start to finish.

To be fair, it should be noted that St. Francis of Assisi was converted to the faith after his God appeared to him while he was dreaming. St. Joseph himself was counseled in a dream to take the Holy Virgin as his bride. The veil between sleep and wakefulness is paper-thin. The distinction between the two is nothing in the face of the eternal. The watchful eye of the creator never sleeps, or so we're told. It persists as if afflicted with perpetual insomnia, forever unable to look away from the atrocities committed in its name.

The details of my unaccounted-for episode can still be called to mind with crystal clarity. Ignatius and his stick puppet were directly involved in its induction. He'd somehow enticed me away from my work one afternoon, having commandeered a section of the parlor. The windows were all shaded, the lights shut out, and a series of flaming candles had been placed at the cardinal directions. One of the eggs I'd stolen for him was involved. It had been carried by the puppet to each of the candles where it was suspended for several seconds above the flame. This seemed progressively to endow the object with a certain tension, as if the inner surface of the shell were being pressed on, very slightly, by an increase in the volume of the contents inside. The monkey's demeanor appeared particularly rapturous as it gazed upon the contours of the consecrated object. Its acerbic grin and frantic eyes were every bit as life-like as the face of the boy who controlled him.

Once suitably prepared, the egg was precariously balanced on one end upon an overturned saucer at the midpoint between the candles. A bright red orchid had been retrieved from a vase atop a nearby end table. This was placed, by way of the monkey's wooden paws, upside-down over the top of the smooth, white shell. I sat directly before the display, stationed opposite the boy, my back to the closed doors of an elegant armoire. I distinctly remember the expression on his face as he turned his eyes toward my own. He was able to convey with a single glance that he was perfectly aware of my relations with his mother. He seemed almost to admonish me for my unease regarding the matter. It was as if he himself had arranged our trysts and was desirous that I place my faith in his designs without a trace of guilt. Without breaking eye contact, he caused the puppet to bow above the egg, its forehead coming down so swiftly and with such force that the eggshell was neatly cracked beneath the covering of the flower.

Upon rising, the doll clasped the orchid in both hands, lifting it above the surface of the violated egg and tossing it carelessly behind him. Thick, white tufts of churning smoke rose from a tiny fissure in the shell. It appeared that the egg had first been boiled so as to keep it from losing its form. Ignatius and his toy puppet withdrew from the room as the smoke continued to emerge. I, for my part, could hardly move at all, as my symptoms were upon me like a pack of wolves.

Events proceeded very quickly from that point, though my recollection is hazy. Within seconds, the parlor was entirely drowned beneath a blanket of rolling fog. At some point during the proceedings, having closed my eyes, I was confronted with an ocean of naked luminosity. By the time I opened them again, the glow had come to subsume everything. There was something different about the pallid light on this occasion. The flavor of my vision was somehow tainted. The invisible essence of St. Severina seemed to pervade it like a perfume. It was as if, now that I'd at last identified her, she chose to reveal her untarnished splendor as the very root and source of my disease.

I don't at all remember my emergence from the embrace of the eternal, nor what happened in the time that followed. The nature of my saint, having come to saturate my senses, gradually came to lose its distinction as I approached the nullity of the Absolute. Like Beatrice during Dante's ascent into Paradise, it seems that she can only accompany me so far. Individual qualities cannot subsist within the all-consuming uniformity of a dispassionate God.

The fact that the episode took place out in the open, along with the absurdity of Ignatius' ceremony, fuels my suspicion that its onset, at least, was contained within a dream. I've learned to take pains to avoid being apprehended at the height of an attack. I can't help but wonder what Kasper would think were he to find me lying insensible on the floorboards. He would inevitably conclude that I'd had a seizure of some sort, and, professional help being duly summoned, I would be made to confess to my history of illness as if it were a sin.

Over the course of the last couple of days, I've noticed minute changes to the way in which Ignatius wields his toy. The creature appears damnably sentient, thanks to the subtlety of its master's art. It seems to regard me as something of a confidant, granting me knowing glances between the rails of the banister or slyly peeking out at me from around the curvature of an urn. A persistent intuition tells me that the boy, like myself, is able to bridge the gap between one world and the next. While I am shaken to the core by the discontinuity, I sense that he makes the crossing without the least bit of unease. How this might be possible, I can't begin to imagine. At times, he seems not altogether human. His mother, on the other hand, comprises a different type of creature altogether. I find myself almost forgetting that they're related.

Emma has returned to the intimacy of my bedroom several times now. Her visits have become a daily occurrence. Night after night, we repeat the same tireless ritual with as little variation as possible. It's almost as if we recite an incantation, the poetry of which lies precisely in its monotony. I can't say that I enjoy our rendezvous, though neither do I find them distasteful. Our relations are like shaving or any other mundane custom—they are a matter of necessity and nothing more.

As my familiarity with the woman grows, I feel more and more that I can discern something of her innate nature. Though hardly remarkable, she is certainly unique. She's intimately bound to the corruption of the world, and thus to the engine of its destiny. This doesn't manifest in her daily life or her vocation so much as it does in the minutiae of her character, in the invisible essence that pervades her body, and in the sequence of contortions that she undergoes while in the heat of our illicit acts. While in my own experience, due to the nature of my illness, the fate of the world is a constantly changing value, for her it is immutable and absolute. If our couplings comprise a sort of prayer, the god that we petition lies beyond all hope of understanding.

Earlier this morning, while the house lay under cover of darkness, I was treated to a cynical remark from my employer. Emma had prepared two cups of strong, black coffee. We sat at a little table in the center of the kitchen, Kasper with his newspaper spread out before him and I seeking epiphanies in the wood grain of a mantle clock that sat upon a high shelf. My host had taken an interest in the recent formation of the Third International in Moscow. "'A new era in world history' they're calling it," he uttered. "Their optimism will fail them before a decade has passed. History is little more than an open wound."

"Much more than that," I wanted to respond. "It is a severed limb, an amputated heart, a phantom pain felt in an absent body."

27 November

As I sip from a glass of my employer's supply of Riesling, the book of photographs lying open on the table before me, I'm gifted with another memory that I can't quite place. Again, I can't be certain if the events truly transpired or if I'd merely dreamed them. My recollection is vague and riddled with holes. I can remember passing through a shipyard after having dined in a favorite public house. My attention was drawn to the vastness of the night sky as I wandered among the rusting behemoths of iron and steel. St. Severina's star resided at an appreciable distance above the horizon, a pinhole in the shell of the created world through which the blood of the eternal seeped in. The other stars resembled little more than ornaments beside her splendor. As I continued on my way through the streets and byways of the sleeping city, I came increasingly to fall beneath the influence of my saint. Little by little, my body became a vessel for her unchanging and imperishable fire.

A creeping delirium pursued me through the open courtyards and claustrophobic side-streets of this little town. The city itself seemed transformed by my disease. I began to imagine that my star had set the very stones aflame. Having not a clue where I was going, I found myself in an area with which I was not in the least familiar. Stumbling up a wide, stone stairway, I was faced with two tall doors that rose to an elegant arch above my head, their surfaces painted a hypnotic shade of peacock blue. Traceries of iron stretched from left to right between the rough stone walls on either side. Without thinking, I reached out to touch them. Scarcely had my fingers brushed the surface than did the rightmost door swing open. I slipped inside and closed the door behind me, thinking it best to ride out my affliction in a place in which I was unlikely to be disturbed.

The interior, much to my surprise, was brightly lit. There seemed hardly any boundary between the holy fire that coursed through my blood and the opulent glow cast from the decorative lamps above. Within seconds, I'd become cognizant of where I was. I stood behind two rows of pews in the very church that appeared in the photographs in Kasper's book. The altar, dome, and chancel were unmistakable, as were the pillars and their connecting arches, the white frescoes and sandstone tiles, the little doors that stood to either side of the pulpit. I stumbled down the central aisle in disbelief as the signs of my affliction continued to rise and seethe within me. The character of Severina suffused the hollows of the nave like an oil distilled from sin.

As my symptoms took me higher, I began to experience the familiar sense of weightlessness. With each step that I took, my perspective grew more distant. My sense of self began to unwind like a thread falling loose from a spool. I recognized the crucial point that marks the onset of hallucination. I clung to the sensation of solidity in order to keep from losing my bearings, clinging to the back of a wooden pew. I knew that any efforts to defer the climax of my sickness would prove futile. When in the grip of my infirmity, I am absolutely helpless. Already, the light that surged within me threatened to engulf my senses.

Furiously scanning the extremities of the church, I at last caught sight of the single feature that I wished to explore before my rapture overtook me. The confessional booth stood partially concealed behind a pillar, crouching in the shadows beneath a window of stained glass. As waves of unrelated imagery began to break upon my inner shores, I made my way with great haste before the open right-hand door. The visible space inside the box was as deserted as the rest of the church, while the priest's door, just as in the photograph, was tightly closed. I wanted desperately to search for the prayer book, the slips of paper half-hidden beneath the implements of the mass, the unfurled scrolls, the graven images, and the hummingbird which I imagined must be flitting about inside the vestry. As it was, I scarcely had time to open the sealed door, though my memory tells me nothing of what lay beyond. From that point onward, I can only recall the ceaseless indifference of the Holy One—an ocean of lucidity that obliterates all trace of feeling, drowning every possibility beneath its inexorable waves.

There is no greater shame than to again confront the world after having suffered the embrace of perfection. The mystic and the exile are united by a bond that runs far deeper than the ties of blood or faith. The fruits of ecstasy and of diaspora sprout from the branches of a single tree. The roots of this tree have no place within the earth. Just as a person cast out from their country can never truly return, the world becomes a foreign territory for the wanderer after having lain for a single night in the arms of its creator.

I don't know how or when I returned to my tiny room in Kasper's house, nor can I ascertain the exact date on which the events that I relate here took place. I'm certain that Emma has visited my room every night since my last entry. Her desire is like the ticking of a metronome—returning to be satiated with a regularity that verges on the mechanical. I'm not in the habit of going out after our encounters. By the time she breaches the door of my bedroom, I've already long since eaten and returned. This notwithstanding, as before, I'm given to a strong conviction that the episode took place within the past week. Is the memory a false one? Perhaps my fugues have progressed to the point where they transpire entirely in my imagination. Another possibility occurs to me—if the world that I inhabited before my most recent attack has been consumed, the period of time in which my symptoms overtook me no longer exists, and thus cannot be accounted for.

I'm tempted to seek out the church in the coming days. The door by which I gained entrance is easily distinct enough for me to recognize on sight. I'm hesitant, on the other hand, to confirm its existence lest I shatter the mystique with which my imagination has endowed it. To tell the truth, I rather enjoy the mystery. I will let it remain impenetrable for the time being.

Meanwhile, Ignatius has increasingly come to antagonize my host. The boy threatens to disturb his equanimity and break the mutual tolerance between them. His stick puppet is utilized with its typical deftness in this endeavor. The figure is made to fix its gaze on Kasper for several minutes at a time, its body shifting slightly in position from one moment to the next, its movements intricately calculated to produce an impression of disdain. This is never done directly within Kasper's line of sight. The infernal toy hovers always on the edge of his peripheral vision. Just before the man turns his head, the puppet is pulled away, hiding itself behind a surface as the boy reveals himself. The tension this produces is nearly unbearable, yet Kasper has thus far managed to control his obvious frustration.

I compose this entry mere minutes after Emma has taken leave of my bed. Her appearance this evening was as punctual as ever, our coupling dispassionate and unsatisfying. Her body blindly thrusts against my own like a hammer striking the head of a nail, affixing my soul to the heart of a world which cannot maintain its composition. Just as steel is tempered by fire and water, I feel somehow fortified by my successive periods of substantiality and dissolution. In this way does my lover conspire with my disease in order to make of me a worthy servant for my patroness.

Emma, in a rare moment of verbosity, left me with an inauspicious omen before returning to her room this evening. "You have only a little time left here," she told me in a perfectly matter-of-fact tone of voice. "You'll abscond, just like the others, and will be no more missed than anybody else."

I don't know who the others are, though I'm bothered by a vague conviction that she refers to shades of myself whose timelines are lost to history.

I have not the slightest clue what time it is, though I suspect it's close to sunrise. I've woken from a persistent vision involving a series of depraved encounters in the hold of a ship. As my ordeal continued, I found myself desperately wishing that the all-devouring waters would swallow me up. I'm not particularly moved to return to sleep.

It's hardly surprising that my rest is disturbed. Earlier this evening, the full extent of my disease was revealed to me. So perplexing are the implications of what I've seen that I'm tempted to pretend they don't exist. Kasper had invited me to dine with him in celebration of the acquisition of a new client. I politely refused, preferring to dine alone, yet I conceded to a single glass of Aquavit at the dinner table in the kitchen. Ignatius made his usual appearance shortly after the drinks had been poured, stick puppet in hand. With the deftness of a master artisan, he marched the figure across the floor and made it climb the wall beneath the high shelf directly across from me. While my host had become quite adept at ignoring the boy's antics, it was all I could do to retain my composure. The wooden monkey took on a degree of comicality that bordered on the absurd. Several times, in the course of his ascent, he slipped back down some distance, only to find his footing in the tiny space between the boards. After each minor setback, he tirelessly returned to his endeavor, never for a moment giving in to the weariness that so obviously hampered him.

Having finally managed to scale the wall and perch himself upon the far end of the ledge, the monkey turned and trained his eyes not on my host, but on myself. Aside from the wooden mantle clock, which is not in proper working order, the shelf is quite profusely decorated. I've come to understand that Emma is in charge of the décor throughout the house.

She's equipped, in contrast to her lack of artistry in more intimate matters, with a surprisingly delicate eye for detail. The ivory petals of several star magnolias rose from a pair of vases placed to either side of the clock. On the side that was nearest me stood a tall jade bottle engraved with characters of eastern origin. The further side was largely occupied by a wooden cabinet of exquisite craftsmanship. One of the monkey's arms was made to rest atop the latter. I thought for a moment that he was going to tilt it forward, causing it to plummet toward a spectacular collision below.

Rather that push it off the shelf, its tiny hand was made to slip into the space behind the knob on one of the cabinet doors. With a single graceful motion, the box was opened and the left half of the interior revealed. An egg leaned up against a partition of rich, dark wood that separated the two sides. Within seconds, the cabinet door was closed again, but what I'd seen behind it had affected me beyond measure. Though I could hardly put it into words, I now knew precisely what it was that lay concealed in the priest's compartment of the confessional. Just as the initiate of the Mysteries of Eleusis, having been prepared by a long and arduous drama, was delivered a crucial revelation by being shown a sheaf of wheat, so have I had the very seed of my affliction revealed to me by a common household object.

In a single, devastating flash, an insupportable barrage of memories came flooding back to me. I understood that my disease had overtaken me with far greater frequency than I'd suspected. My abdications from the world had cast no shadows, produced no reflections, and left no traces of their passing. The incidents that I'd forgotten far outnumbered those that I'd retained. I saw myself emerging from a fugue beneath a bridge in Antwerp, suffering the onset of an attack in a crowded waiting room in Brussels, and returning to my senses in the washroom of a café in which I'd locked myself in a blind panic. I remembered wandering, overwhelmed and in an escalating stupor, through the nighttime streets of Ostend and Bruges. Several dozen episodes in Ghent returned to me, one of which had transpired in the arms of the wife of a magistrate. Hundreds of additional instances appeared all at once before my inner eye in meticulous detail. I suspect still more remain as yet inaccessible. Again and again has all of history been severed only to be cauterized by the fire of God's ambivalence. The spirit of my saint resides forever on the threshold, always ready to administer the anesthetic of oblivion, to tend to my despair, and to see me reborn in a world resurrected from the indifference of its creator.

My host, meanwhile, had no idea what was going through my mind. Not knowing what else to do as the memories washed through me, I simply raised my glass and took a sip of Aquavit. By this time, Ignatius had vanished, leaving a notable tension behind him in the kitchen. I feel that Kasper's approaching the limits of his patience with the boy.

Later in the evening, for the first time, I refused the advances of the maid. I left the door securely locked and ignored the sharp rapping of her knuckles upon its surface. After a minute or two, I was relieved to hear her departing footsteps. I'm inclined to agree with her recent pronouncement. Very soon, the time will come for me to leave this place. I've saved enough money to allow myself to drift in reasonable comfort for a little while. Though something propels me from the convenience of this house, my time here will not have been wasted. I've been brought into contact with the muse of my disease and made to comprehend a little of her mystery. There is some danger, on the other hand, in remaining too long. If I overstay my welcome, I put myself at risk of incurring undesirable liabilities.

Only one incident worth noting has taken place in the time between my last entry and this one. While the event has not affected my decision to abscond, as Emma has so eloquently termed it, it has provided an appropriate degree of closure for the circumstances under which my journal began. A brisk walk to the station upon the completion of this entry will mark the termination of this record. Within its pages lay the scattered fragments of a single, concise statement—the enunciation of an edict from the lips of my saint, itself a footnote to a doctrine necessitated by the eruption of the eternal into history.

I've given no notice of my imminent departure from this house. I plan simply to step out and neglect to return. A train ride to Luxembourg will deliver me to unknown harbors. What awaits me there is not in my control. To abandon one's life to the hands of providence is itself a form of prayer. However careless the act appears in execution, it bestows honors and distinguishments that cannot be attained by more conventional forms of worship.

Rising from my bed this morning, having awoken from a dreamless sleep, I was immediately confronted with fevered thoughts of Severina's star. It seemed to smolder in a place that I couldn't quite identify, its crimson radiance signifying a covenant between the unchanging monotony of heaven and the transitory destiny of the terrestrial world. An answering signal could faintly be discerned in the dark heart of the earth, a rising pulse that seethed and wailed like an animal in distress.

I dressed myself and stepped into the corridor just in time to catch sight of the maid passing into her bedroom. She resembled a penitent Cistercian as she crept into the shadows on the far side of her door. While she hardly discourages him, she has a tendency to bear the guilt for the discrepancies committed by her son. I expected to find Ignatius in the lower section of the house engaged in some insidious game designed to irritate my host.

The light cast from the lamps above me gently overflowed onto the dark wood of the stairs as I descended into the open foyer. From the upturned mouths of six tall urns rose the flower-strewn stalks of an abundance of winter jasmine that Emma had gathered from the garden. A low hum seemed to emerge from the panels on the walls. I could feel it in the hollow at the base of my skull. The sensation gave rise to a familiar inner glow as I stepped through a narrow doorway and into the kitchen. I caught sight of Ignatius' handiwork immediately upon entering the brightly lit space.

Below the high shelf upon which the mantle clock resided stood a truly preposterous display. The monkey puppet had been crucified upon two long, silver serving utensils bound into a cross with a length of twine. The vertical bar emerged from a pyramid of eggs that had been carefully arranged at its base. A small hole had been carved into the puppet's left side, just above the top of its silken gown. The wound was stained with dark red wine which flowed down the length of the gem-studded material and onto the eggshells below. The fluid, so my imagination told me, comprised the nectar of eternity, having sprung from a leak in a point of vulnerability within the fabric of the created world.

My thoughts were inundated with a multitude of disparate associations all at once. I felt certain at that moment that I understood everything: the blood of the saints; the immortal elixir; the passing of the Logos through the body of the son and through his wounds into the earth; the production of unspeakable ores; the propitiation of the star; the subtle wine of prophecy and the drunkenness thereof and the returning of creation to its immutable source. To my dismay, my newfound understanding has proved fleeting. At the time of writing, the knot that bound these threads into a single epiphany has again come undone. At times I feel that I can almost weave them together into a coherent pattern, yet the central motif forever eludes my comprehension.

I don't know how long I remained there. I felt a hint of disappointment to find the puppet entirely devoid of its animating fire now that it was no longer in the hands of its controller. It hung listless on its silver cross, the only element of life being the artificial blood that wept from its side. I wondered if I'd see it resurrected. The vital breath that was withdrawn from it, so it seemed to me at the time, would inevitably seek expression elsewhere. My reverie was broken by the sound of Kasper shouting excitedly from another room. "Ignatius!" His voice was fraught with uncharacteristic rage. "Ignatius, come here at once!"

A quick trip through the narrow passage behind the stairs led me into the parlor. There, I found Kasper frantically trying to extinguish a minor fire before the armoire. With scarcely a thought, I helped him stamp out the flames. From what I could tell a pile of legal documents had been all but ruined. A section of the carpet had been badly scorched as well. Thick rolls of ivory smoke careened up to the ceiling, slowly making their way toward the quarters of the room. No sooner had the blaze been put out than did the armoire doors swing open before us. Ignatius resided inside of the cabinet like a god inside an alcove.

The boy had not a single piece of clothing on, though this was difficult to discern at first sight. His body had been decorated with elaborate markings that covered him from head to toe. Long phrases in stylized letters of red and black had been painted in tight spirals around his arms, legs, torso, neck, and head. These were emphasized by winding serpents, their jaws extending from their open mouths. His hands were extended to either side to the limits of the interior of the armoire. Each palm cradled an egg, their surfaces reflecting the sunlight that streamed in through the parlor windows. The phrases on his body had been written in a language that I couldn't understand, yet I could read their frightful messages with perfect clarity. The boy had transformed himself into a Holy Book. His flesh bore the Testament of St. Severina in characters at once sacred and profane.

He took a step toward Kasper, passing from beneath the shelter of the armoire, his eyes locked on those of the older man. The expression on his face conveyed a knowledge far beyond his years. For one fleeting moment, I beheld the full extent of the boy's genius. He bears within himself the seed of perfection, his actions demonstrating the ineffable mind of a divinity beyond reason. He's beholden to no law and does not concede to destiny. His blood is distilled from the contempt of the undying for everything that passes away. It's hardly any wonder that he refuses to speak. Words must comprise for him a senseless indulgence, an affirmation of the futility of human endeavor in which the baseness of our sentiments is exalted like an idol.

While I was moved to the edge of rapture by the boy's appearance, Kasper was hardly amused. Grasping Ignatius by one arm, he raised a single hand into the air and brought it down with excessive force across his painted face. While the boy hardly reacted to the vicious chastisement, both eggs dropped from his hands. As they cracked open on the carpet, I felt the breaking of a tension that had been with me from the day I first took up lodging in this house. The assault was not yet over. My employer proceeded to lambast the young savant with a scarcely controlled outburst. "You're no son of mine, do you hear me?" he shouted, his eyes like spitting cobras as he clutched the decorated flesh. "You're no son at all!"

Ignatius fixed his assailant with a stare of unconcealed victory before calmly extricating himself from his grasp. He took a single step backward, cast his eyes toward the ceiling in a gesture of derision, and silently headed through one of the parlor doors, presumably to return to the safety of his bedroom. It occurred to me only at that moment that he couldn't possibly have decorated his body by himself. He must have enlisted the aid of his mother, whose complicity I ought to have guessed from the beginning.

"Assuming you still have a stomach for coffee after this ridiculous little drama," uttered Kasper, having swiftly regained his self-control, "I suggest we take it in the nook beneath the stairs."

I politely agreed, and within minutes we were doing our best to enjoy the pungent black liquid. Emma makes the stuff atrociously strong. So far as I know, this is precisely the way that Kasper prefers it. "The boy acts out this way every so often," so my employer calmly informed me. "After doing so, he disappears without a trace for several days. We can at least look forward to an uneventful week while he stays locked up in his mother's bedroom."

Hardly a word passed between us in the hours that followed. Emma, at length, came back downstairs and prepared a conciliatory breakfast: crêpes with artichokes and spinach drizzled over with a glaze of honey. The image of the painted letters that wound their way around Ignatius' body remained ever in the back of my mind. Their message conveyed the inconceivable grace by which the saints commune with the means of their annulment. To the sinners of the world, this inexplicable communion appears like somewhat of a parlor trick. It seems impossible that the nothingness embodied by the Absolute could ever be reconciled with the incarnated soul.

By the time we finished our morning meal, I'd decided the time had come for me to depart from the house. There was hardly any need to gather my belongings, as I possess too little to warrant even the most meager effort. I tended to the day's work with the utmost thoroughness, finding a simple joy in the futility of my tasks. As evening fell, I couldn't help but steal a final glance at St. Severina's page in Kasper's book. I'm certain that I won't have occasion to lay eyes on it again. As I gazed once more upon the body of my saint, my interpretation of her testament was confirmed. The parable presented in her photograph has now been understood in full. What lies behind the closed door of the confessional is the very axis of necessity—it is the desire of the Absolute, the will to manifest from nothing, the temptation to exist against all odds. It's precisely this which constitutes the initial error of the cosmos. The saint's complicity in the photograph denotes the true purpose of redemption. By making her confession to the very principle of original sin, she ratifies the flaw in the celestial design.

To further elucidate what's been revealed to me would be an impropriety. The ability to contain the abomination of true wisdom requires a lifetime of repentance. This must be the true objective of the mortifications of the ascetic, with their emphasis on the extinction of desire. There are other methods. One might reduce oneself to nothing, embrace the ravages of the perverse, or, as in my own case, come to know the ineffable purely by accident. There are costs incurred, no matter what the mechanism used. The germ that so insidiously contaminates my blood at once perfects and negates my humanity. This dubious miracle is accomplished without the slightest volition on my part. Like a reluctant prophet, I'm scarcely given any choice.

In one hour's time, I'll be en route to a city which is entirely unknown to me. The distant call of unfamiliar streets lends an animating vigor to my spirit. Emma has been duly satisfied, or so I can only suppose, and has returned to her quarters without a word. She's left the serenity of a sleeping house in her wake. So far as I'm concerned, this final act marks the completion of my contract. I feel a trace of apprehension lest my infirmity overtake me before I manage to board my train. On the other hand, if my symptoms come before I leave the house, so be it. Having renounced the possession of my earthly senses, I give myself entirely over to the wiles of my patron. One thousand fugues or more await me and I welcome each and every one of them. I am an incidental servant of oblivion and I want for nothing.

THE DREAMING PLATEAU

by Martin Locker

HIGH up on the hills, where eyries lurk in broken crags and clouds take their rest, the vast plateau of T'Singah lay alone, save for the trails of vultures. Down in the village, where peasants cast their eyes to the earth when T'Singah was mentioned, the small rhythms of tea houses and tarnished rice fields rumbled along, mindful of the clamouring beaks far above them.

As a young man I found myself there, primarily representing a small London firm that specialised in gems and antiquities but also in the hope of encountering not one black ball within the forthcoming membership bid for the London Geographical Society. A bookseller in Curzon Street had grudgingly handed over a slim volume written by a Russian during the previous century, detailing his exploits along the Himalayas, one of the last great expeditions commissioned by the Czar prior to his swift fate in a damp cellar. A Tartar by birth, this Petrov Luchenko had spent two decades exploring the valleys and bleak mountains along the Pamirs and the Kush, venturing up into Tibet and conversing with those yellow-hatted Lamas that held sway over the remotest monasteries. His commission being cartographic, Luchenko was eager to know of the distant realms which no known map had yet charted. His Tartar constitution was accustomed to long uncomfortable sojourns; thus, any hint of far-flung forgotten places was like wine to him. It was as he pushed further into the U-Tsang that he came across a vast lake, known only to surviving locals as the 'Dreaming Tear' which sat in the shadow of the Gangdise Shan mountains. According to his account, he had talked extensively with a hermit who spent his days in quiet contemplation near the shore, retreating during the freezing nights to a hearth in the nearby caves. The hermit, known to Luchenko only as "Rdo Kelsang", had told him of his younger days herding goats among the Gangdise Shan pastures and the legends of the great T'Singah plateau which lurked in the cradle of a mountain shaped like a saddle. An unknown age ago, a wealthy and decadent complex stood there, whose dark temples were so perfumed that each breath of wind carried the scents of agar, cedar and snow lotus to towns which lay hundreds of miles away. Some manner of cataclysm had broken the buildings and the inhabitants who were not crushed beneath masonry escaped to far Lhasa. Yet the reputation of their strange rites had preceded them and the Lamas rejected their pleas for refuge. Many would join the caravans that trailed down to Afghanistan, others simply found themselves in the towns of Gurjuratra, where they formed small sects and carried on their strange remote religion in secret.

Once Rdo had ventured there and through the mists he had glimpsed huge pillars that lay cracked and twisted upon the ground, stone halls whose roofs had long since been wrenched to earth, and as he walked further he had stopped at the entrance to a mine. Here the clouds had allowed a brief shaft of light to pierce the gloom, refracting into splinters from the countless crystals which lay upon the cold earth. When Luchenko asked why he had not gone further, perhaps pocketing some of these treasures, Rdo replied that at no point during his wandering in T'Singah had he not heard the wailing and champing of some terrible creature, sometimes nearer, sometimes further, but always within earshot, and within the mine this sound was amplified to an unbearable degree. He had fled back to his goats in terror when a voice appeared next to his ear. For the indomitable Luchenko this was too tempting to bear and the next day he set off, through hard passes and grim pastures, to the village of Dsang. After several days he sighted the collection of stone huts along an unending river and here his account of the expedition to the plateau is fragmented, filled with (what we took to be) hyperbolic descriptions of titan stones, towering walls and the dread fragments of forgotten gods littered across the plain. Most enticing for our firm were his reports of the mines, where every second step would happen up against some jewelled stone, boulders of cragged crystal and glimmering veins that reached into the heart of the mountains. We paid no heed to his words which explained his own rapid departure from that strange place, the mention of ragged breaths in the shadows, a sensation of ever-present watchers and the villagers' faint memories of screams which would echo between the tolling temple bells. No indeed, it would be better had we read less impatiently, but man's attention is ever-riveted to the thought of wealth.

Thus funds were raised, boats were chartered, horses overburdened and six months later myself and eight others found ourselves crossing the threshold of a squalid tea-house beneath the T'Singah plateau, travel-stained and nearly broken but with the keen desire to seek out a selection of antiquities and archaic crystals which would find great favour, and greater prices, among the drawing rooms of north-western London. After stabling our horses we were taken to the see the village elder who, after some initial mistrust and dark glances which were ameliorated by our translator and several handfuls of silver *tangkas*, agreed to house us during our stay. We were then taken to the village outskirts, where a series of rough guesthouses stood assembled around a yard. The gloomy interiors were lit from an open skylight, with carved wooden beams and the pervasive aroma of animal dung settled all around. After his daughters lit fires and began to refresh the buildings from years of disuse, we gathered in the largest house and sat upon the hard, wooden floors. Water was boiled and a bushel of herbs was steeped, and so we began to drink the thick, heady tea of the Gangdise Shan and bent our ears to the old man as he began to speak. As he did so his hands would stray to a wizened string of beads around his wrist and his thin eyes would dart up to the roof's opening; it was clear that the lurid tales of the venerable Rdo were not unique.

The man began by telling us how, many generations ago, the plateau held a singular people almost mythical in their longevity, whose songs were still sung some nights by the villagers. These fragments of verses and the strange droning melodies used to drift down from the high temples, filling the dreams of the village folk hundreds of years ago, so that when they awoke it was as if they had never slept. Trains of horses would lead up and down the mountain every third moon, bringing ponderous bushels of herbs from the Kunlun Mountains upon whose slopes those rare somatic grasses grew which granted the deepest slumbers, and taking away splinters of crystal to adorn necks of women from Jaipur to the Mongol plains. Daoist priests could be seen passing on to T'Singah, their heads grazed with stubble from months of travel, and on some nights the temple dirges did not float down but tumbled in floods, crashing upon the village houses and rendering all who heard them possessed of such a lethargy that their hearts could barely beat. In those nocturnal imaginings the villagers would swim on thick black tides in the darkness, carried by the dull chants beyond the mountains and pastures into a distant pulsing void, illuminated by a far red glow in whose heart there swirled an unimaginably vast maw. Trembling, they would awaken at dawn's first glimmer, wracked with fear and aching from their oneiric tumbling between sound and teeth. But they stayed, for the mountainside was unusually fertile and the spaces between these slumbering visions were made profitable with good yields and the chance of trade with the never-ending passage of visitors. Only in those hours that followed these dreams did their minds wander to the thought of relatives in distant Lhasa, of how unencumbered their lives might be were they there too, and how terrible was the great cycle of time itself. Over the centuries seasons blurred and the sun began to glow less brightly over the Gangdise Shan. As temperatures slowed their dance between Winter and Summer, the trains of herb bales did also, until only a handful would arrive through the year. With this the chants that came to the village began to lose their savage lulls and became fearful, even desperate. The dreams which the villagers endured no longer carried them over opaque black waves. Instead they gained a momentum which took each dreamer over the crest of the maw, where they saw a single dead sphere on whose barren rocks cities lay dead and forgotten among sprawling mandalas of bones and black monoliths. They would awaken, no longer fearful but filled with an eerie feeling of sharp dread, as if they had foreseen the future not only of their village but of the entire cosmos, broken and rusted, lost from any record as it decayed in the margins of space. One day, as the caravans had trickled to a halt and the chants became nightly in occurrence, a blooming cloud of smoke erupted from the plateau, as if a vast bonfire had been lit in supplication. The old man told us that, shortly after this, the bells rang out harsh and shrieking, followed by a long, silent procession that could be seen from the valley below, as hundreds of those who dwelt in T'Singah made their way in to the mountainside itself.

From then on, the plateau was as silent as a tomb. He told us that over the following centuries several visitors, including our dear Tartar, had made their way up to T'Singah, drawn by its history, yet very few had returned. Those that did said nothing as they arrived back at the village, they were pale and quite shaken. Luchenko was similarly reticent in his own report, our book gave us few clues as to what he had seen within the mine. He only recorded that he had left without taking a single crystal nor a coin from the plateau and it was clear from his tone when describing the journey back to St Petersburg that his mind had taken a sombre, brooding tone, filled with thoughts of time, mortality, and a fear that all could end at any moment. He retired back to his Caucasus mountains after delivering his report, never to leave his own village again where, it was said, he would no longer pray nor held any theology in high regard.

However, we were not deterred. We thought these histories entertaining, antiquated and exotic certainly, but not anything which a modern enterprising band such as ourselves needed be fearful of. The elder looked regretful at out insistence on pursuing our mission, yet agreed after much haggling to provide us with some fresh horses and three local guides. Thus we rested and, after rising with the sun and drinking some more of that thickly brewed tea, we set out the following morning with thoughts of wealth and, in my own case, of the report I would submit to the London Geographical Society upon my return.

Over the course of that first morning we picked our way over the grasslands, bent double against the winds and surrounded by billowing green purple herbage. This undulating sea of grass stretched for many miles until it was brought abruptly to a halt by the cragged edge of the mountains which dug sharply against the rising plain. Gradually the clamour of the village receded, the hue and cries of daily existence which had previously eddied around us were no longer carried by the gale and our ears were struck only by the harsh rhythm of the wind. As noon approached we found ourselves confronted by monolithic rocks, great stelae of black stone which stood forlornly against the bleak backdrop of mountains and plains. My colleagues picked over the stones, hoping that some trinket would remain at their base, but these unmarked shards would not yield their secrets. Those who lay beneath were forgotten, the tales of their lives forever silenced, and so we forged ahead with our guides towards the mountains, unsettled by this bleak vision of mortality. Gradually, as the sun begun to find itself cut by the peaks and twilight descended, we reached the base of that precarious path which would lead us up to T'Singah and it was decided that we should make camp and gather our strength for a taxing push the following day. Small caves furrowed the volcanic rock that crowded around the mountains. We lit fires and burrowed into them, escaping the wind's effect but not its constant grinding howl. My thoughts strayed to Luchenko and how like the wolves of his homeland the sound must have been. Despite our best intentions, none of us slept well that night. We told each other that it must have been due to our excitement and fervour to see the fabled plateau, yet for myself I can admit that this fitful rest was caused mainly by the hideous dreams that crept into my moments of slumber. Whenever my eyes closed and my mind sank below the tides of wakefulness I was beset by feelings of unease and visions of some terrible black palace whose walls slowly contracted and expanded as if operated by vast lungs, of corridors drowning in purple fumes and a solitary tremendous figure at its centre, in whose yawning mouth I found myself falling into an endless void. I passed the majority of that night awake and was unusually quick to rise in the morning, packing the provisions and blankets with a rapidity that was echoed by my colleagues. The guides, I noted, had sat up the entire night, brewing a constant stream of the thick local tea that they passed among them in horn cups. Before leaving I made some swift sketches of paintings near the back of the shallow cave which the dawn's light had revealed. They appeared nonsensical to me, exhibiting none of the motifs which I had seen along the chortens and stupas encountered during our journey through the Himalayas. Instead of scripts, solar wheels and swastikas, there were only wavering figures which stood before a single anthropomorph, lain upon some manner of trestle and surrounded by rough stars. On the cave's roof, etched in ochre, a crude mouth leered down at me, within which an unblinking eye floated among the soot-blackened rock. I hurriedly essayed the scene in my notebook and stepped out to join the party as they set off up the cragged path that begun the ascent from the plain.

Many times we stumbled, buffeted by the winds which fairly screamed around us. We began to see the vultures wheel and wander. Their eyries lay high above and no doubt they were keeping a watchful gaze in case we should fall forever in this lonely spot. Sure-footed, the horses kept a slow monotonous pace as we passed over natural bridges, spanning chasms that churned with the thunder of distant waters within which silver shimmers of fish strove against the current to reach higher ground. Stone cairns marked the path, many of which had tumbled into a sea of split stone upon the ground and there were times when I thought that I spied the trace of tanned, weather-beaten bone among those ruins. The hours churned by, the guides coaxing the beasts onward with clicking tongues and our feet followed their hooves, ever upwards, winding between cliffs that loomed over the trail and brought us over miniature passes whose position seemed so precarious that an inopportune gust would send a man falling, to lie broken upon the grasses so very far below. Many a knuckle stood white not from the cold but a desperate grip upon the iron-spiked staves we had purchased in Lhasa weeks ago and which allowed us to crab along spots where the path had given way to time and degenerated into a pebbled slope. From afar we no doubt looked ridiculous, bizarre tripods rocking forward in time with each other, yet we were very grateful that we could progress at all during these moments.

Eventually we crested another doomed pass and the guides began to rush ahead, tethering the horses together and telling us to wait. As the minutes slipped by, some began to whisper that they had marooned us on this hellish peak, that there was no T'Singah, and that it was a ruse to let us perish and then loot our corpses. However, our worries were unjust. After a half hour they returned and explained that they knew the path split a little way ahead, with one route leading swiftly to the plateau and the other reaching a scree slope from which none returned. One of our group asked to see the latter and reported back that the slanting rocks below bore witness to splintered limbs that jutted from the wastes, whose flesh was now taught and beaten by the wind and passing centuries. Despite having made this journey five times apiece, the guides told us that this bifurcation was not consistent, the destinations shifted to deceive the traveller with each passing season, and it was necessary to confirm which was indeed which at this moment in time. A mere hour later we reached the lip of a ridge which looked down upon the plateau of T'Singah.

I was not sure what I had expected to see. Perhaps in my dreams, fermenting over the past months into a cornucopia of exotic visions, I called up the grand and beautiful ruins of the Orient, gilded roofs and bejewelled temple columns, ornate banners that whispered of unknown but fabulous gods. What I beheld as I gazed down upon the plateau seemed instead to be drawn from some ghastly forlorn corner of a nightmare. I saw strewn blocks of stone the size of fifteen men end to end hewn from pumice, shrieking vultures, unbearable dolmens that stabbed against the sky and in the centre the tumbled remains of a complex whose shadows leered out among the grasses. The entire scene spoke of unutterable loneliness, of being truly forgotten by the world and a fulcrum outside of time's movements. Certainly there was something of the grim otherworldliness I had encountered when talking to the lamas of Lhasa. They related their tales of the forbidden Bon Po rites that used to dominate the land, the black-hatted priests and their severance of body and spirit on distant plains, of the sleeping mountain, in whose caverns a living corpse spun the world into being and whose sleep kept it from breaking apart. Far off on the opposite side the mountain yawned open and when the clouds shifted the sun reflected from crystalline seams that ran into its depths. I am not ashamed to admit that my shudders owed nothing to the wind.

The guides refused to go down into the bowl, but insisted that they would set camp against the ridge and watch over us. Our entreaties would not move them, nor would a promise of extra pay. They simply dug their heels in and promised us that they would be here when, or if, we returned. There was nothing to be done, so we began to pick our way down the slopes into the plateau's embrace. Our former bravado had dissipated and it was a sombre party of society men that made their way towards the desolate wreckage of T'Singah, slipping on the loose rocks with clatters that broke the stillness in a horrible fervour. We made our way to the enormous blocks, pockmarked and rough, and neck after neck craned back as we stared up to their zenith. Deep grooves the width of a man's leg lined their upper portions and green stains leeched across. As we traced these around the plateau, fragments of copper could be seen peeking from the soil, and I stooped down to dig with cold hands around the emergent metal lip. The soil was curiously loose and within twenty minutes I had uncovered a deep curvature some fifty hands in width that dove deep into the earth. Suddenly I fell over on my haunches, for I had realised what this voluptuous mystery was. Here was one of the bells the villagers had heard centuries ago, the same ones which accompanied the dirge-like chants that blew down from the plateau into their dreams and left them marooned in some awful timeless void. Picking myself up, I brushed dirt from the partially unearthed lip of the bell and saw engraved around it the very same mouth and eye motif which I had encountered at the mountain's base, painted upon the cave's roof where I had spent such a restless night. To say that my unease was increased would be an understatement. However as only I had encountered these symbols before, and not wanting to scare my colleagues, I said nothing, merely brushing the earth back over the carvings before the others could see them. For their part they had wandered off, following the line of huge stones which snaked around the outskirts of the middle structure, and shortly one shouted for us all to "Come quickly!" He stood before one of those dread dolmens, and it wasn't until we had hurried over and came but ten feet before it that we realised why he had cried out in such shock. What had appeared to be a monolith hewn from black rock was, in fact, an enormous tear-shaped piece of obsidian, fully thirty feet in height and unbroken. Across its huge surface spiralled delicate carvings of men, leading towards the very same anthropoid figure that slumbered in my cave, lain on the now-familiar trestle. But this was not the most curious thing. The dolmen was warm to the touch, not in the way in which a stone upon the beach is warmed by the sun, but as from a pulsing heat from the centre that ebbed and flowed like blood from a heart. Leaning closer I fixed my gaze upon the central dreaming figure, and as the light played upon the smooth surface it seemed to move ever so slightly, like a man shifting his weight in sleep. Looking back, I noticed that it was not just I who had seen this. Several of my colleagues looked quite ill with apprehension and we understood why the guides would not set foot here. We held a small conference, huddled against one of the great pumice blocks. Beneath the gaze of the vultures we debated leaving, for no one could have foreseen what we had found. Yet the call of wealth whispered to us and within my own soul there wavered the siren call of recounting this adventure before the awe-struck faces of London's prominent society men, the honorary invitations to noble houses and the baying of publishers outside my door. Surely to give up now would be foolish, I told my colleagues, we had come so far and this was but a tithe of the discomfort endured by men who had set out from our misty isle to carve out an empire such as the world had never seen, bringing fame and fortune to their names with sheer nerve and resourcefulness. My words swayed them, the reminder of the money which could be ours if we returned, our packs bulging with crystals from this lonely plateau, perfumed by adventure and the mystique of a long-lost sect, lurked within their minds. So it was decided that we should carry on our inspection and locate what we had come to plunder.

Sinews strengthened, wills resolved, our party crossed into the centre of T'Singah and trooped up the broken steps into what appeared to be the main temple, its colonnade open to the clouded sky. We walked among the towering pillars, some standing, others strung across the ground like stone leviathans stranded upon a foreign shore. The sheer scale of things left us dumbstruck, and yet this was not a complex structure. Instead it formed a simple cruciform pattern, leading from the cardinal points towards a single enormous block. Here again, the black obsidian made itself felt, forty feet in length, twenty in width, carved at one end with a huge circular object, concave in the centre. One of our number mentioned that it resembled the sleeping tombs in our own cathedrals, and once seen it could not be unseen. This was a bed, the circular creation a pillow, but of such dimensions that twenty people could lie with their outstretched arms touching and still leave space at either end. What manner of soporific cult had dwelt here in these ruins, devouring bushel after bushel of herbs whose ashes once blew across the colonnade? Most crucially, what had held its slumber on this bed of volcanic glass that also pulsed in warmth like a living thing? I wandered around the "bed", for what else could it be, and upon my third circulation my foot came up against a bump in the soil. Again, I knelt with flurrying hands, and this time my colleagues joined me in my efforts, now with curiosity and terror neatly balanced. For a full hour we scrabbled in the earth until we had scraped a circle of roughly ten feet that dipped down in the centre to reveal a surface of dull beaten copper. Tracing the thing's lip, further digging revealed a definite outline of a vast dish, upon which chunks of fusain the size of a man's head lay broken. It was a brazier, a great or rather a *giant* brazier, still garnished with the relics of its last offerings. At that moment a sliver of wind wound its way between the pillars and threw some of the powdered charcoal into my face. A sharp scent entered my nostrils and the broken temple wavered before me. I saw, treading between the present and the past, the ghostly shapes of black-hatted men tending braziers around the massive dais, deep within the gloom afforded by a timbered roof that no longer existed, and sighing upon the obsidian dais lay a figure of such vast dimensions that I shrieked in fear.

My cry jolted what was left of my senses out from this olfactory hallucination. The others were staring at me in grim horror and rushed to pat me on the back, soothing me with stoic quips and suggestions that, as the light was fading, we should make camp. The thought was a welcome one, but only to a degree. The thought of scrambling back up that ridge put tremors in our already weakened legs, and so one of our party walked out into the open and waved at the guides, signalling that we would rest where we were and that they should maintain their watch. The three distant figures, already seated around a flickering glow, waved back to suggest that, if we were foolhardy enough to rest there, they would not stop us but nothing could prevail upon them to join our company. We settled down among the northern colonnade and started a small fire, protected from the winds by the stone blocks which marked the perimeter. We ate some dry rations and warmed our hands by the flames, yet the mood was decidedly more disquieted than that of the previous night. Gone were the jests, good-natured ribbing and speculation upon what we would find. In their place were faint attempts at humour, quiet inquiries at where we were and weighty, ponderous silences while the company was lost in its own dreadful thoughts. At least the vultures seemed to keep their distance. By the by we slumped down among our blankets and tried to sleep or, at the very least, attempted to distance our minds from ominous thoughts. Eventually only I remained awake, and was moodily prodding the dimming coals when the moon slipped from the sky. A soft wind seemed to hum down into the plateau from the surrounding peaks, bringing with it a thin mist that draped itself over everything. Soon I was unable to distinguish some of my fellows and the stones around me were shrouded in a white veil. As I sank deeper into my blankets, for the chill had markedly increased with the visit of this inclement guest, a sharp scent pricked my senses. It was not the soft, moist freshness of the mist but an acrid trace that wafted through the broken pillars. My immediate thought was that my boots had slipped in the remnants of the fire but this was not the case, it came from beyond our little circle.

By this point I had given up all thoughts of sleep and, wrapping a thick blanket around me, I struggled into my unsinged boots to wander through the ruins in search of the scent's source. The balusters and stone shafts leered out at me between the milky haze, their outlines blurred by a clouded sky through which the stars vainly tried to shine. I trod cautiously, trying to discern the direction from which this smoke came, for that was what I intuitively knew it to be, despite wishing it was not. Through the four colonnades I roamed, shuffling in fear and curiosity, pausing to taste the air like an old hound. I circled back to the huge stone dais, horrible in the murk, and suddenly there came through the distance an unmistakable sound, almost like the lowing of cattle but deeper, gargled yet melodious and pulsing with a tidal rhythm of its own. To my horror it came from beyond the ruins, in the direction where I knew the mine entrance to be. Convinced by now that I was in some sort of dream, I had to follow its call. My pace quickened as I exited the colonnades and made my way the four hundred paces over wet grass to that cavernous mouth. The song grew stronger, the scent grew thicker, and by the time I reached the entrance with its glistening crystal veins there could be no mistake. Both came from within the mountain itself. Surely, I thought, this was some hallucination brought on by the day's discoveries and that damned tea we had drunk before sleeping? T'Singah was dead and had long been beyond living memory, its people scattered down into far India and beyond. And yet, and yet . . . something was underway within the rocks before me. I was compelled, I could not draw back, I had to enter the earth and see for myself. I stepped forth into the blackness, following the plumes of smoke and that undulating dirge of voices that quivered in unison.

The floor turned quickly from earth to rock slick with moisture and the crystal veins ran thick as a man's arm down along the cragged walls. I walked for what seemed like hours, although it may have been merely minutes, feeling my way down in the darkness along the tunnel walls until the blackness began to lift and a very faint luminescence appeared, a glow similar to a wick only just blown out. By now the voices had been joined by a resonant slow drum which seemed to be born of the earth itself, running up my legs and massaging my chest so that it was as if I had two hearts, my own beating nearly out of my chest in apprehension and the insistent yet strangely calming pounding that came from the depths. It was also now possible to discern a dual presence in the chanting. The rumbling dirge had been joined by a fragile, higher chorus that wove in and out of itself, creating a mesmerising sensation that would have been wonderful had it not emanated from such a fearful place. I continued, slowly feeling my way and following the glowing air downward, down into what must have been the very bowels of the mountain, the crystals catching on my blanket as they protruded from the walls like geometric claws, shimmering and refracting the ever-increasing light. Finally, after what seemed an age, the tunnel opened up into a cavern. The word alone could not do the sight justice, for this was more akin to the space conjured by a cathedral, and now in an instant the sounds and smells became clear to me.

What I beheld was beyond anything encountered outside of the most lurid orientalist literature found in club annals across London. I will attempt to describe it here, but I fear that even now, with the clarification of time, it would fail to do the scene justice. Hundreds, possible thousands of small oil or butter filled lamps wavered across the space, forming rings around seated figures whose heads were slumped against their chests, faces obscured by fronds of fabric wreathing their heads upon which black conical caps were perched. Slowly they rocked back and forth whilst from their mouths the slow terrible chant crept out, modulated by that shrill melody which, at close proximity, lost any beauty and now launched itself from wall to ceiling in that endless cave. Braziers mirroring the one we had uncovered upon the plateau gleamed in the light of the lamps and from their vast dishes I could see bundles of vegetation smouldering, issuing huge towers of smoke which billowed around the air and conjured a fog that settled down among the figures. However, this was not the most incredible thing and I wish that it was, for what I am about to relate will haunt me to my death. A natural rise in the cavern's floor formed a tremendous plinth, upon which lay a figure *fully thirty feet long*, wreathed in smoke and with its eyes closed, while its chest rose and fell with huge, glacial breaths.

It was at this point that my mind broke free of its paralysis and a sharp cry left my throat. The nearest figures snapped their heads up and while I was unable to move, captured by this monumental strangeness, they rose to their feet and walked towards me, gripping my arm with hands that seemed formed from only sinew and bone. The horror on my face must have been evident, for they gestured me to be calm and sit. My legs buckled and they helped me to the floor. I began to shout but very quickly one of the men clapped his hand over my mouth and flapped the other to indicate that I must be quiet, which in my stunned state I obliged him. He placed his head against mine and pulled my right hand to his temple. I recoiled but, not unkindly, he gestured me to calm myself once again and this time I followed his wish. As my eyes slowly closed through no volition of my own I glimpsed a milky tendril of the smoke emerge from his head and fall upon my own. Both the sound and smoke began to vibrate within my skull, filling my every sense until I was subsumed by the cavern and its strange rite. Through the miasma of confusion there slowly assembled in my mind a cogent series of impressions that were being imparted to me. Gradually the form of an ethereal mandala began to turn anti-clockwise, dissolving into an image of T'Singah before its abandonment. Above I could see the moon and sun chasing each other across

the heavens until they slowed and a long night fell. The colonnades, no longer ruined but erect and intricately carved,
soared upwards as my spirit drifted through them towards
the dais. One of the black capped men was carrying a vast
bundle of herbs before me, breaking off branches bristling
with leaves and laying them upon the copper braziers, into
which fiery brands were plunged and a multitude of formless
men sat, beginning their unearthly chant. In the middle lay
the giant creature, his mouth forming wordless utterances as
he slumbered and I knew intuitively that his sleep had lasted
since time began. I was struck by the importance of this sleep
and my realisation was forced that this endless cycle of chant
and smoke was devoted to ensuring that his rest was undisturbed. The planets began to follow each other overhead once
again, the song spinning into itself as the months and years
flew by into centuries, the same timeless dirge ensuring the
unconscious dreaming of this giant. Through this maelstrom
of time I approached the figure, leaning my ear to his yawning
mouth, rimmed with white teeth. Strange syllables tumbled
from it and as I turned my head to gaze into that maw I saw,
writhing in its centre, the cauldron of creation, a boiling gal-
axy that oozed together and drifted apart forming the shape
of an eye, exactly as was portrayed upon the cave roof during
my first night's rest. Suddenly, this sombre image was wrested
from me, to be replaced by an overwhelming sense of panic among the guardians. I became aware that these bushels,
whose acrid smoked carpeted the ground and which was so
crucial in keeping this creature under the waters of waking,
were no longer arriving in their long trains, and that in despair
the black caps gathered what stores remained deep into the
mountain. I saw them forming a line of supplicatory hands,
passing each inch of the creature down into a rocky womb,
where the fumes may hold longer and permeate the stone,
where their chants could reverberate more fully, in a desperate

attempt to forestall his waking. All this I understood, albeit in a glazed manner rather than grasping the significance.

As my mind returned to the present, the man saw in my eyes the question. He raised me to my feet and, taking my hand, brought me into the Great Presence. Miming that I bend my ear, as I had in my vision, I leant close to hear these sibilant whispers, knowing that beneath my head lay a microcosm of the heavens. As the strange, hissing mantras wheezed out with each long, laboured breath, I finally knew. The creature was not creating anything, he was dreaming creation, each whispered breath held the continuity of our world and all those that lie beyond our perception. The man raised my head and mimed his own eyes opening, before bringing them together in a movement as if washing his hands. The awful reality struck me. Should this god awaken, for that was what he surely was, we and all things would cease to be, jolted from the god's dreaming plane upon which we were but a perpetual hallucination. It was for this that they chanted each night, burnt their reserves of narcotic herbs, in a ceaseless effort to stifle the inevitable waking that would shatter our reality. We were but the long dreams of a divinity, whims of his unconscious. I own then that my mind fully departed its moorings. I turned and fled, as Luchenko must have done, for nothing else would account for his swift departure both from society and his native religion. I remember stumbling out into a clear night, waking my companions and mutedly signing that we had to leave. My face must have been expressive enough to indicate my sincerity, either through madness or truth, and within minutes our party was packed and heading up the ridge to joing the guides.

I cannot account for the next few months with any clarity. A confusing mixture of memories and dreams (some waking, some I hope not) and the testimony of my colleagues tells me that we reached the village the next night, where I raved about oil lamps, terrible mouths and the perpetual whispers that dwelt in my head from some cyclopean figure. Somehow, I was transported back to Lhasa and spent several weeks in a hospice of sorts, where the nearby temple bells and chanting monks only acerbated my nightly dementia. In desperation, my colleagues used the last of the expeditionary funds to get me across the mountains down into northern India and then Delhi, where I was set to recuperation in a British-run hospital. Eventually my fears subsided enough that I could wear a mask of normality, yet I refused to speak above a muted mutter, as if in church. The few times that the chaplain came to visit me I was told that he would leave deathly pale, and my terse monologues about us being mere playthings of a slumbering god's dream cut through his more prosaic Anglican faith to such an extent that he refused to visit me further. Weeks turned into months and finally I was bound upon a ship, docking in Plymouth where I was taken to London to make my report to the firm. My colleagues had returned several weeks prior and their lack of anything to show for the expedition had engendered such wrath that each had hurriedly told their superiors that it was I who had sabotaged the mission. The inevitable interview was futile for all involved. My claims were ridiculed, I was branded a fraud and a thief. My former dreams of wealthy clients and glorious Society talks were truly damned, although these were of no value to me whatsoever any more. I took my punishment, swore to never darken the firm's doors again and returned to my native Hampshire, where I knew I could find lodging with my sister and her husband. To their shock, I was quite content to join the field labourers, safe in the knowledge that it didn't matter a damn what I did, as every night I was awaiting the awakening of that terrible figure who dwelt beneath T'Singah. The efforts of the vicar to involve me in church affairs drew no fruit, I would merely gaze at him sadly as he talked of Paradise and the kindly Lord's hand, for I knew the awful truth that would tear his world from him in an instant. As of yet, His slumbers have obviously been painstakingly maintained and so I am writing this testimony in case they should outlive my own. But when my weary body lays itself down each evening, I can no longer keep at bay those terrible whispers, the hissing sound of creation that draws itself into my dreams and breaks my rest with the image of a galactic mouth, in whose blackness the spiralling stars draw together as an eye, which must inevitably open and break the oneiric cycle.

ABOUT THE AUTHORS

AVALON BRANTLEY (1981-2017) is the author of the collections *Descended Suns Resuscitate* (Zagava, 2014) and *Transcensience* (Ex Occidente Press, 2015), as well as *Aornos* (Ex Occidente, 2013), a mind-staged hallucinatory tragedy in the classical vein, set in Greece during the Archaic Period. Her posthumous novel, *The House of Silence*, was released by Zagava in 2017. "Under Different Stars" originally appeared under the pseudonym "Navas" in the anthology *Dreams of Ourselves: An Appreciation of Pessoa* (Zagava / Ex Occidente, 2014).

ADAM S. CANTWELL had an early interest in oneiromancy, astral projection, and "paramentals," which has inspired his fiction, which includes *Orphans on Granite Tides* (Ex Occidente Pess, 2013) and *Bastards of the Absolute* (Egaeus Press 2015). "Moonpaths of the Departed" originally appeared in *A Pallid Wave on Shores of Night* (Ex Occidente Press, 2011).

BRENDAN CONNELL was born in Santa Fe, New Mexico, in 1970. His works of fiction include Metrophilias (Better Non Sequitur, 2010), *Against the Grain Again: The Further Adventures of Des Esseintes* (Tartarus Press, 2021), *Heqet* (Egeaus Press 2022), and *Upuaut* (Occult Press, 2024). "The Chymical Wedding of Des Esseintes" originally appeared in the anthology *Cinnabar's Gnosis: A Homage to Gustav Meyrink* (Ex Occidente Press, 2009).

JUSTIN ISIS is a Tokyo-based writer, artist and member of the O.T.O. His works include *I Wonder What Human Flesh Tastes Like* (Chômu Press, 2011), *Welcome to the Arms Race* (Chômu Press, 2015), and *Divorce Procedures for the Hairdressers of a Metallic and Inconstant Goddess* (Snuggly Books, 2016). He has edited a number of anthologies including *The Neo-Decadent Cookbook* (Eibonvale Press, 2020) and *Neo-Decadence Evangelion* (Zagava, 2023). "The Underground Room" orginally appeared in the anthology *Crystal Castles* (Raphus Press, 2019).

COLIN INSOLE lives in Lymington, on the edge of the New Forest, in England. His books include *Elegies and Requiems* (Side Real Press, 2013), *Valerie and Other Stories* (Snuggly Books, 2018), and *The Last Gold of Decayed Stars and Other Stories* (Mount Abraxas Press, 2024). "Flower of the Sun" originally appeared in *Supernatural Tales* in 2011.

MARTIN LOCKER is an archaeologist, researcher and teacher based in Andorra. He runs the Perennial Pyrenees project which produces books and other media based on the ethnography, history and archaeology of the Pyrenees. His books include *The Tears of Pyrene: Archaeology, Folklore & Traditions of the Pyrenees* (Mons Culturae Press, 2019) and *Prisms of the Oneiroi* (Mount Abraxas Press, 2022), from which "The Dreaming Plateau" is taken.

DAMIAN MURPHY was born and lives in Seattle, Washington. He is the author of *Daughters of Apostasy* (Snuggly Books, 2017), *The Acephalic Imperial* (Snuggly Books, 2020), *The Exalted and the Abased* (Snuggly Books, 2021), and *The Explosion of a Chandelier* (Occult Press, 2023), among other collections and novellas. "St. Severina's Fire" originally appeared in the anthology *Wound of Wounds, an Ovation to Emil Cioran* (Mount Abraxas Press, 2017).

REGGIE OLIVER is an actor, director, playwright, illustrator and award-winning author of fiction. His published work includes the collections *The Dreams of Cardinal Vittorini & Other Strange Stories* (The Haunted River, 2003), *The Complete Symphonies of Adolf Hitler & Other Strange Stories* (The Haunted River, 2005) and *A Maze for the Minotaur* (Tartarus Press, 2021), as well as the biography of the writer Stella Gibbons, *Out of the Woodshed* (Bloomsbury 1998). "The Children of Monte Rosa" originally appeared in *Dark Horizons* in 2007.

R. OSTERMEIER has written three collections of stories which explore worlds of peninsular disquiet from folk horror to more contemporary weird fiction: *Therapeutic Tales* (Broodcomb Press, 2022), *Nocebo* (Broodcomb Press, 2023), and *A Trick of the Shadow* (Broodcomb Press, 2020), from which "The Bearing" is taken.

THOMAS PHILLIPS is a sound artist and author who teaches literature at North Carolina State University. In addition to numerous music releases, installations, and collaborations in dance and theater, he has published a number of books, including the novel *Long Slow Distance* (Object Press, 2009) and the collection *The Light is Alone* (Ex Occidente Press, 2013), from which "Alyssa" is taken.

FARAH ROSE SMITH lives in New York City where she is currently conducting research at the intersection of disability theory and supernatural fiction. Her books include *The Visitor* (Ulthar Press, 2017), *The Almanac of Dust* (Wraith Press, 2018), and the collection *The Witch is the Body* (2021), from which the story of the same name in the present collection is taken.

THOMAS STRØMSHOLT, who lives in Copenhagen, Denmark, is an author of weird and occult fiction. His works works include the collections *Splinters of Horn and Ivory* (Mount Abraxas Press, 2015), *The Sorrows and the Furies* (Mount Abraxas, Press 2018), and *O Altitudo* (Ex Occidente Press, 2013), from which "In Search of the Hidden City" is taken—though the version in the present volume has been slightly revised.

BENJAMIN TWEDDELL was born and lives in Somerset, England, where he manages Courtyard Books Glastonbury, a store specialising in rare Occult tomes. His books include *Sermons In a House of Grief* (Mount Abraxas Press, 2019), *The Salix Arcanum* (Mount Abraxas Press, 2020) and *A Crown of Dusk and Sorrow* (Mount Abraxas Press, 2020). "The Dance of Abraxas" was originally issued as a stand-alone book by Mount Abraxas Press in 2018.

MARK VALENTINE is a British writer whose books of fiction include *The Peacock Escritoire* (Ex Occidente Pess, 2011), *The Fig Garden & Other Stories* (Tartarus Press, 2022) and *The Mascarons of the Late Empire & Other Studies* (Ex Occidente Pess, 2010), from which "A Walled Garden on the Bosphorus" is taken. Among his non-fiction books is *The Secret Ceremonies: Critical Essays on Arthur Machen,* edited with Timothy J. Jarvis, (Hippocampus Press, 2019).

RON WEIGHELL (1950-2020) was a British writer of fiction in the supernatural, fantasy and horror genres. His books include *An Empty House and Other Stories* (Haunted Library Publications, 1986), *The White Road* (Ghost Story Press, 1997), *Tarshishim* (Ex Occidente Press, 2011), and *Summonings* (Sarob Press, 2014). "The Four Strengths of Shadow" originally appeared as a stand alone book, published by Sutton Hoo Press in 2013.

OTHER BOOKS IN THE SERIES

The Zinzolin Book of Occult fiction (edited by Brendan Connell)
The Vermilion Book of Occult fiction (edited by Brian Stableford)
The Zaffre Book of Occult fiction (edited by Brendan Connell)
The Alabaster Book of Occult fiction (edited by Brian Stableford)
The Viridian Book of Occult fiction (edited by Brendan Connell)

A PARTIAL LIST OF SNUGGLY BOOKS

G. ALBERT AURIER *Elsewhere and Other Stories*
CHARLES BARBARA *My Lunatic Asylum*
S. HEZOLNRY BERTHOUD *Misanthropic Tales*
LÉON BLOY *The Tarantulas' Parlor and Other Unkind Tales*
ÉLÉMIR BOURGES *The Twilight of the Gods*
CYRIEL BUYSSE *The Aunts*
JAMES CHAMPAGNE *Harlem Smoke*
FÉLICIEN CHAMPSAUR *The Latin Orgy*
BRENDAN CONNELL *Metrophilias*
BRENDAN CONNELL *Spells*
BRENDAN CONNELL (editor)
 The World in Violet: An Anthology of EnglishDecadent Poetry
RAFAELA CONTRERAS *The Turquoise Ring and Other Stories*
DANIEL CORRICK (editor)
 Ghosts and Robbers: An Anthology of German Gothic Fiction
ADOLFO COUVE *When I Think of My Missing Head*
QUENTIN S. CRISP *Aiaigasa*
LUCIE DELARUE-MARDRUS *The Last Siren and Other Stories*
LADY DILKE *The Outcast Spirit and Other Stories*
CATHERINE DOUSTEYSSIER-KHOZE *The Beauty of the Death Cap*
ÉDOUARD DUJARDIN *Hauntings*
BERIT ELLINGSEN *Now We Can See the Moon*
ERCKMANN-CHATRIAN *A Malediction*
ALPHONSE ESQUIROS *The Enchanted Castle*
ENRIQUE GÓMEZ CARRILLO *Sentimental Stories*
DELPHI FABRICE *Flowers of Ether*
DELPHI FABRICE *The Red Sorcerer*
DELPHI FABRICE *The Red Spider*
BENJAMIN GASTINEAU *The Reign of Satan*
EDMOND AND JULES DE GONCOURT *Manette Salomon*
REMY DE GOURMONT *From a Faraway Land*
REMY DE GOURMONT *Morose Vignettes*
GUIDO GOZZANO *Alcina and Other Stories*
GUSTAVE GUICHES *The Modesty of Sodom*
EDWARD HERON-ALLEN *The Complete Shorter Fiction*
EDWARD HERON-ALLEN *Three Ghost-Written Novels*

www.ingramcontent.com/pod-product-compliance
Lightning Source LLC
Chambersburg PA
CBHW050524110726

47899CB00005B/1584